ANNE'S BOUNTY

BITSEY GAGNE

ANNE'S

BOUNTY

BITSEY GAGNE

Anne's Bounty.

Printed in the United States of America.

Self-Published by Kindle Direct Publishing.

Illustrations & Cover Design by Katie Ferree.

Edited by Mary Dempsey.

ISBN Print Version – 979-8-9885007-7-3

ISBN E-Book Version – 979-8-9885007-6-6

To my talented niece, Katie Ferree, who prepared the beautiful illustrations, family trees, logo, and book covers for *The Pirate Series*.

It has been a joy to watch her grow into a charming, gifted lady who does exquisite work. I hope she continues to unleash her remarkable abilities and artistic flair on the many creative projects that await her, including my upcoming book.

THE GANG

Angie Harriott *country singer, songwriter, and author engaged to Thomas Alexander. Angie traces her family line back to Evangeline Alexander, Jacob Harriott, Virginia Dare, and the pirate Anne Bonny.*

Thomas Alexander *Angie's fiancé and the architect/coowner of In Time Renovations, a company that rehabs historic homes on Ocracoke Island. He is the brother of George Alexander and a descendent of Evangeline Alexander, Jacob Harriott, Virginia Dare, and the pirate Anne Bonny.*

Emily White *part owner and manager of the Oxford Pub at the Shepard's Head B&B, which her sister Sarah White Harriott operates. Her ancestors include Emily White Alexander, better known as "Old Emily."*

George Alexander *A/C technician engaged to Emily White. He is descended from Evangeline Alexander, Jacob Harriott, Virginia Dare, and the pirate Anne Bonny.*

Sarah White Harriott *manager and part owner of Shepard's Head Inn. She is Emily's sister and married to Angie's brother, Matt. Sarah is a descendant of "Old Emily."*

Matt Harriott *architect and co-owner, with Thomas, of In Time Renovations. Married to Sarah. Descendant of Evangeline Alexander, Jacob Harriott, Virginia Dare, and the pirate Anne Bonny.*

Sally Harriott Brown *elementary school teacher, wife of Robert, and mother of twins Evie and Jacob. Angie is her sister; Matt is her brother. Her descendants are Evangeline Alexander, Jacob Harriott, Virginia Dare, and the pirate Anne Bonny.*

Robert Brown *physical education teacher, husband of Sally, and father of twins Evie and Jacob. He is the son of David Brown and the late Samantha Brown. He is descended from Roger Brown.*

Isabella Albright Harriott *widow; retired government worker; mother of Angie, Sally, and Matt; and grandmother of little Evie and Jacob. Isabella is* engaged to David Brown. Her ancestors are Evangeline Alexander, Jacob Harriott, Virginia Dare, and the pirate Anne Bonny.

David Brown   widower, retired government worker, and father of Robert Brown. He is engaged to Isabella. He is a descendent of Roger Brown.

Sally Albright White   former manager and owner of Shepard's Head B&B. Her daughters, Sarah and Emily, now run the inn and Oxford Pub. "Old Emily" is her ancestor. She is a distant cousin and dear friend of Isabella, who named her daughter after Sally White.

Jim White   retired owner and manager of the Oxford Pub, which is now run by his daughter Emily. He is married to Sally Albright White. John White, one of the original Lost Colonists, is his ancestor.

Paul Albright   retired teacher and history buff. Mary Greenville Albright is his wife. Isabella is his daughter; Angie, Sally, and Matt are his grandchildren.

Mary Greenville Albright   retired nurse married to
Paul. Isabella is her daughter. Mary is the grandmother of Angie, Sally, and Matt and great grandmother of little twins Evie and Jacob.

Liz Alexander   retired school teacher, wife of Joe, and mother of Thomas and George. She is a descendent of Roger Brown.

Joe Alexander   retired AC repairman, husband of Liz, and father of Thomas and George. He is descended from Evangeline Alexander, Jacob Harriott, Virginia Dare, and the pirate Anne Bonny.

Sam Brown bartender and water taxi operator at the Oxford Pub. He is also a paramedic and the boyfriend of Cindy Smith. Robert Brown is his cousin.

Cindy Smith   nurse at OBX Hospital and the girlfriend of Sam Brown. Sarah and Emily White are her longtime friends; Chloe Brennan is a former classmate.

Billy Alexander aviator who flies small planes. He also works as a stonemason, including for his cousin, Thomas, at In Time Renovations.

THE NEW PEOPLE

John Brennan *EMT in Charleston, South Carolina, and husband of Chloe. He and Angie are related through the pirates Anne Bonny and Calico Jack.*

Chloe Brennan *elementary teacher in South Carolina and John's wife. She is a classmate of Cindy Smith.*

Stephen Bell, Jr. *Jamaica-based scuba diver, fishing boat captain, and treasure hunter. He is the son of Stephen, Sr., who died in a suspicious boat accident. His girlfriend is Violet Morgan. Stephen is related to Angie through the pirates Anne Bonny and Calico Jack.*

Violet Morgan *computer/IT specialist whose parents died in a sinister explosion. She is the girlfriend of Stephen Bell, Jr., and a descendent of Henry Morgan.*

Timothy Bell *Stephen Bell, Jr.'s "Uncle Tim." He is a scuba diver, fishing boat captain, and treasure hunter in Jamaica. He is the father of Hunter and Logan Bell and brother of the late Stephen Bell, Sr. He traces his family history back to pirates Anne Bonny and Calico Jack.*

Logan Bell *tough guy with criminal leanings and questionable friends. He is a scuba diver, fishing boat mate, and treasure hunter in Jamaica. Timothy Bell is his father; Hunter Bell is his brother. He is related to Anne Bonny and Calico Jack.*

Hunter Bell *scuba diver, fishing boat mate, and treasure hunter in Jamaica. Timothy Bell is his father; Logan Bell is his brother. He is a descendent of Anne Bonny and Calico Jack.*

... AND THE SPIRITS

Anne Bonny *famous female pirate from the 1700s and lover of John Rackham, better known as Calico Jack. Her son, Austin Bell, is an ancestor of Stephen Bell. She is also related to Angie through her later marriage to*

Virginia Dare's great, great grandson John Kercher, who changed his name to John Brennan.

Evangeline Alexander *the protagonist of a tragic and longago Ocracoke Island love story. Evangeline is the lost love of Jacob Harriott, and a descendant of Virginia Dare and Anne Bonny. Angie—named for her—traces her family roots back to Evangeline.*

Old Emily (Emily White) *Evangeline Alexander's best friend and sister-in-law. The Whites—Sarah, Emily, and their father—are descendants.*

George Harriott *the late father of Angie, Sally, and Matt and the late husband of Isabella. He is a descendent of Evangeline Alexander, Jacob Harriott, Virginia Dare, and Anne Bonny.*

Reflections of a Time Forgotten

The misty glow of the eyes of a stranger reaches

out to tell us about a Time Forgotten.

Their love was volatile and lustful.

They stormed the southern seas making what

belonged to others their own, her wild

adventurous spirit still manic even in death.

Our existence hangs in the balance if we

can't go back in time to save her soul.

Will the magical powers protect us and bring

her back to a Time Forgotten so our family can

continue to exist?

TABLE OF CONTENTS

Bitsey Gagne

Prologue

We have been home for two weeks following our exciting and memorable vacation to Cat Island, Bahamas. I can't stop thinking how happy I am that my family, friends, and I were able to witness the union of two remarkable souls: Matt, my brother, and Sarah, one of my best friends.

We lost Blackbeard's treasure but soon we'll be starting our next adventure trying to find Anne Bonny and Calico Jack's bounty. We were ecstatic to learn that we are, indeed, related to the infamous female pirate Anne Bonny as well as Virginia Dare, one of the Lost Colonists of Roanoke Island. Even more, my grandfather, Paul Albright, a local historian, is over the moon at our discovery of what really happened to the Lost Colonists. Tonight, my friends, family, and I are at Shepard's Head B&B, Matt and Sarah's home, inspecting the digital wedding pictures that Sarah has opened on the computer in their spacious dining room.

My grandfather and my grandmother, Mary, both come running into the inn carrying a stack of newspapers. "Look at this!" my grandfather exclaims as he drops the papers on the large oak dining room table.

He holds up a copy of *The Washington Post*. "We made the news, big time. Our pictures are on the front page of the *Post*, *The New York Times*, the *Ocracoke Observer* and, from what I hear, just about every newspaper from here to Cape Cod and the Florida Keys. This is so exciting!"

He's grinning from ear to ear and Mary is beaming, her bright blue eyes sparkling with pride as she watches him and points to me, Matt, and our older sister, Sally.

"It's been Paul's dream and your father's dream to find the Lost Colonists for as long as I can remember. I truly can't believe how lucky we were to find the stone indicating where Virginia Dare and her colony disappeared to all those years ago.

"It's a shame we couldn't bring home Blackbeard's treasure," she continues, then shrugs. "Daniel's ghost destroyed any chance of us ever finding that treasure." She lovingly rubs my grandfather's shoulder.

Matt picks up and reads out loud the headline on *The Washington Post*: "Local historian Paul Albright, up and coming country singer Angie Harriott, and a local group of friends from Ocracoke Island lose Blackbeard's Treasure but stumble upon the whereabouts of The Lost Colonists of Roanoke Island."

Matt laughs and pats our grandfather on his back. "This is so cool. I just love the picture of you, Granddad, holding up the stone tablet that we found in Evangeline's cottage with the information about Virginia Dare on it. I can remember when we met Virginia Dare's ghost on Cat Island and how thrilled you were."

Paul lifts the newspaper, remembering back to that momentous day when we found out what had happened to the Lost Colonists.

"It still feels like a dream when I remember how Virginia appeared before us in a mist. I've been searching for clues about their unexplained disappearance for as long as I can recollect. And then, on top of that, to have found—and lost—Blackbeard's treasure! What a crazy adventure we had."

I put my arm around my grandfather. "Well, even crazier is the fact that Virginia is related to us—and that Anne Bonny, the famous female pirate, is related to us, too!" I say. "Plus, we may still discover more about their lives because we can conjure up their spirits at any time. How cool is that?"

I shake my head and raise my eyebrows. "Now, we just need to figure out how the antique watch that we found in the cedar chest in mom's storm shelter—Calico Jack and Anne's secret hiding place—works."

I pause for a minute and think about that challenge. I suspect that holding onto the watch might allow us to conjure up Anne Bonny's spirit, but we need to figure out the key to doing that.

"I guess she didn't want anyone else to be able to figure out how to reach her ghost if they discovered the watch," I add. "Anne Bonny was quite the character. I would have loved to have known her in her day."

Thomas, my fiancé smiles at me. "Angie, you never know what other qualities the timepiece may have. Maybe, we'll even be able to time travel, you just don't know. I mean, think about it. Who would have ever thought, six months ago, that we'd be able to talk to ghosts—and pirate's ghosts at that?"

I look over at my sister, and I can tell that Sally is thinking about how much her twins, Evie and Jacob, have grown in the last five months. She perks up, taking her husband
Robert's warm hand in hers, and declares, "It amazes me how much our daughter, Evie, reminds me of Anne Bonny. Not only do they resemble one another, but Evie even has Anne's wild adventuresome personality."

Sally chuckles before adding, "I just hope our little Evie doesn't end up becoming a pirate one day."

Our mother, Isabella, starts laughing uncontrollably.

"Oh Sally, you make me laugh. I was just imagining Evie in a little pirate outfit!" she says. "I still can't believe that she is crawling already. We're going to have our hands full keeping up with her. Thank heavens for your nanny, Georgia."

Robert, my sister's husband picks up his little girl, tickling her tummy.

"Oh, my tiny tot, don't grow up too fast. Next thing you know you'll be walking and taking your easy-going little twin brother, Jacob, with you on wild adventures."

David, who is Robert's father and Isabella's fiancé, is holding Jacob. His little grandson, ever alert, is watching the adults around him.

"Don't worry Robert. I think we have a while before you need to stress about that happening," David points out. "But, seriously, is anyone else concerned that our popularity—all those news reports—might make it hard for us to keep Anne and Jack's treasure a secret?"

Matt speaks up. "I was thinking the exact same thing," he says. "I just hope that we don't end up with a bunch of crazy, treasure-hunting, wannabe pirates lurking around the island."

Paul looks thoughtful. "You know, I pray you're not right about all this publicity and how it might attract troublemakers and degenerates," he exclaims. "I was so excited about all our findings… I hope I haven't put everyone at risk."

Mary responds to his concerns with reassurance. "Oh honey, don't worry. It's 2023. There aren't any pirates around anymore," she tells the husband she adores. But Matt shakes his head in disagreement.

"Crazy as it seems, Grandma, there *are* still pirates out there," he says, firmly. "We'll just need to be careful not to leak any details about how we found Anne Bonny and Calico Jack's treasure map, antique chest, and the hidden room."

He points down the road towards mom's house. "By the way, I was thinking, we really should keep the chest hidden in the secret room at Mom's home. What does everyone else think?"

My mom has been worrying about dangerous people finding out about our latest discoveries. "I think that's a wonderful idea," she tells us, relief in her voice. "Maybe we should only bring the chest out into the storm cellar when we are investigating the items in it."

My mom hugs Sally White, who is her dear friend and Sarah and Emily's mother. "This conversation has reminded me that I feel like we are missing something important," Isabella says. "Why don't we all plan to meet at our house tomorrow so we can continue looking at everything in the chest?

"For now, though," she adds, "the girls and I have a hairdresser appointment. We want to look our best at the combined Annual Christmas Open House and wedding reception for Matt and Sarah at the inn tonight."

Sarah is beaming, thinking about her island wedding in the Caribbean. "It's feels like we're having two weddings," she marvels. "I'll to get to wear my wedding gown *again*. How many brides get to do that?"

Sarah points to me, Sally, and Emily, who is Sarah's sister and my best friend. "Can you girls come over to help me get ready when we get back from the salon? I can really use some extra hands. I have our staff setting everything up in the pub because it's so much bigger than the inn's dining room."

Sarah steps over to me and gives me a big hug. "Angie, I'm so happy that you want to play your music tonight. It's always so special."

I hug Sarah back, grinning.

"Of course. I can't think of anything better that I'd like to do. I am delighted at how much you like my music.

"Hey," I add, "are you girls ready to go to the Hatteras Island?"

I continue to smile calmly at the group, but inside my head I am beyond excited. I can't wait for Matt and Sarah to hear the new song I've written just for them. It's going to be so special. The ladies laugh and answer in unison, "We're ready!"

Chapter 1

A Special Wedding Reception

We are back from our hair appointments before we know it, and Sally, Emily, and I are helping Sarah into her wedding gown. She slips on the beautiful ivory-colored tea-length gown, her newly styled blonde hair catching the light.

"I'm so nervous," she says, shaking her head in disbelief. "It doesn't make any sense that I should be this nervous. Matt and I are already married."

Emily pours champagne for all of us and hands a glass of bubbly to Sarah.

"Here. Take a sip of this. It'll help ease your nerves," she tells her sister, before adding: "Besides, I want to give a toast."

Emily holds up her champagne flute.

"Sis, I'm so happy for you and Matt. You have found the fairytale love you always wanted." She stops and looks at her sister, then continues. "I hope you two will always be happy together. I love you."

After we raise our glasses and sip the champagne, Emily puts down her glass and moves over to Sarah. She gives her a hug.

Sarah blushes and smiles at her.

"Thank you, Emily. That's so sweet. But what about you and George?" she says. "I can't believe you two finally opened your eyes and realized you were meant for one another. It's so exciting!"

After barely a moment, she adds, "So, when are you two going to get engaged?"

Emily throws her arms up in the air. "Good grief, Sarah. We just got together. Don't you think we ought to date for a little while before we get engaged. I mean really!" Emily is blushing, her cheeks as red as a cherry on top of a sundae.

My sister, Sally, takes a sip of her sparkling wine. "I think it's awesome that we are all in such happy relationships. It's so nice to have weddings on this year's calendar. Hopefully it won't be long before I'll get to be an auntie." We all roll our eyes at her, but Sarah winks.

"Well, we're not doing anything to prevent it. Sooo... you never know."

We squeal ecstatically over the news, but Sarah reins us all back in.

"Please don't say anything to anyone," she says. "We want it to be a surprise. Besides, you never know, it could be years from now before we have an announcement.

"For now, let's get ready to go to the pub for our party," she says

I smooth down my dusty rose bridesmaid dress. "I'm so glad you suggested we wear our dresses from your wedding," I say. "I think we all clean up nicely.

"Cheers," I add as I finish my champagne and set the glass down on the oval silver tray on Sarah's nightstand.

The girls and I step out into the hallway and walk toward the ornate staircase. We waltz down the winding white stairs into the beautifully decorated parlor then cross the breezeway that leads to the pub's door. Green ivy, red bells, and white lights hang from the dear old banister and charming parlor tables. The B&B favors traditional holiday decorations—classy, not gaudy.

"I just love how you ladies have decorated the inn for Christmas," I tell Sarah and Emily. "It is just how I would have imagined it back in Evangeline's day. Of course, minus the strings of electric lights!

"Sometimes, I get these pictures in my head of what the old house would have looked like."

I gesture toward my friend, Emily. "Speaking of the past, have you had any more dreams about the Old Emily?"

As we learned the story of our ancestor Evangeline, who many people think I resemble, we also learned about her friend Emily. We call her Old Emily.

Emily nods. "You know, it's funny you ask that. I dreamed about her last night."

She continues, "It was Christmas and Emily, and her family, Evangeline, William, and Roger were all gathered around the family's Christmas tree."

Emily smiles at the memory. "You know their families remind me so much of our families. They were very close."

I raise my eyebrows. "Did the dream contain any deadly warnings for you or us?"

Emily opens the door to the pub, and we line up to be announced. "Not so far," she answers me. "Hopefully we won't need any more ominous premonitions." She breaks into a smile and adds, "Now let's get this party started."

The DJ that Jim White, Sarah's father, has hired announces us as we enter the pub. The guys join us to make our entrance. Sally looks pretty in her dusty rose bridesmaid dress with Robert escorting her. He bends down to kiss her lightly on her flushed cheek. "How's my lovely wife tonight?"

She blushes like she is a bride, not a wife of over four years. I just love to watch the two of them together. I hope that Thomas and I will have as great a relationship as they do.

Suddenly it's our turn to be announced. I take Thomas by the crook of his arm. My bright blue eyes tear up when I look deeply into his soul. His love for me shines as brightly as mine for him.

"I can't wait to be your wife," I whisper. He nods and kisses me quickly, whispering into my ear that he can't wait either.

Next to be announced are Emily and George. Talk about sparks igniting between two people! It still amazes me that they waited so long to be together. I guess it only makes it sweeter and more precious for them. Emily's pink cheeks and George's twinkling blue eyes say it all. Love shines in both of them.

My hand reaches up to my neck and I grasp my heart-shaped pendant. Immediately I feel and see the spirits of Evangeline, Old Emily, and my dad watching us from over on the other side of the bar. My dad has proud tears sparkling in his captivating blue eyes. He winks at me and places his finger to his lips. He does not want me to announce that he is with us.

Finally, the time comes to present the new couple: the beautiful blushing bride, Sarah, and my handsome brother, Matt. The room explodes in applause and loud warm wishes as they dance their way over to their seats at the head table. I see Matt look in the direction where my father's spirit is watching. Matt salutes our father before turning to kiss Sarah. I smile to myself and look in Sally's direction. She catches my eye and winks at me.

Matt announces a toast, raising his champagne flute. Everyone in the room does the same. "I want to welcome all of you to our wedding celebration and annual Christmas party," my brother says. "Thank you all for coming. It's an honor to have so many loved ones here to support us.

"Cheers and everyone enjoy yourselves," he says, moving the glass to his mouth. We all drink to his toast as Sarah takes the mic. Her tiny, elegant hands are shaking and there are tears in her eyes.

"As Matt says," she announces, glancing at her husband, "we want to welcome you to our home and thank you all for coming."

She takes a deep breath and speaks from the heart.

"Most of you who know me have been aware that I have been in love with this man since we were children running along the shores of Ocracoke Island. He gave me my first kiss. I hope he will also give me my last kiss after we grow old together."

Tears start to enter many of the guests' eyes just as Sarah continues, "Everyone, please. Have fun, dance, drink, and be merry. Oh, and Merry Christmas! Thanks for coming."

She hands the microphone over to her father, Jim. He smiles at his daughter and then at the crowd.

"Yes, everyone please enjoy yourselves at Sarah and Matt's wedding reception and our annual Christmas celebration," Jim says. "It's an open bar, and there is a buffet set up over in the corner, catered by the Ocracoke Oyster Company. The desserts are made by the Fig Tree Bakery. Enjoy!"

The evening continues and everyone is having a wonderful time. It is now time for me to dedicate my new song to Matt and Sarah.

I pick up my trusty guitar, which has been resting in the special oak guitar stand that Thomas made for me. I make my way up to the DJ stand and welcome everyone.

"Good evening. It's a pleasure for me to be part of this awesome celebration. As you are all aware, I love being able to write songs about the people who I cherish. That is why I have written a song for Matt and Sarah."

I see Sarah grin and take Matt's hand up to her lips to gently kiss it.

My melodic voice rings out through the tiny pub. My song tells a love story about two young children who grow up, move away from each other, and finally find each other again. The room sways to my music.

Sarah and Matt take this opportunity to have their first dance together. They are both grinning from ear to ear as they dance and listen to my lyrics. When my song comes to an end, the newlyweds rush to embrace me and thank me for their song.

Matt announces to the crowd, "I love it, Angie. We are so lucky to have a song written about us."

He hugs me again and, as glasses start clinking, he responds to the crowd's request by turning to passionately kiss Sarah. When the kiss ends, Sarah ecstatically hugs me. "Oh Angie, the song is so special— and so us!"

The father-daughter dance is next. Jim looks proudly and lovingly into his daughter's teary eyes. All eyes are on her as she dances with her daddy.

My dad's spirit watches from the corner of the bar. I see sadness cross his eyes, knowing that he can't take his place on the dance floor with my mom, Isabella. Still, he winks at Matt, places his hand over his heart, and blows a whisper-like kiss toward my mom as David takes her onto the dance floor. We all join the others for the bridal party waltz.

And, finally, the cake is cut, and the evening comes to an end. Thomas and I see my mom, David, Jim, and his wife Sally standing next to the bar looking serious. They are talking to Sam Brown.

Sam is Robert's cousin. He runs our water taxi in the summer and is an EMT full time. Tonight, he has been helping us out with bartending duties. I saw him earlier flirting with Cindy Smith, a friend of ours who is a nurse at the local hospital on the Outer Banks. The two started dating last summer after she returned home from Salisbury University, where she earned her nursing degree. They make such a cute couple, Sam with his long blond hair and blonde-haired Cindy with her blue eyes. She's wearing a gorgeous, strappy red dress tonight.

I nudge Thomas and point toward the bar. "I wonder what's going on. Sam and the others look awfully serious for a wedding reception," I say. "Do you think something has happened? Let's go check it out."

Thomas lays his hand on my back as we make our way over to the bar. "Let's hope everything is okay," he says to me as we move through the crowd toward Sam and the others.

David looks up, then points to me. As we get close, he says, "Oh good, Angie. You're here. We might have a problem."

I raise my eyebrows, questioning. "Uh oh, what's up? Has something happened?"

David looks at Sam. "Sam, tell Angie and Thomas what you just told us."

Sam reaches into his pants pocket. He pulls out a card with a name on it and hands it to me. "This couple showed up earlier tonight. I let them know that this was a private party and asked them if they knew anyone here or if they were invited."

Sam continues. "The guy's name is John Brennan and his wife's name is Chloe. He said he is from Charleston, South Carolina, and he thinks that he is related to you and your family. He said he did one of those 23andMe DNA tests and your name came up as a possible relative.

"It was weird. How many people just show up like that? It kind of gave me the willies, if you know what I mean," Sam adds. "I told them they would need to come back tomorrow if they wanted to speak to you."

Sam scratches his bearded chin. "I worry about treasure hunters showing up here after all those articles came out when you came back from Cat Island and your search for Blackbeard's treasure."

Thomas rubs my back as I worriedly run my fingers through my long wavy raven hair. Thomas wants to reassure me. "Well, let's not get too worried just yet," he says. "Maybe he really did do one of those DNA tests like you did, Angie. There is no point in all of us getting worked up until we know something.

"You can call him in the morning," Thomas continues. "But Sam's right. I guess we need to be on alert again. No one should go out walking around without a shadow."

Isabella, my mother, shakes her head and looks at me. "You got that, Angie?" she says with concern in her voice. "I don't want anything happening to anyone. You've already been kidnapped once, and we don't want it happening again."

Jim claps Sam on the shoulder. "Thanks, Sam for the heads up. I'll let the others know."

We are quiet and thoughtful for a few minutes, then Jim speaks up again. "I don't know about you guys, but I'm whipped." He puts his arm around his wife, Sally. Although she is Sarah and Emily's mother, my family has a special closeness with her. That's why my sister was named after her.

"We're going to call it a night," Sally adds.

David looks over toward Matt and Sarah, who are saying good-bye to their guests.

"Well, we know those two are attached at the hip. Sure sign they'll stay together," David says. "Let's not spoil this perfect evening. We'll wait until tomorrow to let them know about our uninvited guest.

"George and Emily left early so we don't need to worry about them. George has an early call in the morning," David adds. "Sally and Robert also headed home a while ago. They said the twins are still getting them up early, plus they had to get ready for Santa. So, we'll leave tonight as it is—but I feel strongly that we need to be on alert again, much as I hate that."

Jim points to Isabella. "Does anyone want to help me search the chest again in the secret room?"

David nods. "I think that's a great idea. Maybe everybody can come over to our house tomorrow morning. Let us be the hosts for once so that you don't have to, Sally."

Sally smiles, thinking about how blessed they've been since she and Jim moved back to the island from Florida after retiring last year.

"I think that's a lovely idea," she says. "Oh, I can't tell you how happy I am that we're living back on the island." She sweeps her hand around the pub, adding, "I have so missed this."

Anne's Bounty

Chapter 2

The Secret Room

The next day, Thomas and I run up the steps to the wide veranda leading into my mother's home. When we reach the top, Thomas turns to me. "Do you think we are going to find anything else in the secret room?" he asks. "I heard from Robert that before Calico Jack and Anne Bonny owned the home, it belonged to Charles Vane. Did you ever hear the history between the two pirates?"

I turn my head to the side as I think. "Didn't Granddad say that when the two were on Vane's sloop Calico Jack had him voted out of his position as captain, then Calico Jack took over Vane's ship, the Ranger?"

Thomas nods. "You're right. So let me try again with another question. We'll see if you know the answer to this little piece of trivia. Where did Calico Jack get his name?"

I laugh. "Oh, that's easy," I tell Thomas. "He got his name from the calico pants he liked to wear. His real name was John Rackham. Jack is often a nickname for John."

I bow in victory after my response. Thomas grins. "Well, aren't you a smarty pants!"

He opens the white oak door that leads from the veranda to the house. "Let's go see if we can find any new clues," he says.

Our group is already gathered around my mom's rustcolored granite kitchen island drinking their morning cups of joe. My mom spots us enter the room, and she comes over to hug us. She points at the coffee carafes on the counter.

"I made regular dark French Roast coffee and some vanilla-flavored coffee. There is vanilla coffee creamer and a mocha mint coffee creamer or just plain half and half to choose from. Help yourselves.

"Oh, and there are Styrofoam cups with lids so we can take our coffee downstairs if we want," she adds.

As we greet everyone, we find out that George had a call this morning and can't be with us. Paul takes a long sip of his mocha latte and explains that they set up two tables in the storm shelter. "David and I pulled the cedar chest that belonged to Calico Jack and Anne into the storm cellar. What do you all think about splitting up into groups of four or five? Each group can examine the items we have found," Paul says.

Jim nods in agreement. "I think that's a great idea. Why not have Angie, Thomas, Emily, Sally, and Robert go check out the secret room? Thomas you've been good at finding hidden latches, so you never know what you guys might discover."

Thomas pats himself on the back and laughs. "I'll do my best," he says, adding, "I like that Robert will be with us since he's done a lot of research with Paul."

Paul rubs his lightly stubbled chin. "That's a good idea," he says. "Why don't Isabella, Mary, David, and I be in one group and Jim, Sally, Matt, and Sarah be in the other group? That means everyone has someone in their group who knows the history of the island and its pirates. Jim and I have done research this way before."

David opens the door leading down into the musky storm cellar. He flips on the switch to light the dimly lit stairs. "Be careful," he cautions. "These steps are a little creaky and steep. Thomas and Matt, one day when your business slows down, maybe we'll get you guys to do some more renovation on Isabella's home."

Matt points his flashlight down the rickety stairs. "Sure thing," he says. "I've been thinking about that since the last time we were in here. That was during the tornado warning this summer."

Thomas smiles. "And maybe we'll find more treasure or, at least, treasure maps. If Charles Vane lived here before Calico Jack, he might have left treasure or a map, too."

David turns the doorknob to the storm cellar, and we step back in time, to a past of lost treasures and forgotten memories.

"Well, here's the old chest," David says. "Why don't Paul, Matt, and I empty its contents on the two tables so we can examine the bottom of the chest. You girls look over the items we put on the tables. Once we've examined the coffer, we'll come help you examine the items, too."

Thomas pushes the latch to expose the hidden passageway within the storm cellar.

"Let's go guys," he says. "This should be fun. I can't wait to see what else we might find."

Sally sneezes and pushes away a spiderweb laced across the dusty tunnel. "Ooh, this is spooky," she says as she holds up a battery-operated lantern that illuminates our way. "Just think, years ago all they had were candles.
Yikes, that would have been even scarier."

I swat at a spiderweb that I manage to get tangled in my hair. "Yeah, that would have been awful," I say. "Can you imagine having to hide down here for days? I wonder if the tunnel leads outside, too."

Matt chimes in. "You know, I hadn't thought about that. What do you think, Robert?"

Robert scratches his head. "It would almost need to have an outside entrance, wouldn't it? Matt, and you, too, Angie and Sally, have any of you ever noticed weird slats of wood or boards outside your house?"

I shake my head. "I've never really looked closely for anything like that but it's possible. There are some huge bushes outside the house. You can't really see what's under them. We'll have to take a look outside the cellar."

Robert points to the darkened oak barrel sitting beside a raggedy old cot. "Emily, why don't you and Angie check out the barrel? And Sally, why don't you see if the cot has any hidden panels or spaces? Thomas and I will examine the pictures on the wall and see if we can find any concealed latches or exits to the outside."

Sally removes the dirty burlap mattress that covers the bed. She flips over the decaying cot and examines the underside of the frame. "Hey, look at this, guys!"

She sneezes as dust mites fly in the stale air. "Hey look at this. There's a compartment on this side. It has a tiny door at the end of the board." She pushes open the cloaked crevice and pulls out a dusty tubular object as we crowd around. "Wow, it's a telescope," she says.

She hands the 'scope to Robert. "This is super cool, but I wonder why they hid it in here and not in the chest with the rest of their belongings?" he says.

He hands the antiquated cylinder to Thomas, and I look over his shoulder at our newfound treasure. "Maybe it's magical? Kind of like the watch that we found that we still need to figure out, so that we can get Anne's spirit to appear," I say.

Thomas turns the 'scope over and looks through the viewfinder. "I don't know, crazier things have happened," he says. "Maybe we can even look back in time and see where Anne left their treasure. I agree with Angie, we need to figure out how to reach Anne."

Robert picks up the old oak barrel and look to see if he can find any more hiding spaces. Then he shakes the barrel, which was used as a makeshift nightstand. We can hear something rattling. "Wow guys, I think there might be another object inside here," Robert says.

He turns the barrel upside down with the help of Thomas. "Look, I think there is a false bottom in the underside of the drum," Robert tells us. "Now we just need to figure out to get into it. It looks like this section can slide."

He slides a little wooden panel to the side and reaches in. He pulls out a thin, crinkly booklet. "Hey, this looks like a captain's log."

He points to an entry on the first page and starts to read. "The notation says, 'Spring 21st day of April 1718 – I became Captain of Charles Vane's vessel after his men voted me in and him out due to a charge of cowardice. I became Captain of the sloop called The Ranger. I sent Vane on his way in one of our other schooners. I heard he left for Honduras.'"

He hands me the journal. "Hey Angie, maybe you can write a book on Calico Jack in addition to your book on Evangeline." He grins at me. "What do you think about that? I guess for now, though, we'll take it to Paul and the others to examine with the other clues." He rests his foot on a slot in the wall.

Thomas looks down at the rung. "Whoa, I didn't even notice this area at the head of the cot. Look up, guys." Emily squeals as she looks up. The wall is notched all the way to the ceiling, where we can see some sort of seams.

"Oh, my goodness. It makes so much sense if you think about it," Emily says. "We are in the basement, so to get out—or in—they would have to go up."

She looks toward Sally and me. "Have you girls ever noticed any trapdoors on your property?"

I shake my head. "I've been all over our land and never noticed anything. What about you, Thomas? You, George, and Matt used to play at our house all the time, did you ever see anything resembling an escape hatch?"

Thomas starts to climb up the rungs. At the top, he pushes on a square opening in the ceiling. It gives way to a secret exit. "Well, well, look at this. There's a bunch of roots on top of this hatch. It won't open all the way," Thomas says. "I guess we're going to have to go outside and come back in from that direction. It's probably overgrown with weeds or bushes."

Thomas points at Robert. "Hey, Robert, can you hand me that pole over there on the floor so I can mark where the entrance is?" Robert nods his head in agreement and hands Thomas the wooden pole. "I think you're right, Thomas."

Robert then points to the door leading out into the tunnel. "I think we've found everything we can for now. How about we go see if the others have unearthed any new objects and show them what we have found."

Emily agrees, shaking her head. "Yeah, I think we're done here for the moment. I can't wait to see what Paul and the others think about the telescope and the pirate captain's log."

I open the old pine door leading into the tunnel. "Oh, here we go back into spider web haven," I say. I cringe thinking about all the spiders that have woven their webs in the passageway over the past two hundred years. I really do hate spiders.

Thomas laughs at me and wraps his arm around my waist. "Don't worry, Angie. I'll protect you from the vicious spiders."

We all laugh as we make our way down the dark and dank passageway so we can show the others our discoveries.

Chapter 3

More Discoveries

The gang spreads out in the basement's storm cellar. Angie, Thomas, Emily, Sally, and Robert have ducked back into the room through the hidden doorway and tunnel they found months ago. Robert is carrying something in his muscular hand.

"Hey guys, look what Emily found in a hidden compartment on the underside of decrepit old cot." He holds up a telescope, then hands it to Paul.

I have come out of the hidden passageway right behind Robert. I also hand something to my grandfather. "Robert found this captain's log in the bum of the drum, the one in the secret room. It was beside the cot," I say.

"Why don't you put that ship's journal on one of the tables for a minute, Angie, while I check out this spyglass," Paul says. He reaches for the telescope and looks through the lens. "That's weird. Why would they hide this 'scope?" He tries to adjust the telescope lens. "I can't figure out why they bothered to hide this telescope, unless it has some special powers or is connected to some secret that we haven't discovered yet," he says.

He looks more closely at the spyglass. "It seems pretty normal to me … hey, wait a minute. There is this small slot here that I've never seen before on an antique telescope. I wonder what's supposed to fit in here?"

I point to the journal on the table. "Is there something in the logbook that explains it?" I ask. "I only just scanned it when Robert handed it to me, but I did see a couple of drawings. Maybe they can help us sort this out."

Thomas, Emily, and Sally are watching the interaction. Thomas is thinking about a tunnel from the hidden room to the outside. Unable to contain his excitement, he turns to Isabella. "Did you ever find any unusual portals or maybe wooden slats in the ground around your home?"

Mom shakes her head. "No, I don't think so, not that I can remember."

Then it hits her. She turns to Matt. "Oh, my goodness, I just remembered your father telling me that one day when he was trimming our bushes, he spotted a weird piece of wood under the bushes. He told me that he planned to investigate it but I guess he wasn't ever able to get back to it before he died. I hadn't really thought about it because I'm not usually the one who does the gardening."

"Well, maybe the time wasn't right," Matt says. "And we know from our last adventure that it's all about the right timing. We'll have to go outside to see if the wood is still there."

Robert points to the chest and the other items now spread out on the tables. "It's amazing to think all these things stayed hidden for so many years. This stuff is so historical."

David goes over to the table and picks up an object, a compass, holding it up for us to see. "This is one of the surprises we found in the bottom of the chest. It was hidden under a false bottom in the trunk. So were these maps. I think they're of Jamaica."

He looks around at all of us. "And it keeps getting better. Show them what you found, Sarah."

Sarah lifts up a dress and pulls at a side pocket. "Look at this," she says. She hands the dress to Robert to examine, as she continues. "There's some sort of secret message or code sewn into the opening. I just found it a minute ago, so we haven't tried to figure it out yet or even remove it from the dress. Pretty cool, though, isn't it?"

Robert carefully holds up the dress, gently turning the pocket inside out. "I think I can get that parchment out." He reaches into his jeans and takes out his trusty Swiss army knife. "I need to be very careful not to tear the fabric—or the paper," he says, concerned.

He manages to extract the tiny piece of parchment without any damage. He takes a deep breath as he sets the delicate note on the white plastic table. "Shooo, that was tricky. I was so worried I would rip the dress or the paper—or both. Now, let's see what it says."

This is what is written on the antique parchment:

Barbara Applies Hogsbreath Amidst Mommas Shelves

Left Elizabeth Applies Dogs Scared

Tominack Only

John Applies Momma Applies Inside Colorful Applies

Robert scratches his chin. "You're right Sarah. It sure looks like some kind of code."

Paul looks at the parchment. "Hmm. Every word in each sentence is capitalized. I wonder if that means something." He waves over at Mary. "Hey, honey. Can you hand me my notebook? I want to try something, although I doubt it's as easy as what I'm thinking."

He writes each capitalized letter on a sheet of the notebook, then reads what he sees:

"Bahamas map leads to Jamaica."

Paul jumps up and down, clapping his hands. "We figured it out! Yahoo! Do you realize what this means? The treasure is not in the Bahamas. It's in Jamaica."

Robert nods. "Well, that makes so much more sense since the two pirates were from Jamaica and that was their stomping ground."

37

I make a check mark in the air. "One mystery solved! Now we will need to figure out how the watch that we found in Anne Bonny and Calico Jack's cedar chest in the secret room and the telescope fit in. I feel the two items are related and will work together, but I'm just not sure how. Maybe there's a way we can ask Anne."

I point to an object that my grandfather placed back on the table a minute ago. "What's that?" I ask.

Paul holds up the device. "I believe it's a compass, but I can't figure out why it was in the bottom of the trunk, along with the maps."

Thomas reaches out and takes the compass. He examines it. "It's a little different than most of the compasses I've seen. This one has a hole in the top of it." He continues to inspect it, then asks, "Was there anything else in the hidden bottom of the trunk that might fit into this hole?" Jim holds up a small candle and hands it to Thomas. "Just this candle," he says. "I thought it was weird to have a little old candle in there with the maps. It was wrapped in burlap." He hands the weathered yellow wax candle to Thomas. It is about six inches long and very slender.

Thomas looks at the candle and then at the hole in the compass and then back again at the candle. "Hey, guys. You aren't going to believe this, but I think this may be a perfect fit for the hole in the compass." To prove it, Thomas slips the yellowed wax taper into the hole. "Wow. Do you think this may be part of the puzzle that is going to lead us to the buried treasure?"

Matt pulls a lighter out of the pocket of his faded blue jeans, flicks it with his thumb, and holds the flame to the wick of the candle. It sputters and smokes for a few seconds before it lights. "Can you tell if the compass needle is moving any, Thomas?" A smoky odor from the lit candle fills the air.

Thomas shakes his head. "No, I don't see anything happening. Let's blow the candle out for now until we figure out what it's for. We might need more clues to see how it works.

"We really need to figure out how to work Jack's antique watch so that we can reach Anne's spirit," he insists.

He turns to the others. "With Evangeline, when Angie and I each touched our matching half-heart pendants, she would appear. Maybe the watch is the item that will make Anne Bonny materialize. Has anyone given any thought to how we can get the watch to work so we can conjure up Anne's spirit?"

I notice that we talk about conjuring up ghosts as if it were nothing. But I remember the first time Evangeline appeared to me and what a shocking—and extraordinary—moment it was. I was staying at the B&B at the time while my cottage was being renovated. My room at the inn faced Silver Lake. As I looked through the window at the water, a vibration ran through me. I think back to the experience.

The air becomes cool, and hairs stand up on the back of my neck. I feel a presence in the room. Startled, I look around. Evangeline appears before me. She is pointing toward the cottage that once belonged to her. "Angie, you must go now," she says. "The time is right. Someone there is waiting for you."

Then she vanishes. I wonder if I am going crazy. She has never spoken to me before. I grab the keys to the cottage and run down the stairs of the inn and through its massive oak door. I race across the gravel driveway. The cottage sits in front of me. The broken screen door slams behind me as I cross the small summer porch to the main wooden door into my cottage.

I turn the doorknob and energetically push the door open.

A tanned, well-built man is leaning over the old, weathered stone fireplace. As he stands up and turns toward me, I see in his muscular hand a silver chain with half a silver heart dangling from it. I reach up, grasping its twin—the fragile necklace around my neck. My beloved silver necklace exactly matches the one in his hand.

I rush across the room and reach out to touch the necklace in the man's hand. My fingertips graze his, and time seems to freeze as the translucent forms of a man and a woman appear. The sight makes us both gasp.

We are cast back into a bygone era, some two-hundred-and-fifty years ago. In awe, we watch as the young man bends down on one knee. He vows: "Evangeline, I will return to make you, my wife." He then pulls two silver heart pendant necklaces from his pocket and places one around her neck. "Evangeline, my love. Wear this necklace until I can bring a ring to wed thee." He keeps the other necklace in his hand.

Evangeline drops down on her knees beside the young man and clasps his hands in hers. "Jacob, I will always be yours," she replies.

"These will remind us of our undying love for each other while I am away," Jacob replies. "I engraved my initials, JH, on your heart. EA is etched onto mine. I will wear you on my heart so that we will forever be close to one other."

We watch the interaction unfolding between the beautiful ravenhaired girl and the young man with long, wavy blonde hair. Tears stream down the faces of the two young lovers as they say goodbye to each other.

Jacob wraps his arms around Evangeline and kisses her lips. The two lovers' passion is so strong that we can feel it, like a force in the room. They whisper their goodbyes, not knowing that this would be the last time they would see each other.

Suddenly, they vanish.

My hand falls and I release my hold on the necklace entwined in the muscular man's hand. I lift my eyes to meet his stormy green ones. I am unable to pull away from his gaze. Strong emotions and sparks fly between us. I have a feeling of déjà-vu, like I've been with him before. The green-eyed man is Thomas. It is the first time we meet—and the moment is electric.

I bring myself back to the present. Jim is turning the old pocket watch over his hands. He pops open the lid on the gold case of the timepiece. "I was looking at it earlier and inside there are two inscriptions. On one side of the case, it says, 'To Jack – Love, Anne.' We already knew that, but what is really interesting is this second inscription."

He points to tiny words etched into the metal and begins to read. "It says, 'Look from within the slot to find what you desire but first you must know what time is right'"

Jim shakes his head and scratches his lightly grown beard. "I'm not sure what that means." He scratches his chin again and repeats the words: "Look from within the slot to find what you desire but first you must know what time is right."

I blurt out. "I think I get it! I think we have to set the watch to the correct time before Anne will appear before us."

Paul nods in agreement. "You might be on to something, Angie. Now we just have to figure out what date or time she's referring to. If you noticed, in addition to the hands on this watch, there is an area that shows the month and day."

Paul passes the watch to Robert then puts his head in his hands. This unconscious gesture is a familiar one. We all know that it means he's thinking hard about something. After a minute, he tells us what he's ruminating about.

"So, you know what that etching inside the watchcase means, right? We must figure out the correct day and time," he declares. "Let's brainstorm. What date and time would have been significant to Anne?"

Emily offers a suggestion. "What about the time that the two met?" George exclaims, "Or when she disappeared.

November 28, 1720, is what I think you told us Paul." Sarah, thinking really hard, then blurts out, "What about when they were captured by Johnathan Barnet, that English privateer?

Matt claps his grandfather on his back. "I think I have it! What are the most significant dates we can connect to both Anne and Calico Jack?"

The room falls quiet while we think. Then Robert grins and says, "It probably can't be this easy, but wouldn't it be the day that Jack died? I just finished doing some research on him. Calico Jack was hanged at Gallows Bay in Port Royal, Jamaica on November 18, 1720."

Do you know what time of day?" Matt asks. "At sunrise," Robert replies.

Matt grins as he pulls out his cell phone and asks Suri the time at sunrise on November 17, 1720, in Jamaica. She answers: "The sun rose on that day in Jamaica at 6:20 a.m." We all start hooting and hollering, laughing at our discovery. Then Matt picks up the watch and we fall silent. Not a whisper can be heard as we anxiously watch him turn the crown at the top of the watch. He sets the date and time to match the exact moment Calico Jack was hanged.

"Well here goes nothing," he says as he closes then reopens the watch case.

A sudden shriek of laughter startles us—and the misty form of Anne Bonny's spirit begins to take shape before us. She brushes back her untamed red hair then waves her arms wildly.

Chapter 4

Anne Bonny

"Well, what took you so long?" the infamous pirate woman boisterously demands.

The ghostly figure of Anne Bonny then touches her finger to her forehead. "I had to make it difficult just in case someone accidentally found the watch before you. You see, I only wanted someone related to old Jacky boy to use the watch to gather the clues to where our treasure is hidden."

Paul excitedly asks Anne, "Before anything else, can you tell us your story? What happened to you? It was as if you simply disappeared after Jack's execution."

Anne grins at him, leans forward, and gives him a peck on the cheek. "Sure, mate! Aye, I can do that, but 'tis a mighty long tale that I tell." Paul sits down on one of the folding chairs in the storm cellar. "We have plenty of time," he says with a laugh. "I can't wait to hear your story."

Anne proves to be quite the thespian, and the saga she tells is filled with embellishments.

"Well, you see lads and ladies, I was but a baseborn wee one from Cork, Ireland. I was spawned from an affair me father had with his maid, Peg Brennan, me ma, in the year 1697. Me father, wanting to keep me close but ashamed of my existence, had me dress as a servant boy in his mighty household.

"But as you all know, the mighty do fall."

Anne runs her hands through her exuberant red hair as she continues her story.

"You see me ma and me da were found out when one of the other serving fellas in the household tried to play a prank on Peg Brennan. Well, the joke led to the downfall of the mighty William Cormac when the affair was discovered by his wife and mother-in-law. Cormac, me da, was a wealthy attorney, and in those days, folks didn't take too kindly to nefarious behavior."

She shakes her head. "What happened next was to be expected. William Cormac was ostracized and forced to leave his home. He took me and me ma away to the new colonies to start a fresh life in a place called Charles Town in South Carolina. He became a prosperous solicitor and merchant again. He was quite bossy, he was, especially towards me."

She laughs as she remembers back to her early years. "You see, all was going quite well until I became a woman at the age of thirteen. At that, I was expected to act as a lady, instead of the tomboy that I was known for on our new land."

She points to her manly pirate outfit. "But me parents could not contain me. I fought and played like a lad. I was rough and tough as they came, and the other fellas couldn't keep up with me." She paused and her voice softened. "But everything changed that year as me ma succumbed to the typhoid fever. My life was no longer mine, and me da threatened to have me married off to one of the rich blokes in the county."

Robert asks Anne, "Was this when you ran away?

Anne grins to hear that Robert knows so much about her. "Aye, laddie. I could never have stood to become a proper lady. I was too wild and adventurist for the staid old life. Instead, I found a mate—a sailor—and I made my escape with him."

She quiets for a minute and looks thoughtful before she continues. "But I made a mistake. I never should have married the cad—I did not love him. He was a bore, and I soon tired of him. James Bonny, he was a pirate aboard a sloop bound for the Bahamas."

She turns to Paul and Robert and a devilish glint hits her eyes as she continues her story. "I met a handsome, virile man, Jack Rackham. He stole my heart and, like me da before me, I became an adulterer. But it wouldn't have gone easy for me because I was a woman. An adulteress? I would have been beaten for my infidelity."

Anne then turns to us girls. "You see, ladies, back then we were mere property. But I was having none of that, so I ran again. Jack and I stole a sloop and slipped away. We left the island to sail the seas in search of bounty."

She raises her hands to her heart. "I fell in love for the first time with my soulmate, Calico Jack. I pretended I was a servant boy—and dressed the part—so I was able to keep my identity a secret on the ship, until one day old Jacky boy became green with envy. He thought I was having an affair with one of the crew members, a lad we had captured from a Dutch ship."

She laughs, remembering that day. "Well, you should have seen Jack's face when he discovered that this crew member was also disguised as a boy. Her name was Mary Read. You can just imagine the rest of the sailors' faces when they were made aware that we were both women. It was a spectacular moment to be had as we had already both proven ourselves to be loyal and vicious pirates. Mary Read was a special friend to me and fierce pirate. She fought harder than most of the men."

Thomas asks a question. "Didn't the pirates worry about the superstition of women being a curse aboard a ship?"

Anne shakes her head and continues her story. "Well, if they did, no one ever said a word to us," she says. "But you have to remember that Mary and I had been on board the sloop for many months without any issues. We were prosperous and gaining a mighty wealth."

Anne looks sad as she begins the next part of her story.

"It was not long before I became with child, and I was taken to a land called Havana to bear our child, a son. Jack and I left him there with the family of an evil pirate, Matthew Bell, and our wee boy became his heir. His name was Austin Bell, and he became as notorious and wicked as his adopted father."

Anne continues her story looking mournful. "Years later I tried to go back for my boy—after I lost my love, Jack— but it was not to be. The child had turned vengeful and hated my guts. He told me that I gave up my right to him when we left him with his adopted family. He spit in my face.

"I have always regretted my decision to leave my child with them."

Anne suddenly laughs her raucous laugh again as she resumes telling us about her life with Calico Jack.

"We continued our raiding sprees and gained a large amount of bounty." She sighs. "But everything always comes to an end. Eventually we were captured and tried for piracy, and my love was hanged. But Mary and I managed to escape a hanging as we were both with child. I did not feel sorry for Jack or our crew as they were so drunk that they weren't able to defend themselves. What a bunch of muttonheads they were!"

She hangs her head thinking about her friend and lover.

"Oh, but I did love him, and I bore him another son after I escaped. That's when I ended up on Cat Island with no other than my good friend Edward Teach. And it was also there that I met and fell in love with Billy Kercher, the great-great grandson of your ancestor, Virginia Dare. Billy raised my boy, John—Jack's son—as his own. I bore Billy five more children of his own."

"So, where did you finally end up?" Paul asks. "And what about your treasure?"

Anne laughs at my granddad's questions. "The first answer is easy, but you'll have work to find our treasure."

She continues: "I had to hide until they stopped looking for me, or I would have surely been hanged. I hid out on the island for several years, but my father finally found me and brought me home. By then I had settled down and was a real married lady."

She shrugs. "You see my papa was an important citizen of Charles Town and a prosperous barrister. He was able to pay off the chancellor so I could return to the colonies. I promised my papa I would behave and live peacefully on a land not far from his home until I died."

I am listening to Anne and suddenly have a thought. "So that means you have descendants that might be living in Charleston, South Carolina?"

Anne nods. "Aye. Why do you ask?"

I excitedly tell her about the request I received from the couple at Matt and Sarah's reception. "We had a husband and wife show up at our party yesterday saying that they are related to me," I explain. I hand her the card with their information on it. "You see it says their names are John and Chloe Brennan."

Looking at the names on the card, Anne responds. "That is possible. When I returned to the colonies, we took my mother's maiden name. But I will warn you that some of my children strayed and joined the pirates, so they could be dangerous."

Thomas speaks up. "That's my concern, too. I worry we might have unleashed a bunch of evil pirate wannabes."

Anne shakes her head in agreement. "You have a right to be worried. There is a mighty big treasure out there just waiting to be found." Then she laughs loudly again and brushes her wild red hair back from her eyes.

"I have made it difficult, though. The only way to find the treasure is to follow the clues. You will need the items I left for you in our trunk— but you will have to figure out how to use them."

47

Anne steps back, gave us all a wicked smile, and added, "At that, I will leave you all to ponder where our riches are hidden. I have left you clues in a coffer full of baubles."

As suddenly as she had materialized, Anne disappears in a haze, leaving us all open mouthed and wondering how to decipher the clues that point to the treasure. We're also trying to decide if our new relatives, the Brennans, will be good or evil.

Chapter 5

A New Relative?

Isabella sits down on one of her folding chairs. "Well, that was enlightening, but I am certainly concerned about her warning."

David puts his hand on her shoulder. "We are just going to have to be on alert like we were when we were searching for Blackbeard's treasure."

I agree and pull my phone out of my back pocket. I pick up the card carrying the contact information John and Chloe Brennan. "Well, here goes," I tell everyone. I punch in the numbers and hear a male voice answering. "Hello, this is John. Is this Angie?"

I answer with a tentative "yes," although I worry that I may be making a mistake by contacting him. "Yes, this is Angie. I got your contact information from our friend, Sam."

"Hi Angie," John replies. "I know it must seem weird. I'm sure you're wondering why we showed up at the inn instead of just calling you. But please don't worry. My wife Chloe and I have enjoyed coming to the island for many years. I even saw you play in the Oxford Pub earlier in the summer."

He pauses and then continues. "Chloe and I have never been on the island at Christmas time even though we've always wanted to. It seems like a cool new tradition to try, spending Christmas and New Year's here."

He takes a deep breath. "I think I owe you a bigger explanation, actually." I can hear him take another breath. "Well, to make a long story short, Chloe gave me one of those 23andMe tests for my birthday in October. I just got the results back. It says we are related. Chloe and I wanted to meet you and your family."

I have my phone on speaker so everyone can hear. "That's so interesting," I say, "and we would love to meet you. How about we meet at the pub later today?"

John sounds excited when he responds. "That would be great! We can be there around 6 p.m. Is that a good time for you?"

"Sure, that sounds fine," I answer.

I hang up and turn to the others. "What do you think? Is it a good idea?"

Thomas puts his arm around me. "I think it's just a meetup. It's not like we have to include him in our lives. We can just meet them and see where it leads."

Six o'clock arrives before we know it. I feel my palms becoming sweaty as Thomas and I open the pub's old oak door and walk in. "Thomas, I'm so nervous," I confide to him quietly. "I feel like I'm getting ready to perform at a large concert."

Thomas stops me and pulls me into his arms. "It's going to be okay. I'm not going to let anything happen to you— not this time," he says, thinking of when I was kidnapped last year by scary treasure hunters who overheard some of our conversations about the treasure maps we found. "And besides, just because we meet this fellow doesn't mean it has to be any more than that."

Thomas kisses me on my cheek. "If you or any of us get any bad vibes, we'll just blow him and his wife off. I already talked to our sheriff—to Bobby—and asked him to do a criminal background check. He was willing, especially after what happened to you last summer."

I frown and look into Thomas' brilliant green eyes. "My mind keeps going back to that night when Ricky and Rusty abducted me. I'm petrified that it'll happen again."

Thomas brushes my wavy black hair away from my eyes. "Oh Angie, I will lay down my life for you," he vows. "Please stop worrying. Everything is going to be fine."

We enter the room, crossing over to join our friends and family. I hesitantly ask the others, "Has anyone heard from John yet?"

Sam is at the bar. He waves and walks over to me. "Hey Angie, John just called and said that he and Chloe are on their way. They were just finishing up dinner at Dajio's so they should be here in the next fifteen minutes or so."

I release a long breath that I didn't even realize I was holding. "Thanks, Sam. How are you doing today?"

Sam hands me a menu. "I'm good. How about you? Can I get you and Thomas anything to eat? I make a mean pepperoni pizza." Sam smiles at me and continues speaking. "I can see the nerves flowing off of you," he says. "But I think you can stop worrying. That couple seemed pretty cool when I met them."

Because Sam is so close to us and because there is a chance that he will overhear things about our latest searches we've updated him on things that are happening. "Let me know if you know what you want," Sam says. "Everyone else has already ordered and gotten their food."

Thomas asks me, "How does a pizza sound, Angie? And a beer?"

I give him a thumbs up. "Sounds good to me, but can we add some veggies to it? Maybe mushrooms and onions?" I ask. "As for the beer, I think I'm just going to have a glass of white wine tonight, maybe a chardonnay."

Thomas gives our order to Sam, who returns to the bar and bring us our drinks a while later. While we wait, Thomas turns towards the others. "I was telling Angie that I asked Bobby to check out John and his wife."

Matt swats him on the back. "Man, you have ESP. I was planning on doing the same thing."

Jim listens to what Thomas and Matt are saying. "I think that's a wonderful idea," he says. "Wait. It looks like we'll have to continue this conversation later. I think our guests have arrived."

Thomas stands up to greet the couple hurrying our way. John is as tall as Thomas with curly auburn hair and Chloe is a petite blonde who comes up to John's shoulder. Thomas extends his hand. "Hi, I'm Thomas. You must be John."

John wipes his clammy palms on his faded blue jeans. "Hi, you're right, and this is Chloe," he says as he shakes hands with Thomas.

Thomas points to me. "And this is Angie." I reach out with my shaky hand, my palm sweaty, as I grab John's hand firmly in mine. I laugh nervously when I realize the Brennans' hands are just as sweaty as mine.

Thomas points to the others around the table and rattles off their names. Then he laughs. "There will be a quiz at the end of the evening." Chloe nods and laughs lightly in response, but she looks really nervous. "Hello everyone.
Thank you so much for meeting with us."

Thomas pulls out a chair next to him for Chloe and points to the chair next to it for John. "Have a seat. We're excited to meet you. Those 23andMe kits are great at digging up long-lost relatives."

John nods in agreement and begins to speak. "It is really quite fascinating, if you think about it. Who would have ever thought that when we saw Angie play this past summer that we were related. You were awesome, by the way, Angie. We really enjoyed your music."

He continues speaking. "And not only that, but to learn that we—and you—have a whole other family out there that we never knew anything about. Who would have ever thought it?"

He apologizes. "Sorry I'm rambling on. I do that when I get nervous." Chloe places her hand on John's arm to reassure him.

I look more closely at them. "Oh, my goodness. I remember you two! I think I even sat down with you at the bar in between sets. This is fascinating."

John nods. "Yeah, that was us. I wasn't sure if you would remember. We had such a nice time talking to you."

I run my hands through my wavy black hair. "Of course, I remember you. That's the nice thing about playing in a local neighborhood pub, as opposed to a huge concert venue."

Chloe sounds enthusiastic when she emphasizes how much she enjoyed that evening. "Your music is so heartfelt," she says. "I have read that you don't plan on doing any concerts. Is that correct?"

I nod. "I just can't help it—I don't want to play anywhere big. I get horrible stage fright," I say. "But, back to you guys. Tell us about yourselves."

John lovingly drapes his arm over Chloe's shoulders. "Well, there's not a whole lot to tell you. I'm a fireman with the Charleston Fire Department and have been for the last five years. Chloe is a second-grade teacher at the local Methodist school. She's been working there for the last year after graduating from Salisbury State University on the Eastern Shore. We got married last summer and came here for our honeymoon. We just love Ocracoke Island and its quaint little community."

Sally is excited to hear that Chloe is a teacher. "What a coincidence," she says. "I'm a teacher at our local school here on Ocracoke Island." She points to Robert. "My husband, Robert, is the PE teacher.

"It's a small world," Sally continues. "We have a friend who went to Salisbury. Maybe you know her, she went there and took the nursing program. Her name is Cindy Smith."

Chloe puts her hand to her heart. "Are you kidding me? She was my roommate all through school. Wow, it *is* a small world!"

Emily speaks up. "That's so cool. You might even get to see Cindy. She's been dating Sam since last summer."

Chloe points to Sam, raising her eyebrow. "Amazing. So, that's the Sam that Cindy has been telling me about. He is a cutie."

She smiles. "Cindy and I still keep in touch. In fact, we're supposed to meet up with her here later tonight."

I laugh, thinking to myself how many coincidences have led us to this moment. "I'm just wondering," I say, "do you have any siblings, John? Aunts? Uncles? You know, it's like a whole new world if you think about it."

John laughs and nods his head in the affirmative. "I have a great grandma who I saw before leaving to come to the island," he says. "Her name is Bertha Brennan, and she lives in Salem, North Carolina. As a matter of fact, that's part of the reason why we wanted to meet with you. Anne Bonny spent the last part of her life living in the house where my Grandma B now resides.

"You see," he continues, "when Anne and her husband, William Kercher, moved to the colonies, they changed their surname to Brennan after her mother, Peg."

He nods his head and continues. "Her father, William Cormac, was a prolific attorney and wealthy merchant who was able to secure her escape from trial, as long as she no longer continued her piracy. According to my granny, at this point Anne had several children and had settled down in her role as their mother."

John reaches into the pocket of his navy-blue hoodie and pulls out a worn envelope. He hands it to me. "It's a letter for you," he says.

I tentatively take the envelope from his muscular tan hands and pull out a parchment, wondering at the age of the ancient, yellowed paper. "What is this?" I ask.

I flip over to the front of the envelope and am open mouthed when I see what is written on it. I hold it out for Thomas to see. "It has our names on it." I turn to John. "I don't understand. How would your grandmother have a letter addressed to us?"

"We were just as shocked as you when we visited earlier in December and she gave me this," he says. "I wanted to call you right away, but we decided it was best to give it to you in person when we met."

He rubs his hands through his curly auburn hair and continues. "So let me back up a little bit. We went to visit Grandma B early in December. I told her about our DNA results. She's old. She was born in 1923, so she's 100 years old. She doesn't have any knowledge of computers or technology, so we had to explain everything to her."

He takes a deep breath and turns to Chloe. "Honey, can you hand me our old family Bible?"

Chloe reaches into her oversized tan purse. "Here you go," she says as she uses two hands to give it to him. "It's pretty heavy."

John takes the Bible and opens it to the first page. "So, this is crazy, right?" he says as he places the old family Bible on the table, being careful not to spill anything. He points to the pages with the family tree. "Okay, so here's what I wanted you to see. It's the part showing my great great-great grandmother. Well, it's probably more than that, but you can see how it links our two families."

He excitedly shows us Anne Bonny's name. The family tree shows her married to one of Virginia Dare's great great grandsons, William Kercher.

My grandfather, Paul looks over John's shoulder, nodding. "That's right. Remember how Virginia Dare married a Kercher on Cat Island?"

John nods and continues. "Isn't it cool? I didn't know that we were related to Anne Bonny until I saw that. I mean, I had heard rumors, but I was never shown anything concrete like this until that visit with Granny B. I've always had a thing for history, and anything about pirates, I find fascinating."

He points to the letter. "I'm not sure what's in the letter but it's hard to fathom that it's for you two. I mean, it's so old. That's too weird to think it's been waiting for you, right?"

John takes a sip of the water Sam set down beside him earlier. "Grandma B had instructions she was given about the letter. They have been passed down through the generations." John rubs his forehead and wipes his brow with one of the white paper napkins on the table. "Grandma B said that her instructions were written on this old parchment paper."

He starts to read from a separate sheet of paper he pulls from his pocket. "Please render this letter to ANGIE AND THOMAS when the time is right. You will know who and when to give this. After finding the two, you must work together to recover what is rightfully yours and theirs. They are our relatives from long ago and without their assistance, our family line will cease to exist. Do not allow this letter to fall into evil hands as they will put you all in peril."

John points to the letter. "I didn't open it. It was really hard not to. My palms were itching to see what it said. I hope that you'll share it with us."

"Um. Can you give us a minute?" I ask. Then Thomas and I pull the others aside and huddle quietly for a minute.

We whisper back and forth and decide to share the contents of the letter with John and Chloe.

I read the letter out loud:

Angie and Thomas,

If you have found this letter, then the time is right for you and my descendants to come to help me, to find me so I can escape my persecution. You may ask how is this possible, but they will share with you the secrets that they have discovered.

You see, in our travels Jack and I were able to find a treasure so remarkable that it will raise the hairs on the back of yer neck. There is a timepiece and other items that will bring you to me at my time of greatest need and peril. You must first figure out their secrets.

Beware of those who will wish to harm you and take what is rightfully yours. They must not be given the clues to our grand treasure, the jewels and wealth beyond your belief.

Please heed my warning and come to help me escape the gallows of Port Royal, Jamaica.

Truly Yours,

Anne Bonny

We all stare in astonishment at each other than collectively let out a long deep breath.

"I think we need to talk about what we should do next," I say. "But maybe this isn't the place for that discussion." Thomas looks around the room, notices another couple has just entered the quiet pub, and turns to the group. "Let's take this conversation back to Isabella and David's home. What do you all think?"

We nod in agreement and start to gather up our belongings to head over to my mother's house. Chloe picks up her phone. "Let me just text Cindy and let her know we'll meet up with her later."

Thomas takes a last bite of his pepperoni pizza and a final sip of his golden lager. Then he says, "We thought we could use the watch in some way to get in touch with Anne Bonny. But do you all realize what this letter from her could be telling us?"

John nods slowly. "I know this may sound like some insane sci-fi movie, but I think she's saying you have a timepiece that will allow you to time travel."

Chapter 6

Other Discoveries

Isabella opens the ornate white door to her home, and I wonder if we are inviting in people who mean to harm us or pilfer the treasures that we have found so far. Thomas knows me well and senses my concern. He pulls me to the side and kisses me lightly on the cheek.

"Angie, I think it's going to be okay. These two are both people who work to help the public. Just think about it, he's a fireman and she's a teacher. Nothing scary about that, huh? I think they can help us, and we can work together with them."

I nod tentatively. "I guess you're right. Besides, we don't have to share everything with them," I say. "And they might even be able to figure out the time travel thing. Wow, how cool is that! Also, a little scary, no?"

Thomas leads me through the door to where the others are standing in the parlor.

David turns and sees Thomas and me. I look at the group and ask, "Should we go right down, or should we talk more about what has happened so far?"

Paul suggests that we all move into mom's large sunroom at the rear of the home. "Why don't we all take a seat and try to update John and Chloe on what's happened so far," he says. "I think it was a good idea to come back here so no one else can hear about our discoveries."

He turns to Chloe and John and starts to explain what has transpired in the last year.

"You see, John and Chloe, I opened up a can of worms by sharing our wondrous discovery of the stone that once belonged to Virginia Dare and her husband, Kenneth Kercher." Paul shows them a photo he took of the old hand-carved stone tablet. It reads: *Virginia Dare Kercher, Born 1587*

Married Kenneth Kercher, 1602

Bore three children Mary, David, and Elizabeth in the year 1602, 1604 and 1605'

Paul goes on to explain the amazing significance of the find, and how it helped explain the fate of the Lost Colony of Roanoke, a mystery that had stumped generations of historians. He reveals how we learned that Virginia Dare and some of the other colonists were abducted by Spanish pirates and taken to Cat Island in the Bahamas. He also tells them how that discovery led us to Blackbeard's treasure—although the unexpected collapse of the cavern where it was hidden snatched the treasure out of our reach and carried it deep into the sea.

"You can well imagine that we have been bombarded with every history buff and wannabe pirate with the additional loss of Blackbeard's treasure," Paul says.

Matt throws his hands up in the air. "It's been really crazy ever since it happened. It's great for business at the inn and the pub but it's been a little bit daunting."

Sarah places her petite hand on his shoulder. "Yeah, it's been great for business, but it's attracted the strangest people to our doors. We have started screening people that are registering to stay at the inn," she says. "I'm not sure if you've ever been in the inn before but it's more of a B&B—a home with lots of guest's rooms. It's very quaint and it's our home, so we really don't want just anyone staying there.

"We already had an incident happen last summer that scared us all to death." She points to me. "Especially Angie."

I pale just thinking about the danger I had been in, but I decide it's a good idea to share what happened to me.

"Last summer when we were searching for clues to where Blackbeard's treasure map was, a couple of hoodlums overheard me telling Emily and George about a clue we had found." I sigh and continue my story. "These two were known delinquents from Ocracoke Island—they'd just recently been released from jail. They decided that they were going to get the details of our clues regardless of who got hurt in the process."

I pause for a minute then continue the story.

"Well, one night when I was on my way home from the pub, they kidnapped me and kept me hidden in a storm cellar. Luckily, we had a guardian angel—or maybe it was a guardian ghost—and our trusty dog, Max, to help find me."

John and Chloe both gasp, look at each other, and say in unison: "You were kidnapped? And a ghost saved you?" They look astonished, but then John scratches his chin and says: "I—we—have always believed in ghosts and
supernatural occurrences. Please, go on with your story." I run my fingers through my raven-colored hair, pulling it up into a ponytail. "Crazy, right? It still scares the bejeebers out of me when I think about it. So, you can understand why we are a little leery of new people."

Thomas puts his arm around me as he notices the goosebumps on my arms. "Yeah, Angie was pretty traumatized by the whole thing, as you can well imagine."

Chloe, who is sitting beside me, reaches over to place her hand on my arm. "Oh Angie, that must have been terrifying. But please, fear not, because we're good people. You can check us out if you want—it won't be the first time," she says, then chuckles. "We have to have background checks every year because of our professions. We're really just nice people."

61

John, nodding, slips his arm around Chloe. "We'll be here to protect you now, too—especially since we are all related. It's like finding out you have a whole new tribe of people. It's so cool. I can't wait for you to meet my brothers, Mike and Tony. They're my younger brothers. One is a police officer, and the other one followed me into the fire department."

I sit down on the comfy white ottoman. "Wow, I never really thought about that side of it. That *is* pretty neat," I say. "Well, John, we have a fairly big extended family, but my immediate family is here." I point to my mom, siblings and their spouses, and my grandparents.

Paul smiles at me. "Yeah, we're a tight-knit family, and we all just moved permanently to Ocracoke Island this summer." He looks around the room then gets serious again. "Let's get back to business. I think it's a good idea to show John and Chloe the secret room."

David and Isabella both stand up. Isabella leads the way. "Follow me but be careful," she states as she opens the door leading to the storm cellar and secret room.

As soon as we step through the door, we are met by musky air. We start to walk down the creaky basement steps. Thomas takes a flashlight off the wall where it is hanging; Matt and George grab two other flashlights from nearby hooks and the three men shine the bright beams ahead of where we're walking, cutting through the dim light of the cellar.

Thomas speaks up, his voice reassuring. "It's pretty tight through here and the stairs are a little rickety but it's safe."

David, who is at the front of the group, steps over to the solid oak door to the storm cellar and opens it. "Earlier in the year, we had a tornado warning and had to hide out here one night. That's when we found the secret room that once belonged to the pirates Anne Bonny and Calico Jack. We think they used the room to hide from the British brigadier who was trying to arrest them."

Thomas walks over to the bookshelves in the storm cellar, reaches in, and pushes the latch that exposes the hidden tunnel leading to the secret room.

"Here it is," he says. "We did some research and found out that the house once belonged to Anne and Jack. The home was originally owned by the English pirate Charles Vane, who was friends of Edward Teach— otherwise known as Blackbeard. Calico Jack was a mate on Vane's ship until the crew called for Vane to step down in favor of Jack. When Calico Jack became the captain of Vane's sloop, Ranger, this house became Jack and Anne's hideaway."

John and Chloe look both shocked and excited. John peeks down the tunnel. "I feel like I'm in a movie or something. It just doesn't seem like this should be real."

I laugh. "You haven't seen anything yet," I say. Then I turn to the rest of the group. "Why don't we conjure up old Anne and get her to come meet her descendants?"

Thomas asks Matt and George to give him a hand pulling out the old wooden chest from the secret tunnel that we had found. "I think it would be easier if we brought everything out here to examine," Thomas adds. "We can put all the items on the tables again."

The guys haul out the old cedar coffer. Thomas opens the lid. "Prepare to go back to a long-forgotten time. We found these things in the chest and in the secret room."

He hands the sepia picture of Anne to John and Chloe. "This is the first clue we had as to who these items belonged to, that and the fact that we met her ghost on Cat Island."

He points to me. "It is a pretty crazy story. Angie, do you want to tell them about how we met Anne?"

I can't help but laugh as I'm looking at John and Chloe, remembering how shocking it was for us at first, even though we had experience dealing with Evangeline's spirit.

"It's a pretty insane story and I wouldn't blame you if you both thought I am crazy," I say. "When we found and lost Blackbeard's treasure down the shaft in the caverns of the coves of Cat Island, we encountered and were introduced to Anne's ghost."

I grin at the awestruck looks on their faces. "She's just as she appears in the pictures and as wild as any stories you might have heard about her. It all started when Evangeline pointed out that she'd brought me into contact with the ghost of my cousin, Virginia Dare, but I hadn't yet met Anne Bonny. She told me that Anne was a long-distance cousin of mine. She married one of Virginia's great-great grandsons."

I smile remembering her story.

"Anne went on to say, 'You might not have been able to reap the rewards of Blackbeard's plunder but mine is ripe for the picking. You only have to find the clues that I have hidden in our old home. You have already found our map, but you will need my help to find my treasure.'

"She went on to tell me, 'Angie, the precious watch I gave Jack will be your link to me. You only have to take it in your hands to reach me.'"

John rubs his hands over his chin. "Wow, that's some story. I don't even know what to say about it."

I laugh. "Well, every word is true. We'll just have to show you," I say.

John shakes his head and comments. "The crazy thing is I believe every word you've said. Being a fireman, I've seen all kinds of weird things. I can't wait to meet Anne. This is so exciting."

Bitsey Gagne

Anne's Bounty

Chapter 7

Anne Returns

I set the watch to the time and date of Calico Jack's hanging. Suddenly, Anne appears before us.

"Well, it looks like you have been busy," she says, pointing to John and Chloe. She steps closer and stares deeply into John's eyes, a look of recognition crossing her brow.

"Ahoy, matey, who have we here?"

I turn toward Anne and point to John and Chloe. "Anne, this is one of your descendants. His name is John Brennan, and this is his wife, Chloe. They are from Charleston, South Carolina."

Anne walks around the two, looking them up and down, and finally says, "Well, he has my husband's eyes, that's for sure. And I did end up living in Charleston after I escaped from Cat Island.

"You trust them?" she asks.

Thomas answers. "I think they are pretty trustworthy. They both have jobs helping the public. Nowadays we have ways to check out people's criminal history, and both of them checked out okay."

I hand Anne the letter that John has given me. "John's great grandmother gave this to him to pass on to Thomas and me," I say. "This letter is from you."

Anne takes the letter from me and nods. "Aye, 'tis."

She points to all of us. "Your very existence relies upon you coming to save me from prison in Port Royal. I shall have to teach you how to go back in time to help me escape the gallows."

Thomas and I look at each other and then back to Anne before we say, in unison, "But how? We have no idea how to time travel."

Anne picks up the timepiece I had set down on the table. "You will need this. You only need to set the day and time to the 28th of November in the year 1720."

She also picks up the periscope that had been sitting next to the watch. She indicates an indentation and then slips the timepiece into the slot on the 'scope. "After setting the time, place the watch in this slot here. You then need to state this phrase while holding hands."

She looks at Thomas and me. "You two must make sure you hold hands, so you won't be separated. It's very important to do that."

She continues in an excited voice. "You must chant, three times, 'Take me to a time when Anne's soul is needing to be rescued from the gallows of Port Royal Jamaica.' Once you find me, you must take me to Cat Island so that I can meet my everlasting love, my husband to be, William Kercher."

She points to me, my siblings, and grandparents. "He is your ancestor, Virginia Dare's great, great grandson," she says. "I must meet him, fall in love, and bear his children. If I do not, none of you will exist. It is imperative that you do this, or it could change the course of history."

We all look back at her dumbstruck. Thomas runs his hands through his curly blond hair and asks, "When exactly is it that we should do this? Isn't it going to be dangerous? What if we are caught?"

Anne raises her hands in the air. "Aye, you could be. But you will have the watch, and it will help us escape quickly. This meeting today was meant to happen—your very survival is dependent upon what you do.

You must leave as soon as you can, but first you must dress to fit the time. Otherwise, you will stick out like a purple elephant."

Paul looks at us and points to the cedar chest. "Well, we have Anne's clothes and Jack's clothes from the past. Angie and Thomas, you can change into those, so you won't stand out."

My grandfather turns to Anne. "But how will they know where they will appear? Will they end up in the gallows with you or outside your cell?"

Evangeline and Virginia's spirits materialize before us. Evangeline reaches out to Thomas and me. "Fear not. We will keep you safe. It is your fate that this should come to pass."

Virginia smiles and exclaims, "It is written in the stars and was meant to be when the time was right."

Everyone is suddenly chattering at once. I take Thomas hands in mine and finally say, "Let's do it. They have kept us safe so far. I know it's crazy, but last summer I didn't even really believe in ghosts and now look at me. I'm conjuring them up. Why not time travel? Just think how exciting this will be when we tell our children."

Anne interrupts me. "Yes, you must do this. If you do not, there will be no children to tell—because none of you will exist.

"Remember that you only need find me and take me to Cat Island," she adds. "When you have me, you must all hold hands. Then say these words: 'Take me to Cat Island.'
"After that, you will be able to return to this day and time by chanting, 'Take me back to my time and where my loved ones are waiting for me in the cellar on Ocracoke Island.'"

I laugh nervously. "You make it sound so easy." Then I take a deep breath and turn to the man I love. "Well, Thomas, do you feel like going to 1720?"

Thomas nods, laughing, and declares. "Okay, let's do this before we lose our nerve."

We both quickly change into the clothes that once belonged to Anne and Calico Jack. Anne hands Thomas a gem-studded sword and she passes me a dagger with rubies embedded in its handle. "Here you two," she says, "take these just in case you run into danger."

As she places the saber in my shaking clammy hands, I notice the intricate carvings on the hilt. She points to an area of my pirate's outfit. "Hide the dagger in this slot. It will be hidden but easy to reach," she says. "You should be able to go right to the cell where I am being held for execution but, just in case there is trouble, you will have these."

I stare at the ornate blade and slip it into my clothes where Anne has indicated. "I hope we won't need these. I've never used a knife before."

Anne laughs. "Believe me, if you are in fear for your life, you will not hesitate," she says.

Evangeline is standing next to Virginia. She speaks up. "We will be with you two every step of the way. Fear not. The time is right," she says.

Thomas looks at me, kisses me on the cheek, and says, "Okay, let's do this."

Chapter 8

A Time Forgotten

My mother and the others reach out to embrace Thomas and me. Isabella takes my chin in her hands and places a gentle kiss on my cheek. "Please be careful." She puts her arms around both me and Thomas. "Thomas, take care of my little girl," she says. A small tear slides down her cheek.

I look into those tearful baby blue eyes. "I'll be fine, Mom. I have Thomas and we have guardian angels helping us."

I sense something and look behind my mother. My father's spirit appears. He looks just as he did before he died so unexpectedly last year. "I'll take care of them, too, Isabella. Don't you fear. You might not always see us, but we will be there if ever you need us."

He waves goodbye but before his ghost disappears before our eyes, he turns to Paul. "They'll be back before you know it—and with tales you never dreamed possible."

My father winks at Paul. "So glad you finally found the Lost Colonists. Who would have ever thought that we were related to them?"

Paul's eyes are watering as he reaches out to my father. "I know. I only wish you could have been there when we found them," he says. "I sure do miss you and all the days we spent researching Ocracoke Island's wonderous history."

My father nods. "I know. But always be assured that I will be here in spirit whenever you need me." He waves goodbye as his ghost evaporates before our eyes.

Anne hands Thomas and me the watch and the periscope. "It's time to go," she says. "But first I must warn you of one more thing. The Anne in the past does not know about this plan," she says. "You see, I did not find out about the watch's magical qualities until I was back in the colonies."

"What?! You mean we might have to fight you once we find you?" Thomas squawks out. "She—I mean, you— will think we're crazy when we show up. Or maybe worse. What if she thinks we're witches?"

Anne reaches into her pocket. "You must give her this trinket. 'Tis a small rabbit's foot I got when I was but a wee one hunting with the lads," she says. "Tell her that you were given this by me in the future. Assure her that there are sometimes things in life we cannot know or understand. Remind her to think back to her childhood days in Cork, Ireland, and the stories that her mother, Peg, told her."

Anne nods her head reassuringly. "Tell her what I have said, explain about the watch, and let her know that she must go with you if she and her child are to survive.

"Now hurry!" she says. "We must do this as the veil is thin now. Take the watch and periscope and repeat after me."

Thomas and I nod. I reach out to take the watch from Anne. "Okay, let's do this, Thomas, before I change my mind."

She points to the magical timepiece. "You have already set the date and time on the watch. Now you must hold hands and repeat these words: 'Take me to a time where Anne's soul is needing to be rescued from the gallows of Port Royal, Jamaica.'"

We nervously hold hands and recite the words that she has given us. We say in unison: "Take me to a time where Anne's soul is needing to be rescued from the gallows of
Port Royal Jamaica."

Chapter 9

What? Time Travel?

The room spins for Thomas and me. We hold onto each other's hands as a time vortex spirals around us. The air is dense, almost sweet, and saturated with the aroma of lavender and mint. Wherever we are, it is dark and glorious. Suddenly, we are rapidly approaching a brilliant light ahead of us.

And then, unexpectedly, we are dumped onto a brown dirt floor.

The sweet-smelling draft that had swirled around us turns putrid, smelling of rotting flesh and rancid body odor. We are in a dingy room with stone walls. It is furnished sparsely with only a tiny wooden desk, a reed-back chair, and an oak cabinet. Thomas is still desperately holding my hands. He looks deeply into my terrified blue eyes. "I think we're here," he says. "Are you okay?"

I dry rub my now-sweating face with my free hand. "I think so. Can you tell where we are?"

Thomas cautiously stands up with my other hand, which is shaking, still in his. "I think we are in a jail, but I'm not sure where Anne is. I guess we'll have to find her."

We hear a whistling coming from around the corner. We quickly hide behind the wooden cabinet. Cautiously, we peek around it to see who has come into the room. It is a British officer dressed in clothes from a long-ago era. Thomas places his finger to his lips and mouths the following: "We must stay hidden until this guy leaves. I really don't want to use this sword. He will have to take a break at some point."

My frightened heart is racing. It feels like it will erupt through my chest. I try to control my breathing as we wait for the officer to leave his perch at the old wooden desk. Finally, he stands up. He stretches and I see a short wooden pipe in one of his hands. "Ah, a smoke break," I think. He leaves and through the window in the room, we see him. His tall, lean frame is propped up against the stone wall as he stares out toward the crystal blue water visible ahead.

Thomas grabs my hand, and we start down the narrow hallway leading past dingy cells with iron bars. A set of rusting keys are hanging haphazardly on a thick iron nail. Thomas reaches up to grab the keys when we hear hoots from the dirty, stinking wenches in the cells. An especially raucous laugh comes from a wild looking—and pregnant—redhead.

"Hey, handsome, so what have we here?" she calls out suggestively to Thomas.

Thomas places a key into the worn latch and opens the heavy iron door. "Anne, come with us!" he orders her. "Your life is in danger. We're here to rescue you."

Anne laughs hysterically. "Oh, matey, I can do as I please." She starts to push past Thomas to get out of the jail cell, but he quickly grabs her slender wrist to stop her. "You'll never get away going out that way," he says. "You must come with us."

She ignores him and tries to push past us. His muscular hand still holds her slender wrist. Thomas pulls out the watch that Anne had given to her love Calico Jack and hurriedly tells her, "I have your watch. You must listen to me and remember the stories your mother told you when you were young, the stories about magical things that you never understood."

Thomas holds up the timepiece and the telescope. "This watch will help you escape." Anger flares in Anne's bright green eyes. She grabs for the watch. "Where did you get that timepiece?" she demands. "It belongs to Jack." Then she looks at me. "And who are you?" she asks, menacingly.

Anne reaches into her ragged boot and pulls out a sharp-edged spoon. Before I know what is happening, she has the deadly blade at my pale white neck, shocking Thomas and—definitely—me.

"If you know what's good for you and you want your woman to survive, you'll let me pass," she says to Thomas.

Thomas nervously reaches into his brown leather pouch and pulls out the small rabbit's foot. "Wait. This will be hard to understand, but the future you told us to give you this—and said you must listen to us." She grabs the dirty, shabby rabbit's foot from Thomas and stares at him with wild eyes. "Who are you people and how did you get my wee trinket? Are ye witches?" she demands to know. "The 'future me'? What are you talking about?"

I try to push the sharp blade away from my neck. I nervously chime in. "It's true, Anne. I know it doesn't make sense, but we have to hurry and get you out of here. We don't know how much time we have before the guard returns. He just stepped out for a smoke."

Anne shakes her head. "You will be getting me out of here? How do ye plan on doing that?"

Thomas holds up the antique gold watch. "This watch has magical properties. We are from the future. Your future self-sent us to save you from the gallows. Grab our hands, don't let go, and say these words 'Take me to Cat Island.'"
Anne jerks her hands back. She looks astonished. "Have ye lost your minds? 'Tis nonsense. I will not do it. I will take my chances on my own."

She tries again to leave just as we hear the front door of the jail squeak open. The British officer is whistling. I grab Anne's wrist and whisper, "Come on. We have to go. You still have a life to live. If you don't come with us, you and your child will not survive."

Anne gazes down at her swollen belly and places shaky hands on it. She nods and takes our hands. "Okay, for my wee one."

"Don't let go of our hands, whatever you do," I say as I tell her to repeat with us: "Take me to Cat Island."

I feel the world swirling. It's inky dark with the sweet lavender mint aroma surrounding us once again. This time we land in soft sand, and I look up to see a gentle waterfall cascading down into a cave. Thomas and I know this place. We were here when we were searching for Blackbeard's treasure. Anne gasps, grasps her swollen belly, and skitters away from us. "Ye are witches. Where have ye taken me to?"

I lay back on the silky sand and look into Anne's eyes. "No, we aren't witches. The watch is magical. You are here because this is a safe place for you to hide. It is one of Edward Teaches hiding places. From what the future you told us," I say, "you were friends with him and met him on Ocracoke Island."

She continues to scramble backward away from us. "But what am I to do here?"

Thomas explains. "According to the future you, you will hide out here until you can safely come back to the colonies. The future you wrote us a letter telling us to travel through time to save you."

Thomas holds up the watch. "Years from now, the future you discovered that this watch has magical properties that could carry people into the past. You couldn't time travel to save yourself from the gallows—it would have warped the timeline—but you figured out a way to tell us to come here."

She raises her eyebrows questioningly. "So, we can go back and save my ole Jacky?"

Thomas adamantly shakes his head. "No, we can't change history. Now, you will stay here—and we have to go."

She tries to grab the watch from him, but Thomas manages to hold it up higher than her reach. He tells her, "If you take this watch from me, what we're doing right now—saving you in the past—will never happen."

She stops reaching for the timepiece. "Well, go on then. Go back where you came from," she says. "I can handle myself."

Thomas and I nod, hold hands, and begin to chant, "Take us back to our time and where our loved ones are waiting for us in the cellar on Ocracoke Island."

I look deeply into Thomas's eyes as we chant. I am praying that we can return to our time. Suddenly the air around us spins and swirls. The sandy beach is gone, and we are thrust back to the future. We land exactly where we left, to the surprised glances and shouts of our loved ones.

Isabella rushes to put her arms around me with tears streaming down her face. "I was so scared for you and Thomas," my mother confides as she takes my face in her trembling hands.

"I am so glad you are back and both unharmed," she adds as she places her hand on Thomas' brawny arm. The others rush up to hug us and Anne materializes before our eyes again. "You are all still here—so apparently you were successful."

Emily is pummeling us with questions. "So how was it? Was it as cool as I think it was? I want to do it next."

Anne takes the watch from Thomas. "That will not be possible as it could change history. But you can take the watch and see into the future."

Emily shakes her head in disappointment. "I was really looking forward to going back in time," she says. "Just think. We could watch as history is unfolding."

We think about this for a few seconds, then Emily says,

"Well, tell us what happened."

I breathlessly answer by telling our turbulent story.

"We went through the mysterious time vortex. It was like being in a dark, swirling, twirling tunnel with the strangest, sweetest aroma of lavender and mint. It was so scary and so exhilarating," I say. "We landed on a dirt floor in the middle of the jail. Luckily, we just missed a British officer that had gone into another room."

I point to Thomas. "You tell the rest."

Thomas continues to tell the others of our escapade. "It was terrifying," he said. "We had to hide behind a cabinet in the room until the British officer went outside and then we searched for Anne."

He shrugs his broad shoulders. "You should have seen that place. It was really crazy. And I had to just stop myself from thinking about what we were doing," he continues. "We managed to sneak down the filthy hallway to where Anne was held captive."

He shakes his head remembering the stench. "It was awful. The place smelled of rotten flesh and decaying meat and feces. The black flies were swarming around the waste in each cell. It almost made me vomit." He points to me. "We managed to get into the cell with Anne. She was as much a character when she was young—maybe more so, if that's even possible—than she was when she was older."

He anxiously laughs. "The future Anne was right about Anne of the past. She was our biggest danger. She sharpened a spoon into a deadly blade and she caught us off guard by holding it at Angie's neck. When I saw a small pin prick of blood well up on Angie's neck, I pulled out the rabbit's foot and rushed to tell her the story Anne of the future told us.

"She finally relinquished and allowed us to help her escape—just in the nick of time. The officer guarding the jail had finished his smoke break and had just come back into the building."

I tenderly put my arms around Thomas's neck and nuzzle my head under his chin as he rubs my hair.

"I was so scared she was going to slice your throat," he confides.

"Finally, we escaped to Cat Island," he continues. "Anne tried to take the watch so she could help Jack escape but, luckily, we were able to persuade her that she couldn't because it would change history... We left her on Cat Island and, thankfully, returned here to this time."

I turn around with my back to Thomas. He wraps his arms around me. "I haven't been that scared since I was kidnapped by Rusty and Ricky," I say. "I was never so glad to see all your lovely faces."

I rub my face with my still trembling hands. "What an adventure! But I just keep thinking how badly it could have gone. What if we had been stuck in the past?

"Right now, I just need to stop thinking about 'what ifs,'" I declare.

Paul grins and touches my cheek. "I was never so glad to see your faces either. When it's convenient, you'll have to tell me all about the jail cell you were in and about Cat Island."

John and Chloe are standing behind the others looking shocked. John steps forward. "You guys are something. I don't know if I could have done it," he says. "Well, I guess I could have if I'd been through the same year you had. Maybe you've become desensitized to danger."

Thomas nods. "Yeah, I guess you're right," he says. "I'm not so sure if we would have done it if it weren't for all the stuff we've been through.

"So, I take it that everyone else has updated you on our escapades of the past year," he adds.

My brother, Matt, looks at his Apple watch. "What amazes me is that you were only gone about half an hour. How long were you back in the past?"

79

Thomas looks at Anne's timepiece. "According to this watch, we were gone for about three hours. It felt like longer, though, especially when we were hiding behind the armoire waiting for the officer at the jail to take a break and leave the room."

The cedar chest is still on the floor, so I reach in and pull out the dress with the secret code in the pocket. "What about these things in your chest?" I ask Anne. "Do we have enough here to find your treasure?"

Anne shakes her wild auburn hair. "Aye, ye have what you need. But you still must figure out to find the treasure." She points to all of us. "I will help as I can, but you first must prove to me that you will work together. And you must trust no out outside this circle. There are others who would love to steal my treasure."

She bows. "I will leave you now so you can work on the clues you have found," she says. "And remember: You can use the telescope to look into the past for answers to questions you may have."

With that, she vaporizes in a mist.

Chapter 10

Hidden Clues

Paul picks up the periscope and examines it. He notices unusual lines and extra dials. "Look. There are notches on the 'scope," he says. "I wonder if we set the watch and then look through the telescope whether we can see what is happening at that particular moment in the past?"

Robert looks over his shoulder and agrees. "I think we might need to be careful, though, or we could end up on a gangplank." He thinks for a moment then adds, "Maybe we should ask Anne."

Paul nervously responds. "You might be right. We'll need to be cautious." He sits the 'scope back down on the table. "What about the paper we found sewn into the pocket of the dress?"

David puts on a pair of white gloves and picks up the delicate parchment. "I think we need to look at what's written here, plus study the map that we found. I also wonder, John, if there might be something hidden in your Bible that could help lead us to the treasure."

John holds up the precious family heirloom. "Maybe. I haven't examined it. It was right before we came here that my great grandma Bertha gave it to me, so I didn't really have time to look at it. She had been instructed to render the book when the time was right."

He hands the Bible to Paul. "Do you want to take a look? It's very possible there's something in it that would be helpful," John says.

Paul lays the Bible on the table, delicately opening it to the front pages where the family tree is located. "Let's look back to when Anne started documenting her family history," he says. We all stand around the table watching as Paul and Robert delve into the family lineage. Paul points to first page. "It shows here that Anne is born in Cork, Ireland. It shows her having a son with Jack Rackham; it says that her first son, Austin Bell, was born in Cuba but there's no other mention of him after that."

He scratches his bearded chin. "She must have lost sight of him. She told us that she went back for him, but he didn't want anything to do with her."

John speaks up. "That makes sense. When I did the 23andMe test, it showed that I am related to a Stephen Bell. He emailed me, but I haven't gotten back to him. He lives in Jamaica."

Paul runs his hands over his thinning hair. "Wow, that's something," he says. "But I think we need to be careful there because Anne said she unknowingly left him with an evil pirate. Bell could be a danger to us. I would tread lightly."

Thomas is pacing, thinking aloud. "But isn't it possible that this Stephen Bell in Jamaica might know how to find the treasure?" Thomas turns to John. "I think you should contact him. We can ask Billy to do a background check on him. I'll ask Billy right now if he can."

John holds up his phone. "I did a Facebook check on him. He owns a diving company and is a known treasure hunter. He has a girlfriend. Her name is Violet Morgan," John says. "Hey! I wonder if she's related to Henry Morgan. He was a pirate back in the day, too."

Matt asks, "Wasn't he a big-time Welsh pirate in the Bahamas and Jamaica?"

David perks up. "Yes, you're right," he says. "Henry Morgan was known in Port Royal, Jamaica. He actually was Sir Henry Morgan, and he became the lieutenant governor in Jamaica. He even owned several sugar plantations on the island. Chances are this Violet is a descendant of his."

Matt pats David on the back. "Now wouldn't that be cool, another pirate treasure to find."

John exclaims, "I'm up for it! I never thought in a million years that I would be looking for a treasure."

Paul continues to slowly flip through the pages of the Bible, looking to see if there are extra sheets or notes slipped between pages of the heirloom. He gets to the back of the Bible and notices that the back flap of the book is lifting up. He slides his finger under the loose flap.

"Well, well, look at this."

He carefully pulls the page up, being cautious not to rip the fragile paper. He gently tugs out a narrow booklet that is hidden under the flap. "I wonder what this is?" he says.

We all gather closely behind him as he reads what's written at the top of the paper. *'Captain John Rackham – Calico Jack Memoir'*

He takes a breath and continues reading.

I am now Captain of the vessel known as the Ranger. In a unanimous vote, the crew took the title away from Charles Vane and bestowed it upon me. In this log, I list some of the booty I have commandeered in my privateering. I have used an Old English cipher to hide the details from eyes that cannot understand.

Dlog Rohcna I detlem nwod dlog srab dna dih meht na a evac ni Aciamaj & Erusaert tsehc si neddih ni a evac ni Acimaj & Erusaert tsehc fo slewej si no Ekocarco Dnalsi

Anyone in possession of my log can take possession of this treasure if they can decipher my code. A map in my log shows the location, but you must first figure out how to read it.

I excitedly exclaim, "Now we just need to break the code!"

I am standing on the other side of the table when Paul holds up the map. I notice an outline of something on the backside of the page. I grab Thomas's arm. "Oh my gosh, Thomas, look. The way Granddad is holding up the map, the light is shining through it. You can see the shape of another map."

I take out my phone and snap a picture of it. I show everyone the photo, and they are as intrigued as I am.

"I'm going to do a Google search and see if this map outline matches some location," I announce. "This is so exciting! I wouldn't have noticed it if I hadn't been standing on this side of the table."

An image pops up in the search menu. "It's Jamaica—just like we suggested! Now we just have to puzzle out what the clues are!" I tell everyone. We all start whooping and hollering. Thomas hugs me and then kisses me on my cheek. "Way to go, honey. That's amazing."

Robert is staring at jumbled words in the captain's logs. "Hey guys, you aren't going to believe this, but I think I figured it out." He looks up at all of us and says, "The words are just written backwards."

To prove his theory, he takes a pen from his pocket and jots down the first line on another piece of paper.

Dlog Rohcna I detlem nwod dlog srab dna dih meht ni a evac no Aciamaj

He starts to reverse the letters: *Gold Anchor I melted down gold bars and hid them in a cave*

He goes on to the second line: *Erusaert tsehc si neddih ni a evac no Acimaj.* It turns out to be *Treasure Chest is hidden in a cave in Jamaica*

Erusaert tsehc fo slewej si no Ekocarco Dnalsi becomes *Treasure chest of jewels is on Ocracoke Island*

That last line, in particular, sparks gasps and laughs. We shake our heads in disbelief. My sister, Sally, hugs Robert and plants a wet kiss on her husband's lips. "Way to go, honey. You're so smart," she says.

Robert laughs and pats himself on the back. "The coolest part of this discovery is that there is a treasure chest right here on Ocracoke Island!"

David turns to Isabella. "It must be hidden somewhere in your house," he says. "That would make so much sense, if you think about it. What better strategy than to separate the treasure into two parts. The pirates never knew where they might end up. This way, if they had to hide out here, they'd have some of their treasure close at hand."

Paul nods in agreement. "I think Isabella's house is a good bet. Now we just need to figure out *where* it is in the house. Is there something we're missing? Maybe another clue somewhere? Could there be a clue in the paper that Anne hid in her dress pocket?" he asks.

I put on the white gloves David used earlier and carefully pick up the paper, examining what Anne has written in code. Then I hold it up to the light.

Sarah squeals in excitement. "Look! There's a clue—it's just like the map, but this time it's some transparent writing that shows through the paper. Let me look closer." She examines the paper. "It says, 'Look to a place that is hidden from view and has kept us safe.'"

She thinks for a minute then points to the secret room. "It has to be in there somewhere," she says, confidently. "We need to take another look."

Matt grabs a couple of the flashlights that we have placed on a shelf and asks, "Who's coming? It's a shame George had a call this morning, but he said he should be here in a little while."

Isabella, Mary, and Sally all shake their heads in the negative as they say in unison, "You guys go."

Paul nods. "I think just a few of us should go, otherwise it'll be too crowded," he says. "David, Jim, the ladies, and I will stay here and re-examine the other clues. I want to look inside the cedar chest again to make sure there is nothing else in there that we're missing."

With flashlights in hand, Matt, Sarah, Emily, John, Chloe, Sally, Robert, Thomas, and I head into the concealed tunnel leading to the shadowy room.

Anne's Bounty

Chapter 11

The Search

We start to meander down the dark, dank tunnel leading to the secret room. Thomas suggests. "Why don't Angie, Emily, and I look along the tunnel wall to see if maybe there is another secret room or hidden compartments. The rest of you can go on straight to the secret room."

Matt nods his head. He has a headlight on his baseball cap, and it shines in my eyes. I laugh and cover my eyes. "Well, Matt, you can light up the whole tunnel with that thing."

Matt takes his lighted hat off. "Do you like it? Maybe I'll get you one for Christmas."

His bright white teeth shine in the darkness. Thomas pops my brother on his head laughing at him. "Gift me one, too. They will be great when we go to Jamaica to explore the caves. I can't believe Christmas is in two days."

Matt chuckles. "Wouldn't it be awesome if we found some of Anne and Jack's treasure today—the ultimate Christmas present!"

Then he adds: "The other area we need to check out is where that ceiling exit goes outside. John and Chloe, are you up for finding some buried treasure? You can help us search."

John and Chloe are grinning from ear to ear. "This is so neat. Never in a million years did I think that we would ever be on the hunt for treasures. When we were kids, Chloe and I and a group of us used to go fortune-hunting in Charleston."

Sally turns and looks at Robert. "Why don't we check outside right now and see if we can find anything under my mom's bushes," she suggests.

"I think it's going to be too crowded in the secret room and I'm already feeling a little claustrophobic in this dark tunnel. Is that okay with you?"

Robert nods his head. "I agree with you. Plus, it smells horrid in here— it's so musty."

Robert takes Sally by the hand and leads her back toward the cellar. "Come on, honey. Let's go find some buried treasure."

Matt, Sarah, John, and Chloe continue forward until they reach the end of the tunnel. They open the door into the cryptic niche. It's the first time they have seen the room. John looks around, taking in all the details.

"Wow, this is crazy. Look at all the old things in here," he says. He picks up a candleholder sitting atop the antique oak barrel. "Just think, this was probably the only light they had when they were hiding out down here. It must have been terrifying to be stuck here in the dark. Can you just imagine them sneaking down here away from the British brigadiers?"

Chloe pulls out a Zippo and lights the nubby yellowed candle. "I would have gone crazy down here," she says. "I wonder how long they had to stay hidden. And do you think this whole hidden area was already here, or did they dig out the tunnel after they got the property?"

Matt explains what we found out earlier in the year. "From what we understand, this house originally belonged to the pirate Charles Vane, so we think that he probably dug this out when he was in command of the Ranger. After Jack became captain, he and Anne took over Vane's belongings, including the house. So, we might actually find things that belong to Charles Vane."

Sarah tucks back some wispy blonde hairs that have escaped from her ponytail. "You know, he probably didn't tell Anne and Jack where he kept his bounty," she says. "I hope we *do* find some of Vane's things. No telling where they could lead us!"

Matt gives Sarah a peck on the cheek. "Well, let's see if we can find anything. A lot of the stuff is already in the storm cellar room, but you never know. We might stumble across something of Vane's."

They search the secret room but to no avail. Meanwhile Thomas, Emily, and I are combing the walls of the tunnel. Thomas being Thomas finds a hidden alcove that leads to another covert room.

We brush back spiderwebs as we enter that cubbyhole, which is set up pretty much the same as the other secret room—with one exception. This one contains a huge wooden bench with storage underneath. Thomas carefully lifts the hinged cover of the wooden bench Inside the lid there is a picture of a pirate I don't recognize.

"Who's this?" I ask.

Emily looks at the hand-painted image. "I think it's Charles Vane, but I'm not sure. Thomas, what do you think?"

Thomas agrees with her. "That's him. Anyway, it makes sense that it's Vane. He owned this house before Jack," he says as he pokes around in the bench. "Oh, look. What else do we have in here?"

He pulls out a captain's journal and hands it to me laughing. "Here, Angie. Maybe you can use it as background to write another book just like the book you are writing about your ancestor, Evangeline, and the story about her being captured by Blackbeard's grandson, Daniel. You're almost done with it, aren't you?"

I shake my head, 'yes,' thinking how I should be finished with the book soon. Then I turn my attention back to the captain's journal. On the front cover, written in English calligraphy, are the words 'Charles Vane, born 1680.'

"You're right. This does belong to Vane," I say, pointing to his name. I take extra care as I open the book and turn its crinkly, yellowed parchment pages.

"Granddad is going to be thrilled about this discovery. He loves this kind of stuff. We'll have to look more closely at the logbook later," I say. "I wonder how everyone else is doing."

We look through the rest of the room but don't spot anything else that might be useful for finding pirate treasure. We decide to pull the storage bench out of the room to show the others.

Thomas points to the bench. "Girls, can you give me a hand dragging this thing out into the other room?"

I pick up the journal and lay it on top of the chest. "Let's bring the captain's log out, too, so we can take a closer look."

As we push the bench out of the room, we encounter Sarah, Matt, Chloe, and John in the tunnel. Thomas points to the room we've found. "Look, guys, there was another secret hiding hole. This one belongs to Charles Vane. Check out this bench."

Matts swats Thomas on the back. "Awesome. I can wait to explore the room," he says. "Glad you were successful. We didn't find anything new in the other room."

Matt puts his hand on the storage chest. "And what have we here? Is that what I think it is?"

I hold up the journal. "Not only that, but we found a diary in the bench. We were just taking everything out to get a closer look at it."

Thomas and Matt drag the chest the rest of the way down the tunnel and into the storm cellar where the others are still looking over the objects from Anne and Jack's cedar chest.

Paul excitedly asks us, "Is that what I think it is? Is it the buried treasure?"

I laugh at my grandfather's hopeful question. "If only! It isn't—but it *is* another chest and another journal, only this time they belong to Charles Vane. We need to examine them more carefully."

I look around, questioningly. "Did Sally and Robert find anything outside?"

Before anyone has a chance to answer, John and Chloe inform us that they have a lunch reservation with Cindy and Sam, and they need to dash. "I am so glad that you included us and we would love to stay, but we already made these lunch reservations yesterday," John says, adding that they will catch up with us later.

Chloe adds, excitedly, "This has been so cool. I wish we could stay to see what happens, but I told Cindy we'd meet her and Sam today for lunch in Cape Hatteras. Now, I know that Sam knows about everything, but does Cindy know about all of this?"

I shake my head. "We haven't said anything to her," I answer, "although we know she and Sam are pretty close."

John opens the storm cellar door to head upstairs. He turns back to us. "Don't worry. Lips sealed," he says as he pantomimes zipping his lips shut. "I'll give you a call tomorrow."

"We'll let you know what we find," I assure him.

As they head up the stairs to the kitchen, I follow John and Chloe.

"I'll walk you guys up," I say. "I know this has been pretty crazy!"

Then I add: "I don't know what your plans are, but I wanted to invite you to join us for Christmas Eve tomorrow night. I hope you can make it. It's pretty casual. We just have a nice dinner with everyone who was here today except we add the twins. They are so cute."

John and Chloe both nod, smiling. "That would be awesome," John says.

"We were wondering what we were going to do for Christmas," Chloe adds. "We're so used to spending the holidays with our families. Maybe we can Facetime them tomorrow so you can meet them."

I smile and nod. "That sounds great. Have fun at lunch—— and see you tomorrow," I say. "Now I'm going to see if Robert and Sally found anything outside."

Chapter 12

Another Tunnel

I am wondering about Sally and Robert as I head back downstairs to let the others know I'll check on my sister. Suddenly, the other door into the basement—the one leading in from the backyard—opens and they both rush inside. They are flushed from running down the stairs from the yard to the basement. They look ecstatic.

Robert points to Sally. "Tell Angie what happened. You guys aren't going to believe it."

Sally is waving her hands wildly in the air. She gestures toward her feet. "We were outside, trying to calculate where that exit from the secret room would be. We thought we were close to the spot when I stepped to the left—and my feet busted through a piece of wood in the dirt! I almost fell through a hole in the ground. I would have fallen right in if Robert hadn't grabbed ahold of me." She rubs her hands over her scraped up ankles.

"It was crazy," she continues. "It looks like there's another tunnel. We didn't explore it because it is too dark down the hole. We'll need flashlights and ropes to check it out."

Robert picks up flashlights and asks," Matt, do you know if your dad left any heavy-duty rope around here? I think we need to make sure when we go down to check out the other tunnel that we are secured. We don't want anyone getting hurt."

Matt reaches into a shelf on the wall and pulls out ropes, bungee cords, and some rock-climbing harnesses. "Will this work? If not, Thomas and I have ropes in our work trucks."

Matt's phone beeps with a message. "It's George. He's on his way downstairs from the backyard. He didn't want to freak us out by just coming in."

Thomas nods. "That's good. He can help us check out the new tunnel. He's been caving with Matt and me before."

Robert speaks up. "I can help, too. Two years ago, I did some caving. But I want to say again that we need to be very careful. If the wood that Sally stepped on is rotted through, there's no telling what condition that extra passageway is going to be in."

George suddenly opens the door and crosses the room to give Emily a kiss. "Did I miss anything?" he asks.

Sally excitedly updates him on her latest find with Robert outside the house, and then Thomas tells him about Charles Vane's room, chest, and the journal.

"We were getting ready to go outside with Sally and Robert to check out the new tunnel," Thomas adds. "You're just in time to give us a hand."

"Cool! That sounds like fun," George says, "but we better be careful. If there's a hidden treasure down there, there might also be booby traps. You know, like Blackbeard had in his hideout on Cat Island."

Emily shivers, remembering when she fell through the cave leading to Blackbeard's treasure and how she almost ended up on one of deadly spikes that were hidden in the dark and lethal cavern floor.

Robert chimes in, "Oh, I didn't even think about that. Also, we need to make sure whatever we find stays hidden. Luckily, Isabella's property backs up to the woods so we should be able to work without anyone seeing us. Let's go. I have the flashlights and Matt has the ropes."

Isabella turns to my grandma and Sally White. "Do you girls want to come up to the kitchen and help me make some lunch while they go check out the tunnel?" The two women nod and follow her up the stairs while the rest of us head outside to check out the latest discovery.

Robert leads the way behind two overgrown azalea bushes that are at least six foot high and back up to the thick cedar forest. He points to a spot on the ground. He and Thomas reach down to remove a decayed wooden hatch. As they pull away the splintered planks, Robert says, "This wood looks ancient. I bet it's two hundred years old. I can't wait to see what's down that shaft."

Thomas suggests that we lower a lantern into the burrow. "I think it's a good idea to put some light in the opening before we lower ourselves down there," he says. "What do you guys think?"

George answers him. "That's a good idea, plus tie the rope with the harness around your waists before you try to get down there," he suggests.

George lowers the lantern into the black void and the guys peer down into a dank, dark space that has several wooden steps that look as old as the wooden hatch. They crumble when Thomas pushes on one of the stairs. "These steps look pretty decrepit. We can tie the rope around this other tree to secure you," George says.

Thomas nods his head. "I agree. We don't know what's down there. Let's not take any unnecessary risks. It looks like they carved out the ground to form a niche. Who knows what we will find when we actually get down there?"

Robert, Thomas, and Matt tie the ropes to their waists and attach them to a tree. George says. "I'll stay up here with David, Jim, and the girls in case you need help."

Robert leads the way. He steps down onto the first couple footholds. Suddenly, the rungs give way, leaving him swinging in the air. "Help! Pull me up!" he yells.

The guys drag Robert up from the black hole. He climbs out over the edge. He's shaky from the experience. "Wow, that was scary. And you were right, Matt. It is booby trapped," he says. "I could see spikes on the dirt ground at the bottom of the ladder. Thank heavens I was tied with the rope, so I didn't drop down all the way. I could have been history."

Sally fiercely hugs her husband. She is unnerved by what has just happened. "Okay. Let's rethink this," she says. "Is there a way to drop a camera down there or something?"

Robert waves his hands in the air. "I don't think we need to do that," he says. "I only saw the spikes at the bottom of the steps. I think we can still lower ourselves down, but now we just know that we need to avoid stepping onto the spikes."

Sally takes Robert by the shoulders, looks into his eyes, and pleads, "Can you please let the other guys check it out first?" she says with emotion. "I just saw your life fly past me. Besides, this new baby needs a father." Robert looks back at her, confused.

"I think I might be pregnant," she says.

Robert is shocked by her announcement. "You're pregnant? How come you didn't say anything?" And then he sweeps Sally up in a huge embrace.

We all hoot and holler, celebrating the two of them and their new addition-to-be. I hug my sister. "Oh, Sally I'm so happy for you guys. The twins are going to be a big brother and a big sister."

Sally shakes her head. "I'm not positive, so don't get too excited. I might just be late because of all the excitement we've been through," she says. "I mean, really, I'd rather wait at least a year before we have another baby. You know, they're still only five months old.

Matt grins and pats his shocked brother-in-law on his back. "Yeah, Robert, I think you better stay right here. Let us go down and check it out first. Just in case."

Thomas also slaps Robert on the back, and then he hugs Sally. Emily and Sarah are laughing. "Oh boy, are you going to have your hands full!" Emily says.

Sally rubs her hands over her face. "I know. Fingers crossed that it's just a false alarm," she says. Then she points down into the dark hole. "In the meantime, I can't wait to see what is down there."

George gives Thomas his lighted hat. "Hopefully this will light your way and keep you out of trouble," he says.

Matt and Thomas lower themselves slowly into the inky hole. Matt has gone down first. He has his phone flashlight on and is recording his journey into the abyss. "It's pretty scary down here," he calls up to Thomas, who is following him down, and to us.

The two eventually reach the dirt floor of an underground vault. The brown clay walls of the chamber are covered with old graying timbers. Caked dirt seeps between the slats in the wooden planks. A tunnel leads from the open space to an alcove. The deadly spikes that Robert spotted appear to be the only visible lethal booby traps, but Thomas is on high alert.

"We need to be cautious just in case there are more traps down here," he warns Matt. "It looks like the cave leads down to a tunnel over here. Let's go check it out."

As they slowly creep into the tunnel, Matt points to a spot where a stick points up from the ground. "Hey, there's the stick from the ceiling area in the secret room, the marker you pushed up from the hatch at the top of the notches leading up the wall by the cot," Matt says. "So, that's where it leads—into this new tunnel we've found. We'll have to come back and explore it later."

The guys notice that there are small chunks of dirt breaking off the walls of the shaft and dropping at their feet. "I'm not so sure it's very stable down here," Matt says, sounding doubtful. "We better hurry."

Thomas agrees. Carefully, they walk down the dark, dingy tunnel that leads into a bigger opening. The cavelike area is approximately eight feet by eight feet and, in one corner, there is a small chest sitting on an old oak barrel.

Thomas exclaims, "Oh, my goodness. Look at that. Do you think we found the treasure? Or is this the box of baubles Anne was talking about? Could it be the small jewelry coffer said to be here on the island?"

They cautiously make their way over to the wooden box. Matt works the clasp up and opens the lid. He reaches inside and picks up a few gold coins that he holds out to show Thomas. Then he reaches his hand back in and pulls out a gorgeous gold necklace with a ruby pendant.

"This is amazing!" Matt says as he steadily shoots videos of the treasures in the coffer.

"What should we do with it?" he asks Thomas. "Should we leave it here or try to take it out of the room and back up with us?"

Before Thomas has time to answer, Matt speaks again. "I think we should get out of here now—and bring the necklace and whatever else we can carry with us. The chest's not that big. The guys can bring it up with a bungee. But I don't want to stay down here any longer. There is dirt and sand coming out of fissures in the wall. It's not safe.

"We will need to come back down here later and shore it up," he adds.

Thomas agrees. They both stuff their pockets with as much of the treasure as will fit. Then Thomas yells up to George and Robert. "Hey guys, we found something," he calls up the shaft. "Send us down some extra rope and bungees. You should see what we found!"

George lowers a basket to them with some rope and bungee cords. Thomas and Matt maneuver the chest into the basket and tie it securely before they call to the guys to pull it up. Then Matt and Thomas start to make their way back out of the entrance of the cave with the help of Robert and George.

Matt emerges first. He reaches into his pocket, pulls out the gold chain with the ruby pendant and holds it up for us to see. "You guys are going to die when you see what we found down there."

We all gasp in delighted surprise. By then, Thomas has emerged from the hole. He swings me around and wraps a diamond necklace around my neck. "We're rich guys!" he announces. "And I don't even think this is the big treasure chest."

Matt starts to show us the videos he's taken. We are astonished by what we see.

Matt describes the manmade cavern, then adds, "I don't think it's very safe down there. We'll need to shore up the walls if we're going to do any more exploring. The walls are leaking sand plus we need to remove the deadly spikes at the bottom of those decrepit steps."

David suggests that we go back into the storm cellar to discuss what they've found. "We wouldn't want anyone overhearing us," he warns.

Chapter 13

Exciting New Finds

We enter the storm shelter just as my mom, Sally White, and my grandmom, Mary, bring down a scrumptious lunch of ham and Swiss cheese on rye, with chips, for all of us. Matt steps up behind my mother and drapes the gorgeous ruby necklace around her neck. "Look Mom, I'm going to cover you in jewels."

Isabella glances down at the beautiful strand of ruby and gold sparkling on her neck. She looks up at Matt, both puzzled and ecstatic. "Wow, what's this? Where did you get it?"

As Isabella turns to hug her son, Matt beams with joy. "We found it," he says. "We found some of the pirate treasure they left on Ocracoke Island!"

Isabella, Mary, and Sally White are stunned. Sarah hands her mom a few of the coins that Thomas and Matt brought out of the crumbling tunnel. "Look, there are even gold coins like the ones we discovered in Evangeline's home," she says.

Sally White grins widely and takes her husband, Jim, by the arms, swinging him around. "We're rich! Yoohoo!" Then she pauses, gets a curious look on her face, and glances around at everyone. "Now what?" she asks.

Jim raises his eyebrows and exclaims, "That's the question we're all asking."

George holds out some of the old Spanish coins as he speaks. "Good question. Do we notify the authorities or wait until we finish our quest for the rest of the treasure?" Paul reaches to take a few of the ancient coins from George's hands. "I think we will need to keep this to ourselves for now or we are going to have wannabe pirates from everywhere invading the island." David and Robert nod in agreement.

"The next question is whether we keep the treasure hidden in the secret room or put it in the safe. And should we tell John and Chloe about what we have found? There are so many questions and no concrete answers," Paul says.

Emily raises her arms up in the air. "I think we've already trusted John and Chloe with all the what's-what about Anne's spirit, so we probably should tell them. Plus, they are a direct descendant of Anne and Jack."

I make an announcement. "Speaking of John and Chloe, I invited them to Christmas Eve dinner. I hope that's alright with everyone. I didn't want them to be alone without family at the holiday."

A sneaky grin spreads across Sarah's face. "I know—let's surprise them tomorrow night when we exchange gifts," she says. "We can give each of them a gold coin."

Isabella laughs at the suggestion. "Now, that would be a really cool gift for our new relatives. They're going to love it."

Isabella then points to the lunch she helped make. "Speaking of eating, there are plenty of sandwiches for everyone. Enjoy, and once we're done eating, the ladies and I are going to go upstairs and make Christmas cookies."

She turns to me, Sally, Emily, and Sarah. "Do you girls want to come help make cookies? I was thinking we could bake some gingerbread so we can make gingerbread houses tomorrow night."

"Absolutely!" Sarah says. "That would be awesome."

My mom then turns to Emily, Sally, and me. "How about you three? Are you up for making some cookies?"

I beam. "That sounds great to me, but Emily and I will need to leave around 3 p.m. to open the pub. I'm singing tonight, and with it being Christmas and all the families visiting the island, I expect we will be busy."

Emily agrees with me. "I'm up for making cookies, and you're right, Angie. We are always busy at Christmas time. Better put on your roller skates."

Isabella points to us. "So, it's decided. The girls will make cookies. What about you guys? What are your plans? And what about the treasure?"

Jim glances around at everyone as he answers her. "I'm going back to the inn to help with the check-ins, so Sarah can have the day off. I think we should hide the treasure in the secret room for now. As for the new outside entrance to that hidden shaft, we need to make sure the hatch is completely covered over again like it has been for years."

Thomas and Matt nod in agreement, as do David, George, and Robert.

"I think that's a good idea," Thomas says. "Matt and I already covered the hatch with the patches of grass we took off it once we figured out its location. We're going to need to go back down there eventually, but I think maybe we should wait until after the holidays when there aren't as many visitors on the island."

Everyone agrees with Thomas. They start digging into the lunch. As they do, Matt whispers to Thomas. "Hey, Thomas, do you want to go work on our job at Bob and Sue's house—or work on your surprise?"

"Both sound good to me," Thomas answers. "I still can't believe tomorrow is Christmas Eve."

Thomas, George, and Matt tell the group that they need to leave to work on their jobs. The renovation company that the three guys started last year has really taken off. In-Time Renovations has so many orders that they have enough work to carry them into next year—and more orders are streaming in every month. Robert stands up, too, and excuses himself. "I've got to head home and play Santa. We bought the twins some things that need to be put together," he explains. "I can't wait to see their cute little faces tomorrow when they see the Christmas tree."

Sally smiles and hugs Robert. "Thanks, honey. You're the best." She kisses him on his cheek, smiling, and he pats her belly. She winks at him.

I follow my mother and the girls upstairs to start our fun afternoon baking cookies. I am so happy that I moved to the island. It will be our new tradition here on Ocracoke. In fact, many new traditions are emerging this holiday season. By the time I get into the kitchen, my mom, Isabella, is already standing at a counter with a bag full of cookie cutters. She gives me a peck on the cheek, then she hands them to me.

"Perfect timing," she says. "We're having a cookie competition. Everyone gets to make one perfect cookie to enter the contest, and the guys will be our judges."

I laugh as I search through the large plastic bag filled with cookie cutters from years gone by. "You're on," I say. "I think I'm going to choose this cute Santa. What has everyone else picked?"

Sally holds up the Christmas gnome she has chosen. Emily has a deer. Sarah has chosen an angel. Mom and Mary both have angels, too. As for Sally White, she has selected a Christmas stocking.

Emily holds up a reindeer cookie cutter. "You just wait," she says. "This is going to be the best cookie of them all." She laughs and then takes a sip of her warm vanilla latte.

Sally picks up little Evie, who is watching us with her crystal blue eyes. "What do you think, my little angel? Don't you think that your momma has this in the bag?" she says to the infant who coos, looking at her mother as she reaches to take one of the cookie cutters from Sally's hand.

My mom quickly tells her, "Well, I guess we'll just have to see about that, won't we?" Jacob, who is bouncing on my mom's lap, watches the interaction among his mom and his sister and his grandmother.

We work on the cookie dough for a while, then Emily and I notice the time. We leave Isabella's house and drive head over to the Shepard's Inn and the pub. When we get to the historic house, we walk arm-and-arm up the front steps, into the house, and through the parlor to the entrance to the pub. Laughing, we open the pub door at just before 3:30 p.m.

I am swept by joy as I look at my friend. "Oh Emily, I'm so happy I moved here. I don't even know what I'd be doing today if I hadn't moved to Ocracoke last summer."

Emily grins and nods. "Angie, it's like you should have been here all along," she says. "Every time you left at the end of each summer to go back to D.C., I missed you like crazy. You have always been my closest friend."

I busy myself pulling out the ingredients to make the pub's famous Oxford Pub Brew. "I just consider myself so lucky to be here living my best life," I tell her. "It's so weird. I feel like I've always been here."

People start to drift into the cozy neighborhood bar. It's a busy evening but, before we know it, it comes to an end. George has turned up and he's helping us clear away the night's clutter. Then he makes his way behind the bar to wrap his muscular arms around a cheerful Emily. I think to myself how cute they are together and how they were just made for each other.

Thomas arrives with our dog, Max. "Hi, pretty lady," he says with a laugh. "Can I walk you home?" I come around the bar and wrap my arms around his neck, reaching up to feel his warm lips on mine. "Hmm, I think that sounds like an awesome idea."

I reach down to pet our excited puppy, rubbing his fluffy ears. "Hi, my boy. Want to go for a W-A-L-K?" I spell out the word just in case

Thomas has already walked him, but Thomas shakes his head to show me the suggestion is a good idea. Thomas puts a leash on Max. "It's pretty chilly out," he says. "It must be down in the 40s, so we'll probably want it to be a quick walk."

I wrap my heavy blue scarf around my neck and zip up my royal blue ski jacket. "Sounds good to me. It's been a busy night," I say. "This place was jam packed, and I'm kind of tired. Plus, we have a long day tomorrow with it being Christmas Eve."

I run my fingers through my raven hair. "Man, what happened to this year?" I ask aloud.

As Thomas and I start to head out the door, I wave to Emily and George. In unison, Thomas and I say, "Goodbye, guys. See you tomorrow."

After a brisk walk along the cold beach, we make it home.

Chapter 14

New Christmas Eve Traditions

I wake up, roll over, and gently kiss Thomas's bearded cheek, swinging my leg over his legs, spooning him. He rolls over to face me. "Good morning, my love," he says softly in a sleepy voice.

His muscular hands begin to touch me delicately in all my sensitive areas. He nuzzles his lips against my ears and makes his way down my neck and to my breasts, where he nips my nipples with his lips. I wrap my arms around him. My breasts rub against him. My nipples are erect, and I can feel his manhood growing hard against my groin. It isn't long before we are taken over the edge into a climax of desire that leaves us both trembling.

I lay my head on his shoulder. "I just love waking up to you and our life together," I whisper to him. "And just think, this is our first Christmas together."

Thomas pulls me up on top of him and rubs my bottom. "Well, if you liked that, I could probably give you an encore—maybe even one in the shower. Why don't I just take Max out for a quick walk and then join you in the shower."

I take his bearded chin in my hands and gently kiss him. "I think a shower together is not such a good idea—I'm afraid we'll end of spending the day in bed, and I don't think the others would like that too much," I say, smiling.
"We have a lot of things planned for today."

I reach down to pet our excited, tail-wagging Golden Retriever on his furry head. He whines and barks to go outside.

"Why don't you take Max out and I'll meet you in the kitchen when I'm done getting ready," I tell Thomas, as I look at the time on my phone. "Later, I have to get over to the inn to help the ladies get ready for tonight's meal, but first I need to make my famous green bean casserole for the dinner."

Thomas is back after I have my shower. He pushes my wet black hair out of my eyes. "Merry Christmas, my love," he says as he kisses me. "And to many more Christmases like this."

Before I finish getting ready for the day, Thomas has already showered, toweled off, and dressed. He starts the morning coffee and begins to make us a wonderful, homey breakfast. I walk into the kitchen to find him happily whistling, 'I wish you a Merry Christmas.' I can't help but feel lucky to have found this dashing, humble man. I wrap my arms around his muscular waist. "Aren't you in a Christmas-y mood?" I say.

Thomas turns to face me, handing me a plate holding a breakfast of smoky hickory bacon and the Thomas-style scrambled eggs that I think are so scrumptious.

"Here you go. Breakfast of champions," he says. Then he adds: "I got out all the stuff for your green bean casserole. I am going to eat, then I have to run off to meet Matt and George to do an errand linked to your Christmas surprise." He is grinning from ear to ear. "And boy, are you going to be surprised!" he adds.

"Oh really?" I say as I gratefully take my plate from him and sit down on our tan leather couch to start eating. "And what kind of surprise do you have for me? Any clues?"

Thomas shakes his head. "No clues for you, young lady. You'll just have to wait until tonight."

We finish eating our hearty breakfast. He takes his hooded, olive-colored jacket off the coat rack, kisses me goodbye, and heads toward the door. He stops to puts a purple leash on Max—and the crazy puppy practically drags a laughing Thomas out the door. I watch them leave, wondering what kind of gift Thomas has in store for me. I hope he likes the gift that I've made for him.

I finish preparing my green bean casserole, one of the side dishes for our Christmas Eve dinner. Then I pick up the bag of gifts for the others that I'm taking to the inn—but I change my mind. I'll take them over later. For now, I throw on my heavy navy-blue jacket with the matching scarf, glad that I brought it with me from Maryland. It will be perfect for today's damp cold. I make my way over to the inn to join the others for our fun day making gingerbread cookies, our new tradition here on the island.

I push open the ornate white door to the inn, and the gloriously warm aroma of cinnamon washes over me. I inhale deeply and hear a giggle from the top of the banister. Looking up, I see the ghosts of Old Emily and Evangeline smiling down at me and waving. I smile up at them and wave. I wonder to myself when it became so normal for me to simply accept the presence of spirits from the past.

The homey inn welcomes me like a warm bear hug as I make my way across the parlor, with its classic Christmas decorations, and through the swinging door into the kitchen. Christmas music echoes through the bright, familiar room.

The girls are already busy in the kitchen, along with Sally White and Grandmom. My mom, Isabella, greets me with a light peck on the cheek. She hands me a tin full of gingerbread house pieces. "Perfect timing, we're having a gingerbread house contest in addition to the cookie competition," she says. "There is candy and also confectionary sugar to make the frosting. We have cardboard pieces to put your house on, along with different colors of Saran Wrap."

"You're on!" I laugh. I start to search through the large plastic bags of candy, picking out special pieces for my gingerbread house. "I think I'm going to pick out this cute chocolate Santa and do Santa's home for my theme. What theme has everyone else decided?"

My sister, Sally, picks up her Christmas gnome cookie. "I'm going to do a gnome house. Emily has chosen a Rudolph the Red-Nosed Reindeer theme. Sarah is going to do an angel theme with Baby Jesus. Mom and Grandmom are going for a traditional Christmas theme."

"Me, too," says Sally White. "It's traditional Christmas for me, as well."

My sister picks up little Evie, who is watching us with wide eyes. "What do you think my little angel?" she coos to her daughter. "Don't you think that your momma has
this in the bag?"

My mom has stepped over to pick up Jacob, who is now bouncing in her lap as he watches his mother and his twin sister. Mom turns to Sally and, using her mock challenging voice, says, "Well, I guess we'll just have to see about that, won't we?"

Our day continues with much fun and laughter. Late in the day, when we're nearly finished working on our houses, Sally makes a happy, but tearful announcement.

"I know I told all of you that I thought I might be pregnant, but guess what?" She grins with tears shining in her pretty blue eyes. "I'm not. I don't know whether to be thrilled or sad that I'm not having another baby."

As she speaks, she is lovingly rocking her now-sleeping red-haired daughter, her wild child, in her arms.

I reach over to put my arm around my sister. "Well, I can't imagine having twins, then turning around less than a year later and being pregnant again," I say. "Did you tell Robert yet?"

She laughs. "I know you might think this is weird, but I'm going to gift wrap the pregnancy test and give it to him for Christmas."

We all start laughing hysterically. Mom stretches her arms around Sally and tells her, "He'll love it. He looked so shocked the other day when you said you might be pregnant. I know he would have been happy either way, but I think this is for the best."

Mom picks up Jacob and rests him on her shoulder, patting his little back. "This way you will be able to enjoy these babies more than ever," Mom says. "They grow up so fast."

Isabella kisses her grandson on his cherub cheek. "I'm just so grateful that I am getting to watch them growing up," she says. "It all goes by so quickly. I can remember when you girls were this age. It seems like only yesterday."

Sally White nods her head in agreement. "You're so right, Isabella. It does feel like it was just yesterday when these four girls were in diapers." She rubs Emily's back then runs her hand through her daughter's strawberry-blonde ponytail.

Emily smiles and takes her mother's hand in hers. "It's so hard to believe we were ever this size," she says, pointing at the twins. She reaches over to tickle little Jacob's belly and casts her eyes on Evie as she naps.

We finish making the gingerbread houses. Sarah's house is precious. She has formed her gingerbread into a barnlike structure. Inside it, Baby Jesus is in a manger. Sarah holds up the tiny plastic baby she is using for Jesus. "What do you guys think about my gingerbread manger?"

All our houses have turned out festive, and we are all pleased with the results. Emily smiles. "This is so much fun having all of you guys celebrate Christmas with us," she says. "I'm looking forward to many more Christmases together—and making more memories."

We'll have the gingerbread house and cookie competition tonight. We've decided that John and Chloe can join the guys as judges. We all help to clean up the kitchen. Isabella puts on her sable-brown winter

111

jacket with the furry hood, and says, "I need to head back over to the house to check on the turkey. I left it in the oven. David's keeping an eye on it, but it should be about ready. I can't believe it is already 3:30 p.m."

Isabella looks over at Sally White. "You said you wanted to have dinner around 5 o'clock, right?"

Emily and Sarah's mother nods in the affirmative, looking at the clock on the microwave. "You're right—I also didn't realize it's so late. I still need to take a shower before everyone gets here."

She turns to me. "Angie, what time did you tell John and Chloe to be here?"

I look at my Apple watch and answer her as I pull on my coat. "I asked them to come over around 5 o'clock or so. They said that they had to Facetime their families first, and then they'd be over for dinner. I guess we all need to go get ourselves together and then come back over.

"I can't wait for the baking competition results," I add. "I just love our new tradition of making cookies and gingerbread houses!"

Emily hugs me. "I'm excited about tonight, too, but for a different reason. I can't wait to see your face when Thomas gives you your Christmas gift." I grab Emily and excitedly ask her, "What is it? Can you at least give me a hint?"

Sarah looks at Emily and pantomimes the act of zipping her lips.

"Nope," Emily says, "you are just going to have to wait until later tonight." She pushes me toward the door. "But, boy, is it good!"

Chapter 15

Special Christmas Presents

Thomas is getting dressed when I walk into the warmth of our cozy home. He greets me at the door with a peck on my cool, rosy cheeks. "Hi, honey. How was the gingerbread house-making day?"

"It was so much fun," I tell him, excitedly. "We have decided to make it an annual Christmas tradition. You fellas are going to get to judge our cookie and gingerbread houses tonight, anonymously, of course."

He scratches his chin and smiles. "I'm glad we won't know which entries belong to which baker," he says. "Otherwise, there might be a lot of biased judges. Me included."

I have been home for about an hour when I look at the clock on the microwave and realize it's time for us to head to the inn. I point to the presents I've placed over by the door. "We need to take our gifts to the inn when we leave—and the green bean casserole."

Thomas nods. "No problem. Let's get Max on his leash, then I'm ready to help." He shows me his muscular arms as Max enthusiastically winds his way between the two of us.

We make our way across the oyster shell driveway, the brittle shells crunching under our feet. I wrap my scarf around my neck and over my ears more tightly. "Wow, it's really gotten chilly out here tonight. It feels like Christmas."

We enter through the inn's heavy embossed doors. We are immediately enveloped by the warmth from the parlor's fireplace. I walk over to the hearth and point at the fire. "Look at that toasty flame. It's a wonderful night for it. And I love that it is a double fireplace with the other side in the dining room." I listen for a minute to the cheerful voices coming from the other room. "It sounds like everyone is here," I say.

Thomas lets an excited Max off his leash, and our puppy dashes toward the dining room and then into the festively decorated den. We try to keep up with him. "Well, I guess we'll just follow him to find everyone," I laugh. "I hope he doesn't knock anyone over."

Thomas nods as we move deeper into the house. We find everyone in the living room gathered around the Christmas tree. Cheerful Christmas music plays in the background.

The others come over to give us hugs, pecks on the cheeks, and a hand with our gifts. Sally White points to the kitchen. "We're setting up a buffet in the kitchen for our dinner," she says. "Angie, just follow me and I'll get you a hotplate for that casserole. I can't wait to try it. That's one of my favorites."

I smile. "I know. It's one of my favorites, too, and so easy to make." I follow her into the kitchen and set the dish down on a hotplate she has placed on the beautiful gray granite island.

She points to a selection of beverages on the counter. "What would you like to have to drink? We have quite a variety."

I pick up a plastic tumbler and get a tall cup of ice water. "Water is good with me for now. I'll get Thomas one, too. He likes his water."

We hear the doorbell ring, and Sally White and I look at each other. "I bet that's Chloe and John," I say. "Let's go together to let them in."

She nods, and we head toward the entryway. Sally White yells back to the others. "We've got the door."

She opens the door and greets our new relatives with a smile and a hug. "Welcome. Come on in, out of the cold," she says. Then she points. "The others are in the den."

John hands Sally White a bottle of white wine, then laughs. "I know you own a pub, but we didn't want to come to your home empty handed."

As we make into the inn, Chloe and John both stop in the pretty parlor and look around. "This is gorgeous!" Chloe exclaims.

Hearing a noise, John and Chloe look up toward the top of the stairway. Their jaws drop open. "Oh my, it looks like with have company," Chloe finally manages to say.

At the top of the steps, the ghosts of Evangeline and Old Emily are giggling and waving at the pair. "Wow, that's amazing that you can see them," I say. "That's a first. The only people who have been able to see them are just our group of family and friends. I guess that means that you are accepted."

Chloe nods but still looks a little shocked. "Well, it might take us a little while to get used to it," she says.

John wipes his brow. "You're right about that, honey," he says. Then he laughs and adds, "But it's cool." He waves toward the images at the top of the stairs.

Sally White guides the surprised couple into the dining room, giving them a tour as she leads them to the den.

When we enter the festively decorated room, everyone gets up to greet and welcome the young couple.

Jim asks, "Did you get to Facetime with your families before you came over?"

"Yes. We'd thought about trying to Facetime so you could all join us and see everyone, but both our families start the holiday early. So, we did a Facetime before we came over. I'm glad we were able to speak with everyone," John answers. "They said to say 'hello' and that they look forward to meeting you all."

"We're so glad that you two were able to be with us this year," Jim says. "It's very casual. We normally do a buffet dinner." He looks around the room and then adds, "So, if everyone is hungry—and I know I am after smelling all the scrumptious aromas coming from the kitchen—let's eat."

In unison, we call out in agreement. Jim leads the way as we follow, with Sally White rounding up the end of the group.

"It's right in here," Jim says as we enter the kitchen. "I normally say a little blessing before we get started. So, let's bow our heads now for a short prayer." We lower our heads as Jim begins to say grace. "Dear Lord, bless all who enter our home and sit at our table and this food that we are about to eat. Bless all our friends and family who are not here with us. Amen. Let's eat."

"We use paper plates and plasticware. They are over on the counter along with drinks," Sally White explains to everyone. "If you see something we need that's not out, let me know. We probably have it in the pub."

John rubs his stomach and puts his arm around Chloe. "My goodness, everything smells heavenly. I'm happy with anything. Please don't feel like you must wait on us. We're easy."

Chloe smiles and hands John a cup. She reaches out another that she is holding so he can fill them both. "I might have a drink later tonight, but I'm good with ginger ale for now," she says, "and I agree that everything looks scrumptious."

We fill our plates then make our way into the large dining room. There are two tables set so everyone can sit and enjoy their food. We laugh and talk our way through a delicious meal.

We all work together to clear away the dinner dishes and put everything away. Sally White graciously thanks us, then announces: "Now it's time for the judging to begin in the Cookie and Gingerbread Competition."

Emily wraps George up in a big bear hug. "This is going to be so much fun," she says, with excitement in her voice. I can't wait to see who wins."

To say that we are out of control over this contest is an understatement. My sister, Sally, pumps her hands in the air holding up a Number 1 sign. "Emily, you know you don't have a chance!" she calls out, bragging and taunting a competitive Emily. I put my arms around both of them, laughing. "You two are ridiculous and so funny." Then I look at our gingerbread houses and cookies, laid out for all to see, and I add: "It's going to be a tough decision for our judges."

The cookie competition is first. In front of each cookie is an overturned card; the hidden side of the card identifies whose cookie it is. I explain to our judges, including John and Chloe, that their votes are secret. "You just need to write your scores down for each cookie, noting which you think is the best on one of these blank cards. Then slip your votes into this box," I say.

Our judges score our cookies and place their ballots in the box. Jim takes out the cards, tallies the results, then announces the results.

"First place goes to whoever's cookie is Number 4. Second place is cookie Number 2, and third place goes to cookie Number 3."

Emily is squealing in delight and teasing poor Sally, who momentarily looks sad. Emily hugs Sally tightly and tries to be conciliatory. "Well at least you got second place," she says. "And Mary, way to go with third place!" My Grandmom bows in acknowledgment.

Chloe shyly says to Sally, "I thought they were all good. It was so hard to choose. I'm so glad it was a secret ballot."

"I can't wait to see who wins the gingerbread competition," Emily says, her competitive spirit alive and well. I point at the gingerbread houses and laugh. "Yes, I'm impatient, too, to see who wins this one. They are all so good."

The next round of ballots is tallied, and it is a unanimous vote for Sarah's creation with Baby Jesus in the manger. Her eyes are teary as she hears the results. "Really, I won?" she says, surprised. "That is so cool. I don't know what to say."

We all congratulate and hug her. As we start to calm back down, Isabella looks at Sally White and asks, "Is it time for presents?" Then my mom looks straight at me. "I've been waiting for this all day. I am wondering what the big surprise is from Thomas to you, Angie."

Sally White puts her arm around my mom's shoulder and the two women, friends for decades, lead the way into the den where gifts are piled under the Christmas tree. We find seats and get ready, then Jim stands, reaches down, and picks up one of the presents. "I'm going first," he declares, as he hands a small box with cheerful red bows and ornaments to Sally White. "Here you go, my love."

Sally blushes. "For me? But don't you want the others to go first?"

Jim shakes his head. "No, not this time," he says. "I want you to go first."

She opens the box. It contains an envelope. She opens it to find two plane tickets to Key West. "Oh, honey! That's so sweet. You know how much I love that place," she gushes. "It'll be perfect when it's too cold to do anything around here."

She leans over and gives her husband a kiss on the cheek. "Thank you so much."

The next gift is to Isabella from David. He laughs as he tells everyone what he gave her. "It's a gift card for the bridal shop. Everyone knows that we've decided to get married in Jamaica when we go to search for Anne's pirate treasure. This is so she can pick out a special dress for the ceremony." He embraces her and gives her a touching kiss that makes her eyes water.

We all comment on what a lovely gift it is. Isabella gushes and hugs David back. "Oh, what a good idea," she says. "I hadn't even thought about what I would wear to get married."

Isabella never thought she would get married again after suddenly losing her husband last year and neither did David after losing his wife to cancer two years ago. The friendship between the two eventually bloomed into love—and both couldn't be happier.

Now it's my turn to give Thomas his present. I am nervous as I hand him the small box. "I wasn't sure what to get you, but since Evangeline and Jacob's heart pendants brought us together, I thought we might want ones of our own. I had them made by one of the local crafters on Hatteras Island."

Thomas opens the package. He is clearly moved with emotion as he examines the detail in the gift. There are two silver half-heart pendants, one for Thomas and the other for me. "I thought that we could each wear these half heart pendants along with the ones that belonged to Evangeline and Jacob to form a perfect heart," I explain. After removing the necklace from around his neck I slide the half silver heart toward it to form a whole heart. "Your love completes me and is a perfect circle of love," I tell him.

He kisses me passionately on the lips. "I love it Angie. What a great idea. It's perfect."

Matt laughs and calls out, "Hello, we're still here. Get a room. LOL."

I swat my brother on the back. "Hush, Matt."

I turn back to Thomas. "I had hoped you would like it," I say. "It carries me back to the day we met."

He hugs me as he says, "It's awesome. Really, such a perfect gift."

Thomas steps away from me and says, "I have been so excited about giving you your gift." He reaches in his pocket and pulls out a small brightly wrapped gift. "Here's yours. I hope you like it."

My hands are shaking as I hesitantly take the present. I am so nervous and excited. "I'm sure I'll love it," I tell him. I excitedly rip off the pretty

Christmas paper, then shake the little white box before I open it. I lift out the small item that is inside. It is wrapped in tissue paper. It feels solid like metal. I turn it over in my trembling hands trying to figure out what it is, then I finally tear off the paper. It's a silver key.

I look up, questioningly, at Thomas. "What is this?"

Thomas laughs, but he looks as nervous as I am. "It's the key to our new house. The house that I showed you last month," he says. "I got a contract on it. I kept it a secret because I thought it would make a great Christmas present." He is rambling but he continues on. "I thought it would be great to buy it now so it would be ready in time for our wedding in June. I hope you like it."

Tears stream down my rosy cheeks. I place my hand over my heart as I answer him. "Oh Thomas, never in a million years at this time last year would I have thought that I would find the man of my dreams and be moving into a brand-new house with him. This is spectacular. I will always treasure this Christmas."

After a pause, I add, "We might have to get another key so we can frame this one!"

The others rejoice in our happiness, congratulating us. Sarah turns to Emily and my sister. Sally speaks up. "Emily, now we can give them the gift from us. "Do you want to hand it to them?"

Emily grins. "Definitely," she says. "I have been itching to give them this since we made it. We hope you like it."

Thomas takes the bulky item in his muscular arms and sits down next to me. We open the present from the girls together. Fabric in muted tones of tan and images of olive-colored ducks have been crafted into an amazing homemade quilt.

"Do you like it?" my sister asks. "The girls have been teaching me how to do quilting. We weren't really sure what pattern to get you guys. We hoped these colors would be neutral enough and that you would like it."

"We love it!" Thomas and I answer Sally at the same time.

We stand up and embrace our friends. Then I hug the quilt to me. "It will absolutely work in our new home. It's so comfy and homey. I can't wait to wake up under it," I say. "You girls will teach me quilting, too, so I can make other quilts and maybe even some curtains and pillows to go with this one."

Mom laughs as she hands us two bulky presents from my parents and Emily's parents. "I think this is the right moment—Sally White and I made these for you," she says. I hand one of the packages to Thomas to open. We unwrap them at the same time, pulling off the pretty Christmas paper that covers them. We see that they are throw pillows that match our quilt.

"Oh, wow. These are perfect," I say.

Thomas and I hug my mom and Sally White and thank them for their thoughtful gift.

"So, everyone knew about my gift from Thomas, right? But when did you guys get a chance to make these other gifts?" I ask. Sarah points to Thomas and answers. "When Thomas showed you the house, he told us that he planned to surprise you with it for Christmas, so we got to work making them. I can't believe we all were able to keep it a secret, though."

Thomas shrugs and adds, "I hope it's okay that I went ahead and bought the house. You seemed to like it as much as I did, so I took a chance."

I have tears in my eyes when I hug him again. "Are you kidding me? I'm so touched by everything," I say. I look around the room at everyone and add, "I just don't know what to say except 'thank you' to all of you."

George stands up. He is blushing—even his ears are pink. Then he drops to one knee and calls Emily's name. He holds out a small black velvet box. "Emily, it's your turn," he says. "Okay, so I practiced this many times. And I've thought about this moment forever."

He takes a deep breath. "Emily, I have been in love with you forever—even when I didn't realize it, I was. Will you be my wife and spend the rest of your life with me?"

Emily falls to her knees beside a nervous George. "Oh my God!!! Yes! I can't believe this. I love you with all my heart."

George takes a delicate, solitaire diamond ring, set in gold filagree, out of the box. He takes her trembling hand and slips it on her finger. "I'm so happy—and relieved," he says. "I was scared you weren't ready yet."

We all gather around the happy couple to congratulate them. Neither Emily nor George like to be in the limelight, so it doesn't take long before both insist that we continue opening gifts. "We need to give Chloe and John their present," Emily declares.

Jim agrees. He reaches into his pocket and pulls out a small white box. "We thought you two might like this," he says, adding, "I can't wait to see the expression on your faces."

John tentatively takes the gift from Jim. "Oh, you guys, you didn't have to get us a gift. But, of course, we really appreciate it," John says. He hands the little box to Chloe, who automatically shakes it and looks inquisitively at it. She holds the box while John lifts off the lid, and both their mouths drop open when they see two antique gold coins sitting on a bed of cotton gauze. Chloe's hand goes to her mouth. "Is this what I think it is? Did you find the treasure?" she asks.

John picks up one of the delicate gold coins and scrutinizes it. "They're Spanish doubloons," he says. "This is so cool. We want to hear the story behind these!"

Chapter 16

Another Relative Discovered

Thomas places one of the gold coins onto John's palm. He starts to explain its origin.

"After you two left the other day, Sally and Robert went outside to look for a hidden entrance into the storm cellar," Thomas says. "While they were looking around, Sally's foot fell through a hole that leads to a tunnel we didn't know about. When Matt and I went down the tunnel to check it out, we found a small coffer of Spanish gold coins and a couple pieces of jewelry."

Matt pulls out his phone and shows the surprised couple the video he took of the excursion into the hidden cave.

"You can see from the video that the tunnel goes to a cavernous room. It was kind of scary. Robert almost landed on some wicked spikes that had been placed at the bottom of the stairs leading into the room."

Robert lifts his arms up in the air. "I almost fell right on them. I thought I was a goner."

I pick up the story at this point. "Yeah, we pretty much have closed up the tunnel until we can find time to go down and make it a little safer. Sand was leaking through the cracks in the wooden-planked walls of the room," I explain. "Thomas and Matt were worried that it was going to collapse."

John holds up the coin, examining it. "Has anyone thought to check out the worth of the coins yet?" he asks. "I'm just curious—and what are you going to do about it? Keep it hidden or what? I mean this is pretty historical."

Paul answers him. "Yeah, we were thinking about that, too. If we document our discovery with the authorities, we are going to have every crazy treasure-hunting nut show up to dig up the island," he says. "We think it's best to keep it a secret until we figure out where the rest of Anne and Jack's treasure is hidden.

"And as far as that goes, I think we still have a lot to figure out," "he adds.

John looks at his phone and then takes a picture of the gold doubloon. "I'm going to do a Google Lens search to check it out," he says. "I mean, what could it hurt."

The search quickly turns up some interesting results. It confirms that it is a Spanish coin from the 1700s.

"Look at this," John says, clearly excited. "It says that some coins were called gold *escudos* and could be worth up to $4,000 apiece! Are you sure you want to give us these? They are really valuable."

Emily shakes her head in a firm 'yes.' "We talked about it. Anne is related to you just as much as Angie and her family are, so we felt like you should be able to share some of the treasure with us."

Chloe places her hand to her heart. "That's so touching. We don't know what to say," she says, with emotion in her voice.

George speaks up to explain his concerns. "We also decided that we need to keep this as quiet as possible," he says, "so, for now, we are asking that you not tell anyone about it."

John nods his head. "Of course. I totally understand where you're coming from," he replies. "Mums the word. We'll keep it between ourselves. So, what's the
next step?"

As he mimics zipping his lips, his phone dings with a new text message. He looks down at the phone, and his eyebrows rise as he reads the message.

"That's crazy," he declares. "Do you remember when I told you that I did the 23andMe DNA test? Well, it came up with yet another relative—a Stephen Bell from Jamaica. This text is from him. Isn't that weird? I wonder how he got my phone number to text me?"

Thomas asks if he can see the message. John nods and hands him the phone. Thomas looks at the message and reads it aloud.

"Hi, John. You don't know me, but I found you on the 23andMe website. It looks like we might be related. Fancy that, we have relatives in common. I hear that we might even be related to that country singer, Angie Harriott," Thomas reads. "If you have a chance, I'd love to have a chat with you and maybe even meet up at some point. My girlfriend, Violet, and I are planning a trip to Ocracoke Island for New Year's. One of your Facebook posts says that you are there. Isn't that cool? We might even get to meet up on the island."

I feel goosebumps rise up and down my arms and spine.

"That's too much of a coincidence for me and it's giving me the creeps," I say. "I don't know why but my Spidey senses are going crazy right now."

My mother comes up beside me and rubs my arms and shoulders. "I'm sure it's just accidental that he texted right after John looked up the Spanish gold coin's value," she says. "Or is it?"

John nervously rubs his hands through his wavy auburn hair. "Yeah, it has to be a coincidence," he says, but his voice carries some doubt. "I wonder if there is some kind of app that alerts people to when different online sources are referenced?"

Paul sounds skeptical when he responds. "You know that the government has ways of alerting them, but I can't imagine that any ordinary person would have access to an app like that. I hope we are just worrying unnecessarily.

"What are you going to do, John?" he adds.

John is still looking at his phone. "I don't know," he says. "What do you guys think? Should we check him out before I get back to him? My brother is with the Charleston Police Department. I could get him to do a criminal background check on him."

Thomas agrees with that idea. "We know the local sheriff here and he can run a check on him, too," Thomas says, "and then we can go from there. Let's try not to worry too much. It's Christmas."

Sally White, being the great hostess that she is, immediately distracts us from the moment. "I have eggnog for anyone who is interested in a little Christmas cheer along with a bit of Christmas carol karaoke. Emily, pull out your microphones and the music sheets so everyone can sing along."

The rest of the evening is fun as we sing all the old Christmas carols. Before we know it, it is time to say good night so that we can all get ready for a festive Christmas Day. Most of us have individual plans for the next day, meeting up with many relatives. Thomas and I will be together with my mom, David, Robert, Sally, Mary, and Paul for an early lunch. Then we'll head over to Thomas's parent's home for dinner. After we marry, I think we'll probably have a combined dinner with everyone. I will definitely need to make that suggestion.

Before we leave for the night, Isabella invites John and Chloe to join us at her home tomorrow.

"John and Chloe, if you don't have plans, we would love for you two to spend Christmas Day with us," my mom says. "It's very casual and you don't need to bring anything. The turkey and ham are all ready to go into the oven and the sides have been prepared in advance. We would love to have you."

John blushes and says, "That's so sweet of you, Isabella. We would be thrilled to come. What time should we be at your house?"

"We will probably start around noon," Isabella responds. "I'm so glad you two can join us."

Chapter 17

Our New Home

I wake to start my first Christmas Day together with Thomas. He is already up when I roll over to see the bright sunshine beaming through our bedroom windows. Prisms are shining on the mellow yellow bedroom walls, making me feel nostalgic. After performing my normal morning routine, I make my way into the kitchen to find Thomas putting out some buttery croissants and pouring some yummy hazelnut coffee.

He comes over to greet me with a kiss and a cheery "Merry Christmas!" He gestures for me to sit down. "I'm just warming these croissants for breakfast. What do you think? Will this be enough to tide us over until lunch at your mom's?"

He hands me a cup of one of my favorite coffees and I take a sip before answering. "I think this is perfect," I say. "Here's hoping that by the end of the day—after meals at my mom's and then your mom's— we'll still be able to roll home."

I laugh as I remember being a young child on Christmas Day. I tell Thomas about it. "When we were children, we used to visit my grandparents on both sides of the family. I can remember being so stuffed by the end of the day," I say.

I lean over to give Thomas a quick peck on the cheek as I reminisce. "I wouldn't have changed it for the world." Then I find myself getting serious as I add: "I still can't believe this is the second Christmas without my dad."

I wipe away a lonesome tear and take a deep breath. "Enough of that, he wouldn't want me to be sad," I scold myself out loud. Thomas gently wraps his arms around me. "Angie, I know that you know this, but it's okay to show those feelings around me. I'm here for you if you ever want to talk about it or anything else for that matter."

I nod. "That's so sweet. I hope you know it goes both ways," I tell Thomas. Then I collect myself and announce: "It's Christmas, so let's have fun."

We finish eating our breakfast. I stand, reach in the pocket of my red Christmas sweater and pull out the key to our new house. "I was wondering, do you want to go take a look at our new house?"

Thomas grabs me and whirls me around. He is as excited as I am.

"Let's do it!" he says. "I left the plans on the island so I can show them to you. I really want both of us to be involved in the planning, so if you think of anything you'd like added, please let me know."

I smile as I look up at him, thinking how lucky I feel to have found someone who completes me and makes me feel loved. It was only a year ago that I was living with my old boyfriend, who always put his feelings and goals ahead of mine.

Thomas and I slip into our heavy winter coats. Outside the cool, damp Carolina breeze is gusting—chilling us to the bone—as we walk down to our new house with our excited pup, Max, in tow. Thomas takes my hand in his. "I think Matt, George, and I can have the major renovations done before our wedding in June," he tells me.

I shake my head in disbelief. "It's so hard to imagine that it is only six months away. This year has flown by. It will be here before you know it."

Thomas still has my hand in his as he unlocks and opens the solid oak door to our home, but he stops me before we cross the threshold. "Wait, Angie. I want you in my arms before we cross the doorstep," he says. He stoops down and lifts me into his arms.

"I know, you'll probably think I'm silly, but I am superstitious," he confides. "Did you know that carrying your bride over the threshold back in Viking times was said to protect them from evil spirts?"

I nod. "I knew it was a custom, but I never heard what the superstition was about," I respond. "That's interesting. There are so many sayings and customs."

Thomas sets me down on my feet once we're inside the house then leads me into the kitchen. "You know, it's so weird," he says. "As soon as I walked into this house, it felt like home."

I face Thomas and brush back the wild curly tendrils of blond hair from his forehead. "That's so funny. I felt the same way when you showed me the house," I tell him. "I just can't believe it's ours. We can raise our children here and grow old here. We'll need to put some rocking chairs on the front porch. I can just see us sitting out there on glorious summer nights watching the fireflies sparkling in the cedars."

Thomas nods, imagining the scene. He guides me over to the old and worn olive-green kitchen island.

"Come take a look at these plans and see what you think," he says as he points to island and the plans dating back to the '70s. "First thing I think we're planning to do is renovate this antiquated kitchen. This ugly green has got to go. My thought is to tear out the kitchen cabinets but see if we can reuse them because they are pretty sturdy. Do you have a preference as to a color theme?"

I look around the galley. "I think I would like to have muted tones of tan, rust, and gray. I really liked the color scheme that you used at Sally and Robert's home," I answer. "What were your thoughts?"

He steps over to the olive-green cabinets and opens them. "That's pretty much what I was thinking, too. I like earthy tones. Maybe have the cabinets in a darker gray with the island in colors of dark gray, tan, and rust. I'm thinking we can have a rust accent wall—with gray on the other walls, but a gray that's a little lighter than the cabinets.

"I'd also like to put in a gas stove, especially since we sometimes have power outages here on the island."

I nod and smile at him. "I can see it in my head. It's going to be gorgeous. I can't wait to move in."

Thomas shakes his wavy blond head. "Well, I'm thinking we can move in by May—maybe even a little sooner. I want to complete the renovations of the kitchen and the upstairs bathroom first," he says. "We'll just have to see how much we get done."

He walks me into the living room. "I think in here we'll just need to do some painting and maybe firm up the stone fireplace." As we climb the beautiful curving white staircase, I point to the exquisite stained-glass window at the top of the stairwell. "I just love that window. It is so pretty," I say. "This house already feels like home."

Thomas nods and leads me into the out-of-date bathroom outside our master suite. "I agree. It's one of the things that made me want to make this our home," he says. "Now, to the part that makes me know that this place needs a facelift."

He points to the mustard-yellow bathroom fixtures. "Luckily, they left this white clawfoot tub in here, and it's in pretty good shape. I don't even think we will need to refurbish it at all."

He places his hand on the plaster wall. "I need to see if we can knock down this wall to adjoin the bathroom to our bedroom. It might be a challenge," he explains. "And then we'll add a second bathroom off the other bedroom. The bedrooms are really huge, so it shouldn't be a problem."

I sigh. "It sounds lovely, but it also sounds like a lot of work," I say, then smile. "It's going to fun watching it transform into our dream house."

Next, he tugs me up the stairway leading to the attic. "You've got to see this, Angie," Thomas says. "I have an idea and want to get your opinion before I renovate this room. If you don't like the idea, we don't need to do it, but I think it will be perfect for us."

He points to the window seat at the far corner of the dusty room. "I want to turn this room into your music room. You can sit in the bay window with your guitar in your lap, writing new music for your albums and working on your book about Evangeline."

I shake my head, viewing it in my mind. "That's amazing—even as you were talking, I could see it, too," I tell him. "I love the idea. And this room is so big that we can even add a playroom or den so that you can be here with me, too. I also love that there's a fireplace up here. It will come in handy on those cold damp winter days."

I reach over and touch Thomas's arm. "I love your plans for the house, honey."

Thomas wipes his brow. "Whew, I was hoping that you'd like my suggestions," he says, clearly relieved. "Just let me know if you want anything else."

"I will have to think about it, but I adore what you are planning so far," I say. My watch beeps with a notification and I take a moment to glance at it. "Oh, it's mom texting. She wants to know if we want to come over a little earlier than noon. What do you think?"

"That sounds good. It's already 11 o'clock," he says.

Thomas takes me in his arms and looks around the attic room one more time before we head downstairs. After walking back into the kitchen, he picks up Max's lead.

"Let's go. I think Max is sleeping on the hearth. You know he'll want to go see his buddies. I'll put him on his leash, and we can head on over to your mom's house," he says. "It's so nice that Isabella's home and our family and friends' homes are so close to ours."

I zip up my heavy navy-blue jacket, wrapping my scarf around my neck, and pull on my gloves. "I know, it's so nice to live so close to everyone," I agree.

Max sees us putting on our coats, jumps up, tail wagging, and whines to be included. Thomas laughs and hooks the leash to the dog's collar. "It's chilly out, but let's take him for a quick walk before we head to Isabella's," he says.

When we reach the sandy shore of the pristine water, we see that there is no one on the solitary beach. A brisk sea breeze blows seafoam while crashing waves burst onto the churned-up coastline. Thomas looks around, sees there is no one around, and takes Max off his leash. Our pup immediately chases a sandpiper into the rough surf.

"Oh no. That might not have been such a good idea," Thomas says.

He whistles and calls Max back before the dog gets too wet. Thomas then turns to me and shrugs. "Whoops. I'm going to have dry him off a little bit, but I think I caught him before he got too sandy."

I laugh reaching down to pet Max on his furry head. "I know, Max," I say to the dog. "You wanted to play for longer, but maybe after all our dinners today, we can take you for a better walk."

I pat my belly, saying to Thomas, "And boy, are we going to need to take a walk after all the eating that awaits us."

Thomas agrees with me. "I think a walk later on is a great idea," he says. "I wonder if the others might want to come with us?"

Chapter 18

Christmas Day

We arrive at mom's house and David rushes to open the front door, as we both have our hands full of wrapped gifts and another dish of green bean casserole. "Welcome guys," he greets us with hugs. "The others are in the living room." He reaches down to pet Max, who licks his hand and is wildly wagging his tail. "Hello, Max."

We enter the familiar home my mother shares with David, and we make our way to the living room. Max finds his furry friends, my mother's dogs Ace and Skippy, and the three begin chasing each other around the house. Mom heads to the back door, calling the dogs. "Boys, come on. Let's go outside." She opens the door and lets them out into the fenced-in backyard.

She comes back inside, hugs us, and offers both of us a warm drink. "I made hot chocolate. I felt like it was a good day for it," she says. "Can I get you guys some?"

I hug her. "Mom, I'll get it," I tell her. "You don't have to wait on us. Let me just take the casserole into the kitchen and while I'm there, I'll get Thomas and myself a mug of hot chocolate. That's a good idea on a brisk day like today."

Mom follows me into the kitchen, explaining that she is all ready for lunch whenever everyone is hungry. "I went ahead and put the food on warmers, so it should be pretty easy. I figure we can eat at the dining room table. I even bought these sturdy disposable Christmas plates, so we won't have many dishes to wash."

I pour two mugs of enticing henna-colored liquid into pretty colored mugs for Mom, David, Thomas, and me. The aroma is heavenly. I add a touch of whipped cream to the top of the drinks. "I haven't had hot chocolate in years. I need to remember to buy the ingredients the next time we go over to Conner's grocery store," I say.

I look over at my mother and add, "If you need any help with anything, just let me know."

Mom answers me. "I'm good for now. Maybe when we get done eating you can give me a hand with the dishes. We're just waiting on Sally, Robert, the twins, and John and Chloe."

We hear the doorbell ring, the sound of the door opening, and my sister calling out to us. "We're here! And John and Chloe are with us."

Mom and I rush to help them. "Looks like you have your hands full," I say as I take Evie and Mom takes Jacob in her arms. "Well come on in. Everyone is in the living room."

I look down to see a furry ball of chocolate brown hair bouncing up and down. I squeal out, "A puppy. Oh, so cute."

Robert is grinning from ear to ear. "It was a surprise for the twins and Sally," he explains. "His name is Biscuit. He loves doggy treats—that's how he got his name."
Sally reaches down to pick up the wiggling puppy. Little Evie and Jacob watch with wide blue eyes as the energetic puppy wiggles in their mother's arms.

"The twins just love him," Sally says. "We have to watch him, though, because he loves them, too."

I move close to my sister and rub the little guy's furry brown head. "This should be interesting to see Biscuit interact with the other dogs, I say.

Robert laughs. "He's already met them. He's been staying at George's house and his parents' house during the day when we are working," my brother-in-law says to me. "I couldn't risk telling you. I thought you might accidentally let it slip to Sally."

I playfully swat him on the shoulder as we make our way into the living room where Thomas and David are sitting. "Hey, what are you trying to say?" I demand, playfully. "I didn't tell her about her secret room, did I?"

Robert nods his head in agreement. "Well, you have a point there," he says.

John and Chloe are right behind us, watching our friendly interaction, then John pipes up, holding up two bottles of white wine. "I brought wine, wasn't sure what type to bring, so I got a chardonnay and a pinot grigio."

He reaches over to pet Biscuit. "That puppy is adorable."

We move through the house into the living room, and the twins watch in awe when they spot the twinkling lights of the Christmas tree. Sally hands Thomas the wiggling chocolate brown lab squirming in her arms. "Can you hold Biscuit for a minute while I get the snowsuits off the twins? I bundled them up since it's so chilly outside."

She takes a blanket out of their diaper bag and places it on the rug. "Angie, Mom, why don't you put those two down on the floor so I can get them unwrapped."

I lay little Evie down and she instantly rolls over and starts crawling towards the Christmas tree. I laugh and reach out to catch her before she gets to the tree. "Wow, aren't you a fast little one?" I tell her.

Sally and Robert both nod in agreement. "Yeah, it's starting to be really challenging watching her," Sally concedes. "Jacob is trying to crawl, too, but it's more of a scooting at this point. But, boy, does he watch what his sister is doing."

Isabella motions to David. "Hey David, maybe we need to give Sally and Robert our gift for the twins now."

David leaves and slips into the dining room. He returns with a playpen. "I think you might need this now," he says. "I'm glad we took it out of the box." Sally hugs Isabella and David. "Oh, that's perfect, especially with a new puppy," she tells them.

Thomas is holding the sleeping puppy. "I think someone is tired," Thomas says. I think Biscuit looks angelic in his brawny arms. "I can't wait to see how this puppy gets along with the other dogs," Thomas adds.

Robert shakes his head as he pulls out a casserole Sally has made for our lunch. "He's met Max, but not the other two dogs. Biscuit and Max were grand friends by the end of their day together," Robert says. "I just have to watch him because he's so little yet he thinks he's a big boy."

Holding up the casserole, Robert asks Isabella, "Do you want me to put the dish in the kitchen?"

Isabella reaches out and takes the dish from him. "That's okay. I can take it," she says. "So, this is my question for everyone When do you want to eat? It's all ready."

John and Chloe shrug. "We're guests, so we are good with whatever time you guys want to eat," John says while Chloe nods in agreement. Robert starts rubbing his tummy. "I'm hungry now. We didn't have breakfast because we got so busy with all the Christmas stuff."

David puts his arm around his son. "That's my boy," he says with a laugh. "But to tell the truth, I'm hungry, too. We only had a quick English muffin at around 7 a.m." "That sounds good to me, too," Isabella says. "Since the other animals are outside, now is probably a good time to eat."

137

We start making our way into the cozy kitchen. Isabella smiles at everyone and says, "I have a buffet set up here in the kitchen. Help yourselves—the drinks are over on the counter and the hot chocolate is on the stove. I figure we can eat in the dining room. The twins are in the playpen, and we can see them from the dining room."

She points to Thomas, who is still holding Biscuit. "Thomas, you can put the puppy in the dog's bed by the fireplace. We can see him, too, from the dining room."

David beckons everyone to say grace, and we bow our heads. "Bless this food, all our family and friends. Keep everyone safe on this holiday today and in the future," David says. "Amen."

We've finished our lunch just in time to hear a little whimper from Jacob. Sally wipes her mouth with the pretty Christmas napkin. "Time to eat for someone else," she announces. "I'll take him into the other room to feed him."

She turns to Robert. "If Evie wakes up, can you give her some of the cereal out of the diaper bag?"

Robert nods, stands up, and heads toward the diaper bag. "She'll be awake soon, so I'm going to get the cereal ready for them," he says. "We've just started introducing them to cereal," he tells us.

He mixes the pablum, and no sooner does he finish when we hear Evie starting to squawk.

Chloe grins. "She is such a cutie and she's so alert," she says. "Look how those bright blue eyes are following Robert around the room."

Robert lifts Evie out of the playpen and pats his anxious and hungry daughter on her back. "She's something alright. We are going to have our hands full when she starts walking," he says.

Sally is laughing as she comes back into the room, carrying Jacob and patting his tiny back. "She already keeps us on our toes," Sally says. "Thank heavens for Georgia. Our nanny is a lifesaver."

Sally hands Jacob to Robert while simultaneously taking little Evie from him. "Ah, that's my girl. Come to Momma," she coos to her daughter. "Let's get you fed, too, little girl."

We clear the table and take care of the dishes, and then it's time to let the animals back in the house. The dogs come running into the den to where we've all retired by the Christmas Tree. Max, Ace, and Skippy immediately head over to sniff the sleeping puppy, which wakes up and barks excitedly.

Thomas grabs Max by the collar. "Down boy, easy boy," Thomas says. "He's little."

Robert scoops up little Biscuit. "Let me take you outside for a potty break," he tells the dog. Then he turns to us, "He's surprisingly house broken already, but not when he's excited." Tiny Biscuit whines and barks, struggling to be let down to play. Robert tells the little fella, "Potty first." He takes the puppy outside.

The afternoon continues with good conversation and laughter and, before we know it, it is time for us to go to Thomas's parents' home. I make a suggestion. "Maybe one day we can do a combined Christmas day celebration with all three of our families together."

Isabella runs her hands through her graying brown hair. "I think that's a wonderful idea. I hate that you two have to leave so early," she says. "Let's ask the others what they think for next Christmas."

Thomas and I say goodbye to everyone then leave the house to walk down the oyster-shell road leading to Thomas' family home. I can see that Thomas is thinking about something. He finally breaks the silence. "This is a momentous occasion if you think about it," he says, "our first Christmas together. I just had a glimpse of us with two children in tow, along with Max. It was really weird. I wonder if it was a peek into our future."

I smile, taking his hand in mine. "Two children. That sounds nice, one for each hand."

I laugh then add, "But hopefully not at the same time!"

Thomas chuckles. "I have to agree with you there," he says. "I don't think there are many Georgias around, so we'd need to find another nanny. We haven't really discussed children yet. So, you want two?"

I nod. "I think two would be perfect if they are healthy," I say, before adding, "Wow, a year ago, I had given up on men and now I'm getting married and discussing children."

Thomas smiles. We walk up the steps to his parents' bungalow. As he opens the door, he says, "Here we go. Are you hungry?" I rub my belly and laugh. "Oooh, not any time soon. I hope they don't want to eat yet." Thomas shakes his head as he responds. "Let's just hope that everyone ate lunch, and they don't want to eat again until a little later. It's a shame my grandparents couldn't make it this year. They went on a Caribbean cruise. It's just going to be Emily, George, mom, dad, and Max, of course."

I smile as I tell him, "Oh, that sounds nice and peaceful." Then I add, "I wonder how Emily is doing since getting engaged."

Thomas chuckles. "She was so funny when George popped the question. She seemed shocked but happy."

We had stopped back at our house to pick up a side dish of corn casserole, another one of my favorite dishes to make. George must have heard us drive up, because he opens the door immediately and gives us a hand. Max rushes between our legs and into the house to say hello to everyone.

"We're all sitting in the den. There's a blazing fire in the wood stove," he says. "Hope you wore layers because it's a little warm in here, and you're probably going to want to strip off a layer or two."

At that, Joe and Elizabeth Alexander, George and Thomas' parents, appear and reach out to welcome us with warm bear hugs. I have known them since I was a young girl. It still amazes me that I never met Thomas before this past June.

Elizabeth, who likes to be called Liz, reaches out for the casserole. "I can take that, Angie," she says. "We figured you two would still be stuffed after lunch at your mom's, so we decided to wait until later to eat. I hope that's okay.

"Emily is in the other room," she continues. "We were working on a new puzzle."

I answer her with a big grin, rubbing my stomach. "You are so right. We are both stuffed, but we can eat whenever you want," I say. "A puzzle? That sounds fun. I love puzzles."

Emily comes out of the den and into the kitchen where Liz and I are standing. George, Thomas, and their father have gone through the foyer into the den. Emily looks so happy as she comes over to hug me hello.

"Hey lady, how's it going? I know you must be stuffed, too," she says. "My mom made a brunch for all of us. When we left my parents, Matt and Sarah were with them, and they were getting ready to go over to your mom's house."

"I know what you mean about being full," I say, then I decide to tentatively broach my idea about next Christmas. "I had an idea about that, in fact. Liz, I've been wondering… what you think about taking turns and having one big family lunch or dinner all together next year? I mean, we are all so linked with Matt and Sarah, Thomas and me, Emily and George."

141

Liz raises her eyebrow and says, "I think that's a wonderful idea!" she says. "That way we all have one big meal during the day. We all have big homes and plenty of room to entertain everyone.

"We'll have to check how the others feel about it," she adds. "And one day, I guess you two girls might want to host our annual Christmas day celebration, too."

Emily laughs at the suggestion. "I don't know how good I would be at it but I'm game. What about you, Angie?"

I nod my head. "That's so funny. Thomas and I went over to our new home this morning to go over his plans to renovate the house. I'll have to tell him a big room for entertaining is a must," he says. "He plans to make it an open floor plan like they did with Sally and Robert's home."

Liz runs her fingers through her pretty blond hair. "Yeah, so consider it settled with us. Now we just have to see what the others think."

Emily tells Liz, "You'll need to come for our annual cookie and gingerbread competitions, too. We launched it this year and it was so much fun."

Liz smiles, points to both of us, and nods. "It's a deal. It sounds like a wonderful tradition. But before we start planning next Christmas, I guess we're going to have to plan two weddings." Emily blushes furiously and looks down lovingly at her new engagement ring. "I know, it's crazy," she says. "I have always loved George, but never allowed myself to show it. He makes me so happy."

I hug my friend. "Your wedding is going to be so much fun. Have you two decided where and when—or is it too soon?"

Emily shakes her strawberry-blonde head. "I don't know what we are planning yet. I guess we'll need to talk about it. Man, there's so much to do. I do know that I don't want anything elaborate. Maybe we'll do something like Sarah and Matt did, a destination wedding."

Liz points to the counter where there are drinks. "You girls, help yourselves, then we can go in and join the others in the den. There's ice in the ice bucket on the counter."

We have a very pleasant rest of the afternoon and evening visiting with Thomas' family and Emily. Before long the day is over, we decide to take Max for a long walk around the point and then head home.

Max is overjoyed to be outside for a walk. He pulls Thomas down the road, his chestnut-colored tail wagging furiously. Thomas whistles. "Down, Max. Sit, Max," he orders as he pulls a treat out of his jacket and turns to me. "Boy, is he excited. You good?" he asks. "Do you feel like walking down to the lighthouse? The wind has died down some so it doesn't feel as cold outside."

I pull my wild dark hair up into a ponytail. "That sounds good to me. It feels nice to be out and to walk around," I answer. "What time do you have to work tomorrow?"

"We don't have to be there until 10," Thomas answers. We're at Bob and Sue's house tomorrow to work on their deck. It should be a quick job."

Then he adds, "The pub is open tomorrow, right, since it hasn't been open for the last few days?"

I nod. "Yeah, it'll be nice to work again. I love the holidays, but I really enjoy my time singing in the pub," I say. "I'm also planning on sending my novel to the publisher tomorrow to have it edited. It will be good to have the final manuscript ready to go."

Thomas hugs me. "Wow, I didn't realize you were so close to being done," he says. "It seems like only yesterday that you started writing it."

I hug him back. "I know, it does seem like just yesterday that I started writing it, but most of the story was already told long before I began it," I explain. "I just embellished the story with the journals from Roger and Evangeline plus all my dreams. Maybe I'll write about Anne Bonny next. Just think, I can call it 'The Pirate Series.' I might even be able to do a book on Charles Vane. Who knows where this could lead with all the pirates there were around back in the day."

Thomas whistles for Max. "Ready to head home, Angie?" I nod, and in no time we are back at our house, sitting in front of our fireplace dancing with flames. Thomas rubs my shoulders and pulls me over onto his lap. "Well, our first Christmas together is over," he says. "I love you, baby."

I turn around and sit in his lap, my legs wrapping around his legs. I passionately kiss his warm lips. Before long, our clothes are scattered on the furry rug. I rub my body up against him and our lust overflows into climax, leaving us both spent in front of the warm fireplace.

The evening ends and our passion is satisfied. We both feel warm and cozy. We retire after spending our first wonderful Christmas together.

I am looking forward to tomorrow. I will turn my new novel into my publisher. Luckily my agent knows a traditional publisher I can use to launch my book.

Chapter 19

A New Day Brings Promises

We rise to find a foggy mist covering the countryside and flowing over the gusty shoreline. Vicious waves crash against the eroded coastline. A nor'easter has landed upon the Carolina coast.

Thomas, always the early riser, has already taken Max out for his walk on the beach. "Good morning, sleeping beauty. How did you sleep?" he says when he returns to the house

I reach up into the kitchen cabinet to grab two coffee cups for us as I answer. "I slept pretty well, but I kept having the strangest dreams. It reminded me of the warnings that I used to get from Evangeline, almost like she was trying to tell me something. I hope it's not an omen."

Thomas pours us each a cup of coffee and reaches into the refrigerator to get the container of French vanilla coffee creamer. "Well, let's hope we don't have any problems," he says. "I keep thinking about all those articles that were written about us. I hope they don't attract a bunch of crazy people."

I rub my hands over my eyes. "Oh, don't say that," I reply. "I wonder if that's why I had those weird dreams about being chased. I don't remember them, but I woke up feeling anxious."

We have our coffee and a quick breakfast of fried eggs and a couple of croissants that we warm up in the oven. As we tidy up after breakfast, Thomas wraps his arms around me and massages my shoulders. "Try not to think about those dreams too much," he advises me. "You have a busy day ahead of you. I'm just so proud of you finishing your new book and a new song."

I run my slender fingers through my untamed hair. "You're so sweet," I say, "and you're right, I *am* going to be busy today. I'm lucky my music agent knew a literary agent and was able to get me that contract with Berkley Publishing. I mean, how awesome is that? Most people never even get accepted by literary agents, much less a traditional publisher. Plus, with me releasing my song about Evangeline at the same time, the book will— hopefully—be a big hit."

I think about how happy all my creative output is making me—and how it is enriching my life with Thomas, too. "You know, I can help with the renovations, anything we want," I tell Thomas. "It would mean a lot to me helping out financially."

Thomas laughs as he puts on his jacket. "That sounds nice to me," he says. "And just think, you can add any special touches or features you want to make it all ours. For now, though, I gotta' fly. I'm supposed to meet Matt at our job at Bob and Sue's house in 15 minutes."

I sit at my laptop. As he walks by toward the door, I reach out to stop him. I give him a quick peck on the cheek. "Have a good day. And keep your fingers crossed that everything goes smoothly for me today." He crosses his fingers and blows me a kiss which I catch, laughing.

"Love you," he calls as opens the door. "I'll catch up with you tonight at the pub."

My mind is racing. I'm beyond excited at the prospect of launching my new book. I am supposed to sign the book contract today. I think of how far I've come—from a meek young singer who entered a country music songwriter contest two years earlier, and won, to someone who makes a living with music. And now with writing! Who would have ever thought that I'd have several Number One hits on my hands and other songs climbing the charts? I am thrilled by all the good things that have come my way.

I stare at my computer screen and review parts of the final manuscript I submitted earlier. I really love the part in the story where I describe how Jacob gives Evangeline a silver pendant shaped like half a heart. Distractedly, I reach up to grasp my own silver half-heart necklace. A vibration runs through me, and Evangeline's vision appears before me.

"Angie, I am in fear for you and your friends' lives," she warns. "It is just a premonition, but I feel a steady emotion coursing through my being, and it is telling me that you are in danger. Take heed! I know not what the peril is, but something is coming to do you harm."

Before I can ask any questions, she disappears from my sight. I start to worry that maybe the danger is related to the contract with my literary agent or my publisher. My lawyer has already reviewed the documents, but could he have missed something? My Zoom call is about to happen any second now.

My computer beeps and a link appears for the video meeting. I take a deep beath, smile, and click my keypad to join the call. "Hello, Donna," I say to my new book agent. "I'm so happy to meet you."

Donna is a petite brunette whose warm smile immediately puts me at ease. "Hi, Angie. It's so nice to meet you, too. Have you had a chance to review the contract we sent to you?"

I nod and hold up some pages. "I went ahead and printed the documents that you sent to me. They look pretty straightforward. I don't see any problems with them."

Donna pushes her fluffy bangs away from her eyes. "I know you're familiar with these types of contracts. They're probably similar to the ones you sign with your recording agent. Speaking of which... I spoke to Phillip, your music agent, and we discussed the possibility of releasing your song about Evangeline at the same time as the book. What do you think?"

I nod in agreement. "It's definitely fine with me. I think it's a great idea." I laugh and continue speaking, "Maybe it will even be a movie one day. Wouldn't that be cool?"

"You never know what could happen," Donna says. "For now, let's get some nuts and bolts out of the way."

Donna shuffles photographs in front of her and then starts holding them up to me. They are some of the book cover designs her illustrators have come up with.

"Our artists have emailed these illustrations to you so you can pick out a cover for your book. The manuscript has been sent to our editing department and comments from that team will be available in the next couple weeks," she tells me.

"What do you think about these?" she asks as she holds up some images.

I gaze at the photographs that she has selected for my review. "Wow, those are all so good. I really like the one with Evangeline standing on the shore gazing out at the sea. It reminds me of the years she watched for her true love, Jacob, to return to make her his wife."

"I really like that one, too," Donna says. "Do you want to make it the cover—or do you want to think about it?"

I shake my head and run my hands over my face. "No, I don't need to think about it," I answer. "I love the design we're talking about. I'd like it for my cover."

Donna looks pleased by my answer. "Perfect. Now we can get on with some marketing strategies for your book and your new song," she says. "When I spoke with Phillip, we decided to advertise both now so we can start generating preorders for them."

I am in awe at the process. "So, you're telling me we will be able to see how well my book will do even before it's published? That's so cool."

Donna smiles. "Absolutely. We'll start the marketing as soon as I get off this call, and we should start seeing some action by the end of the day," she says. "Do you have any more questions for me? If not, I'll let you go and get back to you later in the week."

I shake my head. "No questions. I think I'm good. If I think of anything I'll email you," I tell her.

"It's been nice meeting you, Angie, and I look forward to working with you," Donna says. "Email or call me if you have any questions. We can set up weekly Zoom meetings to keep you up to date. I'll send you a schedule. If any of the dates don't work for you, just let me know. Talk to you next week."

I nod in agreement and disconnect from the Zoom meeting after saying goodbye. I take a deep breath and exhale. I hadn't realized how tense I have been about the Zoom call. I stretch my arms over my head and then I reach for my phone. I text the girls to see if they want to take a walk on the beach.

Sally is the first to respond. "I can leave in about a half hour if that's good." Both Emily and Sarah reply with a heart emoji. I text them back: "Let's meet at the inn in a half hour." They click on the "like" button.

I change into my warm sweatpants and sweatshirt then add a few layers since it is still quite chilly outside. I finish dressing and walk across the driveway leading to the inn. I look up at a crystal blue sky with puffy white clouds and smile.

I open the door to the cozy inn, and Sarah greets me in the parlor. She looks at me and says, "You look awfully happy today. What's up?"

Before I can answer, Emily and Sally walk into the foyer, chatting and laughing. Sally is teasing Emily. "What did we tell you, Emily? George has been in love with you forever. I'm just so happy for you."

Emily is blushing and nodding her head. "I didn't want to spoil our friendship by mixing in romance," she says. "I was so afraid that if we started dating it might ruin what we had." She hugs herself and continues, "But now it's even better. I can't believe how overjoyed I am. I feel like I need to pinch myself to see if this is for real."

Sarah, who is beaming, hugs her sister.

"I am surrounded by happy women—and that is wonderful," she says." She points to me and says, "This one here looks like the cat that ate the canary. She was just getting ready to tell me what was going on when you guys came in."

I pull out my phone and open up my photos. "Look at this," I tell them. "This is going to be my new book cover. I just got off the Zoom call with my book agent, and she sent over these pictures." I show them the image I picked.

"What do you think?"

They look at the picture and squeal—they are as excited as I am. Sally swings me around. "Whoa, my sister going to be a best-selling author," she shouts. "I love the cover design. It reminds me of Evangeline standing on the shore waiting for Jacob."

I laugh. "That's exactly what I thought," I tell her. "It's perfect for the book. But wait—that's not the best part. They are going to start marketing it for presales, and my music agent is planning to release my song about Evangeline at the same time."

Emily and Sarah hug and congratulate me. "I just can't wait to read your book," Emily says. "Maybe it will even become a movie." I nod my head in agreement. "That's just what I said to Donna, my book agent. She said, 'You never know.' Now wouldn't that be cool?"

Chapter 20

Special Warning

The girls and I leisurely walk down the road, passing Ocracoke Lighthouse as we make our way down to Springers Point. There is a cool breeze, and the temperature is in the high 50s today. I am amazed at how much warmer it is than yesterday. We have a lighthearted banter going as we tease Emily about her new engagement.

Sally puts her arm around Emily, asking her, "So is it better than you thought it would be? You and George are perfect for each other. I'm so happy for you two."

Emily blushes as she responds. "I can honestly say it is even better than I ever imagined. When George lived with me this past summer, it was so comfortable. But now there is passion. He's such a warm person— and so caring. I can't believe how happy I am."

Sarah smiles at her sister. "I told you so, Emily. You two are meant to be."

After a pause, she adds: "So, when's the wedding? I want to be a bridesmaid."

Emily looks toward her sister. "I hope you'll be my matron of honor. Can you remember how we used to play brides up in our old dusty attic?" she says. "I need to find a wedding dress. Maybe we can take another trip up to the attic and explore some of the cedar chests up there. I think I might want to wear our great grandmother's wedding gown. I just love the styles from back then."

Emily glances my way. "And Angie, what about you? What are your wedding plans?"

I fix my ponytail as I turn to face the girls. "Well, we are pretty much all set. I found most of my wedding outfit when we were looking for gowns for Sarah's wedding," I tell them. "I'm planning a very simple, casual wedding with just family and a few friends. As you all know, we're having the wedding and reception at the inn. I need to order the invitations and flowers, but I've already hired a wedding photographer.

I add: "I feel like I'm pretty caught up on things." Suddenly I stop and become serious. "Girls, I really need to tell you about my dream with Evangeline."

Sally stops and takes my hand in hers. "Not more scary warnings, I hope. Last time she was right on in her predictions."

I start to describe my dream.

"It was very weird, almost like I was in a fog or something. Evangeline came to me and told me to be cautious as there could be someone wanting to cause us harm. It wasn't a very specific warning, more like a feeling. I woke up feeling so anxious, just like I did when she kept warning us about the caves on Cat Island.

"Maybe we'll need to ask Anne Bonny if she has any warnings for us," I continue. "What do you think?"

Sally answers my question, raising her eyebrow like she always does when she is thinking hard about something. "That's a good idea, Angie. Maybe she can give us some advice."

We stroll down the sandy path and pass by Ikey D's grave. I stop to reach down to retie my black New Balance tennis shoe. I wonder to myself what dangers await us on this new journey to find Calico Jack and Anne Bonny's treasure.

I break the silence. "Emily, do you think you and George might want to have a destination wedding like Sarah and Matt did?"

Emily pushes her strawberry blond hair out of her hazel green eyes. "Not sure yet. I'll need to ask George," she replies.

Sarah chimes in. "Oh, another destination wedding would be great fun. I just loved our wedding, and I can help you with all the planning. I know you really aren't into stuff like that."

We finally reach Springer's Point, and we stop to take in the view. I point in the direction of a majestic blue heron feasting on a small mullet. "Look, he's caught a fish," I say. "It's always like being in a forgotten land when we come down here. Watch the ripples in the water—it looks like there is a ton of bait fish. We'll have to remember to tell the guys. They might want to come down here and go fishing."

Sally looks down at her Fitbit and exclaims, "Oh man, I need to get back. The twins will be getting hungry," she says. "But we really should try to come down here at least once a week or walk somewhere else. I just love our walks."

My phone beeps with a new message. I look down to read it. "It's John. He wants to know if we'd like to have dinner with them tonight." I start a response. "I'll let him know we'll be at the pub working tonight." As I text him back, I wonder if he's spoken to our other relative in Jamaica.

Chapter 21

Another Day of Discoveries

After our hike, we each head back home. I'm feeling happy as I open the screen door to the porch of my home, and then push against the pretty oak main door that Thomas and Matt refurbished for me. I am daydreaming about our new house and how it will turn out. Will it really be ready in time for us to move in before our wedding in June?

I've just finished primping for work at the pub when I hear a gentle tapping at my front door and a female voice. "It's me. Emily. George insisted on dropping me off so we can walk over to the pub together. Are you ready to go?"

I unfasten the door to let Emily in. I pull on my heavy navy-blue jacket and declare, "Perfect timing. I just finished getting ready."

As I zip my jacket, I add, "Yeah, that's right, we must go back to the buddy system. I really hate having to worry about being cautious, but I guess it's better than the alternative—getting abducted or worse.

"I never want to go through that again," I add in a serious tone.

Emily nods in agreement. "Let's hope there's nothing to worry about and that we're just being overly cautious."

As we walk out, I pull the heavy door shut behind us and make sure I lock it. I slip my brass house key into a pocket of my faded blue jeans. "I know, but it's just annoying having to worry again," I say. "I really like being able to come and go as I please."

Emily swings her arm around my shoulders. "Better safe than sorry," she says. "So, tell me again, what did John's text say?"

I open my phone and read the text out loud. "'Chloe and I were wondering if you all were interested in getting together for dinner at the pub.' I answered back that we're working but would love to see them. He didn't mention anything about our other relative, the one in Jamaica."

"Maybe the guy changed his mind about getting in touch with John," she suggests.

"I guess we'll find out shortly," I reply. "They're planning to come over to the pub around 5 o'clock. It's already 3:45 now."

We reach the Oxford Pub, and Emily searches in her pocket for the old skeleton key that unlocks the big oak door. She pushes the door open, holding it for me to enter. "Well, here we are, one of my favorite places," she says. "We're probably going to be busy again tonight. Most of the people on the island visiting family won't leave until after New Year's Day. Better put on your roller skates."

I go into the pub ahead of her. "I'll start taking the chairs off the tables and then I'll make some Oxford Brew. Let me know if you need me to do anything else."

Emily nods. "I think that'll be good. I'm going to set up the bar and get the ice out of the storeroom. Sam helped me stock before he left the other day, so we should be all set."

The local regulars start trickling in with their kin, ready for a joyous evening of good music, delicious food, and a friendly vibe. Luckily, Sam can help with bartending tonight because the place is jam-packed by 4:30. I'm scheduled to play my first set at 5 p.m.

I stop by the bar to talk to Emily for a minute. "I'm going to go ahead and get started. I'll try to give you a hand in between sets if you need me to."

Emily puts an orange slice on the lip of a glass and slides the ice-cold Blue Moon across the bar to one of the locals, Andy. "Sounds good. Are you planning on playing any new music tonight?"

I nod back to her and say hello to Andy. "I'm going to play a lot of my new stuff," I reply. "My agent wants me to play the new songs every night to get them out there in the public since I'm not doing any big concerts."

Emily looks at me, laughing. "I'll never understand you not wanting to go on the road to perform at concerts. But it works for us—we're so thankful to have you here with at the pub." She points to the crowded room. "You're great for business."

I pick up my well-used guitar and sit down on a brown stool in a corner of the bar. I strum my trusty old guitar, and my voice rings out through the small neighborhood pub. I sing my song about Ocracoke Island, the song about the twins, Matt and Sarah's song, and the ballad about my father.

I am almost fifteen minutes into my set when I see Thomas, Matt, Sarah, John, and Chloe enter the bar. They wave at me, and Thomas blows me a kiss. I reach up to catch it, laughing. I finish the set, grab a quick seltzer water, and join them at the table where they are sitting.

I give Thomas a quick peck on his stubbly cheek and say hello to everyone. "Is everyone having a good day? Anything new?"

John sounds tentative when he answers. "I heard from our cousin, Stephen Bell, and his girlfriend, Violet Morgan. They Facetimed me and said that they are planning to come here tomorrow for New Year's and to meet all of us. I didn't know what to say to him."

Thomas looks worried. "I haven't had a chance to get Billy to do a background check on him yet."

John nods. "I had my brother Mike, who's a cop, investigate him. I also checked out his Facebook, Instagram, and TikTok pages," he says.

Matt asks, "Did the background check unearth anything?"

John looks in Matt's direction as he answers. "Everything turned out okay, but he did have a drunk and disorderly charge at one point a few years ago," he says. "It was related to a bar fight."

Thomas continues to look concerned. "We are just going to need to be vigilant about keeping any clues that we uncover a secret from him. In fact, we need to keep everything we learn a secret from anyone outside our group."

John agrees with him. "From his Facebook page, it looks like Stephen and Violet are both pretty heavy partyers. There are a lot of photos and posts with the two of them doing shots."

John continues revealing what he has learned about our new relative. "Stephen's a professional scuba diver, fisherman, and treasure hunter. He focuses on the coasts of Jamaica and the Bahamas," John says. "I'm not sure if that is a good thing or not."

Chloe adds a detail: "They said that they'd be here tomorrow, a little early, so they could ring in the New Year with all of us."

Matt shakes head. "Just because they come here doesn't mean we need to tell them anything about Anne's secret room or anything else we have found. I say we shouldn't even bring up anything related to the treasure when we're with them."

George agrees. Then Matt adds another thought, "Let's just meet them here at the pub and not invite them to our houses. That way there's no opportunity for them to snoop around where we live."

Thomas nods his head and points to John and Chloe. "I also think it would be a good idea to keep the gold coin that we gave you hidden. He might get suspicious if you show it to him."

John pulls the Spanish coin out of a pocket in his jeans. "No problem," he says, slipping the coin away again. "I'm keeping it hidden in my pants pocket."

George looks at John and makes a suggestion. "I wonder if it wouldn't be a better idea to maybe keep it locked up in the safe in your hotel room," he says. "Or, if you want, you can lock it up in the safe at the inn."

John shakes his head. "Nah, I'm good," he says. "It feels like my lucky charm. I really want to keep it on me."

"Okay, man," George says, "but if you change your mind, just let us know."

The time flies and before long it is almost nine o'clock, time for my last set. It's been so busy in the pub that Sarah and I have been helping wait tables. I point to my little makeshift stage.

"Time for my last set," I say to Sarah. I also swing by the table where the others are talking and laughing. "See you guys in a little bit," I call over as I head to the pub's little stage. I pick my guitar and lift the shoulder strap over my head and into position. I take the mic in my hand and ask the crowd, "Any requests? This is my last set so give me a heads up if there is something you would like to hear." The pub erupts in applause and I hear people calling out that they want to hear my song about Ocracoke Island. I smile, give them a thumbs up and play one of my favorite pieces.

The night ends and George, Emily, Sam, and I clean up the pub. Thomas and Matt have left, both having an early morning tomorrow. Thomas had waved to me and mouthed that he'd see me at home before he left. I had nodded and waved back at him.

As we wrap up the work, George says he'll he walk me back to my house. "We don't need any repeats of last summer," he points out.

I cringe remembering that horrible night when I was abducted on my way home from the pub by those two scummy guys, Ricky and Rusty. They're both now in prison. "No argument here, George," I say. "I never want a repeat of that. Just the thought of it makes my hair stand on end."

George walks me right to my door then heads back to the pub to get Emily; she and Sam are finishing up some lastminute restocking. I hug George goodbye. "Thanks. I really appreciate it," I say. "Oh, and congratulations again. I'm thrilled about you and Emily getting engaged."

George blushes and waves me off. "Oh, Angie, I can't believe how happy she makes me. She's always been my best friend, but now she'll be my wife one day soon, I hope."

I smile at him. "'Night. I'll see you tomorrow."

Thomas is already sleeping when I enter our bedroom. He looks angelic—and I love him even more for it. I slide into bed, spooning him. I whisper goodnight. He squeezes my leg and mumbles goodnight back to me. Max, laying on the floor beside our bed, lifts his sleepy head and groans before dropping back to sleep. I think to myself how grateful I am for my little family. But something darker pushes away the good thoughts. Worries about tomorrow's meeting with our new relative crowds my mind as I fall asleep.

I dream again of Evangeline. For some reason, I dream of her capture. The terror I feel is real and I wake up deep in the night wondering if the dream is some type of omen. I'll have to tell Thomas in the morning. And I'll have to tell the girls, too, when we go for our walk tomorrow. Last night we prearranged to meet for a walk since we are all off on Tuesdays.

When I wake, I feel the other side of the bed. It's cool, and I am amazed that Thomas has managed to head off to work without me hearing him leave with Max. I quickly get ready to meet the girls for our walk then look out the window to see George drop Emily off. I smile when I see him reach over and give her a passionate kiss before she gets out of his truck. I open my front door before she can knock, startling her out of her daydream.

"Man, you look a thousand miles away," I say with a laugh.

Emily's cheeks turn pink, and she grins. "I was just thinking about the conversation I had with George this morning. We talked about our wedding plans. He doesn't want to wait and neither do I," she declares. "There, I've said it. Are you surprised?"

I squeal with delight. "Heck no! That's so cool. Now give me the when's, where's and whatever's. I can't wait to hear."

Before she has a chance to answer, we hear a knock at the door. It opens and in come Sarah and Sally. "We're here," they chime in unison.

Sarah looks at her sister's flushed face. "Something's up, isn't it? What did we miss?"

I gently punch Emily on her slender shoulder. "Tell them what you just told me." Emily's still blushing as she announces her plans.

"Well, George and I are getting married—soon! We've decided not to wait," she says. "It seems like we've already waited a long time. You all know that we have loved each other forever."

Sally and Sarah both bleat out, "Yeah! When? Where? What are your plans?"

Emily laughs. "You two sound just like Angie. She asked the exact same thing."

Sarah hugs her sister. "I am so happy for you guys," she says before getting back to the questions. "So, what did you and George decide?"

Emily shrugs. "We're thinking about maybe doing like you and Matt did, a destination wedding. We still need to do some research, though, and figure out where we want to go. Isabella and David are getting married in Jamaica so who knows?"

"Maybe you can help me, Sarah," she adds. "You're good at that sort of thing."

Sarah grins like a Cheshire cat. "Oh, absolutely, Emily. I'd love to help you guys plan your wedding. Mom is going to be so excited."

Sally speaks up. "I can help, too," she says. "I don't go back to class until after January 5th," she adds.

"We need to get going on other wedding details, too," she continues. "We should check out the attic for dresses later today or tomorrow."

I don't want to be left out. "Hey, me, too. I'd love to help," I chime in. "At least give us a time frame. When are you thinking about getting married?"

"Well, that's the tricky part," Emily says. "We were thinking spring break so that Sally and Robert can come with us, but we aren't sure if we can get it planned that soon. What do you girls think?"

Sarah pulls out her phone and looks up a website for Jamaican wedding locations. "This website, under the Frequently Asked Questions section, says a wedding can be planned in as little as a week," she says. "That's pretty crazy, isn't it?"

Emily throws her arms up in the air and takes a deep breath. "Oh, now I'm getting nervous," she says. "This is happening so fast. I love George, so that's not the issue. It's just the whole process, you know."

We do know. Emily is the cautious one in our group. She's not naturally inclined toward quick decisions or action. Sally steps over and hugs her friend. "That is the most important thing, that you love him," she tells Emily. "The rest will just fall into place, you'll see. It's easy peasy."

Emily opens the front door and inhales deeply. "C'mon, girls. I need some air."

We all laugh and follow her as she steps outside. I make sure I shut the door tightly and lock it. Then I say, "I think we should celebrate. Let's get everyone together and go to SmacNally's later today."

I pull out my phone. "You girls know how much I love that fun little waterfront grill. It's just so casual and they have the best food. I'll text everyone. I'll include John and Chloe to see if they're interested."

Emily nods. "That sounds perfect. I just love that place," she says. "It'll be nice to see Frank and Joe. They are such fun bartenders. They were at the pub last night and they both said they're working behind the bar at SmacNally's today."

We decide to take a walk down Back Road, past the visitor's center, down to the water's edge, and back up to the inn. The dazzling sun is peeping out from the early morning clouds when Sarah suggests we head back and check out the attic at the inn to see if there's something Emily can use as a wedding dress."

It doesn't take us long to get to the inn. We walk up the wide wooden steps to the porch, go inside and head upstairs. After we push open the rarely used door leading into the attic, Sarah flips the light switch on the plastered beige wall so we can see up the old wooden stairs. At the top of the stairs, another light switch illuminates the dusty loft.

Sarah turns to ask Emily, "Did you still want to wear Great Grandmom Lily's wedding dress?"

Emily points to a large cedar chest up against the wall on the far side of the attic. "That's what I'm thinking," she says. "I like the style back then, kinda' Roaring Twenties, if you know what I mean."

Emily walks over to the chest, opens it, and pulls out a beautiful, satin tea-length bridal gown. I know the A-line style and ivory lace will be perfect for her. She holds the lovely dress up to her slim figure. "Well, what do you think?"

Sally gasps. "I think that will be stunning on you," she says. "Look in the chest—does it have a veil, too?"

Emily reaches into the chest and tenderly pulls out a bag with tissue paper. "If I remember correctly, this is it," she says. "It's not exactly a veil, more of a beaded headdress."

She places the headpiece on her strawberry blond head. "Well, what do you think? Is it too weird?"

Sarah adjusts the headpiece on his sister's head. "No, I think it is really unique—and so *you*. It will be just perfect for a beach wedding," she says. "It looks like you—festive and not too girly. It's right up your alley."

I can't keep the excitement out of my voice when I urge Emily to try on the gown. "I can't wait to see what it looks like on you," I tell her. Then, after a pause, I add, "Being up here takes me back to when I was a kid. It feels just like it did when we used to come up here and play dress up. Who would have ever thought that one day we'd be up here actually wearing some of these same dresses for our own weddings?"

Emily slips the delicate gown on and stands in front of the dusty antique mirror gazing at herself. "I can't believe it actually fits. I don't even think I'll need to have it altered," she says. She twirls around to show off her new old wedding dress.

"It's perfect and a great fit," Sarah exclaims. "It's amazing. Let's just try on the headpiece with it." Then she has a revelation. "We need to find you something blue, or I can let you borrow my blue sapphire bracelet. Then you'll have something blue, and something borrowed all in one."

The attic light catches the tears in Emily's bright green eyes. "You'd do that? You'd let me wear your special bracelet? It's your favorite," she says. "Are you sure?"

Sarah laughs at her sister. "Are you kidding me? I know where you live."

We all bust out laughing. Then we hear the steps creaking—and in walk Emily's mom and my mom. The two women take a look at Emily, break out in cheers, and hug her. "Oh honey, it's wonderful," Emily's mother says. "You look so pretty, and that style is outstanding on you."

"I agree," my mom declares. "Oh, darling, you look beautiful. You're going to make us all cry, especially George. I can't wait to see the expression on his face when he sees you walking down the aisle in that dress."

Emily suddenly blurts out to the mothers: "What do you think about March for a wedding?"

Emily's mom squeals. "Oh—yes! That sounds great, but how and where? And what's the hurry? You're not pregnant, are you?"

We all crack up. Emily fakes indignation when she answers, "No Mom, I'm not pregnant." Then she adds, "George and I were talking, and we decided 'why wait?' So, we figured we'd get married at spring break so that it's easy for Robert and Sally to be with us, too. And Isabella and David are getting married in July in Jamaica. We were talking and we don't want to wait too long. Angie and Thomas are getting married in June, so we figured we'd get married in March."

"You know your father and I will support whatever you and George want to do," Sally White says, with love in her voice. "But where are you thinking of getting married? Here?"

"No, we're considering a destination wedding like Sarah and Matt, but not sure where yet. Maybe Cat Island— you know, so we can look for a little buried treasure while we're at it."

Her mother laughs, but we can tell she's not sure if the "treasure" part is a joke or for real. The last time we combined a wedding and a treasure hunt, there were some close calls.

"I think that is an excellent idea," Sally White finally says, "but are we going to be able to plan it quickly enough for spring break?"

Sarah perks up. "Earlier we looked up a Jamaican wedding website that said that they could perform a marriage as quickly as a week," she tells her mother. "So, three months won't be a problem. The girls and I are going to help, too. It should be easy."

My sister looks at her watch. "I need to feed the twins, so I'm going to have to leave," Sally says. "Congratulations, Emily. I just love the dress and all the ideas for your wedding. I guess we'll meet you guys at SmacNally's. We said 12:30, right?"

She heads for the stairs, and I follow with our mom in tow. "We're coming with you, Sally," I say. "Remember that no one is to walk by themselves. Mom and I will walk with you to your place. Robert can walk mom to her house afterward."

I look back and wave to the girls. "See you at the restaurant," I say. Then I turn to my sister. "Sally, can you and Robert stop by so I don't have to walk to the tiki bar alone? It's such a short walk to Silver Creek and SmacNally's restaurant."

Then, before we leave, Sarah turns to me. "Or we can swing by your house. Emily, mom, and I are just going to do some quilting before we can out for lunch. Maybe we can all meet at your house. Did the boys respond back yet to your text?"

I look down at my phone and give her a thumbs up. "They all emoji-ed a thumbs up."

Chapter 22

An Unexpected Meeting

I hear a loud banging at the door. It startles me out of a daydream about finding all the exciting objects in Anne and Jack's cedar chest. I jump up off my cozy, tan-colored sofa and rush to answer the door. Robert and the girls have arrived. The whole gang comes into my house.

Robert, acting silly, waving his arms like he is a girl, says, "Are you girls ready to go? I'm famished." Sally swats him on his shoulder, laughing at him for being giddy. "Come on, big boy. Let's go get you something to eat. I know where the twins get their appetite."

We all file out of the house with me at the end of the line, making sure to lock the door. "All secure. I'm hungry, too, from our nice long hike this morning. I'm looking forward to SmacNally's famous fish tacos."

It's nice outside today, maybe high 60s. There is barely a gentle breeze blowing the seagrass along our route. The oyster shell driveway crunches under our feet as we make our way down to one of my favorite places. We get there just as Matt, Thomas, and George are making their way past the golf carts.

As we walk into the restaurant, we see Chloe and John waving to us. They've claimed a table for our large group. Thomas wraps his arm around me and gives me a peck on the cheek. "Hey, Beautiful. Come here often?" I chuckle and kiss him back on his bearded cheek. "I only come here to meet my handsome fiancé."

He laughs at me and pulls out my chair when we reach our table. "For you, madame," he says. He waves at our group. "Hi, everyone. What's everyone having for lunch?

Frank comes from behind the bar and hands us all menus. "Well, well, well, to what do we owe this honor?" he grins as he welcomes us. "What can I get everyone to drink?"

Chloe and John have already ordered their drinks. John holds up his plastic cup. "These peach mimosas are wonderful. Perfect for an afternoon like today."

Sally, Emily, Sarah, and I all nod and exclaim. "Sounds like a great idea."

We are enjoying a special, joyous day when we hear loud, rapturous music bounding out of a large white boat cruising up to the pier. I point to the foolhardy couple on board. "Take a look. I think our new relatives might have arrived. They do look a little wild and crazy," I say.

The boisterous, wind-blown, blonde-haired woman hooks her arms around an auburn-haired man with a scraggly beard and dreadlocks. Both laugh at the scene they are causing. I see the woman pull out a bottle of what looks like tequila, take a swig, and hand it to her happy partner.

John rubs his hand over a shadow of a beard. "Oh no. This might not be good. I hope we don't have problems."

Thomas reminds John, "Just remember, we don't have to tell them anything," he says. Then he adds, "Do you think we should ask them to join us or just watch them for a little while?"

George points to the giddy twosome. "I don't think we are going to have much of a choice. It looks like they are heading this way." He turns to John and asks, "You Facetimed them on Christmas Day, didn't you? He is probably going to recognize you two."

John and Chloe both nod. "Well, I'm glad we already finished eating otherwise it could be interesting, if you know what I mean," John says. As the couple comes into SmacNally's, John stands and walks over toward them. "Hi, Stephen and Violet. Perfect timing—you arrived just in time to meet our group."

He leads them over to our table and introduces all of us. The guys all extend a hand to shake at the introduction. Stephen nods and grins. "Well, this is great," he says. "I was wondering how we would end up meeting." He swings a chair around, sitting on it backwards, and pulls out a chair for his girlfriend. "So, what's good here," he asks. "I'm dying for an ice-cold beer." He turns to his girlfriend. "Are you hungry, Violet?"

"I'm more thirsty than hungry," she answers. "What are you girls drinking? They look good."

I respond to her question. "These are really tasty," I say. "They're mimosas and they come in different flavors, just perfect for a sunny afternoon."

Frank makes his way over to our table to greet his new customers, handing them menus. "Welcome, what can I get for you two?"

"I'll have an IPA and my lady will have one of those girly drinks," Stephen says, pointing to our mimosas. Frank nods and asks, "Any food for you? Mahi-mahi tacos are the special today."

"Just drinks. We just ate before we got here. Thanks," Stephen answers.

An awkward silence falls on the group. Emily breaks the ice with a question for our new arrivals. "So, you guys are just getting here? Where are you coming from? That's a huge boat."

"We came from Jamaica but stopped in Charleston before we made our way up here," Violet says. "We were looking for clues as to where his great, great, great grandmother Anne Bonny might have ended up."

John raises his eyebrows, and we all take a deep breath, wondering what he's going to say.

"Really, that's interesting," John says. "I didn't know you were related to Anne Bonny."

I can feel the tension rising in our group. The hairs on the back of my neck are standing up.

169

John continues with his train of thought. "So, were you able to locate anyone who could help you?"

Stephen looks directly into John's hazel eyes. "Come on, man. You know we're related to her. I'm surprised your great-grandmother didn't call you to let you know we paid her a visit."

I hear John gasp, looking flustered. "You did what? You visited my granny?"

"Yeah, it was a very enlightening meeting," Stephen responds. "I think I made her nervous, though, because she wasn't expecting me."

John looks like he is going to throttle our new relative. "I can imagine that she would feel threatened if a stranger came to visit her out of the blue."

Stephen pulls out his phone and shows John a picture. "She let me take a picture of a sketch that she had of Anne. Amazing how much we look alike—don't you think?"

I can feel the tension grow thicker, like dense fog rising from the marsh. I ask to see the picture. He turns the phone towards me. "What do you think, Angie, my other relative? Do you think I look like Anne?"

I nod and answer him. "Well, you do look a little bit like her, especially the hair. I've seen some pictures of her in history books."

Thomas changes the subject. "So, what brings you two to Ocracoke Island?"

Stephen gets right to the point. "There are two reasons that we are here." He raises one finger then points to John and me. "First off, we wanted to meet our new relatives."

He holds up two fingers and pulls a crumpled piece of paper from the pocket of his torn and faded blue jeans. "Second, I'm searching for Calico Jack and Anne Bonny's treasure, and we thought you might be able to help us, seeing that Angie and you folks found, but lost, Blackbeard's treasure."

Matt reaches for the brittle parchment in Stephen's hands. "Can I have a look at that? I'm also related to you.

I'm Angie's brother, and this is Sally, our sister." He points to Sally.

Stephen pulls back his hand holding the paper. "Sorry, this is for our eyes only, if you know what I mean."

Matt shakes his head. "That's fair. I can understand that" he says. "I'm wondering why you came here out of the blue?"

Stephen points to Violet. "My Violet here is a computer whiz, and we have a program that notifies us if anyone does a search on Spanish gold coins. Lo and behold, John's name popped up, looking up the value of a doubloon."

He looks at John and Chloe. "Amazing, don't you think, John?"

John seems a little nervous, but his voice remains calm as he answers. "That's crazy. I didn't even know there was any such program," he says. "I did look up the value of a Spanish coin after talking to these guys about losing Blackbeard's treasure." He points to us. "They told me that there were hundreds of Spanish coins in the treasure chest they lost in the caverns on Cat Island."

Matt shrugs his shoulders. "Yeah, it was heartbreaking, really awful, when the treasure went down into the depths of the caves. Do you two do a lot of treasure hunting?"

Violet answers. "That's a really good question. You see, I'm related to Henry Morgan, another famous pirate. In fact, that's how Stephen and I met. He took me on a voyage to search for my great, great, grandfather's treasure." She sighs deeply. "Unfortunately, it was a dead end, so we are still looking. And what better place than Ocracoke Island?"

There is a universal look of surprise on the faces of Thomas and all my friends as they stare at Violet.

"Wow, that is so cool," I say to cut the tension. "I'm sure it was quite the adventure."

"Yeah, it was really cool," Violet says, "but a little disappointing. But we decided to keep looking. I can work remotely from Stephen's ship, so it's been fun. It's like being on a continuous vacation.

"So, tell us what happened to Blackbeard's treasure," she adds.

Matt answers this time. "Well, we were on Cat Island, staying at Shanna's Cove Resort for Matt and Sarah's wedding. We found the treasure, but it was booby trapped so it was swallowed into the caverns. It reminded me of one those Indiana Jones movies."

Stephen shakes his head. "That's a definite bummer. I can't imagine finding something so valuable only to lose it like that. Are you sure you can't recover it?"

Thomas raises his eyebrows and responds. "I seriously doubt anyone will ever find it. It went down into a very deep blue hole on the island."

Stephen nods his head. "That's a shame. Was there a lot of treasure in the chest?"

I nod as I answer him. "Yeah, I've never seen so many jewels and gold coins in all my life," I say. "But to get back to the subject, how did you become interested in Anne's treasure?"

Stephen holds up the parchment again. "I found this document in some of my father's belongings after he passed away last spring. I decided to try my hand at finding the treasure. And what about you guys? Any new treasure-hunting schemes?

Chapter 23

A New Parchment Is Found

We are dumbfounded that he should come right out with such a question. George is the first to recover enough to answer. "Nah, man. We got burnt last time. I don't think we'll be trying that again any time soon."

Stephen holds up his crinkled parchment paper. "Are you sure you don't want to join us in our search to find good ole Anne's treasure?"

Matt eyes the ancient-looking vellum. "Just wondering, is it a map?" he asks.

Stephen clears his voice and rubs his bloodshot eyes. "As I mentioned, my dad died this past spring. He was with me searching for the pirate booty and his dive equipment malfunctioned. It was so unexpected. My father has been diving since he was a teenager."

He pulls his braids back into a ponytail and continues his story. "We were with my Uncle Timmy and my cousins, Logan and Hunter, when it happened. Later, we found a pinhole prick in his oxygen tank," Stephen says. "It's not like my dad to neglect to check his scuba gear. He was meticulous about stuff like that, so we couldn't believe it happened.

"Crazy thing was," Stephen continues, "we had just discovered a shipwreck about 30 feet down on the ocean floor." He pulls a sparkly gold trinket from the top pocket of his olive-green Hawaiian shirt. "We had to abandon our search, so we never found any treasure other than this gold doubloon. When we went back to search later, the treasure had disappeared, covered over by the seafloor."

He tosses Matt the gold piece. "Here, take a look. I have an idea how you felt when you lost the treasure on Cat Island," Stephen continues. "I had just found this coin when my dad started gasping for breath and turned blue before my eyes. I couldn't save him. He was dead by the time we got him to the surface."

He looks sad, and we all sense his grief.

Matt examines the doubloon. "This reminds me of one of the coins we found on Cat Island," he says as he hands it to Thomas. "What do you think?" Thomas turns the gold piece over in the palm of his hand, then holds it up so the rest of us get a look. "I think you're right Matt," Thomas says. "It looks really similar to what we found before we lost the treasure."

He hands the coin to George, who's sitting between Emily and John. George holds the coin up so they can see it, too. "Yeah, I'd say it's a pretty good match to what we found, but that does really make sense. The coin dates back to when pirates roamed the shores and stole from the merchant ships, especially the Spanish," he says. "I mean, think about it. Charles Vane, after being marooned on that abandoned island, had just commandeered a Spanish schooner. They never did figure out what happened to that treasure."

Emily nudges George and raises her eyebrows. "Yeah, it's amazing how much this coin looks similar to the ones we found." Stephen, not missing a beat, jumps on her comment. "Oh, you've found more than one coin? That's fascinating."

"Only one," Emily hisses out her answer. "How many have you found?" She then tries to change the subject. "So, how long are you two going to be staying on Ocracoke Island?"

Stephen notices she's trying to switch the conversation away from the doubloons. "We're not sure how long we will be here. We plan to do more research," he says. "It is rumored that Anne and Calico Jack had a house here on the island. Do you know where their house is?"

Sally pretends that she has just received a text. "Hey girls, we need to go. Mom just texted me to say the twins are acting up. She also asked if you girls are going to help fix those sofa covers, she just made."

George takes that as a cue, and he turns to Thomas and Matt. "Are you guys coming with me to see Bob and Sue about finishing up their renovation?"

Matt looks at his phone. "Wow, I didn't realize it was getting so late. Yeah, I think we better get going, too. I'm so glad we already paid the check otherwise we'd be late. Robert, can you walk the girls back to mom's house before taking Sally home?"

"Sure, no problem," Robert says. "I told David I'd stop by to help him with some shutters he was painting on the front of the house." John and Chloe both get up. John tells Robert he also agreed to help David with the shutters while Chloe goes with the girls.

"Stephen and Violet, it's so good meeting you guys," John says. "I guess we'll see you around the island. Where are you staying?"

Stephen laughs and points to his boat. "That's the best part about having a big boat, you never have to worry about finding a place to stay. But, hey, I'd really like to catch up with you all and get to know you better while we're on the island."

Violet just smiles and waves at us as we make our departure, hurrying down the graying wood steps of the tiki bar. We turn back to wave and call out our goodbyes to the couple.

Chapter 24

Can We Trust Them?

I watch Thomas, George, and Matt all climb into George's red pick-up truck before the girls and I, and Robert and John and Chloe turn to walk down Back Road Rd, the odd street name that we all love. I wait until we are out of view before I burst out in exasperated laughter.

"Oh, my heavens, that was crazy. Sally, good idea changing the subject with the story about the text about the twins," I say. "I really didn't want to have to answer Stephen's question about which treasure we were searching for next. I feel like he can see right through us."

Robert grins at me. "I think you're right, but what do you think about them having that computer program that picks up on searches for gold coins? That's just mind blowing if you ask me. I think we are going to have to be very careful around those two."

John runs one hands through his wavy auburn hair. His other arm is around Chloe. "I don't know about y'all but I'm getting bad vibes from them, like we shouldn't trust them."

"I know what you mean," Emily says. "They both seem a little shifty. Hey, Angie, maybe, Evangeline *was* trying to send you a warning, or an omen, like you said earlier today."

I agree. "I'm feeling it too, but I'm not sure how we're going to avoid them while they're here. Did you get that bit about them researching the area because they heard Anne Bonny had stayed here on the island? I mean, really. His great, great grandfather—Austin Bell—was the child that Anne left on Cuba with that nefarious pirate. How could they know where Anne went? We need to conjure her up again to ask about him."

John nods his head. "What really scares me is that his father ended up dead in a diving accident with all that experience. That has me worried. Do you think someone killed him? I mean, we don't really know anything about these two."

Sally responds while texting Georgia to let her know she's on her way back home. "I don't think Stephen was responsible," Sally says. "He seemed legitimately saddened by his father's death. But who knows about that uncle or his cousins."

I pull out my phone while we're walking and Google their names. "Here's a blurb about Timothy Bell in their local paper," I say as I read the headline. "'Local diver's brother killed under suspicious circumstances. Authorities investigating the incident.'"

Sarah reaches to take the phone from me so she can see the article. She continues reading, "'Stephen Bell, Sr. died after a treasure-hunting dive off the coast of the Bahamas. A faulty air tank was found to be cause of the deadly accident.' Hmm, that does sound a little fishy to me."

We all agree. Sally and Robert stop in front of mom's home and say goodbye to us. We've agreed that we need to do more investigating ourselves before we can trust Stephen and Violet with any of our secrets about Anne Bonny.

Sarah, Emily, Chloe, and I knock before entering my mom and David's home. I holler out a greeting. "Mom, we're here. Where are you?" She shouts back from the other room. "I'm in here, in the den."

We find my mom up to her neck in a pretty tan and blue sofa cover. I laugh when I see her because her hair is in disarray, coming out of her barrettes. "Mom, why didn't you wait for us?" I ask.

"You girls know I like to try to get things done by myself. I just can't help myself," Isabella says. "But now that you're here, can you give me a hand? This thing is a beast," she says as she hands one end of the couch covering to me as she continues speaking. "So how was your lunch, girls? Did you have anything good to eat?"

I lick my lips. "I had their wonderful, mahi-mahi fish tacos. They were yummy," I say. "I had a chilled peach mimosa, too."

"Same for me," Sarah says, "but the lunch was the least of it. You should have been there. We got to meet your new relatives—and, boy, are they something!"

My mom raises her eyebrows. "What? They're here already? I thought they weren't coming until New Year's Eve."

David walks into the room just as Mom is asking us about Stephen. "Well, what did you think about him?"

I wave my hands in the air and point towards the docks, down the road. "We were having lunch, and we hear this loud music coming from a huge white boat maneuvering its way up to the docks." I touch my windblown head and continue. "He's wild looking with crazy dreadlocks. He looks like a pirate, if you ask me. What did you girls think?"

Emily picks up the conversation. "Yeah, they were both a little shady if you ask me. I mean Violet isn't much better with her bright green bandanna and her skimpy halter top. And get this, she's related to Henry Morgan, the pirate. It was crazy and they were drinking right out of a tequila bottle before they got off the boat. Quite the partyers—and trouble if you ask me."

I continue detailing our unexpected meeting. "It took us all by surprise. We weren't expecting them at all," I say. "There was no way we could avoid them because they came right onto the deck of SmacNally's pub."

Now it's Chloe's turn to add to the story. "Yeah, and John and I had Facetimed him, so they knew what we looked like," she explains. "We couldn't pretend that we didn't know who he was."

Emily picks up from there. "Get this, he even knew that John had looked up the value of the Spanish gold coin that we gave him!" she tells my mother and David. "Luckily, John made up a story about how we had been talking about the treasure we lost, and John was just curious about how much a doubloon was worth since we lost so many of them.

"It was a good recovery," she adds, "but it didn't matter because Stephen came right out and asked us what treasure we were looking for next. I could feel each of us gasp at that question. You should have been there." David looks astonished. "How did he know that John looked up the value of the coin? That's weird."

"Apparently, there is a computer program. When someone does a Google search, it'll notify you," Chloe explains. "Violet is a computer whiz and set it up for him. Stephen's really into treasure hunting and that's how he met Violet. She was looking for Henry Morgan's treasure. Morgan was her great, great grandfather. Kind of like how John and Stephen are Anne's great, great ... or great—we lost track—grandchildren."

I stop helping with the sofa cover for a second. "I'm afraid we are going to have to be on our toes when we are around those two," I declare.

The sofa cover is finally in place, mom asks us to come into the kitchen. "So glad that's done. Girls, help yourselves to some coffee. I put some on before you all got here," she says. She then asks us to help with tonight's dinner preparations and the hors d'oeuvres for our New Year's Eve celebration tomorrow.

"I figured we could make cream puffs and stuff them with tuna salad, shrimp, and chicken salad plus make some for dessert, too. What do you think?"

I nod. "Do you girls have time to help mom make the cream puffs?" I ask. "Emily, you make a killer chicken salad, maybe you can make that for tomorrow's New Year's Eve Party."

Emily heads over to the sink to wash her hands. We follow her lead. "That sounds good to me," she says. "And Sarah makes a great shrimp salad." She looks over at Chloe and asks, "Do you want to make some tuna salad? Angie, your egg salad is to die for."

Then Emily adds, "I still can't believe tomorrow is New Year's Eve."

Chloe answers right away. "I can definitely help with the tuna salad. Thanks for including me in your party planning," she says. "You guys are already making me feel like part of the family. John told me the same thing earlier today. As a matter of fact, we like the island so much that we were thinking about looking into buying a vacation home here with our family."

Emily whoops and gives her a high five. "Really, that's so cool. We'd love to have you all visit more in the future."

Chloe blushes. "That's so sweet," she says. "You girls make me feel so welcome. So, let's get these salads made for tomorrow's party. How does it work, the party? Do people all bring things or do you cater it?"

Sarah responds to her question. "We normally have a buffet for anyone who is interested. It gets pretty crazy at the pub but it's a lot of fun."

We are almost done fixing all the appetizers for tomorrow's party when I get a text from Sally. I read it out loud to everyone. "'Hi Sis, I was wondering what everyone was doing tonight. I'm trying to see if everyone wants to hang out?'"

"Tell her to come on over and bring the twins," my mom says. "Maybe we can order some pizza, plus I bought lots of vegetables for a huge salad." Then she adds, "I don't know about the rest of you, but I feel like we need to go see Anne and let her know about her descendant Stephen. What do you think?"

I pull my hair higher up in my ponytail. "I think that's a good idea, Mom. I'll let Sally know what you said. And I'll text the guys to see when they are going to be done with their job today."

Emily pulls out her phone. "I'll let George know. He mentioned something to me this morning about how he thinks we need to do more research on Anne and see if we can find any information on Stephen and Violet."

Chloe perks up. "I was wondering what John, and I were going to do tonight. Thanks for including us."

Mom steps over and hugs her. "Oh, Chloe, you are so welcome. Please know that you two can come visit us at any time. You guys are already part of the family. I can't wait to meet the rest of your families."

Chloe laughs. "That's so funny that you said that because our families can't wait to meet all of you."

Thomas texts me back right away. I read aloud what he wrote. "Matt and I will be over shortly. We both need to shower first. We were working outside on Bob and Sue's deck and are pretty scrubby." Emily informs us that George should be here within the hour. He has to run a call over on Hatteras Island first.

Mom points to the den. "Girls let's go have a seat around the Christmas tree, near the fireplace. I had David light a fire since they say the temperature is going to drop into the 40s tonight," she says. "Besides, I just love looking at our Christmas tree. Oh, Angie, just so you know, I already asked your grandparents and Jim and Sally White to come over, too."

I put my arm around mom. "Sounds good, Mom. I enjoy looking at your tree, too. Your den is always so festive on the holidays," I say. "Who would have ever guessed that we would be spending Christmas here, much less living here. It's still like a dream that I have always had, to be here permanently."

She pushes a stray hair out of my bright blue eyes. "I know honey, it's like a dream come true for me too. Last year was so sad and I felt like I was in a bubble after losing your dad so unexpectedly. This year is about new beginnings, and I couldn't be happier.

I wipe a lone tear that has slid down my cheek when I think about my dad not being here. "I know Dad wouldn't want either one of us to be sad, and he is so happy you are getting on with your life. You should have seen him at Sarah and Matt's reception. He was there—and he blew you a kiss when you and David did your dance. I didn't tell you then, but I thought that you might want to know."

Mom places her hand over her heart and sighs. "It makes me feel so much better that he wants me to be happy," she says. "Your father was a wonderful caring man, and I will always miss him. But David has filled that hole that was in my heart." Her voice trails off for a minute, then she perks up again. "But enough of that," she says. "Does anyone feel like singing karaoke?"

Sarah squeals. "I do, I do!" she calls out. "I just love when we sing Christmas carols." Emily laughs and rolls her eyes. "Sis, you are so silly. It reminds me of when we were kids and how excited you would get when we went Christmas caroling with the neighbors."

Mom pulls out the karaoke machine, and we are still singing and laughing when the guys arrive an hour later. Mom has already ordered a variety of pizzas to be delivered later for dinner. It doesn't take long before we are deep in discussion about our new relative, Stephen. We all feel the same way: that we shouldn't trust him. We decide to head downstairs to the basement storm cellar to see if we can conjure up Anne's ghost to ask her thoughts on whether we should include Stephen in on our plans to search for Anne and Jack's treasure.

Chapter 25

A Scary Surprise

We pull the chest out of the secret room and have all its contents scattered across the two white vinyl tables in the storm cellar. Anne's spirit has just materialized when we hear a loud banging on the basement's back door. We all freeze.

We are shocked when we look up and see Stephen and Violet staring through the window of the backyard door into the basement. They both have looks of amazement on their faces. Stephen yells through the door, "I can see you. We tried the front door, but no one answered. Let us in!"

There is no way to hide Anne or any of the items sitting out on the tables. David shakes his head in regret. "It's too late now," he tells us. "We might as well let him in, but let's try not to let him know about everything."

Thomas moves over to the door and lets the two uninvited guests into the storm cellar. "Well, we weren't expecting you two," he says.

Stephen and Violet stare open-mouthed at the vision of Anne's ghost. Anne, being her usual crazy self, goes over to Stephen. "Well, if you aren't the spitting image of my dear olde Jacky boy. You must be related to me, because you look just like him and have my wild hair—except what have you done to it with all those crazy plaits?"

Stephen is gawking. "What is this?" he demands. "Is this some type of trick?" He tries to touch Anne, but his hand goes through her arm. "Oh my God, is she a ghost? What kind of craziness is this?" he says, shocked.

Anne hoots and laughs at him. "Oh, close your mouth, young man, or you'll get flies in it. Yes, I'm a ghost, and you must be related to my first son. I was such a fool back then when I left my wee babe with that evil pirate Bell. I don't know what we were thinking. We planned to come back for the child but, by the time I was able to, your great, great, great grandfather wanted nothing to do with me. It was one of my biggest regrets."

She turns to me and asks. "Well, Angie, where did he come from?"

John answers her. "Same place that I came from. We both did one of those DNA tests and it led us to Angie and her family."

Anne circles around Stephen. "Well, he's here now and he is one of mine, so I guess he'll have to join your search to find my treasure."

We all gasp and look at Stephen and Violet. Paul steps forward and speaks to them. "Okay, so now you know how we have an advantage in finding the treasure. Anne was just getting ready to give us another clue when you got here." He turns to Anne and asks, "So, what other clues do you have for us?"

Anne responds. "Not so fast, mateys. You'll have to use your brains to go where you'll find the next clue," she says. "All I can say is that I wore it aboard my journey back to the colonies."

Emily hollers out and picks up the cryptic message we found sewn into the antique dress. "Here it is. I bet this is it," she says.

Anne chortles and begins to vanish but, as she does, she exclaims, "Huh! You are just too smart, girly."

Stephen reaches out to take the message from Emily's hand. "Whoa, buddy," Emily says, stepping away from him. "You share yours and we'll share ours."

Stephen guffaws. "Fair enough. We'll share with you," he says. He reaches into his jeans pocket and pulls out the paper, handing it to Emily. With George by her side, we all gather around Emily and paper she is now holding.

"It's a map," Emily says. She turns to Stephen, "Do you know where it's from?"

"We think it is of one of the islands of the Bahamas," Stephen answers, "but we're not sure which one."

George grins as he slips the map out of Emily's hand and holds it up. "Well, it looks like we might be heading back to Cat Island. We'll have to give Gregor and Maria a call and book another vacation at Shanna's Cove Resort."

Emily wraps her arms around George. "Maybe we can do our wedding there, like Sarah and Matt did. I mean we already know the routine there," she says, adding, "It would be perfect."

Stephen looks puzzled. "Not sure what you're talking about, but I think we're going treasure-hunting not wedding-hunting," he says.

Emily grins as she explains for Violet and Stephen. "We were planning to go to Jamaica to get married, but this clue looks like it is leading us to Cat Island. So why shouldn't we get married there, while we're hunting for treasure?"

Stephen scrunches up his nose. "Well, whatever floats your boat," he says. "What's our next step—and what is all this stuff?" He points to the objects laid out on the tables.

"These are things we found in a hidden room. They once belonged to Anne and Calico Jack," Paul explains. "Anne Bonny told us that they hid out in the secret room when British officers were looking for them."

Stephen picks up the telescope and peers through the viewfinder. "Looks like a telescope to me." Paul shrugs his shoulders. "Yeah, we know. It was in that chest over there," my grandfather says.

Thomas takes the telescope back from Stephen. "Yeah, the whole chest was full of antiquated pirate clothes and these other things." He puts the telescope back on the table. We all notice that Thomas provides no details about the 'scope's magical properties, and we nod at him.

Violet looks at the dress that held the secret-coded letter and asks, "Did you find any other clues yet?"

I pick up Calico Jack's journal and show it to her. "We found this journal in the bottom of one of the oak barrels that the two were using for a nightstand." Sarah joins in on the conversation. "We haven't had a chance to go through the book with it being the holidays and all. We were thinking that we would take a closer look at it after Christmas."

Stephen takes the journal from me and hands it to Violet. "We can give you a hand with it. Violet is a whiz at things like that," he says. "You should see her work a computer program. She might even be able to put the information in the journal through one of her deciphering programs."

Thomas speaks up. "That would be helpful, but we have pretty much decided that everything stays here in the secret room, away from prying eyes. Which is a reminder—I guess we need to put a shade or blackout curtain over the basement door windows so that no one else can see inside. We don't mean to be secretive with you, but when we were looking for Blackbeard's treasure, we drew the interest of a couple of nasty hoodlums." He points to me. "Two of them even kidnapped Angie. It was scary as hell."

Stephen nods. "Hey man, we're all related. You can trust us," he says.

The hairs on the back of my neck and down my arms are standing on end as I listen to him. I think to myself that there is no way that I can trust him. It's just a feeling, and I wonder if this is the premonition Evangeline was trying to tell me about in my dream the other night.

"Okay, we'll have to wait and see if we can trust you," David says. "As it is, you might be related to them, but we just met you, so you can understand why we don't confide in you yet."

Stephen nods in agreement. "Understood. I guess it goes both ways," he says. "We all want what we think belongs to us." He pauses for a second then continues. "What are your plans for looking over the items in the chest? Can we give you a hand? We don't have any plans for the evening."

Mom steps forward and announces to the two unwelcome guests: "We ordered pizza, and you are both welcome to stay and join us. It should be here in a few minutes. We were just planning to go back up to the den. Let's take you upstairs to get you two a drink while David, Thomas, Angie, and George tidy up down here a bit."

Chapter 26

A Quiet Evening

Paul guides the two uninvited guests up the rickety basement steps in mom and David's home and opens the basement door into the main floor. He invites Stephen and Violet to join everyone in the den. "What can I get the two of you for drinks? We have sparkling waters, sodas, tea, and some beers?"

Violet answers my grandfather. "You know, a sparkling water sounds refreshing. Thank you, I'll have one of those." Stephen adds, "I'll have a beer. Any kind will do."

My grandmother, Mary, points in the direction of the family room. "You two can follow me. We usually sit in the den, especially at this time of year. It has a toasty fireplace."

Violet smiles. "Oh, that sounds heavenly," she said. "I have been cold ever since we got here yesterday. I didn't bring enough warm clothes with me. I told Stephen that we were going to have to go shopping tomorrow. Any stores you'd recommend here on the island?"

Mary tells her that a lot of the shops are closed this time of year. "But you should try going to up to the outlet mall in Nags Head," my grandmother adds.

Violet then asks her about transportation. "Do they have any taxis or Ubers on the island? We don't have our car with us since we came by boat."

My grandmother is tickled by the question. "Oh, honey, it would cost you a fortune. Maybe one of the girls can give you a ride up that way. Sometimes they head up there to go to the mall. Here they are now."

As we come in from the kitchen with drinks and snacks, my grandmother asks, "Are you girls going to Hatteras Island? Violet says she could use some warmer clothes and would like to go shopping."

Sarah smiles at everyone. "Well sure, anytime," she says. "I really love going up to the outlets." Then Sarah turns and asks the rest of us, "Maybe we can go tomorrow. What are you girls' plans for tomorrow?"

"Count me in," Chloe answers with a grin. "I haven't been shopping for a while and have never been to the outlets. Maybe I'll even get a new dress."

Mom, grandmom, and Sally White all decline our offer to go to Hatteras Island. They all say they have things to do around their homes.

Sally looks at her watch, remembering that she and Robert need to go help Georgia bring the twins over to mom's house.

"I can use a new pair of dancing shoes if you go to the outlets, but I don't think I can make it unless we go early," Sally says. She turns toward Robert, who has just come in the room with the rest of the guys. "Robert, can you drive me over to pick up the twins?"

Robert nods as he's looking at his phone. "Wow, I didn't realize it was getting to be this late. Let's go so we can get back before the pizza gets here," he says as the two of them head out the door to gather up their children.

Emily looks my way. "We have to work tomorrow night at 4 p.m. What do you think, Angie? Do you feel like shopping?" I laugh at her question. "Are you kidding me? I love to shop. I'm game."

Stephen tells us the shopping trip fits perfectly with his plans. "I want to do some work on the boat tomorrow. And then I want to explore the island." He asks my grandfather, "So, Paul, where would you search if you were me?"

"I think Springer's Point would be a good place to start," Paul says. "I have some of my research books over at my house. I can drop them off at your boat tomorrow if that's okay with you." Stephen reaches out to shake my grandfather's hand. "That would be great. And if any of you guys want to come see my boat, feel free," he says, before adding, "We can even go fishing if anyone is interested."

Sarah playfully punches Emily on her shoulder. "Hey, Sis, maybe we can stop at the bridal shop to check out bridesmaids' dresses for Angie and Sally. Plus, you might want to look at some of the bridal stuff. Your wedding is only a couple months away."

Sarah shakes her head as she notes, "Just think, tomorrow is New Year's Eve."

George wraps his arm around Emily and kisses her hot pink cheeks, raising an even deeper blush on her face. "Guys, stop, you're embarrassing me. Ugh, you know how much I hate to be the center of attention," Emily protests. "I'm glad we're doing a destination wedding so that way it will just be family."

We all laugh and tease her even more by telling her that she will definitely be the blushing bride. George just grins and rubs her shoulders, being his ever-loving self.

I notice that Violet looks sad as she gazes at mom's Christmas tree. "Does your family get a tree in Florida?" I ask her.

I see her swipe at a lone tear that slips down her cheek. She sniffles as she explains. "I lost both of my parents last year in a boating accident," she says quietly. "Stephen and I were on his boat searching for Henry Morgan's treasure—and getting really close to finding it—when my parents' yacht exploded. The fire department concluded that it was a random accident.

"My dad was a heavy smoker and he was sitting on the stern of his ship when it went up in flames," she continues. "This is my first Christmas without them. I don't have any siblings."

I squeeze her shoulder and point to my brother, Matt. "We lost our father suddenly last year. I know how hard it is, especially around the holidays."

Violet shrugs in resignation. "So, then you all know exactly how I'm feeling," she says. "Stephen just lost his father this past summer, so it is going to be hard for both of us. That is another reason we decided to take the trip to Ocracoke Island. It's kind of an escape for us."

Sarah smiles sadly. "We'll bring you with us tomorrow night. Hopefully that will keep your mind off of everything. We're a pretty fun group of people and I think you'll like all the locals who come to the pub tomorrow night for New Year's Eve."

Violet nods her head. "Thanks girls. That means a lot to me. You guys are so nice," she says, shyly, as she runs her fingers through her blonde hair.

We hear David and Thomas, with Max, shutting the basement door right at the same moment that there's excited barking at the front door. In rushes Sally and Robert's chocolate brown Lab puppy, Biscuit, who is yipping as his little paws slide across the vinyl flooring. The twin's eyes are wide open as Sally and Robert sit the two babies down on their blanket on the floor and begin to remove their heavy snowsuits.

Sally fusses and tells the puppy to settle down, as she hangs on to his collar with one hand and unzips the twins' heavy clothing with the other. "Biscuit, down boy! Come here," she says. "Settle down, fellow. You're going to knock things over."

Thomas scoops up the wiggly puppy, who begins to excitedly lick Thomas on his nose. "I've got Biscuit. I need to let Max out so I can let the puppy out, too." Thomas carries the pup as he leads Max and my mother's dogs, Ace and Skippy, to the back door.

"Come on, boys!" he calls as he opens the patio door and steps outside. The animals all go rushing out, running wild in the fenced-in backyard.

Stephen follows Thomas out the back entryway. "On that note, I think I'll go have a smoke," he says.

Thomas starts to speak as Stephen trails him into the yard. "Maybe I'll take you up on the offer for a fishing trip. It might be fun," Thomas says. "I can show you a few cool places to fish and where Springer's Point is located by boat."

Stephen takes a long drag off his cigarette, blowing smoke through his nose. "Sounds cool to me, man," he says. "So how do you like living here on the island? I read on your Facebook page that you studied architecture in Washington, D.C."

Thomas smiles as he answers. "For as long as I can remember, it's been my dream to renovate all the old homes on the island. I hated the city. I grew up here on Ocracoke Island, and I think you either love it or hate it here. It's very remote. But I love it."

Stephen looks at the dogs, who have chased one another into a back area of the yard. "Well, the dogs seem to like it, but it looks like yours is digging a hole over there behind those bushes."

Thomas freezes when he sees that Max is burrowing out a spot where the tunnel to the cave is hidden. "Crazy dog! Come!" he calls out, before whistling for the dog.

Max comes racing toward him with a piece of the board that was covering the tunnel. Stephen reaches down to grab the weathered board. "Looks like he's dug up an old piece of timber," he says. "I wonder where that came from."

Thomas changes the subject as he takes Max by the collar, wipes the dirt of his feet with a well-used beach towel, and guides him to the patio door. "Enough of that, Max. Go inside," Thomas orders. "Come on Ace, Skippy, and Biscuit. Let's go inside before you tear up the yard."

Stephen crunches his cigarette butt into the heavy, tancolored ashtray near the steps of the wooden deck of the patio. "Don't you want to check to see what he's dug up?" Thomas shakes his head and walks into the house. "I know what it is," he says. "There's an old flowerbed over there and that's his favorite place to dig."

George is just inside the door when Thomas steps in, and he sees the exasperated expression on his brother's face. "What's up, man? Did Max dig up something?"

Thomas answers him with a firmness in his voice. "He was digging up his usual favorite spot behind the bushes," he says. "I'm going to have to go out later and fix it." Thomas then turns to David and Isabella. "Sorry, guys, you know how he likes to burrow holes like he's going to China."

David raises his eyebrows then nods in understanding. "That crazy dog," he says. "You say he was digging over by the bushes? Don't worry about it. I can go out in the morning and fix it.

"Pizza is here if you guys are hungry," he adds.

The incident is forgotten, and the group spends a quiet evening with Stephen and Violet settling into our family life. I still have my reservations about the two of them, but I am warming up to Violet. She seems very sweet. I think to myself that first impressions are not always correct.

The evening ends with the guys making plans to go fishing with Stephen in the morning while the girls meet up to go shopping at the outlets.

Chapter 27

More Ominous Warnings

That night I dream about pirates chasing me on Cat Island. It seems so real that I cry out in my sleep. Thomas gently shakes me out of my nightmare, and I wake up trembling. I tell him as much of the dream as I can remember.

"Oh, Thomas, it was so scary. I dreamed that I was running away from this wretched-looking character with scraggly oily brown hair and a long revolting beard. He kept yelling at me that I was as good as dead, that I might as well stop because he was going to catch me. I woke up just as his vile filthy hands were wrapped around my waist." I take a deep breath trying to calm myself.

Thomas sits up in bed and takes me in his muscular arms, rubbing my shoulders and lovingly kissing me on my forehead. "It's okay, Angie. I'm here for you and no one will ever hurt you again."

I melt into his embrace and feel his strong body next to mine. I rub my warm body up against him, feeling his male hardness awakening against my thigh. He massages my shoulders, running his fingers gently over my skin, down my arms, and across my stimulated nipples. I kiss him, and our passion takes over. The world and my fears disappear as I fall into ecstasy and his body melds into mine.

We collapse onto each other as our rapture subsides, leaving me with a glorious feeling of bliss. He laughs and whispers in my ear. "Not that I want you to have nightmares, but I'll quell your fears anytime."

Rolling over to face him, I give him a gentle peck on his nose. "Anytime, my gallant knight in shining armor or, should I say, shining birthday suit?" I look out the window and notice that it is already light outside. A thick fog is rising over the morning dew.

"Looks ominous outside," I observe. "I wonder if it's going to be like this all day?"

Thomas rises from the bed, stretching his brawny arms above his bedraggled head. "It'll probably burn off once the sun comes up further. But you're right, it *is* a little foreboding," he says. "What time are you supposed to meet up with the girls?"

I climb out of our comfy, warm bed and check the time on my rose gold Apple watch. "I have time. We aren't supposed to meet up until 10 a.m. It's only 7:30," I tell him. "John is supposed to drop Chloe off at the inn with Sarah and Emily. Robert said he's going to drop Sally off, and then we'll stop by the docks to get Violet. What about you guys? What are your plans?"

Thomas pulls himself out of bed and runs his hands over his beard. "When I spoke to the other guys, Matt, and George both felt like we should get a better feel for Stephen—you know, to see if we can trust him. We're supposed to meet at his boat at 10," Thomas says. "I'm just not sure. There's something about him that gives me the heebie-jeebies, but then another part of me wants to trust him."

I agree with him. "It is pretty creepy how they just showed up and inserted themselves into our lives," I say. "It's funny. I didn't get that feeling with John and Chloe and they pretty much did the same thing. I really like having them around, and Violet seems nice, too, now that I'm getting to know her a little better. Did John and Chloe tell you they might buy a home on the island?"

Thomas nods at me. "I trust John and Chloe, too. They are just so likeable. And to be honest, John kind of reminds me of George."

Thomas pauses for a minute then continues. "Not to change the subject, but do you want some breakfast? I can get a quick shower and make us something to eat while you are getting ready to go."

I smile at him then reach up on my tippy toes to kiss his warm lips. "Yum, that sounds good to me. You spoil me."

He grabs his clothes and walks over to the bathroom. He gets into the shower and is out again before I can even figure out what I am going to wear today. He teases me as I pull a long-sleeved purple tie-dyed T-shirt and my favorite faded blue jeans out of the drawers of my pretty oak dresser. "Are you still trying to figure out what you want to wear," Thomas says, "because you look great in anything."

I chuckle as I hold up my clothes. "Stop. You know how I am. I always have trouble trying to decide what to wear. I'll be quick. See you in a flash."

We finish the yummy waffles he's made with peanut butter and bacon slathered on top, helped by a generous helping of maple syrup. "I never would have thought of such a crazy combination of flavors, but it works," I joke with him. "Must be that sweet and salty mix, kind of like Cracker Jacks."

I take our plates into the kitchen, and rinse and put them into the dishwasher. "Are you ready to go? It's almost 9:45," I call over to him.

Thomas reaches up toward a peg on the wall to grab his thermal sweatshirt jacket that is flannel lined. "I'm ready whenever you are," he answers. "Stephen said he had plenty of fishing gear, so we didn't need to bring anything with us."

I pull on my heavy blue winter coat. "It still looks foggy out. I hope it goes away before we get on the ferry. It always feels so gloomy when its foggy," I respond.

"Come on, Max," I call out. Max jumps up and barks as I put his leash on him. We head out the door, locking it behind us. "I feel like it's last summer again when we had to be so careful. It's just an eerie feeling I keep getting."

Thomas squeezes my shoulders. "Try to stop worrying," he tells me. "The important thing is that we stick together, that way we are all safer."

I nod my head in agreement. "I know, it's just me being me."

We make our way across the oyster shell driveway and up the steps to the inn. We go through the entryway then look up to see Evangeline and Old Emily watching us from the stairwell. They both wave. When we wave back at them, they vanish.

Sarah, Emily, and Sally hear us and come into the foyer just as the spirits of Old Emily and Evangeline fade. Emily points to where the ghosts were standing. "Wow, I haven't seen that in a while," she says. "Do you think they are watching us and trying to protect us again like they did before?"

I sigh and shrug my shoulders. "I had another bad dream last night," I say. "In the dream, I was being chased by this nasty-looking guy with greasy hair. Just as he was grabbing me around my waist, I screamed, and Thomas woke me up. It was so scary. Another premonition, I'm guessing."

Sally hugs me. "Don't worry Angie. We are all going to stick close together. No wandering off, do you hear me, Sis?"

Emily pulls the keys to her parents' van off the pin by the front door. "We'll just have to all be careful," she agrees. "But, in the meantime, let's go have some fun shopping.
I'll drive.

"We can go pick up Violet and Chloe," she adds. "Thomas, do you want to catch a ride with us? We're heading to Stephen's boat. John is supposed to drop Chloe off at the boat."

Thomas nods in agreement. "That sounds good to me. The fewer cars we leave at the dock, the better," he says. "I'm thinking the island is going to start getting a lot busier by later today with it being New Year's Eve."

The girls put on their heavy coats and head out the ornate white door. "Why don't you sit up front then Violet can take your spot when you get out at the marina," Emily says to Thomas.

Thomas opens the door to the silver-colored van. "Sounds like a good plan to me," he responds. "So, where are you girls going to go shopping?"

Emily answers him. "I'm thinking we might stop at Fishermen's Daughter first, then head up to the outlet mall."

Sally perks up. "I really need to get a new pair of shoes. Seems like my feet have grown since I had the twins," she says. "Go figure—another of the things that change after you have children."

We all laugh. Sarah, grinning, chimes in, "I can't wait to find out. I really want us to have children sooner than later. I know it's soon but we both decided we want kids now."

Sally chuckles. "Don't stress about it and it will transpire," she says.

We drive down Back Road Road until we reach the marina, and then we pull up to the parking lot of the visitor's center. Emily slips her parents' van into a parking space.

"Now remember, girls," she says, "we have to be careful not to leak too many details of what we have found. We need to wait until we feel like we can trust these two characters."

"I totally agree with you, Emily. They know about us being able to conjure up Anne, but not how we do it. We should keep it that way— we don't want to give them too much power," I say. "And we also don't need to explain or tell them anything that we have learned about the watch, telescope, or the compass that we found. Do you guys agree?"

Everyone nods at once. "Definitely. We need to keep those things a secret from them," Sally says, speaking for all of us.

Emily finishes her train of thought. "That's good. So, no more treasure-hunting talk today. Let's just talk about clothes and shopping."

We follow the graying docks down to Stephen's boat. Paul is already there, and as we get closer to the boat, we see my granddad handing Stephen a few of his research books.

"Now, young man," we hear Paul say as we walk closer, "I will need these back before you leave the island. I do lectures sometimes at the Ocracoke Historical Museum and use them when I am doing my speeches. As a matter of fact, I am scheduled to do one later this week. You and Violet should come have a listen if you are interested."

Stephen, granddad, Violet, John, and Chloe spot us coming down the pier and wave hello. Stephen bellows out a greeting. "Ahoy, mateys. Welcome to my humble ship."

As we climb aboard, I am amazed at the size of the boat. "Wow, this is pretty big," I say to Stephen. "I can't believe all this room. How many people can you carry?"

Stephen looks proud as he casts an eye around his boat. "It can hold up to 14 comfortably," he says. "It has two private bedrooms below deck, plus a head with a shower."

Thomas rubs his hand along the smooth side of the boat. "What do you think, Angie? Would you like to get one of these for our own?"

I smile broadly. "Absolutely! That would be awesome. Maybe this summer after we get married, we can look into buying one of these," I say. "This one is a beauty."

Stephen looks pleased. "I bought this a little over a year ago, about 18 months or so ago. Our first voyage was when we were searching for Anne and Calico Jack's treasure after I found a cryptic clue in the attic of one of my ancestors' homes," he says. He gazes out at Silver Lake, thinking. "Unfortunately, that was the day I lost my father," he continues. "We never were able to find the treasure. It was just like it vanished from the ocean floor. It was so weird the way it just disappeared."

He points to the high-tech navigation device at the helm. "I had the coordinates pinned in my GPS. My Uncle Timmy and my cousins, Logan and Hunter, were with us when we were getting close to finding the treasure." He stares down at his feet, a dismal look on his face.

"I had just found a gold coin when my dad started gasping for air," he says, drawing in his breath. "I told you the rest of the story the other day. I don't really like to talk about it."

Violet is standing beside him, and she rubs his shoulders. "It's okay, honey," she says. "You don't have to relive it all over again. You already told them what happened. Why not take the guys out on the water?"

Stephen seems to be calming down. "That sounds good," he says. "Guys, you ready to go for a sail? Then maybe some fishing?"

Emily points to her parent's van. "Let's go girls. We have some shopping to do and it's already 10:30," she says. "Angie and I must be back by 3 p.m. to get ready for work. It's a good thing we're closed tomorrow. Today is going to be a long day."

The girls wave goodbye to the guys and walk down the fading gray pier towards the parking lot.

"Violet, why don't you sit up front? That way I can show you the sights while we are driving," Emily says as we come up to the family van. "Chloe and John have already been sightseeing, so Chloe knows the area."

Violet nods, opens the door to the vehicle, and climbs into the front seat. "Thanks, Emily. It will be nice to see what's what on the island. When you come in by water, it's hard to spot all the landmarks."

We pass by the pony pens, and Emily explains their history. "You see those ponies over there? One idea is that the first ponies arrived on

Spanish galleons that collided with the shoals along the shoreline way back in the sixteenth century. This island has a lot of history if you like that kind of thing."

Violet cranes her neck to see the horse pen. "As a matter of fact, I have a minor in history, so I am very interested. This is so cool," she says. "I heard there have been a lot of shipwrecks along the Outer Banks."

Sarah confirms Violet's statement. "You're right. So many ships went down that this shoreline is called the Graveyard of the Atlantic," Sarah says. "Your history courses will come in handy when trying to find your ancestor's treasure, I would suspect."

Violet answers in a quiet voice. "I don't know now that my parents are gone. I have kinda' lost my drive to find the treasure—and the treasure map went down with the boat," she says.

Sally and I understand how she is feeling about the loss of a parent, much less two. "That's so sad about your parents. It must have been so traumatic," I say. Sally adds, "Have you been with Stephen ever since you started looking for the treasure?"

Violet turns around in her seat to answer me and Sally. "You know, it's weird. We are kindred souls. I never in a million years thought that I would end up traveling the world in a yacht. It works for me, though— I can work from Stephen's boat remotely. Now I can't imagine not doing it."

Sally nods and starts to talk about how each of us found our soulmates. "Angie, tell Violet how you met Thomas," she urges.

I think back to last year when I met my fiancé. "I had just moved to the island after breaking up with my boyfriend and I was not in a very good place," I explain. "Our father had passed away unexpectantly the previous October of a massive heart attack. I was depressed but also excited to be moving to Ocracoke—even though originally it wasn't a permanent move. I came for the summer to play my music in Emily's pub."

I push my wavy hair out of my eyes and continue. "I had just arrived and was staying at the inn in Evangeline's old bedroom. Evangeline's spirit appeared before me and told me that I needed to go to her cottage. She said the time was right," I say, then pause. "When I entered the bungalow, Thomas was bending over the fireplace. He had just pulled a silver necklace with a half-heart pendant from behind a stone in the hearth."

I show Violet the unusual necklace around my neck, with its dangle showing half a heart and the initials "JH."

"My father gave me this necklace the summer before he died. He told me that Evangeline had come to him in a vision and said the time was right. The necklace I saw in Thomas's hand was its exact duplicate. Before that moment, I had never met Thomas. It was strange that our paths had never crossed before then given that my family had been coming to the island since I was born."

I think back to the extraordinary moment that marked our meeting.

"Well, then the strangest thing happened. Thomas held out the necklace he'd found for me to see. Unconsciously, I reached up to touch the one I always wear," I continued. "Our fingers happened to touch when we were looking at the necklace from the hearth, and suddenly Evangeline and Jacob's spirits appeared before us. Jacob was Evangeline's love, and she was supposed to marry him— but she was kidnapped by Daniel, Blackbeard's grandson. She wasn't able to escape and return to Ocracoke Island until three years later with her young son, William. Jacob never found out that William was his child."

I feel again the astonishment and sadness that had washed over me at the time. "Thomas and I found ourselves witnessing the moment when the Evangeline and Jacob were saying what turned out to be their last goodbye, just before Jacob went to help his family settle further inland.

205

It was heartfelt and so passionate. I still think about how the two never were able to reunite until after their deaths.

"That moment when Thomas and I made the connection with the two necklaces was crazy, and I worried that the feelings Thomas and I had for each other as a result might not be real—but, rather, somehow related to the excitement over the vision," I say. "But I've gotten over that now. And I've never been happier."

I sigh and gaze at my beautiful engagement ring.

Violet stares in surprise. "Are you kidding me?" she says. "I thought that the two of you had been together forever."

I laugh. "It feels like forever, and I have even joked with him about how maybe soulmates can cross from one lifetime to another."

Chloe jumps into the conversation. "Really, I thought you two had been together forever, too."

I shake my head. "No, we've only been together since last June—not even a year yet—but when you know, you know."

Chloe laughs. "That's kind of like when John and I met," she says. "It was love at first sight."

We arrive right as the ferry is loading. "Whoa, looks like we are in luck today, ladies," Emily says as she pulls into line. "There isn't a long line. Let's hope we don't have a long one when we return."

Sarah exclaims about our good fortune. "You're right about that, Sis. Let's try to get back to the returning ferry around 2 p.m.," she says. "We'll just have to see how the day goes. We might have to make our trip to the bridal shop at another time with the moms."

Emily agrees. "Yeah, it might be too much to fit in today. Here's hoping we find what we need at Fisherman's Daughter," she says, before adding, "I used to really like the Hanes store, but I sure wish that they hadn't changed it as much as they have. You girls really would have loved that store."

Sarah speaks up. "And what about the Kitchen Store? I used to love going in there, too," she says. "I really miss it. I still can't believe that the mall got rid of it. I found so many things that I didn't even know I needed."

Emily follows the ferry attendants' instructions to park close to the front of the vessel. We are sitting in the van, and we continue chatting about where we want to go. "Well, there are plenty of other stores," Emily says. "What are you ladies wanting to shop for while we are here?"

Violet answers first. "I really am in need of some warmer clothes. I didn't realize it was so chilly up here this time of year," she says. "Oh, and I guess I need something to wear to the New Year's Eve party."

Chloe chimes in. "I was wondering, does everyone get dressed up or is the evening just casual?"

"I like to get dressed up," Sarah answers her, "but it all depends on the people. It's a come-as-you-are or get dressed up type of party. I'm going to see if I spot a fancy dress or maybe a cute pantsuit."

"I'm not sure yet what way I'm leaning tonight. I could go either way. It all depends on what we find," I say. "There's an Eddie Bauer and a Gap store for warm clothes, plus a couple other stores for sweatshirts and stuff like that. As for dressier, you might be able to find something in Belk's if you don't see anything you like in Fishermen's Daughter."

Emily laughs at us. "You girls can do what you like, but I'm going for a more comfortable approach. Jeans and maybe a fancy top."

Sarah just shakes her head at her sister. "That's the nice thing about Ocracoke Island, everyone does their own thing and it's okay," Sarah says.

As we sit in the van, Sarah points to the horizon. "I can't believe how foggy it is today. It's like pea soup. I don't even know if I want to get out of the car for the ride over."

"Me either," Sally says as she rests her head on the seatback, yawning. "I think I am just going to stay in the cozy warm van. The twins had me up last night at around 3 a.m. so I'm tired."

We all agree to stay in the vehicle, and the time goes by quickly as we continue chattering on about the local gossip and where we want to go shopping. We also tell Chloe and Violet about the traditions connected to the New Year's Eve party.

The ferry docks and we drive off. I pull my curly windblown hair into a ponytail when we get out of the van at the first store. "You know, New Year's Eve is pretty new for me, too," I say. "I have only spent one other New Year's with you girls, and I think I was only sixteen last time. It's going to be so much fun."

Emily smiles. "It usually is a blast. The pub is always packed, and the music is blaring," she says. "Just think, this is your first time playing for us at the pub on New Year's Eve. I can't wait to hear you."

We trudge up the steps to the Fisherman's Daughter. We are excited as we enter. The store has many new styles and outfits that would be perfect for a fancy New Year's party. I quickly find a beautiful sapphire-colored jumpsuit to wear with a matching shawl. As I pay for them, I announce: "I am so thrilled with my choice. I look forward to wearing this new outfit."

Sally is drawn to a soft aqua cashmere sweater and a pair of black leggings to go with it. "I just love this!" she says. "It's so soft and practical. I can even wear this when I go back to school."

Sarah decides on a sparkly gold form-fitting dress that accentuates her slender figure. "What do you girls think of this? Is it too much?" she asks.

"Heck no," Chloe exclaims. "I think I might go for the same type of outfit." She finds a glittery red dress that looks absolutely adorable on her.

Emily being Emily comes up with a pair of leather leggings and a flowing peasant blouse that suit her personality. "Well, not as fancy as you girls, but I love it," she declares.

Violet is undecided. She tries on a sparkly black-and-gold mini dress. "Oh my, is this okay? I really like it," she tells us. "What do you guys think?" She twirls around in front of the mirror.

I laugh as I answer. "Wow. That's gorgeous and perfect for you."

I walk over to a rack and pull out a black sequined shawl. "I spotted this cute shawl earlier. It will keep you warm if we are out and about," I tell her.

Violet squeals. "Oh, that's wonderful! It will be perfect," she says. "I didn't bring any dressy coats—I only went back once to my condo since I met Stephen."

She becomes subdued as she adds, "I need to figure out what I'm going to do with my parent's condo. And I still need to finish going through my parents' things. I was living with them before the accident because I had just started a new job and didn't know where I wanted to live." She rubs her hands over her face. "Enough of that," she says. "I don't want to think about it now. Maybe after the New Year."

Sally squeezes her shoulder. "We went through the same thing last year. It's finally starting to get a little better, but we are lucky to have such a tight-knit group of people around us," she acknowledges. "You can hang out with us as long as you want."

Violet wipes a silvery tear from her cheek. "I'm so touched. You guys are so nice."

The rest of the day flies by, and before we know it, we are back on Ocracoke Island meeting in the pub for our New Year's Eve party.

Chapter 28

New Year's Eve Party

The cozy neighborhood pub opens at 4 p.m. and Emily, Sam, and I arrive early to unlock the old oak door and get set up. Emily laughs as she belts out, "Here goes the craziness! I hope you two wore your roller skates. Depending on the weather and the crowd, we might expand the party to outside."

Two of the women who work in the inn—Joyce and Marie—have come over to the pub to help wait tables. Sam starts removing the bar chairs from the tables.

"I think you might be right about us being busy," he says. "I spoke to Cindy, and she had to wait for the ferry for over an hour. When she finally got on, there were still a lot more people waiting in line. I tell you, post-COVID has really made this island busier than ever."

I nod in agreement. "I noticed something similar when Thomas and I stopped by 1718 Brewery the other day for a cold beer. There was a long line there, too," I say.

Emily wipes down the gorgeous golden oak bar and starts cutting up limes and lemons for drinks. "Angie, do you mind making the Oxford Pub brew? Everybody loves the version that you mix up. We might need a double batch tonight. What do you think?"

"Sure, no problem," I answer as I head back to the kitchen to get the supplies for the delicious punch. "Do you want me to go down and get some more beer for the coolers?"

"That's okay, Angie," Sam interjects. "I can go down and get beer and some ice for the drinks."

Before we finish setting up, about ten people arrive. It's clear that they already started partying before they got here. I think to myself, "Before the night is over, things could get interesting with this group."

We have a table reserved for our family and friends—and it's a good thing. The pub is packed before 6 p.m. The weather has cooperated, so we are able to open the doors to additional outside seating.

Thomas, George, John, Chloe, Sally, Robert, Matt, and Sarah arrive by 6:30 p.m. Our parents have decided to wait until midnight to come over to ring in the New Year. The place is in full swing with the music blaring from Joe the DJ. I will be doing a couple sets of my music. I plan to go up on stage at 7 p.m. for my first set.

When the time comes, I swing my guitar over my shoulder, walk up to the microphone, and bellow out a greeting to everyone. "Thanks, Joe. Good evening, welcome to the Oxford Pub, and Happy New Year!"

I open with my song about Ocracoke Island since it is always a big hit. The crowded room sings along and sways to my music. I am midway through my set when I look up and see Violet and Stephen walk into the pub with three dodgy-looking characters. One of the men is a rugged looking six-foot-tall guy with long thinning gray hair pulled back in a greasy ponytail. He is standing beside Stephen. Beside him—and at about the same height—is a scruffy mid-twenties male with red hair, a scraggly beard, and raggedy faded blue jeans. As they move into the pub and pass close by the stage where I'm playing, I can see crosses tattooed above the gold rings that sit on his fingers like brass knuckles.

Next to Violet is a scroungy-looking man whose greasy auburn hair peeks out from under his black bandanna. He is sporting a gold hoop earring. He is missing a couple teeth and the front teeth that are still in place look rotten and discolored. He's a little shorter but more muscular than his two companions. All three are menacing looking figures.

The guys in our group stand up. They clearly feel intimidated, and that makes me anxious. I raise my eyebrows but continue with my music.

Even as I sing, I keep an eye on the table. I watch the guarded introduction and know in my heart that these must be Stephen's relatives.

The hair raises up on the back of my neck. I sense that our ancestors' spirits are here and when I look behind my family, I see the spirits of Roger, Jacob, Dad, Evangeline, Anne Bonny, and Old Emily guarding our beloved group. "Whoa," I think to myself, "even they must feel the evil emanating from this group of newcomers. Even the spirit of Roger, who helped Evangeline escape from her capture by Daniel Teach, Blackbeard's grandson is with them."

It seems even weirder that the spirits of both Roger and Jacob have made their presence known to me. I wonder to myself if any of my friends can sense or see the ghosts standing guard behind them.

I finish singing my first musical set and the room explodes in applause. I bow and speak into the mic. "Thanks, everybody! I'll be back shortly. Meanwhile, enjoy the party." I point to Joe. "Take it away, Joe. I'll see you all again in a little while."

I tentatively walk back to our table to stand beside Thomas, who is talking to Stephen's relatives. Thomas puts his arm around me as he makes introductions. "Angie, this is Stephen's Uncle Timmy and his cousins, Hunter and Logan. Guys, this is my fiancée, Angie."

I hesitantly nod at them. "Hello," I say. "We weren't aware you fellows were coming to town. Are you here for the party?"

Stephen answers for them, grimacing. "I didn't know they were coming either. It was a big surprise for Violet and me when they showed up at my boat. We were getting ready to head over here for the party when they arrived."

Uncle Timmy responds to my question. "We heard my nephew was heading to Ocracoke," Uncle Timmy says. "We were thinking it might be fun—and even prosperous—to come along to meet our new cousins."

Stephen looks flustered and Violet looks concerned when Thomas responds. "Well, the party is open to the public," he says, "but I'm not sure how prosperous this island will be for you."

Hunter responds with a comment that chills me. "We know that Stephen and Violet like to follow leads on treasure hunting, so we figured he might be coming here to search for buried loot."

Violet cringes and Stephen looks frustrated, angrily protesting, "I told him we were just coming here to meet our new relatives and nothing more, but they didn't believe me."

Matt steps forward and extends his hand to our new relatives. "Hi, I'm Matt and I guess that makes us related. This is Sarah, my wife." He then points to my sister. "And this is Sally, my sister, and her husband, Robert. Why don't you three head up to the bar and order drinks. If you're hungry, there's also a buffet."

The three men offer their hands. "Nice to meet you all," Logan says. "That sounds good, a drink and dinner. Nice little bar you've got here." Hunter, Logan, and Uncle
Timmy head up to the bar and then to the buffet. I see Emily look my way, along with Sam, before they take their orders.

Stephen apologizes for his uninvited guests. "Hey guys, I'm really sorry. I didn't know that they would follow us up here."

Thomas shakes his head. "I believe you, but we are going to have to be very careful. I don't want those three knowing about our quest to find Anne's treasure," he says. "Sorry, but I didn't get very good vibes from them. As a matter of fact, I feel a little threatened."

Violet flushes and answers him. "I don't understand why they would just show up unexpected like this," she says. "It doesn't make sense."

Stephen guardedly responds. "Unfortunately, they feel like any treasure I am hunting for is partially theirs because we are in a partnership together. I'm hoping that I can buy them out one day, but right now I am kind of stuck, if you know what I mean."

Matt nods sympathetically. "That is quite a pickle you've got yourself in. Maybe you need to sit out on this adventure."

Stephen shrugs. "Or maybe we can just keep this secret from them and then I can pay them off with the profits we will hopefully make off the treasure," he says.

He points in the direction of his uncle and cousins. "They're coming back now," Stephen says. "Let's just not talk about treasure while they are around. Can we do that please?" We all nod in agreement.

Logan places his heaping plate on an empty spot at our table and sits down, munching on a piece of steamed shrimp. "Great vittles. I love a seafood spread," he says. He looks at me and asks, "Is this place always so busy or is it just because you've started playing here? Looks like you've got your own local fan club."

I blush as I answer him. "It's always busy on New Year's Eve," I say. "I guess maybe it's a little busier since I started playing here this past summer."

Hunter squeezes in beside Logan, and their father sits beside Hunter.

"That's pretty cool that your songs are doing so well," Logan continues. "Too bad about you guys losing the treasure this month. That really sucks if you ask me. What a bummer."

Thomas feels me tense up after the comment, and he squeezes my shoulder to reassure me. "Yeah, it was really disappointing," I say. "I guess it just wasn't meant to be. From what Stephen has told us, you guys had a similar situation in Jamaica when you found a treasure but then it disappeared after what happened to his father."

215

Uncle Timmy stiffens and grimaces at Stephen. "It was awful," he says. "I still miss my brother." He has a grim look on his face as he turns to his sons. "I would trade any treasure to have my brother back, right boys?"

Both Hunter and Logan shrug. "It was crazy the way that happened. One minute it was there and the next minute it was gone," Logan says. "Stephen even found a Spanish gold coin. But to lose Uncle Steve that way..."

Stephen looks sad. "I'd really rather not talk about that day, if it's okay with you guys. I'm still a little raw when it comes to remembering that whole incident," he says.

Violet hugs him. "I agree. Let's just enjoy the party," she says.

Logan lifts his mug of beer. "Let's do a toast. To Uncle Steve, we miss you!" He takes a big swig of his beer and salutes his cousin, Stephen.

We all toast to Stephen's father, taking a sip of our drinks. I can feel the tension between the outsiders and Stephen and Violet. It's like Uncle Timmy, Hunter, and Logan are bathed in a big black cloud of wicked aura. Our ancestors' spirits continue to loom over and guard us. I can only wonder what they are thinking. I can't wait to ask them why they are so concerned.

My spirit of my father catches my eye. He lifts his eyebrows in the direction of the evil threesome and mouths, "Beware and do not trust them!"

I look over at my brother, sister, Thomas, and George and I see that they have just witnessed my father's warning. I frown and raise my glass. "And let's have another toast to all those loved ones we have lost."

I see Stephen squeeze Violet's shoulder before taking a sip of his drink. "I'll second that. "To Violet's parents and your father, Angie, Matt, and Sally. May they all rest in peace."

Violet turns her head and swipes a tear that has escaped from her pretty green eyes. "To all of those who we have lost," she agrees. She takes a large swallow of her Oxford Brew and shivers. "Wow, what's in this stuff? It kicks quite a punch."

I laugh. "It's some good firewater but be careful. It'll sneak up on you— just ask Sally and Sarah," I say, happily.

Violet smiles. "Is there a story behind that?" she asks. "If so, I'd love to hear it."

Sarah chuckles and puts her arm around my sister. "Do you want to tell the story, or do you want me to, Sally?"

Sally shakes her head. "No, you go ahead. You tell it much better than I do."

Sarah begins her tale, trying not to laugh hysterically as she remembers the Night of the Oxford Brew. "Okay, so here goes. I hope you guys don't think we are all crazy or anything."

She raises her hands in the air as launches into the story. "One night a few years back, the group of us had taken a gallon jug of that mighty concoction down to the beach. We were all sitting around the bonfire enjoying ourselves, singing, laughing, and telling tales about buried treasure and lost loves." She points to me. "Well, we let Angie make it because she is usually so good at it, but this was only the second batch she made for us, so it was super strong."

Laughing, Sarah, continues with her story. "I think you said that you forgot you had already added the liquor, so you added more. You can just imagine how strong it was. Anyway, us girls being girls, we had to go use the facilities and we went together. Sally and I were traipsing down the beach, arm in arm, laughing and stumbling."

She is laughing so hard that she snorts as she remembers that night. "The next thing you know, we end up in Silver Lake," she says. "A huge rogue

217

wave crashed up on the shore right about the time that we were weaving our way down the beach."

She is laughing so hard that Sally has to finish their story.

"Matt, Angie, and George came running into the water to save us just as another wave comes crashing onto the beach, dwarfing us," she says. "We were all rolling around in the surf like seals and making enough noise that our parents came running down to check on us. Next thing we know we were all in the water, even our parents."

She laughs, trying to catch her breath. "It was the funniest thing ever. Thomas, it's just a shame you were away at camp."

Chloe chuckles. "I can only imagine the whole group of you splashing around in the surf. It sounds like you had a great childhood with all of you being so close," she says.

I stand and wrap my arm around Emily who has joined us in time to hear the story. She has a tray of champagne glasses for all of us.

"We really did have a great time growing up and spending our summer vacations on the island," I say. Emily adds, "I wouldn't have changed it for the world. We were so lucky to have all those summer nights and days."

She looks around the pub, assessing the crowd. "Can you believe it's almost midnight?" she says. "Looks like everyone in the bar has drinks. It's time to start the countdown to midnight."

Our parents and my grandparents arrive from the inn with champagne glasses already in their hands, ready to ring in the New Year. The DJ starts the countdown, and everyone gathers around the TVs to watch the ball drop. "Ten. Nine. Eight. Seven. Six. Five. Four. Three. Two. One. Happy New Year!"

Auld Lang Syne blares over the speakers, and we hug and kiss each other to begin another year. Thomas takes me passionately in his brawny arms and whispers in my ear as he kisses me. "Happy New Year, Angie. I can't wait to see what wonderful, exciting, new things we share together this year. I look forward to making you mine!"

I take his face in my petite hands and kiss him back. "I love you and look forward to being your wife."

I'm so happy—and still so surprised that I met this amazing man and fell in love. A year ago today, I was in a miserable relationship with my wretched old boyfriend, Larry, not looking forward to the future and missing my father.

Thomas and I look around at all our friends. We notice that Stephen is holding Violet and giving her a Happy New Year's kiss when Logan intervenes and wraps his arms around the pair. He's been drinking heavily, alternating between shots of tequila and fireball whiskey, along with several cups of the Oxford Brew.

He takes out his wallet and pulls out a wad of hundred-dollar bills. "Drinks on me!" he shouts.

His father, brother, Stephen, and rest of us stare at the collection of bills in his hand. Stephen's eyebrows rise and his face turns bright red. "Where the hell did you get all that money?" he demands. "Did you find some treasure and not let me know about it?"

Logan stammers and slurs out a response. "It's cool, man. I just sold my bike and brought the cash with me."

He points to his dad and brother. "Tell them, man, that that's what I did." Then he turns back to Stephen. "And what's it to you, anyway? You don't control me—and don't think you ever will."

Hunter nervously answers, eyeballing Logan as he tells Stephen. "That's right, man. He sold his bike before we left. I didn't even know he brought all that money with him." He swats his brother on his shoulder, glaring at him.

Uncle Timmy shrugs his shoulders, looking royally pissed off at his son. "I didn't know he had all that money, either. It's a surprise to me, too."

The tension has risen dramatically in the room and Thomas, Matt, George, and Robert try to jockey themselves into position between Stephen and his cousins. Thomas looks straight at Logan, Uncle Timmy, and Hunter and quietly, but firmly, says, "I think it's time for you guys to leave. We don't want any barroom brawls in here. This is a friendly place. Sorry, man, it's just the way it has to be."

Uncle Timmy grabs his sons by the collars of their shirts. "I have to agree with you, Thomas. I'll get these two out of here. We don't want any trouble." He looks at the two guys, shaking his head. "Do we, boys?"

Uncle Timmy pushes the two toward the patio door. As the three leave, Stephen remains standing and fuming. "They are lying," he says, angrily. "I always wondered how we could have lost that treasure when my dad died. Now I know that they must have gone back and stolen it from under my nose. It makes me wonder now whether what happened to my father was actually an accident.

"I've had my doubts about dad being so careless to make a deadly mistake like he did," he adds. "But now it really makes me wonder."

Violet looks scared as she tries to console him. "Do you realize what you're saying? You're accusing them of killing your dad. That's crazy."

She pauses and then gasps. "Do you think they may be responsible for my parent's death? Maybe it wasn't an accident, either." Tears spill out of her eyes.

Stephen looks forlorn as he answers her. "I don't know, baby. I just don't know," he says, shaking his head. "I would hope that they aren't capable of murdering people, especially people that they love. You know though, Logan is pretty hooked on drugs and gambling, so who knows."

He is wildly running his hands through his dreadlocks as he speaks. He looks devastated. Thomas tries to calm him. "Take it easy. Maybe he is telling the truth about selling his bike," he says.

Stephen hesitantly nods. "I don't know. Did you see the look on my uncle's face when he pulled out that chunk of cash?" Stephen asks. "He looked as surprised as me. I'm going to have to ask him if Logan actually sold his bike."

I look around and notice that the bar is starting to empty. Emily already left my side, along with our parents and my grandparents, before all the excitement with Logan and Stephen. I see Sam, Emily, and her two helpers are busy cleaning up the pub, sticking to the plan to close up at 12:30 a.m.

George, Thomas, and I excuse ourselves. "We're going to go help Emily and Sam close up," I tell the others. "I guess we'll see everyone tomorrow. Mom has invited you all to her house for New Year's Day dinner."

I squeeze Stephen's shoulder and hug Violet as I pass them on my way back up to the bar. John, Chloe, Stephen. and Violet, say goodbye and all leave together.

Sarah and Matt stop by the bar to speak with Emily and me before they go home. Sarah puts her hands up to her face in horror. "Whoa, what was that? Do you guys think Logan might have killed those people?" she asks. I could hear the alarm in her voice even before she added, "I'm scared!"

I answer her. "I'm wondering the same thing myself. Did you see all our ancestor's ghosts standing guard behind us, even Jacob and Roger's spirits were guarding us. It was really weird. My dad even whispered to me, 'Do not trust them!'"

Sarah fidgets. She looks frightened. "Really? I didn't see the spirits." She turns to Matt and asks him. "Did you see them, honey?" He nods yes. "Why didn't you tell me?" she asks.

"I didn't want to ruin the moments we were sharing," he tells her. "I didn't put two and two together until now, that they might be shielding us from the vile trio." He shakes his head. "Wow, that makes sense that they would guard us from them."

Thomas puts his arm around me. "Okay girls, make sure none of you goes off on your own. These guys might be even more of a threat than Ricky and Rusty because, as far as we know, those two never killed anyone.

"I think we need some hanging-out time on our own. Let's get this bar cleaned up and head down to the beach," he says. He points to the door. "I'm going to go get Max and bring him here, then let's do a bonfire."

George nods in agreement. "Sounds like a great plan to me. We are just about done here. By the time you get back with Max we should be finished."

He laughs as he asks, "How's about we bring a couple gallons of Oxford Brew with us?"

I lick my lips. "Uhm, yummy. I didn't really drink anything tonight since I was working. I'm game. Let's just not end up in the bay this time," I chuckle before I add, "It's a shame Sally and Robert had to leave early to be with the twins. Hey Sarah, why don't you text Chloe and John to see if they might want to join us?"

Then I grimace and shake my head as I add, "I don't think we should invite Violet and Stephen just in case the gruesome trio might try to tag along again."

Sarah happily texts Chloe, who sends a thumbs up and texts back: "Awesome, we weren't really ready to end the night. We will be right back."

Chapter 29

Great Friends, Old and New

Chloe and John knock on the locked door to the bar and Sarah lets the cute couple back into the pub. John is smiling. "Thanks so much for inviting us back. We weren't really ready to call it a night, and we haven't been to a bonfire in years," he says. "It's such a nice evening. This should be fun." He swats Sarah on her shoulder, laughing. "Oh, and by the way, Sarah, let's not take a swim tonight. It's not that warm outside."

We all crack up at his joke. Sarah, blushing, laughs, too. "It's a deal. I promise," she says. "So, is everyone ready to go?"

We all head toward the door, carrying blankets to sit on and a container of the famous Oxford Brew to enjoy. Max is thrilled to have so many people with us. His tail whips back and forth and he barks excitedly. It doesn't take us long to gather enough kindling and driftwood for our little fire. The flames crackle on the quiet, lonesome beach while the cyclic moon shines above our heads against the inky Carolina sky. A gentle breeze blows the dry golden seagrass on the sandy dunes.

I sigh, reaching my slender arms above my head. "Wow, what a gorgeous night. I was worried it would be too cold, but this is perfect," I say. "I'm just so glad that the bar is closed tomorrow."

Thomas pulls me over and squeezes me in his arms. "It is pretty awesome tonight," he agrees. Max is on his leash, tugging to get to the shoreline. "No buddy, not tonight. I'm going to take you for a walk in in minute," Thomas says. Max excitedly wags his whole body, licking Thomas on his hand. I reach down to pet Max's golden-brown hair, and he whines at me, jumping up on my legs. I tell Thomas, "Let's take him now and then we can come back and join the others." He nods his head in agreement.

As we head down the beach with the dog, we walk hand in hand, both of us deep in thought. Thomas is the first to speak. "I'm really concerned about Stephen's cousins. I'm not so sure about his uncle but I think his cousins are bad news."

I nod at him, frowning as I answer. "Yeah, those guys are pretty scary, and the fact that all our ancestors were standing behind them, keeping guard on us, really unnerves me." I pause, then ask: "Do you think they really could have killed Stephen's father—or even Violet's parents?"

Thomas stops walking, turns to me, and raises his shoulders. "I don't know, but it's kind of looking that way. I think we will need to be on our toes around them," he says. "Hopefully, they won't stay here too long."

Our puppy turns and starts leading us back to where the others are sitting. I laugh. "I think he's ready to rejoin the party." Thomas nods his head. "Looks that way. Let's go back and ask the others what they think about Stephen's family."

We reach the cozy group, and the fire is crackling like popcorn, emitting a pleasant aroma of cedar. It automatically carries me back to so many pleasant memories. "Oh, I just love the smell of a good bonfire," I say. "It reminds of so many moments of our treasured childhood."

I sigh and sit down on the blanket, joining the circle of my friends, old and new. I no sooner relax back on the blanket, with my body shaping the soft sand under it, when a ghostly vision appears. It is Evangeline, Anne Bonny, and my father.

Chloe gasps but recovers quickly. "I don't know if I will ever get used to these visions," she says in a quiet voice.

My father, George, blows me a kiss and then starts to talk to us. "Your concerns about Stephen's brother, Logan, are correct. You must at all costs stay vigilant when around him. He is very dangerous."

Anne blows out a long sigh. "Yes, mateys. Take heed. I traveled in time to see just what happened to Stephen's father and Violet's parents. I watched as Logan poked a hole in a long tube. George here says that it would have caused Stephen's father to perish."

My father picks up the story about the day Stephen's father died. "From what I could tell, it was only Logan— not his brother, Hunter, or Stephen's Uncle Timmy."

Anne finishes the story. "But it was Logan and his swine friends who went back and stole the treasure that they had found. I never should have left my poor boy with that vicious man in Cuba. I was so young and dumb way back when I was running the seas with ole Jacky boy. And now, generations later, the badness that started then still continues " She looks pensive and forlorn remembering her past mistakes.

Evangeline has been silent up until this time. Now she speaks. "Aye, they remind me so much of their ancestor,
Anne's son Austin Bell. I met him once when I was with Daniel, Blackbeard's grandson. Austin's crew was devious and cruel to their captives."

Anne looks despondent as she continues. "When I was young, all I cared about was myself. It wasn't until after my incarceration in Jamaica and when I was on Cat Island that I became a good mother. I have never forgiven myself for leaving my boy Austin with that family."

"Oh Annie, it is too late to fret about such things," Evangeline tells her. "What is done is done. There is nothing you can do to change it."

Sighing Anne looks at us through knowing eyes. "I am sorry that my mistakes are causing you young folks such problems today."

My father speaks up. "Well, there isn't a thing you can do about the past. But now we need to keep these kids safe." Then my father turns to us, "You guys need to be very careful around the others, meaning Uncle Timmy, Hunter, and Logan. I'm not getting good vibes from any of them, especially Logan. The three of us will try to keep you free from harm, but please take what we're telling you seriously."

With a sadness, he adds, "We must go now, but heed our warnings." At that, the three ghosts evaporate into a mist.

John runs his hands through his windblown auburn hair. "Wow, that is just crazy!" he says. He looks around at the rest of us and adds, "You folks don't even seem fazed that we were just visited by our ancestors' spirits."

Sarah laughs, wrapping her arm around Matt. "We have been exposed to them a little bit longer than you two. After a while, it just seems normal," she says. "I don't know about you guys, but it's comforting to think that they are looking over us and protecting us."

"I guess but I'm not so sure I will ever get used to it," says Chloe, who has been smiling but now starts to yawn, hugging herself. It is now about 2 a.m. She turns to John. "Honey, I'm not sure about you but I'm getting tired. Do you want to head back to our beach house?"

John strokes her silky blond hair. "Sure thing, babe. I'm getting a little tired myself. A lot of excitement today." He turns to Thomas, George, and Matt. "Are we still going fishing again with Stephen tomorrow? I think he said to be there by 11a.m."

Matt scratches his chin and answers. "Yeah, I think that is a good idea. You girls can take Violet with you to Mom's." Matt gets up and wipes sand from his legs, then reaches his hand down to Sarah to help her up from the blanket.

George extinguishes our bonfire. "It'll be fun going fishing," he says. "I might have to get my own boat one day. What about you, Thomas? Didn't you say you might be interested in getting one? Maybe, the three of us can buy one together—a big one so we can go treasure hunting."

Thomas turns to George. "I'd love that, but I need to wait until after we finish working on our house," he reminds his brother. Then Thomas smiles at me and winks. "Only the best for my girl, Angie."

Thomas squeezes my hand, and our puppy stands up beside us trying to get some attention. When we get to the driveway of the inn, I call out, "See you all tomorrow.

Guys going fishing and girls doing wedding planning." I laugh and lightly punch Emily on her shoulder.

Emily blushes and exclaims, "Yeah, I guess I need to do that, don't I? See you all tomorrow—and let's start by checking out the attic to see what other wedding attire we find."

Thomas and I wave good-bye to the others and head toward our home. "As we walk away, I can hear the chatter as everyone else disperses.

Anne's Bounty

Chapter 30

A New Day and a New Year

I have a fitful night of sleep and wake up exhausted. I roll over and see Thomas trying to sneak out of our room. He sees that I'm awake and he sits back down on the bed, ruffling my hair and gently kissing my forehead. "What were you dreaming about, Angie?" he asks. "You were really talking in your sleep, tossing and turning last night."

I reach for my journal on our pretty oak bedside table. I pull back my long dark hair and pick up my pen. "I know. I'm tired this morning. I feel like I've been running a marathon," I answer, as I start to write down the details of my dream. "I was dreaming about Logan and some nasty-looking guys chasing me down a long, winding trail. I didn't recognize where I was at first, but Emily, Sarah, Violet, and Chloe were with me."

I explain more. "We were able to escape because we hid behind some gray rock cave. As a matter of fact, it kind of reminded me of the stone pathway leading to the beach on Shanna's Cove Resort on Cat Island. Remember the Man 'O War walkway we went down when we were at Matt and Sarah's wedding?"

Thomas nods his head. "Yeah, I remember it well. We ran down it when we were chasing Emily after she ran off because George was flirting with that outrageous woman at the wedding. That memory—the fear I felt when we couldn't find Emily—still gives me chills when I think about it."

I grimace and continue telling him about my dream. "It was crazy, and I felt like I was really there. I could feel my heart beating out of my chest. I could hear Logan telling his friends, 'We have to find those girls and get the map from Angie before they find the treasure, otherwise it's lost to us forever.'"

229

I can feel my heart beating as wildly as in the dream. "Logan had a gun on him. But Hunter kept telling him that he wasn't going to be a part of killing anyone like when Logan killed their uncle and Violet's parents. They didn't know we could hear them. I heard the girls gasp beside me, and I feel Violet trembling as tears rolled down her cheeks."

Thomas raises his eyebrows. "Is this just a dream or do you think you're having premonitions of what is to come? I wonder if Evangeline or Anne is channeling these dreams to you as another way to warn us about impending danger?"

I shake out my hair and think for a minute. "I don't know. Maybe we can ask them later today. I wonder if there's a way, we could look back in time to see what exactly happened on those days?"

Thomas nods, stands up, and walks to the door. "Yes, let's go down into the secret room later today to see if we can get Anne to appear so we can ask her. We can go see your Mom and David later today."

I sit up in bed, crisscrossing my legs as I continue writing down what I remember of my dream. "Definitely, that's a great idea," I say. "I'm going to text David for the details of the plan for today's New Year's Day meal with him and Mom.

"What time are you supposed to meet the guys?" I add. "We're fishing at 9, so Matt, George, Robert, John, and I decided to meet at around 9 a.m. John and Chloe are going to stop by and pick up Violet then will bring both girls to the inn. He said he'll pick up Matt and me when he drops Chloe and Violet off. George and Robert are going to drop off Sally and Emily then head down to the docks."

I smile at him. "Good plan. That way everyone has someone with them, just in case," I say, before adding: "I wish Stephen's uncle and his cousins would just go back to Jamaica."

Thomas laughs at my comment. "I can't see that happening, but it would be nice. Listen, I'll walk you over to the inn when you're ready. Did you want breakfast before we leave? I can fix something up really quick if you like."

I grin and shake my head no. "Sarah is going to do a continental breakfast with those yummy croissants from the bakery."

Thomas and I get ready and head out the door with Max in tow. We reach the inn at the same time that Violet, Chloe, Sally, and Emily are being dropped off. We all hug like long-lost friends. I think to myself how close we have become with Chloe and Violet. It's nice to be surrounded by so many friends.

Violet is all smiles as we walk up the steps to the inn. I was worried that she would be upset about everything that happened last night. By the time we get inside the door of the inn, she can no longer control herself.

"Guess what? Stephen and I got engaged!" She squeals as she holds out her hand to show us the pretty diamond ring that flashes in the sunlight filtering in through the windowpanes. "Isn't it gorgeous? I'm just so excited. I know it seems soon, but I'm so in love with him."

We all gather around to examine her beautiful gold filagree diamond ring. Emily laughs. "It must be something about this island and Evangeline spewing love spells over everyone," she says. "The ring is so pretty— and it looks like you. Now tell us the how, when, and where. Details please!"

Violet is beaming and blushing as she describes the proposal. "Stephen planned to do it after the ball came down at midnight, but Logan spoiled that with all his commotion. When we got back to the boat, Stephen pulled out a bottle of champagne he had chilling in the fridge. He had me wait topside while he went down to get it and dropped the ring into my glass."

She laughs as remembers the moment. "I almost swallowed the ring, but the moonlight caught the sparkling diamond just in time. It was so romantic. Stephen dropped down on one knee and asked me to be his forever."

We give her another group hug then Sarah proclaims, "Well, I guess it's good that you're here because we're going up into the attic to get things for Emily's wedding. Maybe you can find something borrowed for your wedding while we're up there."

Sarah points to the sunroom. "Let's go get some breakfast first and then we can head up to the attic to check things out."

The breakfast is heavenly—a great way to start our day. Afterward we all help clean up our dishes. Sally White is in the kitchen baking chocolate chip cookies for our New Year's Day meal at mom's and David's home.

She holds up a cookie from the batch she's just taken out of the oven. "Cookies, anyone? Try one while they're hot."

She doesn't have to ask any of us twice. Chloe sums it up for all of us when she says, "They smell so good. I never could turn down chocolate."

Violet timidly tells Sally White, "That's so sweet of you but if I keep eating like I have been, I'm going to be too fat to find a wedding dress."

Emily and Sarah's mom looks puzzled for a minute then breaks into a big grin and congratulates Violet. "Oh, that's wonderful! When did that happen? And as for fat, you have a long way to go before that ever happens," Sally White says.

Violet tells her story and smiles at Sally White, adding. "You're so sweet. You kind of remind me of my mom." A silvery tear slides down Violet's cheek. "I just wish my parents were here."

Sally hugs Violet and puts her hand under her chin looking into her eyes. "You can use me for your mom. I know I'm not her, but you are now part of our family and don't forget it." Sally pulls Violet into a big bear hug, wrapping her arms around her and resting her head on her shoulder. Tears flow from Violet.

Violet's crying breaks all our hearts, especially mine and my sister's. With our father' death, we experienced much of the same emotional rollercoaster. I reach out and touch Violet's arm. "You've got Sally and me and all the rest of us. Look at us—all your new sisters. We are here for you." We give her another group hug.

Violet wipes the tears from her face, takes a deep breath, and bravely states, "Oh, you girls are something. I can't even express how much this means to me. I never had any siblings growing up so this is so special to me."

We are quiet for a moment, then Violet adds, "Enough of all this sadness. This is a happy occasion. Let's go look for some things for your wedding, Emily, and yours too, Angie."

Anne's Bounty

Chapter 31

Something Borrowed

We climb the stairs into the dusty memento-filled attic. I can't help but smile when I think back to my childhood. Memories come flooding back of long-ago rainy days and playing dress up in the attic with my sister and my friends, Emily and Sarah.

Sarah leads the way and opens the creaky door to the room with our ancestors' cedar chests. "Chloe, Violet, this is where we used to play on days that we weren't able to go outside," Sarah explains. "Evangeline's chest is up here along with that of Old Emily, plus those of my grandparent, great grandparents, etc.

"There are many old treasures for you to choose from, Violet," she continues. "Do you know what type of dress you might like for your wedding? That way, we can figure out which chest to look in for accessories."

Violet looks sad as she answers. "I always thought I would wear my mom's dress. It's a knee-length princess-cut ivory gown, an A-line. It belonged to my great grandmother. It has beading along the neckline. I guess that's what I'd like to wear."

Emily grins and walks over to her great grandmother's chest. "I think I have just the thing for you," she says. "There's a cute little handbag in here that sounds like it would be perfect for your outfit." She opens the coffer and rifles around until she pulls out a small ivory purse with beading. She holds it out to Violent. "Well, what do you think?" she asks. "I think there is even a veil to go with it if you want to borrow that, too."

Violet's eyes are teary as she takes the bag from Emily. "You aren't going to believe this, but I think it might be a perfect match," she says. "Hey, would any of you girls be interested in going with me to visit my parent's condo in Florida? I need to go through their things, and I have been putting it off. My mother's wedding dress is there."

Emily reaches back into the chest. "Oh, here it is, the veil I was looking for. What do you think?"

Violet takes the delicate headpiece from Emily and walks over to the antique mirror. She places the veil over her hair and tears start to fall. "I'm so sorry to be blubbering," she says, apologetically. "I cry at the drop of a hat ever since my parents died. And I can't stop thinking that they won't be here for my wedding to Stephen." She sighs and wipes the tears from her face.

Sally and I remember back to when our dad died suddenly, and we both hug Violet. "I'd love to go with you," Sally says. "I just need to make sure I can coordinate the time away with Georgia, our nanny." She turns to me. "What do you think, Angie? Can you get away for a couple days?"

I nod and ask Emily. "I know I'm on the schedule to work and perform at the pub, but do you think it would be okay if I went with them? I totally understand what she's going through."

Emily gives us a thumbs up. "You know, Sam was asking me for extra hours. Maybe I can go, too. He's so good at taking over for us when we go away. I'm game."

Chloe chimes in. "Me, too. I still have a few days before our Christmas vacation comes to an end."

Sarah shrugs. "Well, if all you girls are going, I want to go, too. Dad will cover for me at the inn," she says. "We can make it a girls' trip." She winks at Emily. "And while we're there, we can do some wedding shopping for both of you ladies."

Violets swipes the tears from her pretty green eyes. "Really, you guys would do that for me? I'm so touched. I've lost contact with all my friends, and it was just me growing up. Both my parents were only children."

Emily pulls out her phone and before we know it, we have tentative reservations to fly to Florida to help Violet with her parents' condo.

"Billy says he can fly us there," Emily says, "so now we just have to make sure we can all go. Once we nail that down, I just need to pay for the flights.

"Hey," she adds as an afterthought. "Do you think Cindy would want to go with us?" Chloe answers right away, "I think her schedule at the hospital makes it difficult to take time off."

Sarah makes a suggestion. "How about we find something for Chloe, too?" The girls search through their great grandmother's chest and find another handbag which is a pale ivory. Sarah holds it up. "How's this, Chloe? You can use it for the weddings and I'm sure it would be okay if you kept it since we are all related."

We do a group hug and Sarah turns to Emily. "Do we have everything we need up here for now? I wonder how the guys are doing?"

Before she can finish her text her phone beeps with a picture of a huge tuna that Matt has caught. She holds up the phone with the photo visible. "Well, speak of our devils," she says. "Look at the size of that tuna. Matt says they are on their way back to the island. He asked me to get the grill out because we're going to have a seafood feast."

Chapter 32

Wedding Plans

After we all make our way back down from the attic, we go into the kitchen where we find Sally White getting ready to whip up some salads. She has just taken a pot of boiling potatoes—for potato salad—off the stove, and she has the ingredients for coleslaw on the counter. "Perfect timing, girls," she says. "Does anyone feel like helping me peel potatoes or grate some cabbage and carrots for coleslaw?"

Sarah laughs as she puts an apron on to cover her blouse. "That's so funny because we came downstairs to start helping with the food. Matt texted us to say he caught a huge tuna and wants to have it for supper." She shows her mom the photo Matt sent her.

Sally White smiles. "He must be proud because he sent *me* a picture, too," she says. She then turns and asks, "Angie, can you phone your mom and grandmom and invite them to lunch? Oh, and maybe Thomas's parents, too?"

Sally White pulls a large can of black-eyed peas from the cupboard, opens it, and pours the contents into a Dutch oven with a piece of ham. "You know we have to have black-eyed peas for good luck," she says before looking over at Chloe and Violet. "Do your families have this same tradition where you live?"

They chime in together, laughing. "Definitely"

"Does anyone know how that tradition came about?" my sister asks.

Chloe answers. "From what I remember, it's a tradition in southern states and it's supposed to bring good fortune and wealth in the coming year. We usually cook ours with collard greens. Do you?"

Sally White pulls out another large can and holds it out for Chloe to see. "We do. Unfortunately, I wasn't able to get fresh collards from the store. But this will work." As she opens the can, she asks, "Do we know what time the guys will be back?"

" Within the hour," Sarah says, "so probably by the time we get done with these side dishes."

I call Thomas's mom to invite her to dinner, explaining that the guys caught a bunch of fish that we're planning to prepare for a New Year's Day dinner.

"We were just talking about what we were going to do for dinner, Angie," his mother says. "I made some macaroni and cheese earlier today. I'll bring that—how does that sound?"

"Perfect," I tell her. "We're here in the kitchen making coleslaw and potato salad. We'll probably eat around 5 p.m. but come on over to the inn whenever you like. My mom, David, and my grandparents will be over, too. It's our usual crowd—with a few extras you met last night."

"The more the merrier!" she replies. "You know I've always loved friends and family get-togethers. We'll be over shortly."

I answer back cheerfully, happy to have Thomas's family so close to ours. "Okay, sounds good. See you in a little while."

I smile, thinking how Thomas's parents, Liz and Joe, have always been a big part of our summer vacations on the island over the years.

"Thomas and George's parents will be over shortly, too," I announce to everyone. "Liz says she has a big pan of macaroni and cheese that she's bringing."

Emily grins as she comes over to me. "It still feels weird to me sometimes that George and I are a couple, but it also seems so right," she says. "Just think, Angie, when you and Thomas get married and George and I get married, we'll be related again."

240

I chuckle. "I know. We'll be sisters-in-laws times two with Matt being married to Sarah and you and me being married to the guys. How cool is that?"

Chloe and Violet both hear our interaction. "I guess that makes us all cousins or cousins-in-law," Chloe says. "That's awesome." She then turns to Violet. "We're just going to adopt you so that will make us all related!"

Teary eyed, Violet hugs Chloe. "That's so sweet," Violet says. "You guys make me feel like I am home."

Sally White steps over and wraps her arms around Violet. "Honey, you are welcome here. Please come visit anytime."

Violet hugs her back. "I feel so honored to be included in your family. Thank you for making me feel so welcome."

The door bursts open and in scrambles Max, his tail wagging wildly and his toenails sliding across the kitchen floor as he tries to reach me. Thomas is chasing after the dog, calling his name and trying to catch him. "Sorry, ladies," Thomas calls out as he rushes by. "He got away from me and he really loves parties—and Angie."

Max jumps up, almost knocking me over. "Hello, buddy. I see you, buddy," I tell him as I pet his furry head. I make him sit and pull a dog treat out of my pocket.

Thomas, George, Matt, John, Robert, and Stephen file into the cozy kitchen. To my surprise, Stephen's Uncle Timmy is at the rear of the pack. He holds up his hand to explain. "I hope it's okay that I'm crashing the party," he says. "I sent Logan home after what happened last night. I had Hunter take him back to Jamaica. I'll deal with Logan later."

We all look a little stunned, even Violet. But Sally White quickly recovers. "Welcome to our home," she says. "Please come on in. Can I get anything for you fellows to drink? There is coffee in the carafes and cold drinks on the bar in the sunroom. Help yourselves."

Matt and George are carrying a cooler full of fish. Matt holds up his prize tuna fillets.

"Look at these beauties," he says proudly. "And we have blues and mahi mahis. We are going to have quite the feast." He points to the dishes we're working on and looks over at Sally White. "Yum, Sally, I just love your potato salad—and your coleslaw, too."

She pats him on the back, smiling. "I know, honey, and there's lots for everyone," she says. "Liz is bringing mac and cheese. And I think your mom is making her famous buttermilk biscuits. Your grandmom is bringing apple pie with vanilla ice cream."

She then points to the stove. "We even have black-eyed peas and collard greens. We are going to have quite a feast," she adds.

Uncle Timmy looks surprised and points to the pot. "We usually have black-eyed peas for New Years Day, too!" he says. "This all sounds wonderful. Thank you so much for allowing me to join your New Year's Day meal. It means a lot to me."

He bows his head, looking sad. "I usually spend the day with my brother and Stephen. This is our first New Year's without Stephen's dad."

Jim, who has just come in from the den, pats Uncle Timmy on the shoulder. "You are always welcome here, and we're glad you can make it today." He points to the den. "Can I interest you fellas in a little whisky to warm you up? I got a new bottle of Glenfiddich for Christmas."

Uncle Timmy rubs his hands together warming them. "Oh, that sounds awesome. I'm not used to this cold weather and me bones are achy," he says with a laugh before looking over at the guys. "But do you guys want help with the fish? I can help if you need me."

Matt, George, Thomas, John, and Stephen tell him to relax and enjoy the whisky. The guys head outside with the fish while Jim escorts Uncle Timmy to the den, where the fireplace is roaring.

Robert has hung back in the kitchen, and he places a kiss on his wife's cheek. "I'm going to run home and get the twins. Do you want to come with me?"

Sally nods. "I was getting ready to ask if you wanted to come with me to get them," she says. "Georgia has plans to visit her cousin for dinner." My sister is texting Georgia as she and Robert walk out of the kitchen. She pauses and turns back to us. "See you in a little while," she says.

I look around the kitchen and float in that warm feeling I get when I am surrounded by my loved ones. This year I am forever grateful for everything I have and for all my friends and my family.

"It's so nice having everyone here. Old and new friends and family," I say. "It's amazing what a difference a year makes." I think back to how miserable I was last year when I was still living with Larry, my old boyfriend. I am so glad that part of my life is over. It makes me appreciate my new life here on the island even more."

There is a knock at the kitchen door and in walks Liz, Joe, my mom, grandmom, granddad, and David. Greetings and kisses follow as we wish everyone a Happy New Year. Then we all file into the large den.

David and Paul raise their eyebrows when they see Uncle Timmy sitting with Jim. Uncle Timmy stands and holds out his hand to shake with the two men. "I'm sure you're surprised to see me here, and I want to apologize for my boy, Logan. I had Hunter take him back home to Jamaica. I was just catching up with Jim."

David and Paul both shake hands with him. "Sometimes you have no control over what your children do," Paul says.

"Oh, look," Paul continues. "It seems that Jim has broken out the Glenfiddich." Paul smiles as Jim hands each of the two newcomers a warming glass of the amber whisky.

"Happy New Year to you all," Jim says. He raises the glass and takes a sip, savoring the glow sliding down his throat.

I am standing near the doorway that leads from the kitchen into the den, and Violet moves over to where I am and says, quietly, "I'm so sorry, Angie. I didn't know Uncle Timmy was going to be here. I will have to speak to Stephen and find out what happened."

"Maybe they made up or maybe he wasn't involved in everything that happened last night," I whisper back. "We'll just be careful but … Oh, wait. I think you might find out right now what's going on. Uncle Timmy is coming your way."

We watch as Uncle Timmy crosses the room and makes his way to where we are standing. I excuse myself after saying hello and asking how the fishing was.

"I caught a big mahi mahi and a huge blue. They gave me quite the fight," he says. Then he turns to Violet and asks, "My dear, do you mind if we talk?"

She nods and he guides her to a quiet corner in the den. "Okay, I'd really like to hear what you have to say," she tells him.

As they huddle, talking quietly, Emily, Sarah, Chloe, and Sally White come into the den with pitchers of lemonade and iced tea that they set down on the wet bar. I move into the den with them. Sally announces to everyone, "I brought in some cold drinks if anyone is interested. Please help yourselves. Matt says dinner should be done shortly."

The girls see Violet over with Uncle Timmy. They come to stand near me, as I gaze into the fireplace. Not intentionally, I can overhear the conversation that is taking place between Violet and Uncle Timmy. I hear him express his concerns about Logan.

"Violet, I want to apologize for Logan," he says. "His drunken behavior was unacceptable. Unfortunately, since Hunter took Logan back to Jamaica, that leaves me with you and Stephen for the time being. I'll try to make myself scarce. Jim has offered to let me stay in one of the cottages attached to the inn. I hope you can accept my apology."

Violet looks at him tentatively. There is sad regret in his eyes.

"You have nothing to apologize for," she says. "It was Logan who made a fool of himself. What really concerns me, though, is the wad of money he had in his wallet." She raises her hands in the air. "I mean, really, did he actually sell his bike? Or was it that he went back and stole the treasure from the dive site after your brother died?

"I'll be honest with you, this whole situation scares the devil out of me," she adds as she takes a big breath and then exhales slowly.

Uncle Timmy grimaces. "That's my question, too, Violet," he replies. "I'm not sure where he got the money. You know, he's been hanging out with several dangerous, grungy characters lately. I know he's been gambling and I'm pretty sure he's been doing drugs again."

Uncle Timmy shakes his head with disgust. "He was in rehab a few years ago and I thought he had turned the tide but now I'm not so sure."

His weathered hand reaches out for hers as he notices her beautiful engagement ring. He brings her petite hand to his lip, gives it a kiss, and asks, "Oh, honey, have you got news for your Uncle Timmy? Here I am just blubbering on when I should be celebrating your engagement. Welcome to our family, my dear."

She takes his hand in hers. "Thank you. Stephen proposed last night. New Year's Eve—and, boy, was it a surprise!" She nervously laughs, looking down at her sparkling diamond ring. "He said the ring belonged to his mother and that he had been wanting to propose since he met me. It was so romantic." She looks away, dreaming back to last night.

Uncle Timmy pulls Violet into a big bear hug. "Oh, I'm so happy for you two. It's been such a dreadful year with all of the accidents and loss. You both deserve some happiness. You have become like a daughter to me over the past year," he says. He sadly looks away as he thinks about losing his brother and how Violet is still grappling with last year's loss of both her parents.

Violet smiles sadly. "Yes, it was quite a year. I hope this year is much better than last year."

She notices the guys returning and points toward the door. "Oh, look, here's Stephen now. I figured he would have told you that we got engaged last night."

Stephen reaches their side just as Uncle Timmy explains what happened at the boat the night before. "You see, right after you left, we had a huge disagreement with Logan and that's when I told Hunter to take him back home. Stephen was so upset with Logan that he wasn't thinking happy thoughts at the time, and neither was I."

Uncle Timmy pauses. "I'll catch a flight back to the island later. I am really worried that my son has gotten himself hooked up with some pretty evil fellows, real pirates," he says.

Stephen listens to his Uncle Timmy as he puts his arm around Violet. "I'm sorry, honey, that I didn't let you know Uncle Timmy would be joining us for a while. I figured it would be better if I explained it in person," Stephen says. "I don't think Uncle Timmy had anything to do with all the tragedy that happened over the past year."

Stephen looks at his new fiancée and he exhales a deep breath that he didn't even realize he was holding. Violet lightly kisses him on his bearded cheek. "Your uncle was just updating me on what has been happening but not all the details. You can tell me about that later," she says.

Uncle Timmy swats his nephew on his back.

"Congratulations on your engagement! You have picked a winner," he says. "I was just telling Violet how I think of her like a daughter."

The three happily hug each other. "I only wish my brother—your father—was here to see this," Uncle Timmy tells Stephen. "He would have been thrilled."

Stephen nods in agreement. "He would have been so happy." He puts his arm around Violet. "He really loved you like a daughter, too."

Violet turns to Stephen, and I overhear her telling him about our upcoming trip. "Speaking of weddings, the girls and I are going to take a flight to my parent's condo in Florida to find my mother's old wedding gown so that I can have it altered to fit me," she says. "I figure I can meet you back in Jamaica after that. Didn't you say you had to get back for a fishing charter after next week?"

Chapter 33

Old and New Friends

Dinner is served and what a lovely time we have celebrating the New Year and Stephen and Violet's new engagement.

Emily, Sarah, Sally, Chloe, Violet, and I confirm our plan to leave the next morning for Violet's home in the Florida Keys. Luckily, we know a pilot, Billy Alexander, Thomas and George's cousin. Billy can fly us from here to the Keys. I sense Violet's sadness but also her excitement about the upcoming wedding.

"My parents bought the condo in the Keys about five years before their boating accident last April. We moved around a lot when I was growing up, so I never had many close friends," she says as she sweeps her eyes across all of us. "It's so nice to be included in your little group."

She smiles then continues. "We can go to my house, find the wedding dress, and I can show you around town." She nudges Emily. "Maybe we can even have a bachelorette party for you, Emily. After living in the Keys for the past few years, I know a couple of nice restaurants and tiki bars."

Emily smiles and blushes, uncomfortable with being the center of attention. "Okay, that's cool—as long as you don't make me wear a tiara or a sign saying 'Bride.' I really feel silly when people look at me. Sometimes Sarah will make me wear a boa when it's my birthday and I feel ridiculous."

Sarah laughs and wraps her arm around her sister. "I promise we won't do anything that bothers you. Anyway, I haven't had time to prepare for things like that—I'll have to save them for Angie's bachelorette party."

I grimace, remembering how last year on my birthday she made me wear a tiara and a birthday boa. I turn toward Sarah and say, "Really, Sarah? Ugh! Do I have to?"

Emily, Sarah, and I laugh hysterically remembering back to my last birthday. I catch my breath and tell Violet and Chloe the birthday story.

"Last year I fell off the pier at SmacNally's, and I almost strangled myself in the water with that crazy boa. Thomas had to jump in the water after me. Boy, did it cause quite the scene!" I wipe the tears that are streaming down my face from laughing so hard. "I still don't know how I did it. I mean, I just bent over the piling to look at a duck and the next thing I knew I was in the water. I hadn't even had but a sip of my strawberry mimosa yet."

Holding her sides and still giggling at the memory, Emily adds, "Yeah, we aren't the most coordinated group of girls, are we?"

My sister, Sally, thinking to Sarah's Oxford Brew in the bay incident, agrees. "Yeah, the Harriott and White girls are a tad bit clumsy if I do say so myself. What is our risk level down in the Keys?"

Violet smiles then declares, "I'll make sure there is a rail on the docks that we go to!"

Once the laughter settles down a bit, Violet adds, "I think it will be great fun with all of you ladies, and I'll get to show you some of the spots that the locals love."

Chapter 34

The Keys

We finish dinner and all head home for an early night. We plan to meet Billy at the Ocracoke Airport at 7:30 a.m.

Morning arrives and I shower quickly and get ready to go. Thomas is already up. He kisses me goodbye and heads out the door with Max. He's going to a job at Sue and Bob's house to finish their deck and gazebo.

I grab the bag I packed the night before just as I hear a knock at the door and Emily's voice. "We're here and ready to go!" she says.

I open the door to see Emily standing in the doorway in a bright pink tank top and her purple flannel shirt. "Have you spoken to Billy yet?" I ask her. "Is he going to be ready when we get there?"

Emily nods. "It's all set. He told me to have all of us at the Ocracoke Airport at 7:30. It's 7:15 now and the other girls are in the truck ready and waiting to go. This is going to be so much fun."

I close the pretty oak door behind me, making sure to lock it as we walk out through the cozy screened-in porch. This is the life, I think to myself. I mean, how many people can hop on a plane for a couple of days at a beautiful tropical beach?

We both climb into the back seat of Sally's blue Ford Explorer. I bellow out a greeting. "Hello, ladies. Let's get this party started."

They all laugh at me and whoop-whoop to my comment. I lean over the seat before I buckle in and ask my sister a question. "Sally, how are you doing with leaving the twins? This is your first away trip without them, right?"

Sally turns around in the seat to answer me. "You know, Angie, it's funny, part of me is sooo excited but another part of me will really miss those two little boogers. Don't get me started. You should have seen me when I went to leave this morning. You would have thought that we were going away for a month, not just a couple days."

Violet pops in with an announcement. "I promise you, Sally—and the rest of you girls—that it's going to be a busy few days. The time will fly," she says. "After I went back to the boat last night, I went online and got reservations at Snapper's Restaurant for tonight. It has a tiki bar."

She pulls out her phone. "Then tomorrow, I'll take you girls to John Pennekamp Coral Reef State Park where we can snorkel, scuba, or go out in the glass bottom boat. This is what the park looks like," she says as she passes the phone around, open to photos on the park website. "Does that sound like a good plan to you girls?"

Emily is looking at the pictures as she chimes in. "Oh yeah, this sounds awesome. We may even be able to practice our scuba diving, ladies," she says. She looks at Violet and Chloe as she adds, "Sarah, Angie, and I took lessons and went scuba diving for the first-time last month when we went to Cat Island. It was so cool."

I respond with excitement. "That sounds like so much fun. Chloe and Violet, do you know how to scuba dive, too?"

Violet answers my question first. "Yeah, I go with Stephen all the time since I started living on his boat. Sometimes I even help with his scuba diving tours when his cousin, Hunter, can't make it."

Violet turns to Chloe and asks, "What about you, Chloe?"

Chloe answers with exuberance. "Oh, I am a *big* fan of snorkeling and scuba diving. John and I took lessons a couple years back and did some scuba diving when we went to Aruba for our honeymoon two years ago," she says. "Scuba diving in the Keys sounds like great fun. It's just a shame my college friend on Ocracoke—our mutual friend Cindy—had to work at the hospital and couldn't join us."

We arrive at the airport and climb out of the SUV with all our bags. Billy rushes over to help us with the luggage. Emily, Sarah, Sally, and I hug him. I thank him and then introduce him to Violet and Chloe.

Emily continues to offer our appreciation. "We're so lucky that you are able to do this on such short notice, Billy. Thanks so much."

Billy smiles. "No problem. I always love a trip to the Keys, and I decided to turn this one into a quick vacation. I have a few friends down there that I'm going to visit." He chuckles then continues. "How many people get paid for going on vacation?"

Violet laughs along with him. "Who are the people you're going to be staying with," she asks. "Maybe I know them?" Billy's still smiling as he answers. "I doubt it since they're from Miami, but their names are Mary and Harry. Mary is actually from Maryland, too, and she knows Angie. That is how I met them—on one of my visits to D.C. to see Matt and Thomas."

Violet nods. "It's a small world. And get this, I know a Mary and Harry from Miami. Maybe we do know the same people! Are they coming to Key Largo, too, or are you going to Miami?" she asks.

Billy shakes head and runs his fingers through his curly blonde hair. "They bought a little condo on the beach a few years back and it just so happens they're planning to be in the Keys this week. What are the chances of that?

"Their last name is Bradley. Does that ring a bell?" Billy asks Violet.

She shakes her head. "Drat. I don't think I know their last name. We've just met casually."

He throws the bags into the cargo hold and opens the hatch to let us into the plane. "Your chariot awaits you, ladies. It should take us about an hour or so to get to the airport in the Keys."

We all climb in and take our seats. "Can I be your copilot, boss?" Emily asks. "I don't know what help I can be, but I've always wanted to say that."

Grinning, Billy hands her a pair of headphones. "I'll give you your first lesson in flying," he tells her.

She looks like the cat that swallowed the canary as she puts on the headphones and gives him a thumbs up.
"Cool, dude."

Billy runs through his preflight checklist with Emily and shows her how to work the controls. She is in seventh heaven. She turns around to us to say, "Guys, I think I might get my pilot's license. For real! Just think how helpful it would be if I could fly us everywhere we wanted to be."

We laugh and yell back at her, "Sweet Dreams!"

The flight is as quick as Billy said it would be, and before too long we are coming to a controlled screech on the runway at the little Marathon airport. When we get out of the plane, Violet tells us that she has an Uber coming for us. "They should be here any minute, according to the app," she says. "I just love these Ubers. They are so handy."

We help Billy pull our luggage out of the cargo hold and hug him goodbye, thanking him. Emily squeezes his shoulder. "Thanks for my flying lesson and the plane ride here," she says. "They don't believe me, but I'm serious about learning to fly. I'll have to get with you later and see what it takes to get flying lessons."

Billy nods, smiles, and tells us, "You guys are laughing, but I can easily see Emily getting her pilot's license." He points to an SUV pulling up. "That must be your Uber," he says. "Harry and Mary are picking me up in a few minutes. I'll see you girls back here on Friday."

We thank him again before we get into the van to take us to Violet's condo, and we wave goodbye as we drive off.

I can tell Violet is anxious, even before she nervously says, "I haven't been back here since my parent's funeral. Luckily, we had good neighbors who have been kind of watching the place."

It is a leisurely drive to Violet's home, taking about an hour in the large SUV. The Uber driver offers to take us wherever we want to go while we're on Key Largo. Violet exchanges contact information with him, then asks: "Can you pick us up here around 5 p.m.? We have dinner reservations at Snapper's at 5:30."

He answers in a slow melodic voice, and you can tell he's on island time. "Sure, man, whatever you need. My chariot awaits you ladies," he says with a wink after he pulls down his Ray-Bans.

Violet nods and gives him a thumbs up. Then she turns to us as we stand looking up at the beautiful building where we've been dropped off.

"Here we are at my humble abode. We're in a condo on the second floor overlooking the Atlantic," she says. She reaches into her faded blue jeans shorts and pulls out a key. "This is it. It's been so long since I have been back," she says as she unlocks the main door. "I guess I should really just sell it or rent it out or something," she adds as an afterthought.

We follow her into the building, dragging our duffel bags behind us, and she shows us to our rooms. "Angie, I put you and Sally in this one," she says, pointing. "Emily and Sarah, I've got you in the other room, and I figured Chloe and I can bunk in my room.

"Settle in and help yourself to anything you want. I have groceries coming in the next hour or so. There will be fresh fruit and Danish for our breakfast brunch. I'm going to get some coffee going."

Sally and I drop our bags in our bedroom and meet the other girls out in the living room where Violet has opened up the French doors leading out onto the patio. She spreads her arms wide as she shows us the view

255

from her deck. "It's really quite lovely all year round. I always enjoy sitting out here. My neighbors hired someone to clean it while I was away," she tells us.

The doorbell rings and we hear a knock. Violet calls out as she heads toward the door. "Oh, that must be our groceries. I didn't order a whole lot since we weren't going to be here that long, only a couple days."

I hear her grabbing the groceries. I go to offer my help in putting them in the beautifully decorated kitchen. "Here let me take a couple of those bags from you," I say. "Umm. Something smells good. Is that a quiche?"

She nods as she answers. "It's a surprise. I think I remember someone saying that they like quiche and fresh pineapple," Violet says. "We've also got lots of baked goods. No dieting this week."

I smile appreciatively at all the goodies. "I didn't even realize I was hungry," I say. "And, oh boy, does that coffee smell heavenly."

Violets hollers for the others to come in and fix themselves a brunch plate. "Girls, get it while it's hot," she announces. "Lots of yummy breakfast food. I don't know about you all, but I'm starving."

We take our over-piled plates out to the gorgeous deck and sit at the ornately decorated outdoor table. Violet speaks first as she sits down. "I just want to thank you all for coming here with me. This is just so hard. You wouldn't believe how I have been dreading this day." Sally, who is sitting closest to Violet, reaches over to take her hand. Sally and I both remember how it was when we lost our father.

"Believe me, Angie and I know exactly how you are feeling," Sally says. "We lost our father more than a year ago in October, but it still feels like yesterday. I'll tell you, too, that even though it hurts when I think about him, it's getting better."

Across the table from my sister and Violet, I nod. I'm thinking about my last visit to our family home in Ripley, Maryland.

"I remember the very last time my mom, brother, and I went to pack up our old house," I say. "It was before we moved to Ocracoke Island permanently. It was heartbreaking. Please know that we are all here for you."

Violet looks so sad as she responds. "Thanks, girls. This really means a lot to me," she says. After a few minutes, she asks, "When we finish eating, do you guys want to see my mother's wedding dress? I can't wait to see how well it matches the veil and handbag you're letting me borrow.

"We need to go into the study to see the dress," she says.

Chapter 35

A Warning from Above

Emily, Sarah, Chloe, Sally, and I go into the room that Violet has pointed to, and we stand next to a huge golden oak desk. It looks masculine to me.

"I wonder if this was her father's desk," I say, quietly. "I remember how hard it was when Matt, Mom, and I went back to our old house in Ripley to finish packing for the move to Ocracoke Island. I was a nervous wreck, and it was heartbreaking. My father's desk… oh that was hard to pack up because I just kept imagining him sitting at it."

I turn to the girls just as Violet returns holding the precious veil and antique ivory beaded handbag that belonged to Sarah and Emily's great grandmother. I'm so happy she agreed to borrow them for her wedding. Violet looks sad. I know she is thinking about her parents.

"Violet, I know this is hard," I tell her. "Last year around this time my mom, Matt, and I went to our old home to deal with our dad's belongings. I thought my heart would shatter in thousand pieces."

Sally moves over and places her arm around me as she picks up the conversation thread. "I had just started teaching at the little Ocracoke Island School so I couldn't go help. I felt so bad that I couldn't be there for you guys."

I give my sister a quick peck on the cheek. "It's okay, Sally. We knew you couldn't take time off after just starting a new job."

I continue with the story. "My mom had already packed up the majority of my father's belongings, so we just had his office to take care of. This was just after we were first introduced to Evangeline's spirit. Little did we know that she would visit us at our old home that day." I pause for a minute, thinking back to that day like it was yesterday.

My mother comes out of my dad's office. She is holding a tiny cedar box, the same one that once held the necklace my father gave me. "Look what I found in your father's office," she says. "It looks just like the boxes we found that belonged to Evangeline."

My brother and I are amazed to see that the box she is carrying is identical to the ones we found on the island over the summer, the little boxes that held clues from Evangeline. I reach out to take the box from my mom. "I remember the vision that we had on the day dad gave me the necklace that belonged to Evangeline," I say.

As I grasp the small coffer in my hand, a vision of Evangeline appears before us.

"The treasure is close to being found," Evangeline's spirit says. "You must be very careful on your adventure as there could be peril. Beware of the caverns and tunnels. They could be dangerous. Keep the clues a secret. There are threats around every corner." Then she vanishes before our eyes.

I remember searching through the box. "Look, there are other jewels. Here's a gorgeous garnet hair comb. There's an emerald broach, a pearl necklace, and a diamond ring in here," I tell my mother and Matt. "Hey, these gold coins look just like the ones we found under the floorboard at Evangeline's cottage! When Dad gave me the heart pendant, he told me it was among other keepsakes passed down through the generations for the last two hundred and fifty years."

Matt then rifles through the box and, unbelievably, holds up a small notebook with Evangeline's name on the cover.

"Do you think this was Evangeline's diary?" I ask him and my mother.

Matt smiles and hands me the journal. "This should help you write your novel about Evangeline. I can't understand why Dad never shared these things with us."

I tell the girls about the memory.

"You see, when we were at the house in Ripley, Evangeline came to visit us after my mom found the box that held Evangeline's precious silver heart necklace. Evangeline explained that the time was right for us to find the treasure. It was crazy."

I take a deep breath and continue. "And that wasn't all that happened while we were there. We found out that my dad could visit us and protect us just like Evangeline had been doing. I finally got to say goodbye to my dad." I feel a tear slide down my cheek. "That night when I went to go to bed in my childhood bedroom, my father's spirit came to see me. He helped me remember all the precious times we had spent together."

I finish telling them about the dream about my dad. "I watched just like it was a movie of my life, with all the times my dad was there for me— from scraping my knee when I was learning how to ride a bike, to ice cream after losing a tee ball game. I even got to see him proudly watch me with tears in his eyes when I won the songwriter's award that started my career as a country music artist."

Violet starts to sob. Tears run wildly down her tender face. "It's just awful. I didn't get to say goodbye," she says. "When the boat exploded, there was nothing anyone could do to save either one of my parents. I relived that nightmare every night for months after the explosion."

She frantically rubs the tears from her cheeks. "I never got to say goodbye. That was the hardest part," she repeats.

After a quiet minute, she continues speaking. "Stephen's boat was, luckily, docked at another one of the piers but we were close enough for us to see my parents' boat. Stephen had to stop me from running to try to rescue them. It was the worst thing I have ever been through in my whole life. My family was gone and there wasn't a thing I could do about it. I was devastated."

She has a vacant stare as she finishes telling us about that day. "The fire department, police, and EMS arrived, but my parents were both burned beyond recognition." Violet gasps for air, turns her head, and takes my hand. "Do you think I could get my parents' spirits to visit me, just like your dad visited you?"

All the girls turn to me, wondering what I'll say. "I don't know what's possible, Violet," I tell her. "But maybe we could get Evangeline and Old Emily and my dad to bring them through—you know, like a medium does at a séance or reading."

"It's worth a try," my sister, Sally, says. "We can always ask."

I agree and tell them that I'll try to get my father to come to us right now. I quietly speak into the room, not sure if this is even possible. "Dad, are you there? Evangeline, Old Emily, are you there? We need your help."

A mist envelopes the den and all three spirits materialize before us. Chloe and Violet are not used to having spirits just appear like this and both look scared. I step forward to speak to the ghosts.

"Can you help us?" I ask them. "Violet, our friend, lost her parents last year to a violent explosion on their boat. She wants to say goodbye. Is this something you could help us make happen?"

The three ghosts turn to each other, and we hear them murmuring to one another in low voices. After they confer, my father answers my question. "Normally, we aren't allowed to get involved in things like this, but we feel that you all need to hear what her parents have to say," he tells us.

He closes his eyes and calls to Violet's mother and father. "Alfred and Abigail Morgan, mother and father to Violet Morgan, we ask for your presence. By the powers that be, please make your auras appear before us."

I hear a swish and two apparitions materialize before us. All of us are surprised and step back except for Violet, who reaches out. Her hand passes through the ghostly mist of her parents. She sadly voices her love for them. "Mom, Dad, is that you? I can feel your love all around me."

A whisper of her mother's hand glances her cheek as her father responds. "Oh, honey. We miss you and love you. We can only stay for a brief second to say goodbye to you. Know that we will always be in your heart and that these three spirits will help protect you from the evil characters that lurk around you." He points to the ghosts of Evangeline, Old Emily, and my father as he continues his message from the beyond.

"Now, you must listen carefully to what I have to tell you. It's a warning from above, a communique, a premonition of what has been and what could be if you don't heed this advice. Your mother and I should still be with you. I know this in my heart." He reaches his strong hands toward her. "One of Stephen's relatives must have disconnected the blower and fuel line on our boat to have such a massive firebomb of an explosion. It shouldn't have happened. I am just not sure which one is responsible.

"You also must know something else—and I am sure of this—a small hole was punctured in Stephens's father's airline, causing him to perish." Violet gasps as her father adds, "We must go now as the veil is thin. We left a letter for you in the closet in the event we weren't here for the day you get married." The ghostly images of Violet's parents vanish from our sight.

Violet looks heartbroken as she wipes her tearstained face. We gather around to hug her tightly, but we know we can't take away that type of pain. Only time can lessen her grief. She suddenly cries out to the missing apparitions.

"Don't go. Please. I need you. I'm all alone now."

My father's spirit comes to stand before Violet. Pointing to Evangeline's and Old Emily's ghosts, he states, "Know that we will protect you and that you have found a new family with these girls who stand with you in times of grief and times of happiness." He turns to face Sally and me. "Girls, listen to what the Morgans have foretold. I can feel the evil negative auras around Stephen's relatives, but I am not sure about all of them. I feel like there is only one wicked soul among them, but time will tell."

He pauses and then adds, "For now, beware of the Bells. I feel danger lurking around them." He throws us a kiss.
"I love you girls. Please heed what I say. I must go now."

His spirit and the ghosts of Evangeline and Old Emily fade away, leaving us all dismayed at the warning.

I am the first to speak, and I take a gigantic breath before the words come out. "Oh my, this reminds me of last year when we got the warnings about the caves," I say to Violet and the girls. "But what about the accusations from Violet's parents? Do you girls really think that one or all of Stephen's relatives could have been responsible for the deaths of Stephen's and Violet's parents?"

Violet tries desperately not to cry as she answers me. "I feel it in my bones that neither one of those disasters should have happened," she says, her voice and breathing ragged. She takes another deep breath and explains. "Number One, Stephen's father was obsessed with his diving equipment and safety. He always pushed us to make sure we checked our scuba gear before a dive." She continues, "Number Two, my father was anal about keeping his boat maintained. He was very safety conscious."

She paces around the small room and around us girls, desperate to remember the specific details of the two deadly incidents. "Both Stephen and I talked about our fathers' focus on safety. When the investigations ruled that they were accidents, I feel like we both had our own doubts."

She stops pacing and throws her hands up, exasperated. "I don't know. Good grief, it's just too much for me to wrap my head around. But even if we did think that someone was responsible, how would we prove it?"

I can tell that Emily, always the inquisitive one of our group, has been thinking. "I might have an idea," she says to Violet, "but I will have to let you know later."

I know Emily's wondering whether we can use the watch and telescope to travel or look back in time to both of the occurrences. Of course, she doesn't say this out loud because we haven't mentioned either item to Stephen or Violet.

I raise an eyebrow at Emily. "Hey, let's try to make this a happy day for Violet. We'll think about danger later." Facing Violet, I ask, "Do you want to pull out the wedding dress your mother found for you?"

Sarah, who loves weddings, is suddenly excited. "I can't wait to see your dress," she says. Violet opens the door of the office closet, reaches in and pulls out a white plastic garment bag. She unzips it and gently pulls out a beautifully beaded ivory wedding gown. She also finds an envelope, with her name on it. She gasps as she recognizes the handwriting.

"It's from my Mommy." She holds the treasured message from her mom close to her heart and exclaims. "This is crazy."

Chapter 36

The Dress and the Letter

She looks thoughtful, then props the envelope on the desk in the office. "I'll take a look at that in a minute," she says, lifting the beautiful A-line dress up against the front of her body. Sarah holds the ivory beaded handbag up next to the dress and beams.

"It's a perfect match!" she announces. "Did this dress belong to one of your relatives?"

Violet gazes down, mesmerized by how the dress and purse seem tailor-made for each other. "It's a dress that Mom found in the attic at her parent's home. It had a note that said it belonged to her grandmother—my great grandmother. I believe it was a gift from a relative of my great grandmother's somewhere in North Carolina."

Violet stops to recall what the note had said. "We lost touch with that side of the family so I'm not sure about all the details." She stands in front of a mirror on the back of the closet door and puts the veils on her wispy blond hair. "What do you think? The veil's a pretty good match, too, isn't it?"

Sarah looks at her amazed. "It's almost as if they were made for each other. Weird really," Sarah says. "Just curious—what was your grandmother's name? Our great grandmother's name was Patricia Albright."

Violet raises an eyebrow and looks at Sarah. "It was Albright. She was originally from North Carolina, but she married my grandfather and they moved to California. I think it was a cousin who gave her the dress as a wedding gift because she loved it so much. My relatives were very poor so she couldn't afford a dress."

Sarah and Emily both stare at each other, then Emily loudly blurts out. "Do you know what I think this means?"

Violet is taken aback by the emotional response from Emily, who continues talking. "My great grandmother gave away her wedding dress to a cousin of hers for the exact same reason you just mentioned!" Emily wildly runs her hands through her hair. "Violet, it means we might be related!"

Sarah is bursting with the same realization. "How cool would that be? We might be cousins, you, Emily, and me," she says to Violet.

Violet is overwhelmed by the news. Tears stream down her delicate cheeks, even as she starts to laugh. "Wow! Wouldn't that be crazy?"

Then she suddenly adds, "Wait! I know how to check. We have a family Bible around here somewhere."

She starts glancing around the office as she says, "Let me think. It's probably in this closet." She lays the heirloom wedding gown on the beautiful oak desk and starts moving things around in the office closet. With trembling hands, she pulls the out the Bible and places the family treasure beside the dress. She opens the cover of the delicate old Bible and carefully starts to turn the pages at the front of the book.

With shaky hands, she points to the family tree. "Oh my God! I can't believe this. Look—it's right here. We're related."

Sarah, Violet, and Emily squeal and hug each other. "You see? You really aren't alone," Emily tells Violet. "I can't wait to tell Mom and the others. I mean, what are the chances?

"That means you are related to the Old Emily, too," she continues, "so you have a special guardian angel watching over you."

Violet collapses into the desk chair and places her face in her hands. Tears are spilling and she stutters out a response. "You just don't know what this means," she says. "I have been feeling so alone. Now I know I'm not on my own any longer."

Sarah laughs. "Oh, believe me, girl, you have a *large* family. Even more, all this makes you related to Sally and Angie, too. Just think about it—Sarah is married to Matt, who is Angie and Sally's brother."

Sarah is grinning from ear to ear as she turns to Chloe. "So that means you are also related to Chloe since Angie and Sally are John's cousins."

We squeal with joy as we all do a group hug.

Violet can't control her broad smile. She is ecstatic. "I can't wait to tell Stephen! Boy, is he going to be surprised. Wow, wait, I guess that makes me distantly related to Stephen, too—somehow," she says with a laugh.

She picks up the wedding dress and holds it in front of her again. "This dress means even more to me now. It connects me to my entire family. I think it's time to try it on."

We fidget impatiently in her father's office while Violet is in the other room, slipping into the dress. Before long she waltzes back into the office. "Well, what do you think?"

We all gasp in surprise. The dress looks as if it were made for her. It's gorgeous. Sarah reaches over to place the matching veil on Violet's head. "This is perfect. I think it was meant to be," Sarah says. After a second, she adds, "I wonder why Evangeline and Old Emily didn't tell us that you were our cousin."

At that, the spirits of Evangeline and Old Emily appear before us, giggling and chatting to each other. Old Emily's spirit comes forward and answers Sarah's question. "Girls, I know you wonder why we didn't let you know that you were related. We needed you to become friends before you became family—and we wanted the time to be right."

Sarah nods her head. "I agree. I understand," she says before turning to Violet. "I'm glad we got to know you before we found out we were related. This way it means more to all of us."

Sarah barely finishes her sentence when Evangeline and Emily's spirits vanish before our eyes. We are all speechless for a moment, and then Violet remembers the letter from her mom. She picks up the envelope and gingerly pulls out the letter. Another piece of paper is attached to the letter. She takes a deep breath and reads the letter out loud to us.

Dearest Child,

If you are reading this letter, it means that your father and I aren't here to give you this precious wedding dress. It breaks my heart to know you won't walk down the aisle on your father's arm—something I have waited to see since you were a little girl.

When we embarked upon the journey to find your father's ancestor, Henry Morgan, we knew there would be risks. If you are reading this, it means we are gone because those risks were too real.

Stephen is a good man, and we are so glad that he makes you happy. We had hoped that one day you would find a man who would be not only your friend but your soulmate. We want you to know the joy and love of a marriage like the one we had and a family of your own one day.

I had the dress dry-cleaned and pressed before we left to meet you and Stephen's family to begin the quest to find Henry Morgan's treasure. Your father being your father, and always thinking ahead, made a copy of the treasure map. It is attached to this letter. We hope that you have a blessed life. We will love you always.

Happy treasure hunting, our beautiful daughter.

Our love always,

Mom and Dad

The letter is spattered with the tears that have fallen as Violet read it. We all have tears in our eyes as we listen to her mother's words and think of Violet's loss and grief. I am standing on one side of her and Sarah is on the other side. We each place a hand on her shoulders.

It takes Violet a few minutes to compose herself. When she does, she says, "I just can't believe they wrote this letter. It's almost as if they knew they wouldn't make it back home." She turns to me and wraps her arms around my waist as she sobs. Her tears soak my shirt.

Sarah runs to the kitchen and returns with a glass of water. "Here, drink this—or would you rather have something stronger?"

Violet shakes her head. "No, this is good. Thank you." She takes a sip. "I feel so drained. I think I need to lay down for a minute," she says. "You girls help yourselves to anything that's here. Let's try to leave for the park in an hour or so. How does that sound?"

We tell her that we're good just staying here with her at the condo if she wants. She shakes her head. "No, my Mom and Dad would want me to keep going and enjoy my life, and that's what I'm going to do. I think a day in the park will be just what the doctor ordered.

"Let's plan to leave here around 1 p.m. We can bring clothes with us to change at the park then head to the restaurant after we do some snorkeling or scuba diving, your choice. Later we can take a look at this map and share it with the others," she says.

Chapter 37

Scuba Fun

True to her word, Violet comes back out of her room in less than an hour to take us on an adventure at the John Pennekamp Coral Reef State Park. I can tell she is trying to put up a brave front. "You know, Violet, it really is okay if you'd rather just hang out. I remember how Sally and I felt after we lost our father."

She firmly shakes her head. "No, girls. I'm fine really. I have shed so many tears over the past year. I know my parents wouldn't want me to be sad," she says. "I ordered us an Uber and it should be here in about 15 minutes. I figure—if you want—we can shower and get ready at the park for dinner rather than coming back here. That will give us more time to stay at the park."

Emily perks up to answer. "If you're sure, we are up for it. We've already packed up our duffle bags, so we're ready to go," she says. "While you were resting, we pulled up the website on Angie's laptop. The park looks awesome. It sounds like we're going to have some great fun."

Emily hugs her new cousin and Violet seems more upbeat.

We all go downstairs to wait for the Uber. Once we're in the vehicle, Violet gives us a guided tour of the touristy sites we're passing as we make the short ride from her condo to the park. "One day, hopefully, the whole gang can come down here and we'll do a proper tourist visit instead of a quick trip to the Keys."

She points to one of her favorite restaurants as we pass it. "Sharkey's Sharkbite Grill is one of the best on the island," she says. "There are so many places to go and things to do here."

Sarah turns to Emily. "Are you sure you don't want to get married in the Keys? Or are you down for a Cat Islandand-Shanna's Cove Resort wedding?"

Emily thinks about the question. "I don't know. George and I still need to figure out what we want to do," she says. "I won't rule out something different. Mostly, we just both know we don't want to do anything huge, just family and maybe a few friends."

Sarah smiles at her sister. "I totally understand that. And we all know that you don't like being the center of attention."

Sarah is thinking about her wedding to my brother, Matt, on Cat Island. "In many ways, Cat Island is ideal for the type of wedding you and George have talked about, especially since there are only five bungalows," Sarah tells her sister. "Oh, and the beaches are spectacular. Plus, Shanna's Cove Resort is so quaint. Gregor and Maria are perfect hosts, and that gourmet food they served every night for dinner was to die for."

Emily smiles and nods. "We'll see what happens and see what George wants to do," she replies. "We might need to go back there to follow some clues from Anne Bonny since she lived there for a couple years before moving to South Carolina."

Chloe joins in. "You know, when Billy drops me off in Charleston on the way back, we should really go to Anne's home and meet John's great grandmother, Bertha. She's quite the character—and still sharp. I can't believe she is 100 years old.

"What do you girls think about taking a quick trip to see her?" she asks. "Billy told me he wanted to go visit some friends since he was dropping me off. John should already be home by the time we get there, and he can take us there to see her."

We pull down the drive to the park's entrance. The Uber driver drops us off at the front gate. "So, I'll pick you girls up here at 4:45 p.m. to take you to Snapper's Restaurant in time for your reservation," he tells us.

"Sounds perfect," Violet says as we climb out of the van. "Over here, girls," Violet says as she points toward the scuba shop where we need to pick up our gear for our 1:30 p.m. outing. "I think you are really going to love the coral reefs that they take us to. They are so colorful."

We get our equipment and head to the water. We board the open bow boat and before long we drop anchor. We roll over the edge of the white boat to enter the balmy aqua water. I give a thumbs up and follow Violet to the closest coral reef. We swim past and through muted greens and brilliant blues, gliding among the yellow and blue tangs that move around the reef.

Violet leads us toward an underwater cave. She points to an eroded iron anchor as we enter the cavern. This place is like nothing I have ever seen before. Tiny tenacle-like arms of coral flutter in glorious colors, from bright yellow to dazzling blue. We are all amazed at the beauty surrounding us. Bright blue and brilliant red algae line the craggy cavernous area while orange and white
Clown anemonefish peep in and out of the dark crevices.

Time flies and, too soon, it's time to return to the surface. We all have loved the awesome underwater experience. "That was so cool," Sarah says to Violet on the boat ride back to shore. "Angie, Emily, and I haven't had a chance to do any dives around coral reefs before. I couldn't believe all the vibrant colors we saw. It was like being inside a kaleidoscope." Sarah is beaming as she relives the dive.

Back on dry land, we grab our belongings from the lockers the park has provided, and Violet guides us to the showers and dressing rooms. As we get ready, I make a suggestion. "I think the guys would really enjoy a trip to the Keys. We should ask them when we get home," I say.

Sally is immediately interested. "I truly believe that the guys would love this place. I agree—let's try to plan a trip here."

"That would be wonderful," Violet says, "and you could all stay at my condo. It's a four bedroom and the office has a pullout sofa-bed, plus there's an extra bedroom on Stephen's boat. It would be perfect."

Her phone dings with a text message. "Speaking of Stephen, this is him now," she says as she looks down at her phone. "Oh, he says he's going to sail Uncle Timmy back home to Jamaica and find out what the deal is with Logan. He'll give me a call tomorrow."

She looks a little apprehensive. "I just hope everything is alright with that situation. I don't trust that, Logan. He hangs with some pretty shady characters," Violet says. "I worry about Stephen—especially after what happened to his father and my parents."

She picks up her bright purple duffle bag and swings it over her shoulder. "Whatever. Let's not think about that now," she says, changing the subject. "I think you're really going to like Snapper's."

We nod in agreement, grab our things, and go out to meet the Uber, which is already waiting for us. "Hi, girls. How was your dive?" the driver asks us. "I bring my girlfriend, Scarlet, here on the weekends sometimes. She really loves the glass-bottomed boat ride. You should try it sometime."

"Maybe next time we come down here," Emily says. She then turns to Sarah. "You know you might be right, Sis. I think a wedding in the Keys could be perfect for George and me. Like being on island time, you know. I love the laidback feel of Key Largo. Getting married here would make it our special day and place."

Sarah, sitting next to her in the Uber van, pats Emily on the shoulder. "I'm sure they do destination weddings here." She turns to Violet and asks: "Do you know of any wedding planners in the area?"

Violet nods her head. "As a matter of fact, one of the girls from Snapper's Restaurant is a wedding planner. If she's working tonight, we could ask while we're there. I know people have had their receptions right at the restaurant."

The Uber driver pulls up to the entrance of Snapper's Restaurant. He gets out of the van to let us out, "Just call me when you are ready to be picked up," he says. He waves goodbye as he drives off.

We wave back to him as Violet takes a deep breath and says, "Well, here goes, girls. I hope you like the food and atmosphere as much as Stephen and I did the last time we were here." She checks us in with the receptionist. "Table for six. We have reservations under the name of Violet," she tells the hostess.

The hostess scans down the guest list. "Here we are. Your table is ready. The waitress will let you know about the specials we have for now, but I suggest you try the Funky Monkey Citrus Punch. It's the bomb."

The hostess guides us to our table overlooking the bay, which captivates us with its soft azure color. Almost immediately, our perky raven-haired waitress appears, her arms covered in intricate tropical flower tattoos. "Welcome, ladies. What can I get you girls to drink?"

Violet answers. "The hostess says the Funky Monkey drink is good. What do you think?"

"Awesome choice. And for food, I recommend the fish tacos or the grilled mahi-mahi over a bed of wild brown rice with a pineapple mango salsa. It's one of my favorites." The waitress then points to an item on the menu. "The coconut shrimp are also really good."

We place our orders for drinks and while we wait for those to appear, we look over the menu and decide to share several appetizers as our dinner. We laugh and tell jokes and stories, recalling our antics over the years.

Emily tells the girls the story about how we used to have bonfires on the beach, watch for falling stars, and take midnight swims off the warm shores of Ocracoke Island. "Every summer, Sally, Angie, and Matt would visit. We had such fun times growing up. We would go to the point most nights when they visited. There was always a big crowd." Emily points to me. "Angie usually brought along her guitar, and we would sing around the bonfire. She always told the story of Evangeline and Jacob and how Evangeline was kidnapped by Daniel Teach, Blackbeard's grandson."

Emily leans over and whispers to us. "Who would have ever thought that one day we would actually meet their ghosts, and they would lead us to Blackbeard's treasure."

Sarah laughs and picks up the reminiscing from her sister. "It was those nights on the beach that made me know I would marry Matt, or I always dreamed it, anyways. So sometimes dreams do come true," she says. "On those beach outings, George always sat close to Emily, but never touching. I'm so happy that they finally got together."

Sally chimes in. "You could always tell that they belonged together. It just took you nearly being killed, Emily, before he opened his eyes," she says.

Chloe and Violet raise their eyebrows in alarm. "What are you talking about, Sally?" Chloe asks. "I haven't heard this story. Tell us."

Sally starts to tell the story then turns to me. "I wasn't actually there when it happened. Angie, why don't you tell the story."

I start by telling them about Shanna's Cove Resort. "We all went to Cat Island in the Bahamas for Matt and Sarah's wedding and to search for Blackbeard's treasure." I pull up the resort's website on my phone and show them some of the pictures. "It was absolutely the most beautiful resort and island you ever wanted to see. We stayed at Shanna's Cove Resort and the owners, Gregor and Maria, were the most accommodating and gracious hosts you would ever want to meet." I laugh and point at Sarah. "Well, apart from Sarah's great work as the hostess at the inn, of course!

"The wedding was charming, and this was the first time George had ever seen Emily in a dress," I continue. "He was floored, to say the least. Then the trouble started."

She rolls her eyes when she remembers the incident. "The sparks were flying between the two of them until Sandy, a little twit, one of the groomsmen's girlfriends, started flirting with George. He really hurt Emily by flirting back with her."

Emily nods and I continue my story. "Furious, Emily takes off through the woods and we couldn't find her. She was headed to the cave and the waterfall where Evangeline used to take young William."

I take a deep breath and finish telling the tale. "Luckily, George had put a tracer on her phone after I was kidnapped and he hadn't taken it off yet, so we were able to find her location." I build up the tension. "When we got to the spot, we found her phone and her lonesome silver sandal in the sand in the cavern—but Emily was nowhere to be found."

I let out my breath, remembering that day. "We were at a loss. We had no idea where she was. But then we heard a mumbling coming from behind the wall of the cave. Luckily, I remembered from one of my dreams how there was a hidden entrance to another section of the cave."

I mimic pushing on the wall. "George was beside himself. Thomas, George, and I pushed really hard, and the wall finally budged open, exposing Emily, who was trapped behind it."

I run my hands through my wavy black hair. "We thought she was dead. She was so still, and her head was bent down. It was very dark, pitch black, and George rushed to reach her first. He picked her up and, to our horror, we saw a pit of spikes with a skeleton three feet from where she had landed. It was so scary. She was so lucky that she wasn't killed."

Emily dreamily reveals the rest of the story. "George lifted me up in his arms. He had tears in his eyes, and he told me how much he loved me and never wanted to lose me. He apologized for flirting with Sandy. We kissed an amazing dreamy steamy kiss."

She sighs and hugs herself. "And you guys know the rest. We got engaged and haven't been apart since that worst and best day of my life."

Violet smiles and says, "You two act like you have been together forever. It's hard to believe you two just got together in December."

"I had the same thought," Chloe says.

Sarah laughs as she explains, "That's because they have been best friends all this time but were afraid that if they crossed the friendship line it would ruin their friendship. So silly, the two of them." She ruffles her sister's strawberry blonde hair.

Chloe calls the waitress over so we can each order shots of limoncello to toast to Emily's engagement and wedding. The tangy shots arrive, and the girls make an 'Up Yours' toast, leaving us all laughing hysterically.

Then Chloe says to Emily. "May your love be never-ending and your friendship last forever. Cheers! Er, I mean 'Up Yours,' as you girls would say."

Violet, exhausted from the emotional day, glances at her watch. "Are you ladies ready to call it a night? Sorry, Emily, I didn't see the waitress who is also a wedding planner tonight. I will try to contact her later," she asks us. "I can call the Uber to pick us up. We can continue this at home if you want."

Sally, the practical one among us, seconds the idea. "Yes, time to head back to the condo. We have to meet Billy at the airport tomorrow at 9 a.m.," she says. "Boo! I can't believe we leave tomorrow, but I'm so glad that I was able to join you girls. Just a few more days then school starts."

Sally then turns toward Chloe. "When does your school start back? Our classes begin on Monday."

Chloe nods in agreement. "We're back in the classroom on Monday, too. In some ways, it feels like the holiday break just started but in other ways—because so much has happened—it feels like it's been going on a long time." We all concur.

Violet texts the Uber guy and he texts back that he's already waiting outside. "He said he figured we would be ready soon, so instead of picking up another ride he decided to wait for us," Violet explains. "Let's go."

We divide the bill, pay the tab, and head outside for our ride. Violet looks up at the sky. "We can sit out on the patio when we get home if anyone wants," she says.

No one wants the night to end. When we reach the condo, we thank the Uber driver, give him a good tip, and request a pickup in the morning to take us back to Billy's plane.

Chapter 38

A New Map

Violet slides the brass key into the white condo door and swings it open. "Let me get you guys a drink. We have beer, White Claw, and a chilled bottle of white wine."

"Why don't we have a glass of wine to end our evening," I suggest.

I help her get the wine glasses down from the oak kitchen cabinets. The other girls have made their way out to the patio.

Violet opens the refrigerator door, and reaches into the wine cooler, pulls out a bottle, and hands it to me. "Angie, can you open this for me? I'll grab some pretzels just in case anyone wants a little snack."

I pop open the bottle of chardonnay and pour the wine into the delicate crystal goblets. "These are so pretty. Where did you get these?" I ask her. "I have been looking for something just like these for our new house."

Violet chuckles. "That's good to know. Didn't you say you're getting married in June? They would make a great wedding gift."

The two of us carry the glasses of wine out to the terrace. Sally takes a sip from her glass. "Umm, what a perfect way to end the evening," she says, gazing up at the night sky. "So Violet, what are your plans when we leave tomorrow? Do you have to work?"

Violet points to the living room. "I really need to clear out some more of the things from my parents that I'm not going to use. I managed to get a lot done the last time I was here," she says, "plus I want to let Stephen know about the map."

She stands up. "As a matter of fact, let me go get it. I want you girls to look at the map, too. I wonder if maybe I should make a copy of it to give to you for safekeeping."

Emily grimaces at what she is suggesting. "Let's just hope you won't have to worry about anything happening to you. But, sure, we can keep a copy in the secret room at the inn," she says.

Violet goes inside and then returns a few minutes later with the map. She spreads it out on the glass-topped patio table. "Well, here it is, my heritage. Did you know that Henry Morgan was not only a pirate but also a plantation owner and lieutenant governor of Jamaica?"

She takes a deep breath. "Look at this spot on the map. It shows an X at one of the sugar plantations that he owned," she says. "But I don't know about any buried treasure there. I did hear that they found what's left of a ship of his that capsized somewhere near Panama. Everyone's wondering if it carried treasure. It's also rumored that there was another ship in his fleet that they never found.

"Who knows?" she continues. "My father and Stephen's Uncle Timmy were researching everything when the accident occurred last April."

She wipes her watery eyes. "We stopped searching when my parents died because the treasure map went up in flames. There was nothing left of the boat. It was such a big explosion." Sarah is sitting next to Violet and puts her arm around her, squeezing her shoulder. "I'm so sorry. That must have been horrible," Sarah says.

Violet nods her head and covers her eyes with her trembling hands. "There was nothing any of us could do." She takes a deep breath. "That's enough of that." She looks at her phone. "Oh, my goodness, do you realize it's after one in the morning? I to need to go to bed. I want to make you girls a nice breakfast tomorrow."

Sally looks at her phone. "Wow, I haven't stayed up this late in years." She laughs. "Sometimes the twins wake me up this early, though." She puts her hand to her heart. "My little munchkins, I wonder how they are doing. Robert Facetimed me earlier and they were so cute. They looked like they actually were saying mama, even though I know it's way too early."

I smile and tell my sister. "They are such adorable babies and so precious. Of course, I'm a little biased."

We all agree it's time to call it a night. We take our wine glasses into the kitchen. "Breakfast at 8 a.m. if anyone is interested," Violet says. In unison, we all express our pleasure at the thought of a scrumptious breakfast. Then we say goodnight and head to bed.

Before I know it, the sun is shining brightly through the stained-glass window of the bedroom where I'm sleeping with my sister. Sally rolls over in bed holding her head. "Oh, I really am *not* used to going out and having so much fun."

I laugh, reaching for my phone to check the time. "Not since those babies of yours keep you up at night, anyway." After a pause, I add, "I bet you miss them and Robert. I know I would. For sure, I am missing Thomas and my fur baby, Max."

Sally stretches her slender arms above her head. "Yeah, I have had such a great time, but I sure do miss them." She sits up and slides her legs over the side of the bed. "Let's go get dressed and have breakfast. It'll be time to go before we know it."

In the kitchen, Violet is heating up the quiche from the local grocery store. All of us girls have filed into the kitchen, and we are sitting on stools around the pretty ivory-colored granite island. "I find that these quiches are some of the best I've had," Violet says. "They make them locally, and all I have to do is heat them up in the oven.

"There's fresh fruit salad on the island," she adds. "And help yourself to the coffee in the pot."

As we eat the delicious breakfast, I look at my rosecolored Apple watch. Our luggage is already sitting at the front door. "Oh no, it's almost 8:30. What time is the Uber guy supposed to pick us up?"

Violet looks at her phone. "He'll be here in fifteen minutes. Don't worry about the dishes. I'll clean up when I get back upstairs."

We meet our ride downstairs and say our goodbyes to Violet. I worry about leaving her alone after everything that she has been through since we got here. "Are you sure you're going to be okay," I ask her. "Know that you can call us anytime you need to talk."

Violet nods and looks solemn. "I'll be fine. I have Stephen and I know you girls are only a phone call away. Plus, I am not alone anymore— you are all my family now. That really makes a difference."

"Violet, come back and visit us soon on Ocracoke," Sarah says. "You are always welcome at the inn. You and Stephen will always have a place to stay—and when you come up, I'll help plan your wedding."

"Thanks, Sarah." Violet hugs us all goodbye. "Girls, it has been such a nice weekend."

Chapter 39

A Special Visit

It's a short flight to drop off Chloe and to meet John's great grandma in Charleston. It feels like we've barely boarded Billy's plane when we're coming in for a landing. John picks us up at the Charleston Airport. He kisses Chloe then helps grab our bags. "Hi, girls. How was your trip? Are you all ready to go meet Grandma Bertha—or Granny, as I call her?"

As John drives the half hour to Grandma Bertha's house in the little town of Goose Creek, we tell him about our trip to Key Largo. Chloe sits in the front seat of the SUV that John has rented so there's enough room for all of us. The rest of us are in the back. When we finish our travelog, John starts to tell us about his great grandmother. "My Granny is quite the character for her age. She's going to love telling you her stories about Anne Bonny."

Sally, sitting next to me, points out the window at the Spanish moss draped on the trees we're passing. "I know this is changing the subject, but are you girls seeing all this Spanish moss? I just love Spanish moss. I don't know why, but it fascinates me. It always reminds me of South Carolina.

"Do you know that some people call it grandpa's beard?" Sally adds.

John laughs. "That's so funny. The only bit of trivia I've heard is that it comes from the Meanest Man Who Ever Lived. It's said that a man's white hair grew so long that it got caught on the trees. It amazes me how many different folk stories there are about places or regions."

As we drive, John points up to a mountainous area and the narrow winding road that ribbons over it. "We're going up there, Goose Creek," he says. "You'll just love my Great Grandma Bertha's home. It's like a time
capsule."

I perk up, thinking about all the old folk tales I've heard. "I love all the Appalachian stories. I can't wait to hear your great grandma's story about Anne."

Sally exclaims, "Maybe you can write a book about Anne like you've written about Evangeline. By the way, have you heard any more from your book agent?"

"She texted me earlier today. They are supposed to start marketing next week for presales," I say. "Fingers crossed that all goes well."

Chloe turns around in her seat to face me. "I just think it's so neat that you have written a book and it's going to be published. You are so lucky. There are so many books out there. I know it's not easy to get a book agent, much less a traditional publisher."

I blush at her compliment. "I think I've been lucky all the way around. After all, if I hadn't won the songwriter's contest, maybe none of this would be happening."

Chloe smiles and offers encouragement. "Well, we all love your music, and if your book is anything like your music, you are going to hit the bestseller list." I blush again and thank her for the compliment.

John pulls onto the threadlike dirt road that leads to his great grandma's home. "This next stretch is a little bit bumpy and windy with lots of potholes," he warns us. "Hold on, girls." I laugh, turning to Sally, Emily, and Sarah as we shudder over ruts and holes. "No kidding," I tell the girls. "I feel like we are back on the roads on Cat Island. Remember that?"

Sally nods. "John, you think this is bad," my sister says, "when we got to Cat Island, the airport was on the southern end of the island, and we had to drive 47 miles on a small bumpy roadway. Emily even said it reminded her of a murder mystery novel where you all go in but only a few come back out. Kinda' like Hotel California by the Eagles."

Sarah chimes in. "Yeah, it was crazy. We got to the end and had to go up a steep driveway—a lot like the incline we're climbing now—but what we were hitting were craters, not potholes." She smiles remembering our trip. "I thought we'd never get there. But, boy, was it ever worth it," she continues. "If you and Chloe ever get the chance, you should think about going to Cat Island."

Now it's Emily's turn. "It really had the nicest beach I have ever been to. It had the softest, silkiest white sand and prettiest aqua blue water, a little private paradise," she says. "I hope it never gets too populated. I'd rather keep it our own little secret. Maybe if George and I get married there, you all can come to the wedding."

She smiles wistfully. "Now that I'm thinking back on it, maybe George and I *will* get married there. The chef at the resort served the best gourmet meals—five-star cuisine—every night for dinner. You two would have loved it."

John looks at us in the rearview mirror. "Wow, it really sounds awesome," he says. "Chloe, I think we really should check out Cat Island."

John reaches his great grandmother's house and parks the silver rental van next to a beat-up red truck. As he turns off the ignition, he points to a fairly large wooden bungalow. "Here's Granny's house. And that old truck is Granny's, too," he says. "So far, they haven't taken away her keys, but she only drives into town to the store and one of my great aunts usually rides with her."

He chuckles as he continues. "She still was splitting her own logs this past winter, but I can tell she is a little bit slower than she used to be."

287

Grandma Bertha is sitting on her well-worn wooden porch. She's a petite hunched-over lady with gray hair that she wears piled on top of her head in a bun with bobby pins. "Well look at what the cat drug in," she says, stretching her arms out toward John. "John, Chloe, it is good to see you. And look at all these other pretty ladies John brought with you."

John can't help but chuckle as he introduces us and gives his great grandmother a hug and a quick peck on the cheek. "Granny, these are the girls I was telling you about on the phone the other day, our newfound relatives. This is Angie, Sally, Sarah, and Emily."

Grandma Bertha pushes up her wire-rimmed glasses to inspect us properly. She reaches for my hand, taking it in her own weathered palm. "Welcome ladies. It's so nice to see all of you. And you," she says to me, "you're the Angie I've been waiting to meet all these years. Aren't you a lovely one at that."

She then points to John. "Well don't just stand there, sonny, let the girls into the house. Let's head back to the screened-in porch. It's not too hot today to sit out, and I made some sweet tea and lemonade for anyone who is interested. There are glasses on the sideboard. Help yourselves."

I am impressed by how alert and clear her mind is for her age. And she doesn't look a day over 80. We file into the house and follow John to the back porch. As we walk through the cozy house, I can see what John meant about a gold-themed '70s look. "The house was renovated probably fifty years ago," John says. "Granny likes everything just as it is—she wants no changes."

Granny shrugs and smiles at his comments. "I love my home just the way it is," she says, "even if the young'uns in the family are always wanting me to update things in here. Oh well, it's mine and I love it like this."

John turns around to grin at his great grandma. "It's okay, Granny. We'll just keep up with the repairs when they're needed." He tells the rest of us, "This house is probably over 300 years old. Its basement and root cellar are like being back in the tunnels or secret room at Isabella's house."

He pushes open the door onto the screened in porch. Beyond it, we see a garden oasis with pink, white, and red vincas still in bloom and peeking out from the well-manicured terrace. "Here we are," John announces. "I love your porch, too, Granny. It's like being in the forest with all the overgrown oak trees and pecan trees that are as old as the house, plus all the vincas, lilacs, and rose bushes."

"It's charming out here. What an enchanting haven," I say. "It's surprising that this is so close to the city. Is this the house that Anne Bonny came to when she left Cat Island?"

Granny brushes back the tendrils of gray hair that have escaped from her bun. "Oh yes, honey. She came here with her husband, John Brennan. They changed their names from Dare to Brennan to hide away from other pirates who might try to find them while searching for the treasures she and Calico Jack had." She picks up what looks like a journal that is sitting on the glass coffee table and flips to the first page. She hands it to me, and I see Anne's name on the page. "Here, Angie. I think she would have liked for you to have this," Grandma Bertha says. "It might have other clues on how to find the treasure."

I reach for the book with one hand and place my other hand on my heart to show how touched I am by the gift. "Really? Are you sure? You just met me."

She nods. "Oh certainly. I've been waiting my whole life to get this to you. I never imagined I would be alive to give it to you in person."

I feel tears welling up in my eyes. "Please, can you tell us a story about Anne?"

John's Granny gestures for us to help ourselves to the lemonade or tea. "Girls and Johnny, get yourselves something to drink—both the lemonade and sweet tea are fresh. I just made them this morning. Then settle in and I'll tell you, her tale."

She gets herself a cup of sweet tea and clears her voice.
"It's a mighty long story. Where should I start?" "Granny," John says, "why don't you start with when she is in the brig in Jamaica?"

"Oh yeah, that's a good place to begin," she replies. "Well, as you know, Anne, Calico Jack, and Mary Read, along with the crew, were captured and tried for piracy. That was around the end of October 1720." She reaches for Anne's diary, which I have my lap. I pass it over and Grandma Bertha opens the journal and points to a page.

"Here it is, the part of when they were taken captive. You see, Anne and Mary were both with child, so they weren't executed like the rest of the gang." She stops and turns toward me. "And this is the part where you and Thomas come in. Most people would think she's telling a fairytale if they read this book."

She clears her voice again and takes a sip of her sweet tea. "I have read this diary many times, but it feels funny for me to read it aloud." She begins to read.

A bewildering thing happened the day that I escaped from the gallows of Port Royal. I was sitting in my cramped, mangy cell, and I had just finished sharpening me spoon into a cutter. Out of nowhere came these two young'uns telling me they were from the world to come. They said they were here to help me escape. Well, you can just imagine me brawling with them. I was going to make it out of the jail on my own. I took the girl by her scroungy neck and held my cutter to it. Then that exquisite blond-haired man held out the timepiece that I had given to olde Jacky boy. I was madder than a hatter because I thought that they had stolen it.

Then this blond man holds out my lucky piece, an olde well rubbed rabbit's foot. I couldn't believe my eyes. How did he ever get his hands on that? I tried to take it away from him.

Granny takes another sip of her sweet tea, smiling. She continues reading.

You would not have believed what happened next. The guard had just come back into the jail from having a smoke and these two strange people told me we had to hurry. They spun this tall tale about the watch being a piece for time-travel. Then they said that the future me had sent them into the past to save me.

Granny shrugs and grins as she reads on.

Well, I told them they were crazier than a loon and I was not going anywhere with them. They finally made me believe it. They said we had to save my child and that none of our futures would exist if I didn't come with them, so I did.

Granny interrupts herself. "Now comes the exciting part," she says before looking down to read the diary again.

The next thing I know, they order me to say, 'Take me to Cat Island.' And, poof, we landed on a soft sandy beach.

John's great grandmother giggles as she finishes the story.

I thought they were witches and I was terrified of them. I went on to live on Cat Island, where I met and fell in love with John Dare. He raised my son as his own, and we had two more children on the island before my father came and found me. Through me Da's influence, we were able to move back to the colonies. We had to change our name after I had left piracy long behind and now I gave my time to mothering my children."

John's great grandmother stops again for a second, takes another sip of her tea, and shifts in her rocking chair.

Before we left Cat Island, we went to where Jack and I had buried some of our booty and we took that treasure back with us to the settlement where my father lived.

Grandma Bertha taps her forehead and says, "Now this is where you future children come in."

Years later, I tried to go back and get my first son, but he said he hated me. He wanted nothing to do with me.

She closes the journal. "Well, you may know most of this, but I bet you didn't know that she brought some of her treasure back here. She left clues. Maybe if you follow them, you can find it." She hands me a paper with three clues that Anne has written down for me. I read them out loud to the others.

Anne's first clue is: *Sometimes what you seek is right in front of you and all you need do is reach out and grab it. But first you must follow the clues.*

The next clue is: *Go to the holiest of hills, the highest most majestic view you will see. But do not touch the carved coral or you will be cursed with the obeah.*

The next clue says: *Go to the farthest point, past the mangroves to a place where the wild meets the calm, past the point where the mangroves grow and the faire houses lay.*

I shout out to the others. "Do you realize that she is talking about Cat Island? The path of the mangroves to the Man-O-War and the Hermitage!"

Emily smiles and raises her arms in the air, as if in surrender. "I guess we'll be making another trip to Cat Island after all. Looks like we might have our answer to where George and I will get married."

Grandma Bertha laughs and reaches over to take my hand. "There are probably more clues in the journal. It's yours to keep."

I hug her and feel like I have known her forever. "Thank you so much. We will let you know what happens."

John's Granny squeezes my hand. "You are very welcome, dearie, but heed Anne's warnings because there are still others out there that mean you harm."

John is looking at his watch. "Believe it or not we've been here for over two hours. I need to get you ladies back to your plane and your flight home."

Chapter 40

The Planning Continues

After hugging Grandma Bertha goodbye, we pile into the silver SUV to make our way back to the airport. John seems deeply grateful that we made the effort to meet his great grandmother. "I just want to thank you ladies for going to see my Granny," he says. "She doesn't get a lot of company and really appreciates whenever someone comes to see her."

We tell him how much we loved meeting Grandma Bertha and how grateful we are for the information she shared about Anne Bonny.

It's a short drive back to the airport. When we pull into the paved entrance, Billy is already waiting next to his airplane. He waves and comes over to help us with our bags. "Hello, girls. Hey, John. How did your visit go with Granny?"

I excitedly hold up Anne's journal. "Hi, Billy. It was a really nice visit. She's so cute and look what she gave me," I say. "I'm going to write another novel—this time it's going to be about Anne Bonny."

"Well, look at that. That's awesome," Billy replies. "I can't wait to read it. You know how much I love pirate adventures.

"Hey," he adds, while he stows our bags in the cargo hold of the plane, "have you found any new leads on where the treasure is?"

Since he is a close cousin of Thomas and George, as well the pilot on our adventures, Billy has been included in a lot of our planning. I tell him that we've come across a few more clues that we'll share with everyone when we get back to Ocracoke. I also mention that we might need to plan another trip to Cat Island.

Billy puts on the tan OBX baseball cap he was holding in his hands when we pulled up. As he climbs aboard the aircraft, he says, "That's cool. I

295

really loved Cat Island." He starts up the Gulfstream G650 charter plane and gives Emily, sitting next to him, her precheck instructions. Emily is grinning from ear to ear, blissed out by this jumpstart on the flying lessons she so badly wants.

"This is beyond cool, Billy. Thanks so much for teaching me the ins and outs of flying a plane," she says before turning around to give a thumbs up to Sarah, Sally, and me.

Sarah rolls her eyes laughing. "Go, girl, but don't get us killed while you're at it."

Billy chuckles. "Don't worry, Sarah. She's only helping me. I have full control of the plane. We should be back to the airport on Ocracoke Island before you know it."

He isn't kidding. We are back on the island after about an hour or so. The small aircraft screeches to a stop with Emily as the copilot. Billy jumps out and helps us all climb down from the plane, then he collects our belongings from the cargo hold. "It's been nice flying you, ladies," he says, as he tips his hat.

"Any time you want to go somewhere, just let me know," he says. "Isabella told me that she and David were planning to go to Jamaica to get married. I've put it on my flight schedule to leave July 21 and come back July
25."

Sarah reaches up to give Billy a quick hug goodbye. "That sounds right to me," she says. "I know they had to coordinate with your schedule and with Sally and Robert's schedule. The majority of us are more flexible."

The rest of us hug Billy, say goodbye, and climb into the blue Ford Explorer we left at the airport. I sit in the passenger seat next to Sally. "Well, that was a fun trip," I say. I pull Anne's journal out of my duffle. "And I can't believe John's Granny gave me Anne's diary. I never expected that.

"What do you girls think about everything that happened this weekend? Poor Violet, I feel so bad for her. It was like losing her parents all over again," I say with emotion.

Sally answers me, looking sad. "I just can't imagine losing both our parents at once. It was hard enough just losing Dad. And for Violet to lose both her parents so suddenly—and not to be able to do anything about it."

Emily and Sarah also feel bad about Violet's situation. "And to think that it could have been planned by Logan to get the map to Henry Morgan's treasure map. That just gives me the heebie-jeebies," Emily says.

Sarah agrees with us. "It would be awful to have to deal with so much loss—and scary that it could have been caused by Stephen's cousin, Logan."

Sarah points to the parking lot by SmacNally's and we look over to see Matt, Thomas, and George in George's truck in the parking lot. We pull up beside them and call out "Hello!" They are going to lunch. George comes over to the window, Emily rolls it down, and he kisses her, making her blush. Then he leans in and asks, "How about you girls join us for lunch?"

Sally says she has to decline his offer. "I need to get back to my babies. But you ladies go ahead," she adds.

We say goodbye to her and get out of her truck. "I'll drop off your things at the inn since it's on my way to your homes," she says as she gets ready to drive off. We all thank her and then head into my favorite restaurant for a quick lunch with the guys. I hug Thomas, he kisses me, and I say to the others. "You know the places that we ate at were good, but I've always loved this little pub."

We update the guys on our trip to Violet's condo and Grandma Bertha's home. I keep the journal hidden in my duffle, away from prying eyes.

"John's Granny is so sweet—kinda' like what I would think an old Anne would be like, come to think of it."

Emily continues sharing details about the time we spent with Granny. "Yeah, she was so sweet, and you can also tell she is quite sassy. I can't even imagine how she was when she was younger.

"Hey, Angie, tell them about the journal," she adds.

"Oh yeah, I was going to surprise them," I reply. Then I lower my voice as I tell the guys, "You see, when we were there, she gave me Anne's diary." I smile just thinking about it. "She gave me Anne's journal, and it has more clues in it! We need to conjure Anne up so we can ask her some questions, but I don't want to go into any more detail about that here. So why don't we meet later at Mom's to go over some more plans."

Thomas pulls out his phone and sends a group text inviting everyone to meet later today at my Mom's home. Sally messages back that she's not able to come because she needs to spend time with the twins. "Robert will be able to make it, but I really miss my babies," she writes. "He will update me on any new plans. Don't forget I dropped off your bags at the inn."

I answer her back. "No problem, Sis. Thanks for reminding us and enjoy the twins." She sends me back a heart emoji.

Emily, Sarah, and I decide to get our bags later. We girls, plus George, Matt, and Thomas head over to meet with my mom, David, Robert, Jim and Sally White plus my grandparents. As we start to open the door to my mom's house, she hears us and comes to the foyer.

"Hello, I'm so glad you could all come over. I had some ideas for the wedding, and we need to go over plans for our treasure hunting adventure," she says.

My grandparents and Jim and Sally White are already at Isabella's house, just finishing the lunch they had together. We all settle in to the den by the glowing fireplace when Robert comes in. He is excited to hear about our latest plans.

"Hi, everyone. Did I miss anything?" he asks.

"We were just waiting for you," Paul tells him. "Angie wants us to go downstairs to contact Anne."

I pull out the journal that John's Granny has given me. "It looks like we are going back to Cat Island, in addition to Jamaica," I say as I open the book and point to the clues about the mangroves and the Hermitage.

My mom goes over to a table where she's left her day planner out and starts flipping through the pages. "David and I set a date for our wedding—July 23rd in Jamaica," she says. "We scheduled it to coincide with the summer break for Sally and Robert's school. We're planning to fly to Jamaica on July 21st and I've already spoken to Billy to confirm our flights."

"Cool. I'm here and I'm in," Robert says, standing in front of the fireplace warming his hands. "As for Anne Bonny, I can't wait to hear what she has to say. Let's go downstairs and find out."

We make our way to the basement. Thomas and George open up the secret room in the storm cellar and bring out the cedar chest belonging to Anne. Thomas opens the antique chest and pulls out the special watch and timetravel telescope. He places the watch in the slot, adjusting the time and date to allow us to call her. "Anne, come see us," he says. "We have questions for you."

She materializes in front of our eyes. As always, she is as excited as we are, especially when she spots her journal in my hands. "Well, well, well. What have we got here— my diary? You must have been to my old homestead."

She points to the diary as she speaks. "That is the lifeline to me past. It holds so many dear memories. It also holds clues to finding me treasure," she says. "As ye have probably gathered, we left some of it back on Cat Island. Ye see, John and I were never certain we could safely stay in the colonies, so we kept some of our booty hidden elsewhere. It was just a precaution, but life got in me way and we couldna' go back to retrieve it. So, me and me dear John figured that if Angie and Thomas could come from the future to save me from the gallows, we would give those riches to our descendants."

She reached her arms out towards us. "Aye, sure, we brought a lot of the treasure with us. We used what we needed and hid the rest." She pointed to the small treasure chest. "This is one of the chests that olde Jacky boy and I stashed here when we was hiding on Ocracoke. We was thinking that one day—after we was done pirating—we would come live here. But it never happened."

Paul shakes his head as he listens to what she says, jotting down her remarks so that we will have it documented. He opens the small treasure chest and asks her, "So this is only a tiny portion of what you have hidden? Is that what you are saying?"

Anne cackles and reaches out to touch my grandfather's cheek, making him blush. "Aye, we had bundles of bounty, loads of jewels, silver coins, and gold bullion. But we couldna' haul it all with us because we never knew where we would end up. Those days the British were after our blood. Aye, it was rough work keeping from capture."

It's David turn to ask her a question. "So, we can find your treasure in many different places, is that what you are saying? And what about the watch and telescope? Can we use them to look back in time to see where you left your treasure?"

She moves close to him and saucily rubs her hand on his chest. "Well, are you ever the smart one," she says. "Aye, ye do that—but ye need my clues to know the island that they are on."

Emily, thinking about the accidents that took the lives of Stephen's father and Violet's parents, asks, "Can we look back to a time that you weren't there? Like, can we use the watch and scope to see what happened to Stephen's dad and Violet's parents."

Anne cackles a little bit louder, walking closer to Emily. "My girlie, now are ye not the smart one. Aye, you can. But I must warn you—do not accidentally transport yourselves to that time or ye could be caught up in the danger."

We all stare in amazement at her comment. After a pause, George asks her one final question. "So, you're saying we can use the scope to go back anywhere in history to watch it unfold?"

We all gasp at what Anne replies.

"Ye can do that, but I will warn ye that you cannot change history. You cannot cause time ripples. If ye were to go back to try to save them, it might be ye that succumbs to death because fate has already decided that someone must die."

She waves her arms in the air. "Now I must go because the veil is thickening," she says. "Until we meet again." At that, she vanishes, leaving us all standing with a startled expressions on our faces.

Chapter 41

Anne's Journal

After our meeting with Anne and learning the powers of the timepiece and the telescope, we decide to wait until later to determine what actually happened to Stephen's father and Violet's parents. We all help put everything back in the chest, but I keep the journal with me so I can read it later for additional clues.

Mom and David, Paul and Mary, and Jim and Sally White start to head to the stairs. "I know the kids have other plans, but how would you folks like to play some Pitch?" my mother asks them. In unison they agree that a card game sounds like fun. But just before they head upstairs and into the den to play cards, my Mom suggests that we girls go with her into town tomorrow to the bridal shop to buy dresses for both her wedding and Emily's wedding. We all say that sounds like a lovely idea. We decide to meet at the inn at 9 a.m. to catch the ferry into town.

Robert heads back home to tell Sally about the day's events and tomorrow's plans to go dress shopping in town. Emily, Sarah, and I catch a ride with the guys to the inn to pick up our belongings. We each get a little smooch from our beaus as Thomas, Matt, and George drop us off in front of the B&B and say goodbye.

Emily, Sarah, and I run up the steps to the inn. Just as we reach the front door, Sarah turns around and suggests that we look at the journal that John's great grandma Bertha has given me.

"Let's see if we can find any more clues to where Anne might have hidden the treasure in Jamaica," she suggests.
Emily and I both nod "yes."

"I think that's a great idea," I say. "The more eyes on it, the more clues we might spot."

Sarah suggests that we head to the sunroom where the light is bright, noting that it will be easier to read the journal there. As we near the kitchen, Emily points and asks, "How about some iced tea, soda, or something?"

"Ice water is fine with me, but I can get it," I reply. "You don't have to wait on me." I follow Emily and Sarah into the kitchen to get drinks before moving into the sunroom, where I plop down on the cushy white wicker sofa and pull the journal out of my duffle bag.

"Okay, so most of this Anne has already told us about. But there are still some more details she didn't mention," I say. "Look at this map, for example, and this entry from Cat Island."

I read aloud what Anne has written.

My husband John and I left, leaving the children with his mother, so we could go in search of my first son. I have never forgiven myself for being so selfish when I was younger. How could I have left Austin with that evil pirate Bell in Jamaica? My son spit in my face when I went to try to get him to come back home with us. He called me dirt and said he wanted nothing to do with me. There was nothing I could do, so he stayed with that villainous man's family.

I look up from the diary entry. "I bet she did feel guilty about leaving her son on the other island," I say. "No wonder her son didn't want to go with her. I mean can you imagine?" Emily and Sarah both nod, agreeing with me.

I read the next line in the journal.

John and I arrived in Jamaica. I had to disguise myself so I was not discovered and hanged at the gallows. We managed to find the buried treasure that Jack and I had left on the island. We smuggled it out of there in the dark of the night.

I pivot my head towards Emily and Sarah. "Do you realize what this means? The treasure isn't in Jamaica."

I continue reading.

303

We decided to divide the bounty between two islands, Cat Island and Isla Juana. We feared that if we left it all on Cat Island and it was discovered, we would lose everything.

Emily pulls out her phone. "I'm going to Google where Isla Juana is. Have either of you heard of it?" She holds up her phone to show us the results. "Wow, that's interesting," she says. "It's between Cuba and Cat Island. Ha! Think about it. It makes sense and is pretty smart of them to separate the booty so that it doesn't get stolen or, if someone finds some of it, they don't lose it all."

Sarah turns to Emily. "Wow, this changes everything. Emily, you should definitely think about having your wedding with George on Cat Island."

Emily nods, blushing. "You know, I was leaning that way anyhow because that was where George and I ended up together—so it's a special place for us. Besides, Shanna's Cove Resort and Cat Island are gorgeous."

I am grinning because I, too, have so many fond memories of the island. Then I start to wonder about one of Anne's clues.

"Well, one of the clues had Anne on the top of Mount Alvernia at the Hermitage but remember that the Hermitage would not have been built back then. It wasn't built until 1939 by Monsignor John Hawes, the man all the locals called Father John. That means that there must be a hiding place somewhere on the mountain," I say.

I pull Mount Alvernia—the highest point on the Bahamas—up on my phone and show the girls the
Wikipedia version of the description. "Look at this, it was called Como Hill. I wonder where that name came from?"

Emily does another Google search. "It looks like the word Como stands for masters of masons who carved rock into stone bricks to make buildings in numerous places, from Germany to Italy. They were architects of their time. Some of their carved stone buildings are still standing today, a thousand years later," she reads.

I smile at the girls. "Well, the Hermitage was absolutely beautiful and amazing. I can see it being around in another thousand years," I say. "The structures are stunning, and the actual history is fascinating. Imagine making the Stations of the Cross out of carved stone from the mountain."

Sarah nods. "The whole place is so unbelievable and majestic. I mean you can see all the way around the island from up there," she says. "But, boy, was that ever a hike up. It reminded me of when our family went to Chichen Itza, and we climbed 'The Castle.' Those steep steps to get to the top of the mountain were so scary."

Emily pulls her strawberry blonde hair up into a ponytail as she speaks. "I would love to go back up to Mount Alvernia and back to Mexico sometime," she says. "What about you girls?"

I point to the picture of the Hermitage. "Definitely. And let's explore it a little bit more thoroughly next time," I say. "Anne might have left more clues there, but my intuition tells me that what we're looking for is past the mangroves and on Man-O-War Point. I mean, what better place would there be to hide a treasure? It's so remote and it could be anywhere. I wonder if we can find a map or something?"

Chapter 42

The Dresses

The afternoon turns into morning before we know it, and it's time to rise to go into town to search for dresses for Emily and George's wedding and for Mom and David's wedding. Mom asked Sally White to be her matron of honor. My sister, Sally, and I will be her bridesmaids.

We reach the ferry quickly and are on our way. The bright sun is shining down on us as we get out of the car to enjoy the fresh air on the ferry, but there's still a bit of a chill. I rub my hands together to try to warm them up a bit before I put on my gloves, zip up my navy-blue winter coat, and wrap my scarf around my neck. "Brr, it's a little chilly today, although the sun feels warm," I say. "I just love riding on the ferry early in the morning."

Mom wraps her arms around me, gazing into the wake from the back of the ferry. "It is beautiful, and I can't remember when I've felt so happy and at ease. I have my family and friends with me, and I'm getting ready to marry my best friend."

Sally stands on the other side of our mother, smiling. "Mom, we are all so happy that you and David have found each other," she says. "He's such a nice man, and we can see how happy he makes you."

Soon we're all standing beside her—Emily, Sarah, their mother, my grandmother, Sally, and I all blissfully happy for my mom. Sally White asks her friend, "Isabella, any ideas of the type of dress you want to see at Weddings By The Sea Boutique?"

"I'm thinking about something in a pale ivory or maybe pale blue since it's a second wedding for both of us, but I'll just have to see what they have to offer," my mother replies.

Sally White thinks about her comment. "I agree, and I just love the idea of a different color. Pale baby blue would look lovely on you with your eyes," she says.

"That might be interesting." She flutters her eyelashes as she changes the subject, turning towards me. "So, did you girls get a chance to look at Anne's journal yet? I'm curious to know what she wrote."

I look around to make sure no one is listening to our conversation, shake my head in the affirmative, and excitedly tell her, "I was planning to wait to tell everyone together, but now is as good a time as any. Besides, I'm sure that Emily and Sarah must have told George and Matt like I told Thomas what we discovered yesterday."

I push tendrils of my windblown hair out of my eyes and lean over to whisper to my sister, Sally White, Mom, and Grandmom. "There was a big revelation. The treasure's not in Jamaica," I say in a low voice. "Anne Bonny and her husband went back to get it on Jamaica, and they moved it."

I look around again to make sure no one is listening to me. "They brought part of it to Cat Island and the rest to some island close to Cuba. We are going to need to tell the others and look for a map."

Emily reminds us, "Remember, Angie, that we found a map in the bottom of the cedar chest that once belonged to Anne and Calico Jack? We'll need to pull it out to see if there are any marks on it indicating where the treasure might be."

I nod, remembering the map. "Oh, that's right. And there was a compass and a candle, too. We'll definitely need to pull those out— plus we need make plans to go back to Cat Island."

I point to the shoreline. "Look, we're here already. I guess we'll need to get back in the van."

The ferry chugs up to the port and the attendants guide us as we drive off the ferry. Traffic is light on Hatteras Island. As we pass by Buxton Books, I exclaim, "I'm going to have to stop by one day soon to see if I can get my new book in the store, maybe even do a book signing."

Sarah smiles at me. "My friend the musician, and now local author. How cool is that?"

I blush as I respond. "It's really surreal if you think about it. I never in a million years thought that I would be able to follow my dreams and become an author *and* a country singer."

Emily just laughs at me. "Well, I always thought you would make it big!"

"Enough of that, girls, or you'll make my head explode," I reply as I throw my hands up in the air in exasperation. I quickly change the subject as we cross over the Oregon Inlet Bridge. "That was fast—no traffic today," I observe. "We made good time. We are almost at the bridal shop."

Minutes later, Sally pulls into the parking lot of Weddings By The Sea Boutique. "Here we go, girls. We have arrived," she says. "Let the fun begin."

Mom says, "I feel like the blushing bride. This is silly, but suddenly I'm nervous."

Sally slips her arm through Mom's arm and guides her through the door of the bridal shop. "Aw, Mom, and such a beautiful bride you're going to make," she says.

A dinging bell on the door announces our arrival. Almost simultaneously, my mother turns to Emily and asks, "Do you have any idea what type of dresses you want for your bridesmaids?"

"I don't know," Emily says. "Let's make this your day, Isabella."

Isabella tuts as she replies. "That's silly, Emily. Why don't we go ahead and get all the girls' dresses while we're here?"

Emily timidly asks, "Are you sure you want to share your day?"

Isabella hugs Emily. "Oh, honey," my mother says, "it'll be fun sharing the day with you. Let's do it."

Marie, the shop manager, greets us with a smile. "Hello, ladies. You girls must have love spells going on down there on Ocracoke." She turns to Mom and Emily. "I hear you two are getting married soon."

Isabella smiles, answering right away. "Yes, it seems that way. Angie, Emily, and I are all engaged now. Emily is getting married in March on Cat Island, so we need dresses for that wedding. And I'm thinking about trying a pale baby blue gown or ivory-colored dress—something that works for a beach wedding in Jamaica?"

Marie leads her over to a rack of dresses. "You know, Isabella, these dresses just came in two days ago. I think there's one that might be just what you're looking for." She pulls out a dress and hands it to Mom.

Isabella's eyes are twinkling with sparkly tears as she takes the gown from Marie. She lifts her hand up to her mouth. "Oh, my heavens. It's perfect. It's just what I was thinking of for my dress." Isabella holds it up in front of her and stands in front of the mirror. "Well," she says over her shoulder toward us, "what do you think?"

We all gasp. We tell her it looks like it was made for her. She carries it to the dressing room to try on. Minutes later she comes out wearing the dress and twirls around for us. We can tell she loves it—and it looks beautiful on her. My sister and Sarah squeal, and the rest of us clap. Sally White hugs my mother. "That is the perfect dress. It matches your eyes, Isabella," she says. "What do you think?"

Before she can answer, my grandmother interrupts to say that she, too, thinks it perfect.

Isabella twirls around, smoothing down the silky chiffon. "I love it. It is exactly what I had imagined. I absolutely adore the color. I'm saying 'yes' to the dress!"

Mom then turns to Emily. "Did you see anything you like for your bridesmaids' dresses?"

Emily holds up a dusty rose gown and turns to ask Sarah, Sally, and me. "What do you girls think about this dress? I figure it is something you could wear again since it is knee length."

Crazily, the shop has all our sizes in stock, so we go into the dressing rooms to try on the dresses. When we come out to show Emily and her mother, Emily grins. "Oh, I really love them on all of you. They are perfect."

I have to laugh. "You don't mess around, do you?" I say. "I hope I can make my decision that fast when I pick out my attendants' dresses for my wedding."

Emily leans over and hugs me. "It's not the dress that counts, but the ladies who are wearing them that count." I give her a peck on the cheek. "Right back at you, my friend." I turn to my mom and ask her, "What about you, Mom? Did you see anything that you'd like us to wear as your bridesmaids?"

Mom has been looking around the shop, and she now points to a pale cream—a very light yellow—dress. "I think I like these," she says. "What do you girls think? Marie, can we get these ordered in time for my wedding in July?"

Marie assures her that the dresses will be ready in plenty of time if Mom chooses them.

"Oh, Mom, I love that color," I say. "It will go perfect with the baby blue." I take the dress off the rack and hold it up against me. "Well, it looks like we've got two down. Shall we make it three?"

I pull a light teal off-the-shoulder tea-length gown from the rack beside the one my mom has chosen. "You're not going to believe this, but how about this one for my bridesmaids? I think it will look so pretty with my dress," I say.

I giggle as I turn to Marie. "Boy, your shop is going to love us," I tell her. "Girls," I add, "let's go try them all on. Maybe we can check off all three weddings right now." We put on the dresses and primp before the mirrors. It's clear that all three choices are going to work. It's a sweepingly successful day at the bridal shop. We'll need to return later to pick up the dresses for my wedding and for mom's wedding, but we're able to take the bridesmaids' dresses for Emily's wedding back to Ocracoke Island with us.

When we get back out to the parking area, Emily opens the door to the van and smiles at us. "Thank you. I have been dreading picking anything out, but you girls made it easy for me," she says. "Now, let's go home."

Chapter 43

Cat Island Plans

We all head back to our homes after agreeing to meet at mom's house later that evening to look over the map, compass, and candle in the cedar chest in the storm cellar. We will also need to finalize plans for Emily and George's upcoming wedding on Cat Island.

Thomas greets me as I step through the door. He's finished his job at Bob and Sue's early. "Hi, honey," he calls out. "How was your shopping trip?"

I take the pretty dusty rose gown out of its garment bag and hold it up. "Look, we found bridesmaids dresses for Emily and George's wedding. "What do you think?" I ask him. "I really like the way this fits.

"And guess what? We were also able to pick out dresses for Mom's wedding and—get ready for this—*our* wedding! Can you believe that? I found these gorgeous light teal dresses for the girls. They'll really complement my dress. One shop and we have all three weddings covered. It was amazing," I add.

Thomas kisses me on my cheek. "Angie, you look beautiful in everything you wear," he says. "I've got to say, though, that when I think about it, I really like the idea of teal for our wedding."

He pauses for a minute, and I know he's thinking about what he still needs to do for the wedding. "Teal is kinda' beachy. The guys can wear teal cummerbunds or ties or something. I guess we need to order those soon," he says. "I know we decided on khakis for the guys. I guess we can order or look for teal or cream-colored shirts. What do you think?"

I cup his chin in my hand and kiss him softly on his lips. "If you want, I can get Sarah and the girls to help me order for you guys, now that we have the dresses picked out. Easy peasy. I am getting so excited."

He grabs me and swings me around. "I can't wait to watch you walk down the stairs at the B&B. My heart is melting just thinking about it."

My love for this man is overwhelming. He makes me so happy. "Can you believe it's less than six short months away?" I say. "If you want, I can handle all the details. I'll just run them by you as we figure out everything."

Thomas nods in agreement. "Definitely. Anything you want works for me. That way I can concentrate on getting our house ready. You can tell me details for the wedding, and I'll share updates on the plans for the house. That way, we'll both be able to offer input."

I am overjoyed with his suggestion. "I can't remember ever being this happy," I tell him. "Oh," I add, "before I forget—I didn't want to call you at work, but the girls and I are thinking we should all get together tonight to go over plans for Cat Island. I hope that's alright, especially now that we have the new information from Anne's journal."

Thomas turns around, laughing. "You ladies were thinking the same as us guys. We—as in Matt, George, and I—already spoke to David. We wanted to meet at your mom's place around 7 p.m. I'm so glad that you girls decided to have Sam cover at the pub tonight."

"Yeah, that was Emily's decision," I reply. "She thought we really needed to get together to talk wedding plans. Now that way we've got the time to also go over more of the clues." I chuckle thinking about how in sync we all are with each other.

Thomas walks into the kitchen, opens the oven, and pulls out a baked chicken. A scrumptious scent floods the kitchen. "Hope chicken is okay with you. I thought you might be hungry when you got home, so I picked one up at Conner's grocery store while I was over on Hatteras Island. I had to get more supplies for our house."

I breath in the aroma of the chicken and giggle. "Wow, and he cooks, too. How did I get so lucky?" I say as Thomas laughs. "I love you."

We sit down to a homecooked meal of baked chicken, green beans, and baked sweet potatoes. I savor the first bite. "Thanks so much, honey. You cooked so I'll clean. That way you'll have time to relax a bit before we meet up with the others."

I look at my watch and see that it's almost 6:30. "Once we finish eating, I'll put the kitchen in order and we can head out," I say.

Thomas laughs and announces, "And she cleans, too! How about that?"

He adds, a bit more seriously, "Your thoughtfulness is one of the reasons why I love you so much. There are a not a lot of women out there like you, Angie. How did I get so lucky?"

We finish eating and I hurriedly tidy up the kitchen before we hustle over to Mom's and David's house. A damp breeze swamps us as we open the door and step onto our porch. "Brr, it's really gotten chilly tonight," I say.

Thomas reaches down to put the leash on our happy puppy. "Let's walk to your Mom's. I know it's cold, but he needs the exercise." I nod. "Great idea," I say. "You know how much Max likes to walk, plus I need to walk off that delicious dinner that you spoiled me with tonight."

The walk is rejuvenating, and we reach Mom's home quickly. As we open the door, warm air rushes out to greet us. I can smell the heavenly scent of Christmas cookies from her Bath & Body Works plug ins. I smile thinking about how much that scent reminds me of home. I holler in the door, "We're here."

Max scrambles into the house with his toenails sliding across the hardwood floors. He's excited to greet his buddies, Skippy, Ace, and the new puppy, Biscuit. Thomas follows Max into the den and whistles for him to sit. Our dog comes to a halt, but his tail is wagging so furiously that it makes everyone laugh.

The others are already in the den. Mom, David, my grandparents, and the Whites are sitting on the sofas and loveseats by the fire while Emily, George, Sarah, Matt, Robert, and Sally are standing next to the bar against the back wall discussing our trip to the bridal shop.

Sarah already has her computer opened up as she explains, "I spoke to Maria at Shanna's Cove today and asked if she could provide the same wedding package for Emily and George that Matt and I had. She was thrilled and happy to accommodate us. So, we're scheduled to be there in
March."

Emily is blushing and so is George. "Wow, that was fast, and I didn't even have to do anything," Emily says. "Thanks, Sis!" She hugs Sarah. "So, it's all set. Everything?"

Sarah nods her head "yes," and Emily dramatically swipes her hand across her forehead and lets out a long deep breath. She then gives George a squeeze and a kiss.

"That's the great thing about destination weddings," Sarah explains. "They handle everything except the wedding attire. That's up to us, but we girls now have our dresses. The only thing left is for the guys to get their outfits."

George announces, "Emily and I spoke and agreed the guys could just wear khakis shorts and white tops to make it easy."

Thomas laughs and says to his brother, "That's so funny because Angie and I just had the same discussion before we came over tonight." Matt runs his hands through his wavy black hair and adds his input. "I like the sound of khaki shorts. With three weddings in the next few months, the easier the better."

Mom and David overhear our conversation and both nod. "That sounds great to us, too," David says. "We were thinking the same thing—khakis—with maybe cream-colored shirts to match the girls' dresses."

We hear a knock on the front door. "That's probably Mom and Dad," George says. "They wanted to be included in the plans. It's just a shame Mom couldn't make it to the dress shop today because she had another appointment."

Thomas and George's parents come into the den and warm wishes are exchanged with all of us. "Thanks so much for trying to include me today," Thomas and George's mom, Liz, says. "I'm sorry I wasn't able to make it. George told me that the girls found dusty rose dresses."

She pulls up a picture on her phone. "What do you all think about this dress for me? It's a pale pink off-the-shoulder that I thought might look good." All the ladies peek over her shoulder. Emily is grinning. "Oh, I love it, Liz," she says. Everyone else agrees.

She is thrilled by the unanimous vote. "That's good. I'll place an order for it now," she says. "It says it should be delivered by Monday.

"So, what are the guys going to be wearing?" Liz asks.

George answers his mom. "We decided on khakis with cream-colored shirts. We're going with the same look for all the upcoming weddings to make it easy. Since all the weddings are casual, it works out perfectly."

His father, Joe, grins. "That sounds great to me. I can't believe all the weddings this year. It's truly remarkable. I guess Evangeline's spirit has been busy casting love spells."

He pauses for a minute then asks, "I know we're here to discuss the weddings, but aren't we also going to talk about the treasure-hunting plans?" George and Thomas have been keeping their parents up to date on all the happenings, even though Joe and Liz haven't been directly involved in the hunt for pirate treasure.

Thomas answers his dad. "That's what we were just getting ready to discuss when you got here." Thomas points to the basement door. "Do we want to go downstairs and take a look at everything now? You two can come, too," he says to his parents, "so you can see what we've been talking about for the last couple of months."

Both of his parents nod and we all head downstairs into the storm cellar. Thomas opens the door to the secret room. His dad gasps. "And to think this room has been hiding here for over two hundred and fifty years or so?" Joe says, incredulously. "That is amazing. And it was a tornado warning that caused you to examine the bookshelf against the wall, Thomas?"

We agree that the serendipity of the situation astonishes all of us.

Liz is looking around the room and spots the dress sitting on the white vinyl table. "Is this the dress you guys found with message sewn into the pocket?" she asks. "It looks so old.

"This whole situation is so exciting," she continues. She looks at her husband. "Do you remember when we were in Cancun, and we went snorkeling in the Exuma underwater cavern? I always dreamed—and I know you did, too—of finding buried treasure. Now to think you guys are actually searching for buried treasure! What fun."

Joe picks up the watch and the telescope. "Are these the two pieces that allowed you to go back and save Anne from the gallows?" He examines the telescope turning it over in his muscular tanned hands. "So, you can look back in time with these two objects, too?"

Paul answers him, taking the two items. He places the watch into the slot in the telescope. "It's amazing really. We can either look back in time or actually go back in time. Pretty cool, huh?"

Joe and Liz both nod. They are in awe over all the old items and clues that we have accumulated. I pull out Anne's journal from my blue duffle bag. "Even more exciting is that we were given this journal from John's

Great Grandma Bertha." I open up the journal and flip to the page that indicates where the treasure might be buried. "Look at this page everybody. Emily, Sarah and I were reading it yesterday and found this entry."

I read the page to them and then summarize what it says. "Anne and John were able to go to Jamaica and move the treasure. They took part of it to an island between Cuba and Cat Island and the rest to Cat Island. So that's why we need to go back to Shanna's Cove Resort. We can search the areas that she mentioned earlier when she referenced the mangroves and the Hermitage."

Thomas continues explaining to his parents. "When we were on Cat Island, we hiked the Mangrove Trail that led to Man-O-War Point at the far end of the island. There is a lot of land to cover but it would be the perfect place to bury the treasure. When we were there, we were thinking that maybe Anne left a clue on Mount Alvernia. But we didn't think they'd leave the actual treasure because we assumed it would be too heavy. But, if you remember from our search for Blackbeard's treasure, there was a port at the far northern end of Cat Island."

He points to the cedar chest that belonged to Anne and Jack. "We were planning to look at a map we found in the bottom of this cedar chest and maybe conjure up Anne at the same time."

Joe and Liz both look excited. Joe can barely contain himself. "We're going to meet Anne?" he says. Paul laughs and pats Joe on the back. "Maybe we should have included you sooner. I didn't know you liked these types of things."

Joe turns to Paul, laughing. "I've always loved history, buried treasure, and ghosts," he says. "When I graduated from college, I had a major in architecture and a minor in history." He points to his wife. "Liz got a degree in nursing and a history degree when she graduated from UMD, so we have always had an interest in all the history of the island."

Thomas and George look surprised. "I had no idea that you two would be interested in being included in our treasure-hunting excursions," George says.

"That's so funny," Joe replies. "I wondered why you never asked for our input. I have lots of research papers on the different pirates that roamed the Outer Banks, the Bahamas, and Jamaica. I will have to share them with you all."

Paul raises his eyebrows and grins. "That's awesome. I would love to collaborate with you to see what you have in your research. Do you have anything on Calico Jack, Anne Bonny, or Henry Morgan?"

"Absolutely," Joe says. "I have tons of research on most of the pirates who were carousing in the waters around here in their time." He taps the table grinning.

"Wow. Do you mind if I come over sometime to see what you have?" Paul asks, looking hopeful.

"Better yet, why don't I bring it all over here to see if it helps pinpoint where the pirates might have left their treasures!" Joe looks excited.

Everyone is interested to see what Joe and Liz have gathered over the years. "If you're free tomorrow, why don't you two bring the material over and the retired folks can browse through what you have," David suggests. "Robert, you can come, too, if you like, since you're still on a school break. I know the girls have other plans tomorrow. They want to get ready for these weddings."

Robert nods at David. "I'd be thrilled to see all your research, Joe and Liz. I can't wait. Paul, Dad and I have been poring over everything Paul has gathered over the years. It will be nice to expand out those findings with new details."

Robert picks up the watch and telescope and asks all of us, "Should we get Anne or look at the maps first?"

We decide to study the maps first. Paul unrolls one map. "It definitely looks like a map of Cat Island," he says, pointing to locations. "This is the northern end of the island. On the southern end, here is a picture of a mountain. It must be Mount Alvernia."

Thomas pulls out the compass and the candle. Matt, standing beside him, pulls out his lighter. "Let's try putting the candle in the compass and light it to see if it shows us anything," my brother suggests. Thomas slips the candle into the slot. "Well, here goes nothing," Matt says.

The old candle sputters and finally lights, illuminating and casting shadows on the map. We all gasp as Matt points to a shadow at the far northern end of the map.

"Well look at that," Matt says. "There's a circle with an X through it over at the far end of the mangroves on the Man O-War-Point. On the map, it looks like it's on some rocky feature."

He's so excited that he stutters out. "Wow. Do you think we might have found it? Or at least the general area?

"We need to conjure up Anne and ask her," he quickly adds.

We all high five each other, whooping and hollering. Paul says, "Absolutely. We need to get her in here, so we know if we have found it before we get to the island in March. We only have two more months before we leave and, once we get there, it won't be easy to conjure her up secretly."

Matt jumps in. "Let's do it!" he says. "Here's the watch. I'll put the dials to where they need to be and conjure her up." He laughs again and turns to Joe and Liz who are standing beside Thomas and me, looking both nervous and excited.

"You guys are going to love her. She's a hoot—and quite the flirt," my brother tells them.

Matt dials the settings on the watch and David calls out for Anne to appear. The crowded room watches as the misty spirit of the wild auburn-haired pirate appears before our eyes.

"What have we here, mateys. I am back so soon—not that ye will see me complaining. I always loved being on this side the universe," she says.

She throws back her head then turns toward Joe and Liz. "Well, well, who have we here?" She walks over to Joe and runs her hands over his chest. "You are a mighty handsome one if I do say so myself." She looks at Thomas and states. "I reckon he must be yours, as you are the spitting image of him."

Thomas answers her. "You are absolutely right, Anne. These are my parents, Joe and Liz. So, I guess that makes them related to you, too. They will be coming with us to Cat Island for the wedding and to search for your treasure."

Anne cackles, brushing back her untamed hair. "So, you figured it out, have ye? Smart ones you are, if I do say so myself."

I hold up her journal, showing her the page I read to the others. "Granny Bertha gave me your diary that told us that the treasure is on Cat Island. We just looked at the map and it pointed to the mangroves."

"That is right, dearie," Anne replies. "We separated the treasures. We kept part with us and split the rest—half hidden on Isla Juan and the rest we left on Cat Island. That way we would be safe if things did not work out in Charleston.

"You have it figured out," she continues, "but you will need to go to Mount Alvernia to find the clue with the exact location. You see, we had to make it difficult so only the ones who truly should get the treasure could find it." She points to the mountains on the map of Cat Island, indicating where we'll need to go to find the next clue. Then she evaporates before our eyes, chortling as her spirit disappears.

321

Liz and Joe are standing with their mouths and eyes wide open. Thomas hugs his parents. "She's a wild one, isn't she?" he says to them. "Now that it is settled, I guess we know where we need to go."

While we all digest what has just happened, Thomas speaks up. "How's about we get everything put away. It's already 9:30 and we—Matt, George, and I—have an early start at work tomorrow. I think we need to call it a night."

We help put away all the extraordinary items we pulled from the chest that once belonged to Anne and Jack. David turns to ask Liz and Joe another question. "Would you two be interested in checking out the secret room tomorrow when you bring over your research material?"

Liz answers as Joe nods. "Definitely," she says. "I can't wait to see it. The night just flew by."

She stops for a minute than adds, "You were right, Matt. Anne is quite the character and a flirt, too." Liz can't help but smile thinking about the apparition.

Chapter 44

Time Flies

Over two months have passed since the night when Liz and Joe were introduced to the spirit of Anne Bonny and told all that had been happening. It is the end of February and there are only a few weeks until we leave for Cat Island. Emily and George's wedding plans are finalized, and we have our flights scheduled on Billy's plane. We have separated out all the clues we need to find Anne and Calico Jack's treasure. We'll bring the clues with us in our carry-on luggage.

I am delighted that we have included Liz and Joe in our treasure-hunting plans. Even though I have known them all my life, I am learning so much more about my future in-laws. They are particularly helpful as a source for information on pirates in our area. They have shared their pirate research with David, Paul, and Robert, and it turns out they have an especially impressive amount of knowledge about Violet's ancestor, Henry Morgan.

Matt and George have been working hard with Thomas to get our new home ready for us to move in before our wedding in June. Our wedding plans are pretty much completed except for making some doilies or souvenir gifts for the guests.

My novel about Evangeline is still with the publisher, getting the finishing touches completed before it can be released in the spring or early summer. I have been busy with my music, including a song for Emily and George. I haven't told them—I want it to be a surprise. As always, I second-guess myself and worry whether they'll like it, but Thomas says he really loves the song. Since he's known the bride and groom since they were born, he's helping me fine-tune the lyrics.

Just two weeks ago—on Valentine's Day—John and Chloe settled into their second home here on Ocracoke Island. His family members helped them get the house set up, and Violet and Stephen booked a stay on the island so they could be here for Chloe and John's housewarming.

Between trips to Ocracoke, Chloe and John have been keeping in touch with us on FaceTime. We're excited that they'll be with us at Emily and George's wedding on Cat Island. Our group of friends and family has grown close to them—and with Violet and Stephen as well. I've even warmed up to Uncle Timmy. Once you know him, he's a big teddy bear. But I'm still not sure about Stephen's cousin, Logan, who gives me the willies.

Emily, Sarah, Chloe, Sally, Violet, and I speak weekly on FaceTime. We've been helping Violet with her wedding plans. Sarah, especially, has been a help. She thrives on wedding planning and has even expanded her B&B to offer wedding packages here on Ocracoke Island.

We have a meeting at Mom and David's house tonight in the storm cellar to make sure we are ready for our upcoming trip. John, Chloe, Stephen, and Violet arrived last night; they're staying at the inn with Sarah, Matt, and the Whites. Violet thinks it's too cold to sleep on the boat and, frankly, I have to agree with her. This time of year, the damp air chills right to your bones and makes them ache.

Thomas and I have just finished dinner and are heading over now to Mom's house to join up with the others. I want to know if anyone has discovered anything new since we last talked. As we get ready to go out the door, Thomas pulls me into an enormous hug before putting the leash on Max.

"I can't believe there are only two more weeks before we leave for Cat Island," he says. "I'm glad Chloe, John, Violet, and Stephen could make it here to help us go over the plans."

We've all agreed that Stephen and Violet are trustworthy and it's time to show them everything we have. "I can't wait to see Violet's expression when she sees how much information my father and mother have turned up on Henry Morgan. I was astounded at it," Thomas continues.

I think to myself how much I just love this man and the way he gets excited for our new friends.

"I know. Violet's going to be thrilled when she learns what your parents have discovered," I reply. "Let's go so we can walk Max before we see everyone. Even he looks excited!"

As we reach my Mom's house and start to walk hand-in hand up the front steps, Max struggles to get into the house. Thomas opens the door and Max barks. Thomas responds with a command. "Sit, boy. Down. And no jumping."

As usual we are the last to arrive—but just barely. Sally and Robert walked in a few minutes earlier, and they are taking the twins out of their snowsuits. The babies' rosy, red cheeks are still cold from the bitter breeze off Silver Lake.

I take Evie from Sally, giving my sister a quick hug and peck on the cheek. "So, how's my little angel today?" I say before turning to tickle Jacob on his tubby belly, making him drool and grin. "And you, too, my little cherub, how are you?"

Sally looks flustered. "Oh, you wouldn't believe it, Angie. These two are pulling themselves up in the crib. Aren't they too little to be doing that? Next thing you know they'll be walking—and I am so *not* ready for that!"

I laugh. "I know nothing about babies," I tell my sister. "You're going to have to ask our mother. But I'm pretty sure it will be double trouble when these two start walking."

Sally nods in agreement. "I know that's right. I'm having a hard enough time, even with Georgia's help, catching them when they are crawling," she says. "I guess it's a good thing Georgia offered to keep them for us while we're on Cat Island for the wedding."

I am surprised by that decision, even though I know Sally's right. The twins should stay home for this trip, especially since it is going to be a short one and action packed. Still, I ask, "Aren't you going to miss them, Sis?"

Sally puts one arm around me—she has Jacob on her hip on the other side—and guides me into the den where the others are waiting for us. "I love my kids, but it will be nice for it to be just Robert and me. It'll be like a honeymoon for us."

We both make the rounds, hugging and greeting everyone in our group. Chloe, John, Sarah, Matt, Thomas, Violet, and Stephen are standing around the bar looking at Sarah's computer. She has it open to the website for Shanna's Cove, describing what to expect at the resort.

"Violet and Stephen, I know you're staying anchored in the cove, but you'll have to eat with us at the resort. You'll just love the restaurant. They have the best gourmet meals—surprisingly, I know, for a restaurant that's so remote."

Violet looks up from the webpage and smiles. "It sounds lovely, and the pictures of the sandy beach and aqua water are gorgeous," she says.

As Sally and I walk up, she turns to us. "So how are you two ladies doing? Those twins are getting so big. I swear they have grown in the last two months."

Evie's big blue eyes are watching Violet, intrigued by her sparkly gold hoop earrings. She reaches out to grab one when Sally quickly steps back. "Oh, we are good but watch out for this little one. She has quick hands. If she gets ahold of your earring, she'll pull it right out of your ear.

"I was just telling Angie that they are both pulling themselves up in the crib and playpen," Sally adds.

Violet grins and takes Evie's sticky fingers in her hand, speaking to her. "Aren't you a pretty one? Are you a little wild one, like our Anne?"

I chuckle as I answer her. "I think they are definitely related. Luckily, they are not in the same time zone, or we would have big trouble." I point over to the others and ask, "Have you started yet or were you waiting for us?"

My parents, the Whites, Liz and Joe, and my grandparents are sitting in front of the fire chatting about the weather. My grandfather overhears me, stands, and comes over to place his arm around me. "We were just chitchatting while we waited for you and Thomas to arrive and everyone else to get settled. I think we can now go downstairs to review everything that we've found."

He points in the direction of the stairs to the storm cellar, and we all file through the kitchen and downstairs.

"David and I got all the items out so that we can review them," my grandfather informs us. "Joe brought over all his research on Calico Jack and Anne Bonny." He turns towards Violet and Stephen. "Plus, Joe and Liz have a lot of information on Henry Morgan that we thought you two might be interested in looking at."

Violet and Stephen are both keyed up over what Joe has uncovered.

"Really, Joe and Liz, I didn't know you two were big historians like Paul," Violet says. She reaches into her large black laptop bag and pulls out the cherished map she found in the closet of her parent's home. "I've brought the map we found attached to my wedding dress with the letter from my parents. I was hoping that you guys could keep it safe because I'm not sure how safe it is sitting in my condo."

We are all standing around the white vinyl table, which is covered with all clues we've found. Thomas explains the specific items to Violet and Stephen, starting with the watch. "You two should be aware that this watch is not just a device to conjure up Anne's spirit, it is also a time travel instrument."

Stephen and Violet both stare at the watch, then at Thomas. In unison, they gasp and reply, "What?"

Thomas picks up the watch and places it the slot of the telescope that he's holding. "We haven't tried one of the things that the pieces can do yet, but we were told that we could even look back to see a previous time period. We can also have the device transport us to a time in the past but, if we do that, we have to be careful not to change the past. Otherwise, we could change the world as we know it and cause a time warp."

Paul speaks up, stressing the importance of this concept with all of us. "I know that you have all watched sci-fi movies about time travel and time warps and have heard of the dangers. We must be *very* careful if we ever use the watch and telescope to go back in time."

Stephen tentatively reaches to take the telescope from Thomas. "Oh my God. Are your telling me I can go back and see what happened to my dad and Violet's parents?"

Paul raises his eyebrows. "Quite possibly, but I wouldn't advise it. It could cause a time rift—or even something worse. But we can see back in time by looking through the scope, so technically I guess we could do that to see what happened."

He questions Stephen. "Are you worried that your father and Violet's parents might have been killed intentionally? Do you realize what that means?"

Stephen looks anxious as he responds to the questions. "I know how careful my dad was with all his scuba gear. Honestly, I don't think it was an accident."

Paul gently places his hand on Stephen's shoulder. "I think that we might want to look back in time then, if you're sure you want to know. But think about it. What if someone you love was responsible for one or all of the deaths? I mean, they are your family."

Stephen answers Paul. "That is a problem, but I would rather know so that I can protect myself and everyone else. I just don't know if we can prove it. Can we try it?"

We look at one another. For one thing, this way we would definitely know who we could or couldn't trust. It is decided that we should take a chance and look into the past.

David has a warning for Stephen. "When you look through the telescope, you want to say, 'Show me back in time to when my father died,' not 'Take me back to the time that my father died.' We don't want you time traveling—or time warping or whatever you want to call it.

"We just don't need that happening," he says with true concern in his voice.

Stephen takes a minute. He seems deep in thought before he says, "Okay, I'm ready. What do I do now?" He already has the telescope in his hand. Paul slips the watch in the slot and offers him instructions.

"You need to say, 'Show me back in time to when my father met his peril and the circumstances surrounding his accident.'"

Stephens looks through the viewfinder of the telescope and repeats exactly what he has been told: "Show me back in time to when my father met his peril and the circumstances surrounding his accident."

Stephen nervously tells us what he is seeing through the telescope. "This is so amazing. I can see the serene aqua blue water, and I am watching my father check his gear. Violet and I are downstairs in the boat getting ready for our scuba dive. I see Dad walking down into the galley. He's calling us, telling us to hurry up, that it is time to go."

Stephen gasps and continues. "Oh no, it's Logan. He's looking down the steps going into the boat and over at my uncle's boat. Now I see him sneaking back. He's taking a razor blade from his pocket. Oh no, he just cut a hole in the tubing leading to the oxygen tank!"

Stephen lets out a grief-stricken sob and sets the telescope down on the table. He explodes in tears of frustration and grief then cries out in anger. Violet rushes to hold him to her chest. "Oh, Stephen. I'm so sorry. He's your cousin. That's so awful."

The rest of us try to console him. Then Paul says, "Now we know. But the bigger problem is how to prove that Logan sabotaged your father."

David offers a suggestion. "Maybe we can get him to confess. I don't know how, but let's try to think of something. After all, we can't go to the police and tell them we looked into the past. They would think we were all crazy. We're going to have to be very careful about how we handle this," he adds.

Isabella has gone to the refrigerator in the basement and taken out a cold bottle of water. She hands it to Stephen with a few tissues. "Here, honey," she says, as she hugs him. "We're all here for you, son. We're all so sorry about this."

Stephen takes the tissues, thanking my mom, and turns to Violet. "Do you think he was responsible for your parents' accident, too?" he quietly asks her.

A tear slides down Violet's cheek. She whispers to him. "I can't bring them back, and right now I don't really want to know."

She is silent for a minute. Then she asks Stephen, "How are we ever going to face Logan? And what about Uncle Timmy and Hunter? Do you think they had anything to do with it? Do you think they know?"

Stephen shakes his head. "I don't think so. When I was watching, Logan kept looking down at our boat and then over at their boat, trying to make sure no one saw what he was doing."

Stephen looks so sad and broken. It breaks my heart. Then he looks up at all of us. "Logan's really gotten hooked up with some pretty evil scoundrels lately, with his gambling and drug habits. But I never imagined him capable of this. I'm sorry that I might have put everyone in danger. I'm just so glad Logan isn't invited to the wedding," he says.

Matt is standing beside Stephen, and he pats him on the shoulder. "Don't worry," my brother says. "We'll be super careful. If Logan follows us to Cat Island, we'll avoid him at all costs. Nothing is your fault. You're a victim here, so please stop worrying about us."

Grandma steps forward, looking straight at Stephen and Violet. "You are our family now and that hasn't changed. You kids have a home here with us and will always be welcome."

After a pause, she adds, "Well, you did tell me there are still pirates out there. I guess you were right."

Our whole group nods in agreement. We offer our condolences and reassure the two of them that they are officially members of our family. Robert, seeing how much this has drained everyone, makes a suggestion. "Maybe we should try this again tomorrow. You have to be upset, Stephen and Violet. What do you think?"

Stephen blows his nose and wipes the tears from his face. He squeezes Violet in a hug. "I'm good," he says. "It's a shock, but I already thought something was fishy. Let's keep going. We need to go over everything."

George nods and pulls out a map of Cat Island. "Okay, so while you folks were away, we discovered that the treasure is actually on Cat Island," he says. He opens up the map and lays the compass on it. He then places the candle in the hole in the compass. Matt lights the candle and John, Chloe, Violet, and Stephen are visibly surprised when the map is illuminated to show the areas where the treasure is hidden.

It takes the stunned foursome a minute to process what they're seeing. Violet is the first to speak. "Oh, my goodness, look at that! Didn't you say that one of the clues mentioned Mount Alvernia and Man-O-War Point on Cat Island?"

She puts her hand on her hips. "Well, how about that?" she says, shaking her head in disbelief.

Matt points to the areas on the map that are highlighted. "We conjured up Anne and she confirmed the treasure is here. But she also said that to determine the exact location we need to find one final clue on Mount Alvernia.

"That apparition was crazy," Matt adds, chuckling as he thinks about Anne's appearance. "You guys would have loved it." By now my brother is laughing. He points to Liz and Joe. "It was the first time that these two had met Anne, and she was her usual charming self. She's too much."

Joe and Liz are smiling broadly, agreeing with Matt. "Oh, you should have seen her flirting with Joe," Liz says. "She's so brazen. What a character!"

Liz turns to Violet. "So now that we all know where on Cat Island, we need to look for a key clue. Would you and Stephen like to see some of the research we have done on Henry Morgan?"

Violet nods. But then she glances over at Stephen, who looks filled with remorse. "Would it be okay if we looked at it all later, maybe tomorrow morning?" she asks. "I think Stephen needs to take a break. Maybe we should take a walk to clear his head."

She puts her hand on his shoulder and asks him, "What do you think? How about a walk on the beach for some fresh air?"

Thomas looks at his watch, realizing that it is almost 10 p.m. "Wow, I didn't realize it was getting so late. We should head out. Are you ready, Angie?" he asks me.

I nod. Max hears the word "walk" and he gets up, stretches, and starts whimpering to go out. "Looks like someone else is ready to go," I say.

"I can let you guys out through the basement door if you want," David offers.

"Great," I reply. "I'll run upstairs and grab our jackets and Max's leash."

I turn to Violet and Stephen. "Do you want me to get your jackets, too?

Violet answers. "Stephen, why don't you help the guys put things away and I'll go upstairs and grab our coats."

After Violet and I bring the jackets downstairs and we head out the basement door, I am the first to speak. "Stephen, I'm so sorry you're going through this. Please let us know if there is anything we can do to help you get through this."

"Thanks, guys," he replies. "It means a lot having everyone's support." He runs his hands through his dreadlocks.

As we walk, we all agree to meet at mom's house tomorrow so they can look at the research Joe and Liz have collected. Thomas and I walk with them as far as our cottage, then say goodbye as Stephen and Violet continue on down to the beach. Max clearly wants to follow them and take a bigger walk, but I point him into our cottage. "No, boy, we need to give them their space." He whines but heads toward the door.

Chapter 45

Dreams and Visions

The night ends and I fall into another restless sleep, reliving the dream where I am chased down the path on the Mangrove Trail. I wake up feeling exhausted. I tell Thomas about the dream. "It's awful. It's like a bad omen," I say, with concern in my voice. "Do you think we need to be worried about what we learned last night?"

Thomas wraps his arms around me. "Don't worry, Angie.
We are all planning to protect everyone when we are on Cat Island."

"Okay I guess, but I'm still worried," I say, pushing my bedhead hair out of my eyes. He hugs me. "I promise it's all going to be alright. I'm not going ... we aren't going ... to let anything happen to any of us. I mean, Logan isn't going to be there. He doesn't even know we are going to Cat Island."

"Let's hope he doesn't find out," I say. "I guess I better get going. I'm supposed to meet the girls for a walk this morning. Are you getting together with Matt and George?" I sweep my hair into a ponytail and pull on a pair of sweatpants and a heavy sweatshirt.

"We are doing a little demolition today," Thomas answers, leaning over to kiss my cheek. Stephen and John coming by to give us a hand. Maybe when you girls get done, you can stop by the house to take a look."

"Sounds like a plan. See you in a little while," I tell him. We kiss goodbye and Thomas goes out and jumps into his gray Dodge Ram truck. I stand at the door, and he waves at me as he drives off. I can see Max in the front seat.

I chuckle to myself as I walk over to the inn. Once I get there, I climb the front steps, open the beautiful inn door, and enter the large parlor.

Suddenly I have the sensation I get when Evangeline is close by. I glance up and see her standing at the top of the grand staircase to the second floor with Old Emily, Jacob, Roger, and my father. They are looking down at me.

My father throws me a kiss and says, "We will be there to protect all of you. We will keep you safe." Then they vanish in a mist, leaving me clutching my chest. Emily walks in just as the final glimmers of the spirits dissipate.

"Are you alright? I can tell something's wrong," she says as she rushes up to me. "I suspect you just saw a ghost." After a pause, she adds, "But shouldn't you be used to that by now?"

I start to explain and then the other girls come in. They're all listening to me.

"I'm having bad dreams again, premonitions about being chased by scary people," I say. "Evangeline, Old Emily, Jacob, Roger, and Dad's spirits were just here. My father told me that they are watching us, protecting us all. It terrifies me to think of what is going to happen on the island. I mean, I know Logan isn't supposed to be there, but I'm certain we are in danger."

Emily, Sarah, Sally, Violet, and Chloe look shaken. Emily reacts first. "Don't worry," she says. "You know they will protect us." I hold my head and shake it. "I hope I'm just being silly," I say. Then I take a deep breath and change the subject. "So, what have you girls been doing this morning?"

"I got here early," Violet says. "Joe and Liz brought over some of the documents they have on Henry Morgan, and I was able to look them over. They left a couple minutes before you got here. You know, I was a history major, but I had no idea about some of the things Morgan did. He was even dubbed a 'sir' in his time. Pretty crazy, huh?"

"That's really neat," I answer. "I'm so glad they've uncovered such cool details about your ancestor. I can remember when we were investigating everything on Evangeline, and we found out so many interesting things about her and our family."

I sigh, still trying to shake myself out of my funk.

"It really is a lot of fun and so enlightening, the things that we have discovered. John and I really enjoyed researching Anne Bonny and Calico Jack," Chloe says. "Well, are you girls ready to walk? John wants to leave by 2 p.m. today."

"Sounds good to me, but we better bundle up. There's a brisk gale on the beach, and it might be cold," Emily says as she zips up her heavy purple coat and puts on her matching gloves and scarf. "How do you like the new winter coat George gave me?" she adds. "He says he's tired of me always being cold. He thinks this might help."

The walk is refreshing. The sand blows over the tancolored dunes and the sea grass blasts wildly on the shore. On our way down the beach, I make a suggestion. "Hey, do you girls want to go by our new house and see what the guys are up to? They're supposed to be demolishing the kitchen today."

Emily rubs her hands together to warm them. "That sounds like fun. I can't wait to see what they come up with, maybe even another pirate's treasure map."

"Wow, that would be really cool," I reply. "And you never know since the house used to belong to Lafayette the pirate. I need to do some research on him. I just know that he moved to New Orleans eventually."

As we walk away from the beach, I shiver from the crisp ocean breeze and pull my scarf tighter around my neck. I point down the street to our new house. "We're almost there and thank goodness. I don't know about y'all, but I'm freezing!"

I walk up the now familiar steps and turn around to Chloe and Violet. "Now, give it a chance. I know it's going to be a mess, but it is quite charming," I assure them, opening the pretty oak door. I poke my head in and call out, "Hi, guys, we're here." Dust mites and cinders from the demolished plaster walls between the kitchen and living room are floating in the air.

Thomas hollers from the kitchen. "We're in here, girls." We walk in to find Thomas, George, Matt, Robert, John, and Stephen all covered in a white film of plaster and all drinking beer. Thomas holds up his beer bottle. "Beers, girls?" he asks. "We finished knocking down the wall with the help of all these guys. Stephen was a brute, blasting out his frustration on our walls. You should have seen us. We knocked it out in two hours."

Stephen lets out a loud boisterous laugh. "Yeah, it was awesome. And, boy, do I feel better. I told Thomas and Matt to give me a call whenever they want to knock something else down." He puts his arm around Violet. "What do you think, honey?" he asks her. "We can plan a trip to coincide with Thomas and Matt's demolition jobs and maybe even get a house here on the island when we make it rich."

She grins and gives him a smooch on his lips, the only spot that's not covered in plaster. "I'd love that. I could visit with the girls while you're doing your man thing."

The conversation continues with a lot of joking and carrying on. I think how much I adore this cherished group of friends and family. Chloe, realizing that it is getting late, asks John, "Did you still want to leave around 2? I can drive since I haven't had anything to drink."

John grimaces. "Yep. Back to the real world," he says before turning to the guys. "Man, I'm going to miss you guys but think, just two more weeks and we'll be in the Bahamas."

He turns back to Chloe. "I just need to take a quick shower and change and then I'm ready to leave," he says.

Stephen takes his cue from John. "What about you, honey," he asks Violet, "are you ready to get back to the real world, too? We can stop by your place in in the Keys before we head home."

"You're so smart. I was thinking the same thing," she replies. "I still need to go through some more of my parents' things to make sure I haven't missed anything."

Sally, Sarah, Emily, and I decide to walk back with them and leave George, Matt, and Thomas to finish cleaning up the mess they made tearing down the wall. We agree to meet later at the pub since Emily and I have to work tonight.

When we get to my cozy beach cottage, I say goodbye to our friends and tell them that I can't wait for our next adventure on Cat Island. I remind them that the trip will be here before we know it. Then I wave goodbye as I step inside and close the door.

Chapter 46

Cat Island

The next two weeks fly by, and I can't believe it's time to leave for Cat Island. There's so much ahead of us, including Emily and George's wedding and the search for Anne Bonny and Calico Jack's treasure. We've had several FaceTimes with Violet, Stephen, Chloe, and John to firm up the trip plans.

In the days before the trip, I have several more nightmares in which I'm chased by villains on the Mangrove Trail leading to Man-O-War Point at the far northern end of Cat Island. Thomas and the others have tried to reassure me that they will keep me safe, but my instinct tells me otherwise. I can't help believing that the dreams are premonitions and warnings.

Whenever we talk about the upcoming wedding, Emily is suddenly the blushing bride and George becomes a blushing groom. I think he is just as excited as Emily and that's why he flushes whenever we mention the wedding. It is quite heartwarming to watch their love blossom before my eyes.

The day arrives for our trip, and I make sure to tuck Anne's journal in my luggage when I pack. We're scheduled to meet Billy at 8:30 a.m. I glance at my watch and realize it is already 8. Thomas pokes his head into our bedroom as I give my suitcase one more look. "You about ready?" he asks. "George and Emily are supposed to here in ten minutes."

I zip up my bright blue suitcase and swing my guitar over my shoulder as I move toward him. "Yep, I'm ready. I'm so glad I packed up everything yesterday," I say. "And thanks for putting my dress in your garment bag. That way it doesn't get wrinkled."

I glance at our bags piled at the front door. "Look at this luggage. You'd think we were going for a month and not just four days!"

"I know. We've got a lot of stuff," Thomas says. Then he hears the horn on George's truck. "Time to go," he calls out as he picks up his duffle bag and the garment bag. "I'm so glad that Sam was able to take care of Max for us. I sure hate when we leave him. He always looks so sad when I drop him off.

"Let's go," he adds as he opens the door.

"I'm right behind you, and I can lock the door," I tell him. I slip the brass key into the lock. "All done."

We store our luggage in the truck then climb in. George and Emily, both grinning, welcome us. I slide into the back seat with Emily and Thomas jumps in the passenger front seat.

"You guys ready to get hitched?" I ask.

Emily brushes her pale hands over her blushing cheeks. "I can't believe it's time," she says. "Yes, I'm ready but I'm so nervous—even though I can't wait to spend the rest of my life with this fella."

She reaches forward to the driver seat and squeezes George's shoulder.

George laughs. "I'm on the same page as you. I can't wait to make Emily my wife, but I'm nervous, too," he says. "You know that neither one of us likes to be the center of attention."

Thomas swats his brother on his shoulder. "It'll be fine. By next week, it will be a happy memory, and you'll wonder what you were so worried about."

George and Emily both nod in agreement. The drive to the airport takes us no time. George points to the roadway leading to airfield.

"Looks like most of us are already here. I see all the parents and grandparents, and Sally and Robert are pulling in right behind us," he says. "Looks like Billy's already loading everyone's luggage into the plane." Then George takes a deep breath. "It's happening folks. We're on our way. First stop after landing, Mount Alvernia."

As we board the plane, there is a lot of joking around with the happy couple. After a quick flight, we gaze down from the plane's windows at the beautiful oasis that is our destination.

"We'll be landing soon, folks," Billy announces. "Make sure you have on your seatbelts." The landing gear comes down and in no time, we screech to a proper halt on the runway.

Billy tells us that a taxi is waiting for us in the parking lot. We take the luggage out of the plane and go over to greet our driver, Fred, a jovial Bahamian who was with us on our last trip.

"We want to stop at the Hermitage before heading to Shanna's Cove," Thomas tells him. "We figure we'll take a look since we're close. It's quite an excursion to get here from the other side of the island."

Fred nods and helps us load our luggage into his supersized van.

"Sounds good," he says. "And you guys are learning. I remember your last trip here and how you rented a little tiny car and then had to maneuver along these rocky, crater-covered roads. You ended up returning the car and calling me to come and get you."

We're all laughing. Matt concedes Fred's point, adding, "You were a lifesaver. We thought that rental car was going to lose its rear-end in some of those potholes."

It's a short drive from the airport to Mount Alvernia. Fred navigates the climb up the steep mountain leading to the Hermitage then offers to wait for us since he isn't very busy today. Once we're out of Fred's vision, Thomas discreetly pulls out the map that Anne has given us.

"Okay. So, we marked this spot on the map, and it looks like it should be beside the winding rocky road in the curve of the road," Thomas says.

Then he scratches his head as he asks, "Do you think this road was here long ago or do you think it was added when Father John carved out the Hermitage?"

"Good question, Thomas," Paul says. "It's really hard to say but I'm thinking the road wasn't here in Anne's time. Let's assume it wasn't. But there were probably caves."

David studies the map for a minute. "There's something here that looks like an indentation. Let's spread out and look for an opening in the ground." We pair off, then stretch out in a line of couples, using the same strategy as police search parties. Before too long my grandmother, Mary, calls out in a shrill whisper. "I think we've found something."

As we all run to see what she's discovered, I pull out Anne's journal. I read aloud her description of what to watch for. "It says here to look for an opening with three large rocks placed into the center." I pause for a minute then continue. "Then it says, 'Look beneath the rocks to find a wine bottle to find my next clue.'"

"There's some sort of opening here," Mary says.

Thomas, George, and Matt start pushing aside the stones around the spot where she's pointing. Soon we see a clay wine container.

"By golly, I think you've found something, boys!" Paul says. He anxiously reaches down and pulls the fragile bottle from its hiding place. "Look," he adds, "the cork is still intact. What are the chances of that?"

He hands the bottle to me. "Angie, you do it. Anne Bonny would want you or Thomas to reveal the clue."

My hands are shaking as I take the bottle from him. The cork is tightly lodged in the bottle, and it takes several attempts before I can yank it out. "Man, this cork is tight," I say, just before my hand springs back and the cork flies out of the bottle. "Now let's see what we have here."

I can see a piece of brittle parchment in the neck of the bottle. I try to pull it out with my slender fingers, but I have no luck. I ask to use the tweezers in Thomas's Swiss army knife.

"The paper is stuck," I say as he passes the tweezers to me. Everyone waits nervously as I try to retrieve the piece of parchment. "Ahh, here it is," I say a few seconds later. I hand the paper to Thomas. "Here. You read it."

He nods, gently unfolding the note before reading its cryptic message. "It says, 'Go to the farthest end of this paradise, past the mangroves, down to the most glorious beach that you will ever see and follow my map to find the treasure that we have hidden,'" Thomas reads. Then he adds, "Beware of the pirates of your day because they may be waiting to steal what is rightfully yours.'"

We high-five and hug each other, celebrating our discovery of a new clue. Then Mary asks us, "Do you think we really need to be concerned about pirates? I mean it looks like it's just us here right now."

Paul places his arms around his wife. "You just never know, so we'll all be careful. Everyone, be mindful of your surroundings while we're here."

Paul looks at his watch and then points in the direction of Fred's van. "I think we really need to get back to Fred so he can take us to Shanna's Cove and the other reason we're on Cat Island," he says. He smiles at Emily and George who are wrapped in each other's arms. "It's time to celebrate the two of you," he adds. "Let's go."

Sarah nods and then recites the agenda for the day. "Maria has lunch waiting for us. Tonight, we have the rehearsal and rehearsal dinner. Tomorrow is the wedding. And the next day we go find the treasure."

"Sounds like we have our days all figured out," Paul says, looking down at his phone. "Hey, John just texted to say they're already up in the restaurant at the resort."

We make our way back to the vehicle and Fred safely drives us to Shanna's Cove. Just before we arrive, Emily asks, "Do you guys remember the last time when we drove to the resort?"

We burst into laughter. "How can we ever forget?" Sarah says. "Remember how Sally said it was like a scene from the beginning of one of those murder mysteries. Kinda' like Hotel California—you can enter but you can never leave."

"Yeah," I chime in, "it felt like we were going to the end of the world. It was so remote, and the roads were full of craters. And remember how windy it was? It was really scary. But once we got there, it was like heaven. Just beautiful."

At the end of our long forty-seven-mile journey, we see Gregor and Maria come out to greet us. They are so welcoming. They make us feel like we're coming home. Maria goes over the resort's agenda with us while Gregor distributes the keys to our cozy bungalows. Thomas and I have the Turtle Bungalow again, with its gorgeous views of Shanna's Bay.

Maria explains that we can order lunch and then go drop off our bags at our rooms, freshen up, and return to eat. "Your friends walked down to enjoy the beach," she says. "They'll join you for lunch. We'll see you back here in a little while."

By the time we return to the restaurant, John, Chloe, Violet, and Stephen are waiting on the festive deck. We greet one another excitedly. Marissa, who is Maria and Gregor's daughter, is busy making us her latest concoction, which combines pineapple, blue liqueur, and banana rum.

She laughs and winks. "I'm not giving out the recipe," she announces. Then she winks again and hands each of us a copy of the instructions for making the ambrosial drink.

We relax on the wooden deck where aromatic tropical flowers blow gently in the warm breeze. The girls and I savor our cocktails as the light wind caresses our bodies. The guys have opted for Kalik beers.

George holds up his beer, wraps his arm around Emily's waist, and offers a toast. "I just want to thank you all— old friends, new friends, and family—for coming to help us celebrate our wedding. It means the world to both of us."

Emily nods and continues the toast. "As many of you know, I hate being in the spotlight. But I want you to know that I love all of you and am so thankful. You are making this wedding memorable for us."

She pauses for a minute, then continues. "Being back here on the island reminds me of when George and I finally opened our eyes and realized that the love we were searching for was right in front of us. Thanks so much, everyone."

Emily takes a big sip of her drink and self-consciously sits down. Then she adds: "And thank heavens that the little flirt Sandy wasn't invited to this wedding."

We all roar with laughter, remembering Sandy's outrageous flirting at Sarah and Matt's wedding. John, Chloe, Violet, and Stephen have already heard about how Sandy set her sights on George, and they laugh along with us. When we finish our lunches of scrumptious fish tacos and fresh fruit salad, Emily suggests that we all head to the beach for some much-needed relaxation before the upcoming rehearsal and rehearsal dinner.

After changing, we meet down on the silky pink sandy shore overlooking the brilliant aqua bay. I sigh as I pull off my beach cover-up to reveal my new royal blue bikini. I yell as I run into the balmy water. "Last one in buys the next round of drinks."

Emily hollers, "Hey, no fair!" She sprints past me in her hot pink bikini and dives into the sea, followed by all the others while our parents and grandparent shake their heads and slowly make their way to the shoreline. Grandma laughs and exclaims, "Well, I guess I'm buying." She slowly enters the warm Caribbean water and lays back to float in the briny sea.

We laugh and frolic on the beach until it's time to get ready for the evening festivities. Emily taps me on the shoulder and turns to the other girls. "Hey, do you ladies care to help me with my hair and makeup? I want to look nice for the occasion. George is going to stay with his parents tonight."

We agree to meet her at the Seahorse Bungalow that she and George will be sharing after the wedding. We finish our showers, get ready, and head over to help her. When we arrive, she's in her robe and her hair is dry. Violet works her magic on the makeup. Sarah and I help Emily curl her wispy strawberry blonde hair, then we sweep it up into a loose bun with tiny tendrils of hair falling around her pretty face.

Emily pulls on a turquoise sundress that has tiny hummingbirds, parrots, tropical flowers, and palm trees on it. She looks so beautiful. Almost angelic. When Emily looks at herself in the mirror, she asks, "Do you think it's too much? Do you think George will like it?" She tentatively pulls the skirt of her dress, twirling around to face us.

My sister, standing beside her, smiles. "Oh, Emily, he is going to love it," Sally says. "You look spectacular."

"Really, you're not just saying that to make me feel better?" Emily nervously asks.

Sarah and I both reach out to give Emily a hug, which turns into a group hug to reassure her. Sally snaps a picture of the bride-to-be. "I'm going to take lots of candid shots, and this one is perfect—the bride, her sister, and her best friend. I can't wait to get these photos developed."

Sally looks at her watch. "Ladies, are you ready? It's time to go meet the others."

Emily takes a deep breath and heads for the restaurant. We follow her onto the stone pathway leading to the rehearsal dinner. Maria and Antonese, the fabulous chef at the resort, have turned the deck and dining room into a romantic tropical oasis.

George sees Emily walking up the steps and he throws her a kiss and lovingly says, "You look beautiful."

He comes over to hug her and kiss her freckled cheek. She tenderly reaches up to take his bearded face in her hands and kisses him delicately on his soft lips. "You're not so bad yourself, honey," she says.

Maria leads the rehearsal, and everything goes off without a hitch. The multi-course gourmet rehearsal dinner is delicious. As Violet takes a spoonful of the cool, creamy cucumber soup, she announces, "I don't think I've ever had such a delicious meal. This is better than all of the gourmet restaurants I've been to in New York and Paris."

We all enjoy the scrumptious fresh fish and mouthwatering shrimp, and when we finally push away from the table, we are sated and happy.

Suddenly we find ourselves yawning. It's been a long day, and we decide to make it an early night. It is already 9:30 and we have an early start tomorrow and a wedding. We wish each other sweet dreams as we say goodnight, and we agree to meet in the morning for an early breakfast.

Chapter 47

The Wedding

The morning blooms and we start our day with fresh fruit, cheesy vegetable omelets, and smoky dark coffee. The meal melts in our mouths. Over breakfast, we lay out plans for what we'll do in the hours before the wedding.

Chloe, John, Sally, Robert, Violet, Stephen, Sarah, Matt, Thomas, and I go get into our bathing suits to take a relaxing walk along the pristine beach to the other side of the cove. When we reach the end of the secluded cove, the silky sand feels soft on our winter white feet and the beach's natural untouched beauty is awe-inspiring. We reward ourselves with a refreshing dip in the tropical blue water. It feels great to cool off a bit from the Bahamian sun.

The swim feels almost therapeutic, leaving us delightfully relaxed. By the time we make it back to the captivating resort, it is already noontime to eat a light seafood salad up on the restaurant's stunning deck.

Emily and George have decided on 4 p.m. for their wedding ceremony. After lunch, the girls and I have our showers and dry our hair before heading to Emily's cute bungalow to have our makeup and hair done by the ladies Maria has hired from the island and to help Emily get dressed for the nuptials.

I make my way to Emily's bungalow, walking over the carved rock walkway lined with beautiful tropical flowers. The air is laced with an exotic floral scent intertwined with the briny breeze. It makes me think that this might be what it's like to walk to heaven.

I knock on Emily's door, and she answers it looking a little frazzled. Her cheeks are flushed as Chloe, Violet, Sarah, Sally, her mother, and my mother help her get ready for her wedding. Maria has left fresh fruit out for us, as well as champagne chilling in a decanter. Chloe and Violet are steam pressing the bridesmaids' gowns and Emily's stunning wedding dress while the hair stylist, Jasmine, works on curling and sweeping Sally White's pretty brown hair into a lovely bun. Liz is next in line for the stylist's chair and her makeup. The mother of the bride and mother of the groom are enjoying the memories that are being made.

The photographer, Lila, is capturing many of those special moments, while being careful to guard our modesty. We are laughing and feeling lighthearted, but it also doesn't take long before my mother and my grandmother, who are also in the bungalow, decide there are too many people. To tamper down the flurry—and make the atmosphere more calming for Emily—they decide to slip out and meet up with us at the ceremony.

The makeup artist, Abby, is adding the finishing touches to Emily's mother's makeup. But Sally White looks worried. "What do you think? It's not too much, is it?" she asks us.

As we reassure her, Emily comes over to stand beside her mother. "Oh, Mom, you look lovely," she says. "I can't wait to see Dad's expression when he sees you." Lila snaps a photo of the heartfelt moment between mother and daughter. I can't stop thinking that soon it will be time for Thomas and me to be married.

Sarah, Sally, and I slip into our pale dusty rose bridesmaids' gowns. Emily and everyone else in the room loves how the dresses look.

"You girls look awesome—and so pretty," Violet says. Then she casts a sweeping glance at everyone, adding, "Thanks so much for letting me be a part of this day with you." Sally and I are standing beside her, and we both give her a hug.

"We are so happy you could be with us today," I tell her. "Remember, you are part of the family and cousins with Emily and Sarah, so that makes us all related."

Before too long, it is time for Emily to take a chair to have her makeup and hair styled for her big moment. She anxiously pulls at her satin white robes and taps her toes as she nervously sits down. Jasmine delicately curls Emily's hair, giving her an elegant updo and then gracefully framing her petite freckled face with tiny curling tendrils. Emily will wait until after her gown is in place before putting on her lovely veil.

After the hair styling, it is time for the bride's makeup. Abby works her magic on the angelic face that rarely ever uses any makeup. When Abby finishes, Emily gazes into the mirror and seems happily surprised. "Wow. This is amazing," she says, laughing. "Do you think George will like it? Even more, do you think he'll recognize me?"

Sally White lovingly kisses her daughter's cheek. Her voice is tender when she replies. "Oh, I think George is going to love it—and he will *always* recognize you. Honey, you look fabulous with or without makeup." Liz, who is standing beside Sally White, takes Emily's hand in hers and says," My son has always loved you, Emily. He is going to be awestruck when he sees you." Emily looks touched.

At that moment, Sally White raises her hands and announces, "Now it's time to get you into your wedding gown." We all call out in agreement.

Emily stands as Sarah reaches to pull the delicate 1920s wedding dress from its protective plastic covering. The pale ivory pearl-embossed knee length gown matches Emily's unique personality. As it slips over her head, it flows down and around her slender body. To complete the look, Emily's mother reaches into her handbag and pulls out a long pearl necklace and pearl drop earrings that she inherited from her grandmother. She lovingly places the necklace around Emily's slender neck.

A silver tear drips down Sally White's cheek as she gushes, "Oh, my little girl is all grown up!" The mother and daughter embrace, and Lila lifts her camera to capture the moment.

Then Sarah reaches into her handbag and pulls out the sparkling blue sapphire bracelet that she wore for her wedding to my brother, Matt. She delicately wraps the bracelet around Emily's tiny wrist.

"And here is your something blue, Sis, and borrowed," she says. She beams at her younger sister. "You look magnificent. I can't wait to see George's expression— he's going to cry when he sees you."

It is such an emotional moment that we are all dabbing at our eyes, trying to not to destroy our makeup.

Next, Abby places the elegant, pearl-studded headpiece atop Emily's hair and adjusts its delicate veil. Emily gasps when she sees herself in the cheval mirror. She slowly turns in front of the mirror then takes a deep breath. "Well," she says, "I guess it's time. Let's get the show on the road. The more I stand here the more anxious I'm getting."

The photographer is snapping candid shots as we leave the bungalow and march down the carved rock stairs to greet the rest of the wedding party and the guests waiting down on the silky seashore. Sally leads the way down the narrow floral walkway. I follow, with Sarah behind me. The groomsmen wait patiently to accompany us to the flowered arch where the nuptials will take place. Sally White walks with her daughter as far as the bottom of the steps, where Emily's father waits.

Jim White gasps and tenderly grasps his daughter's petite hand in his. With tears in his eyes, he gently places a delicate kiss on Emily's cheek. "Oh, my dear, Emily. You look so exquisitely beautiful. Where's my little girl? You're all grown up."

Emily dabs at the emotional tears welling up in her eyes. "Oh, Daddy, stop," she says. "You're going to make me cry." She gazes out at the gathering of guests and nervously whispers, "Aww. They are all looking at me."

Her jovial father chuckles. "They are supposed to, honey. It's your wedding day and you're the bride."

Emily then takes her father's arm, and they walk together to where her beloved George is standing.

A guitarist plays the Wedding March as father and daughter make their way onto the satiny beach and over to the tropical flowered arch where the attendants and the handsome red-haired groom are waiting. George is swept with emotion when he sees his lovely bride. Tears brim in his brilliant blue eyes, and he places his hand to his heart and says, "You look so lovely, my Emily."

Jim White kisses his daughter's cheek and joins the two lovers' hands. Then, before he gives Emily one final kiss on the cheek, he says to George, "Take care of my little girl. She's yours now to cherish, too, just as I have since the day she was born."

George nods. He tenderly squeezes Emily's trembling hands. "I love you, Emily," he says. She answers, "As I love you and always will."

The officiant starts the wedding ceremony.

"Friends, we are gathered here today to join these two souls into one, the forming of an everlasting love and union. The couple has written their own vows. George, do you want to give your vows to Emily?"

George bows, gets down on one knee, and begins to speak. "Emily, you have been here beside me throughout my whole life. I've watched and cherished you from the time you were a skinny long-legged child until you transformed into the beautiful caring woman that you are today. Know that my love is endless and that I will love you and cherish you forever."

He then stands up and places the antique diamond ring with gold filigree on her slender finger. "Emily, will you take this ring as a sign of my love and know that I will always stand by you and protect you?"

Emily nods and says, "I do."

She grins at George as she places the gold ring on his muscular finger and says, "George, will you take this ring as a sign of my everlasting love for you? I have been in love with you my whole life. I cherish and love you with all my heart. I have watched you grow from a precious child to a caring and wonderful man. My love for you knows no bounds, and I can't wait to sit on the sandy shores of Ocracoke Island and grow old with you."

The officiant places his hands on their shoulders and says these words: "By the powers vested upon me, I pronounce you man and wife. You may now kiss your bride."

A passionate love-filled kiss is shared by the two childhood friends— now to be lifelong partners—and cheers erupt from our small crowd. The photographer captures Emily and George's first moments as newlyweds.

The officiant announce that the reception will be held up on the restaurant deck, but before we begin to move, Lila asks the families of the bride and groom if they will wait for photos.

"Before you all head up to the reception, I would like to take some pictures. I promise not to keep you too long from the reception," she says. "Can the whole wedding party stand in front of the flowered arch? Then let's have the bride and groom with the bridal party. After that, we'll do the bride's family and then the groom's family."

Pictures are taken against the backdrop of glorious aqua water sweeping gently onto the silky pink shore. The sky behind glows with ebbing amber and peach as the sun starts to set and reflect off the water.

After the photos are taken, we happily make our way up the illuminated carved rock stairs leading to the deck of Shanna's Cove Restaurant. The deck has been decorated with romance in mind and it looks gorgeous.

Special tropical cocktails are served, and the atmosphere is festive and jubilant. The newlyweds give a welcome speech, as do the maid of honor, best man, and father of the bride. A scrumptious five-course meal is served, and then the bride and groom cut the velvety wedding cake.

The first dance is announced. Emily and George have chosen the song *A Thousand Years*. That is followed by the touching moment when Jim White stands, takes his daughter by her hand, and leads her out to dance as the song *My Wish* plays. Among those watching, tears flow freely then are gently wiped away. The bridal party then moves onto the dance floor and soon everyone is dancing. The evening is filled with the laughter and love of a closeknit group of friends and family.

As the special evening comes to an end, we look up at the magnificent star-studded sky. Suddenly, a shooting star flashes across the heavens. We gasp, wonderstruck.

"Thanks for making our wedding so spectacular," George announces to all of us. Then he looks up at the sky again. "And thanks, Mother Nature, for the wonderful
lightshow."

We murmur in agreement before George adds, "I'm looking forward to our next adventure tomorrow. See you in the morning." Then he winks at all of us, and we laugh and head back to our lovely bungalows.

Chapter 48

The Search is On

We wake to brilliant sunshine streaming through the sliding glass door of our room. I stretch my arms above my head and push my wild untamed hair away from my face to see Thomas standing over the Keurig. He turns to smile at me as I gaze out the window at our view: the glorious calm waters of Shanna's Bay.

"Good morning, sleepyhead." Thomas hands me a cup of freshly brewed coffee and touches his lips to the tip of my sun-kissed nose. "Your coffee, madame. Breakfast awaits us on the deck. The others just texted to see when we would be ready to meet them up there."

"Thanks, honey. This is awesome. Coffee in bed," I say, as I take a sip of the heavenly brew. "Can you text everyone and let them know we'll be right up?"

We rush to get ready and meet the others on the deck of the restaurant. It's another scrumptious breakfast. I have a veggie omelet with crisp bacon and more richly flavored coffee. I hold up my coffee cup. "Here's to another spectacular day on the island," I say. "Can you believe this weather for March? It's already 84 degrees outside. It's going to be a hot one."

We finish breakfast and it is agreed that we'll take a hike over to Man-O-War Point down the mangroves path after we finish eating. My parents, grandparents, and George and Emily's parents will spend their day on the beach in front of the resort.

After breakfast, the newlyweds and Sarah, Matt, Chloe, John, Sally, Robert, Violet, Stephen, Thomas, and I agree to meet on the carved stone steps at the entrance to the Man-O-War path at 10 a.m. "Don't forget to wear your bathing suits," I remind the others before leaving the deck. "Remember our last adventure and how we wished we had worn our swimsuits to take a splash in the refreshing bay?" Everyone seconds that idea.

We go back to our bungalows and get our backpacks ready, packing up water, the treasure map, Anne's journal, the latest clues, and beach towels.

We assemble at the stone pathway around 10 a.m. I can feel the excitement swirling around this new treasure hunting adventure. Thomas points down the path. "Well here goes nothing," he says. "Let's hope we find what we are looking for and that we don't meet any danger like we did the last time."

We are halfway down the trail when Emily looks at her arm with some concern. "Man, I think I'm starting to get pink. I totally forgot to pack sunscreen," she says. "Did any of you girls pack some?"

We all check our backpacks and realize that none of us have any sun protection. "Emily, why don't you and I go back to the cottage and get some or you're going to get fried?" I suggest. "We know the trail. We can hike back quickly and join up with the others once we get the sunscreen."

Emily agrees with me. "That sounds good, Angie. I would hate to end up with sun poisoning on my honeymoon."

George and Thomas both look concerned. "I don't know about you two going off on your own," George says. "What if something happens?"

Emily holds up a muscular arm. "We're strong! Besides, we'll be together. Nothing will happen—we're using the buddy system."

George hesitates then nods in agreement. "Okay, but make sure you keep your cell phones on you and call if you need us."

Emily and I turn around and head back along the crackly rock path. After a little while we hear loud boisterous laughter coming from the shoreline. We peer between the jagged rocks that bank the mangrove-lined trail and see a large white fiberglass boat anchored nearby on the shoreline. Shocked by the sight of a boat at this unlikely spot, I tell Emily. "Something's not right. I need to text the guys!"

As I try to get a signal on my cell phone, Emily keeps watching the boat. Then she says in an urgent voice, "Look, there's Logan! And he has a couple of his druggie goons with him! We have to let everyone know."

My heart drops as I realize that we are out of range of the phone signal. "Emily, we have to get back to the rest of our group to warn them before those creeps find them. Let's go!"

We rush through the underbrush in the direction of where the others should be searching for the treasure. Before we can reach them, however, Logan spots us and gives chase. My heart is racing, and I am sweating profusely. I yell to try to get the others' attention. "Help, Thomas!!!! Logan is here and he is chasing us!"

It doesn't take long for Logan and his goons to catch up to us and, when they do, I see that they have guns—which they point at my head and Emily's head. I start to scream again, but Logan roughly clamps his hand over my mouth.

I bite down hard and stomp on his foot to break his hold on me. He yelps then shouts at me, "You might as well stop fighting or I'll kill you just like I did my Uncle Steve and Violet's parents. Don't make the mistake of thinking I won't!"

He then starts pushing me through the leafy mangroves. "Take me to them," he orders.

I can see Emily is struggling with one of the other vile characters who has her in his grip. She stops fighting when she hears what Logan is saying.

Stumbling through the brush and over rocky ground, we reach the others just as they are closing a large, ancient looking, brown chest.

They are shocked to see that we are being held captive by the vicious modern-day pirates.

Suddenly, our ancestors' ghosts materialize before them, and my father says, "You have to let them take the treasure or you will all perish at the hands of those dangerous scum." Evangeline, Roger, Jacob, Old Emily, Anne, and my father are standing guard over my friends and family, but they are not able to help Emily and me.

It is clear that the only choice is to surrender. "That's right, my cousins, you can't win this battle," Logan shouts. "But we'll let you survive. All you need to do is hand over the treasure, making it rightfully mine just as it is yours."

Then Logan turns to Stephen and screams out a warning. "You think you can betray me and hide this treasure? That will never happen."

Logan points to his degenerate scumbag comrades and barks out an order, "Snare that chest and take it to our boat waiting on the shore."

As his gang starts to carry off the chest, he turns back to us and bellows out a warning. "Don't try to follow us or we'll kill you just like we did Stephen's father and Violet's parents—though you'll never be able to prove it!" The two vile gangsters holding Emily and me in their powerful grip start to drag us back toward the boat, their guns still pointed at our heads.

Anne's spirit races toward the shoreline. She is loudly cackling, "Ahh, you scoundrels, you shall never have Jacky boy's or my treasure. Never! You will be the ones to perish at sea." Her apparition floats quickly down to the waiting vessel, and she pulls out the plug of the boat, laughing hysterically as she throws it into the sea.

Of course, the criminals are not able to see her, so they load the chest into the boat. Then they push Emily and me away as they climb aboard, kick in their motor, and start to power away from the shore.

Emily and I both fall down onto our shaky knees. We cling to one another as we collapse onto the sandy shore. Suddenly the guys rush down to us. George pulls Emily up from the ground and wails, crying into her tangled hair. "Oh, Emily, I almost lost you," he says, the emotion gutting him. "I couldn't protect you. I thought our life together was over before it even started."

Emily cradles his cheeks in her trembling hands. "There wasn't anything you could do. They had us at gunpoint. You're here, we are all safe, and that's all that matters."

Thomas is holding me in his arms and tears are cascading down both of our cheeks. I feel him shaking. "Angie, I'm so sorry. There was nothing I could do. I'm so glad you are alright. I love you so much."
I desperately kiss away his tears. "I know, Thomas. But they're gone and we're safe," I say. "It happened so fast, and they had the advantage over us." He hugs me tight.

After a pause, I ask, "Did you hear Logan confessing to murdering Stephen's dad and Violet's parents? But it doesn't do us any good, does it?"

Violet triumphantly holds up her cell phone. A video is playing on it. "You're wrong there, Angie. I was able to record and videotape everything that monster said. He was so busy gloating that he didn't even realize he was on camera."

We stare in disbelief then surround her, rewarding her with the mother of all group hugs. After we step back and give her room to breathe, Stephen—still with his arm around her—happily declares, "That's my smart, precious girl, Violet. It's just a shame that the treasure is lost to us—that boat will be sinking shortly. At least we still have the treasure chest we found on Ocracoke Island."
Stephen turns and points to Anne's spirit and the other spirits standing behind her.

"Thank you all for keeping us safe," he says. "And Anne, thanks for not letting them get away with the treasure. It's lost to us, but it's lost to them, too."

The spirits bow to us and evaporate in a mist on the sandy shore.

Violet has a mischievous twinkle in her eye when she surprises us with a reminder. "Well," she says. "We still have Henry Morgan's treasure to find."

Acknowledgments

Anne's Bounty, the third book in The Pirate Series, came together thanks to the support of many people. I am grateful to my friends Terri Domenici, Wendy Schofield, Kelly Foster, Teresa Simpson-Garriott, Toni Cantrell, Joanne Crowley, Margaret Hayes, Patty Miller, Peggy Durney and Holly Reese for pushing me to continue writing and for their many helpful suggestions along the way.

I can't say 'thank you' enough times to my mom and dad, Doris and Dave Pipes, who have stood by me this whole time, rallying behind my dream of becoming an author. I also want to give a grand thanks to my father-in-law, Harvey Gagne, who has also supported and encouraged me to keep working on this long project.

Special thanks to my Uncle Con, Harry Knott, for always asking when my next novel was coming out because he wanted to read it. His nudges have kept me on track through three books—and I have no doubt that he'll be there for my next book, too.

My siblings, Theresa Ferree, Debbie Herman, and Jason Long, also were among my cheerleaders, encouraging me to finish writing *Anne's Bounty,* as well as *Cat Island*, the book that preceded it.

I can't forget my editor, Mary Dempsey, who took the time to guide and support me on this writing. Thank you so much for all your encouragement.

Last, but not least, a powerful thank you to my husband, Matt Gagne, who has lovingly reassured, encouraged, and supported me in my journey as an author.

Other Books by this author:

The Pirate Series:

Evangeline Shores of Forever.   Book One

Angie's Soulmate.   Book Two

I hope that you have enjoyed my novel, and I thank you all for your support. I am a frequent visitor to the Outer Banks, especially Ocracoke Island. I am fascinated by all of the history of the islands of the Outer Banks, and it is where I got the inspiration for my stories. I am currently working on Book Four of the series and the next one will be about the infamous pirate, Henry Morgan.

Bitsey Gagne

www.ingramcontent.com/pod-product-compliance
Lightning Source LLC
Chambersburg PA
CBHW080716020726
47501CB00010B/2448